CELTIC COMPASS
Part I

a novel by
Sherry Schubert

Published by Sherry Schubert McAllister
P.O. Box 5825
Twin Falls, Idaho 83303-5825
mcallistersh@yahoo.com

Cover design by Molly Jayne McAllister
Cover art by Sherry Schubert

ISBN 978-0-9829563-2-8   (pbk)
ISBN 978-0-9829563-3-5 (ebook)

Dedicated
to

Mel and Jayne
who sowed the seeds of imagination

Acknowledgements

Claudia Creek for her unwavering support and counsel
Molly McAllister for her plot analysis, character critiques
and technological expertise
Numerous friends who have encouraged me to "keep
going," including an unofficial marketing cadre led by
Sonia Alexander
Joyce Ballard
and
Eleanore Burkhart

Books by Sherry Schubert

Puffin Island
Celtic Compass, Part I
Celtic Compass, Part II
Celtic Circle~for Better, for Worse
Celtic Circle~Forever

CELTIC COMPASS

Part I

Chapter 1

Kirin Koyle gazed up through the branches of her Christmas tree. From her vantage point on the floor beneath it, she thought it one of her best creations. Granted, her trees remained much the same from year to year, childhood ornaments interspersed with the latest baubles. Twinkle lights danced on the ceiling, and the unicorn, her namesake, hung perpetually near the top guarding the evergreen, and Kiri herself, from harm, sadness and disappointment. The branches of the tree splaying out above her represented all the possibilities life had to offer, all the choices Kiri had the freedom to make. Yes, her best Christmas tree ever shimmered with magic, and she hated to see it wasted on the most horrible holiday imaginable.

The independent thirty-year-old balked at traveling during the holidays. She longed to stay at home in Denver with her snow and her mountains and her tree with the unicorn at the top. She wanted the same Christmas Eve dinner they always had, the same Christmas Eve service at church with the candles during "Silent Night," the same Christmas breakfast and stockings, and sleeping under the tree on Christmas night. Dublin might not even have snow or Christmas trees, she scoffed.

Why was *her* family the one expected to travel? Pretty obvious. Kiri and her older brother Kurt—young, unattached adults—numbered only two on her mother Paula's side. The O'Connell family, besides Thomas, boasted eight adults and *ten* little children. Yikes! Other peoples' kids! Surely the worst holiday ever loomed before her only an overnight flight away. Maybe she could catch the flu on the way over and stay in bed the whole time. Despite holding a graduate degree and a management level job in one of the premier banking institutions, Kiri acted like a spoiled child, she knew. But, hey, family tradition was family tradition, and hers risked untimely demise in 2008 from a hoard of foreigners across the sea.

* * *

Michael O'Connell sped to the Dublin airport, late as usual. He had one duty today—to pick up Paula's kids and whisk them through customs with as little hassle as possible. This honor fell to him because his press pass allowed him to skip through security and right to the gate without a boarding pass. He had a picture to identify the two Americans in his charge—ordinary looking, nothing special—but he wondered what baggage, literally and figuratively, they would drag along. They could not be too happy about this forced family holiday.

His sisters definitely were not looking forward to the "togetherness," as they called it. Anne, Meghan and Emily accepted Paula as a constant fixture in their father's life, at least for the short term. But her kids? That assumed too much good will from his sisters and brother Tommy. And at Christmas!

Christmas was their family time. Christmas belonged to their mother who died almost six years ago. When she became ill, sister Anne kept it going: the same Christmas Eve supper, same Midnight Mass, and the same Christmas breakfast with each family at its own home now that there were so many kids. Their premier tradition was a really grand Christmas dinner with the entire family around one long table. This year it would be altered by the addition of Paula in their mother's chair and her two adult children. The Koyles could not possibly realize how much they would intrude on his family's holiday.

He felt a little sorry for them, the Americans, walking into all this ruckus. The obedient younger son really did not object to his father's getting on with his life. Once Thomas found Paula again after forty years, his father became a changed man, a relaxed, fun-loving, affectionate man, one Michael did not see throughout much of his adolescence. Paula was good for him, and the sisters leaned toward that way of thinking too. But to force all these strangers together into one happy family at the most stressful time of year.... What were those two old codgers thinking?

Michael felt confident he could identify Kurt and Kiri from their photos, but he doubted they would recognize him. Three days' stubble covered his square jaw and flat chin. Wiry allspice hair erupted in curls and waves, dashing in all directions like a young lion's mane to overshadow his deep-set blue eyes. The husky young guy sported comfy torn jeans, T-shirt and sweater, and loafers, the left one beginning to separate from its sole near the toe. His old leather flight jacket, stained and well-worn, completed the outfit.

His was not the usual garb of an international reporter, but he liked to be casual when at home. Laundry was not at the top of this single thirty-year-old's list. Ditto, for cleaning his apartment—his cold, lonely, flat where most of his possessions remained in boxes from his move there three years ago. Michael—on assignment more than in Dublin—came home for the holiday season this year, and he looked forward to a pleasant, friendly time at his father's house, but now...

...Now he searched for Kurt and Kiri, the Americans. "Please don't let them be 'ugly Americans,'" he prayed. What kind of a name was Kiri anyway—some holdover from the hippie days? He thought he detected a little of that spirit in her mother. His father Thomas and Paula were pretty tight-lipped about when and where they met, but Michael had his suspicions. No matter what the truth, at least his imaginings made for interesting speculation.

*   *   *

Thomas O'Connell paced from living room through den in anticipation of Kurt and Kiri Koyle's arrival. He had to admit his cleverness in contriving the perfect holiday. A year ago—even six months ago—he could not imagine the possibility of such happiness. Now it lay only minutes away. Last year he lived alone, a retired widower in an empty house. Six months ago he reacquainted with Paula, a summer love from his youth; 1968, it was. His family and friends had called theirs a summer romance, a phase experienced by every hot-blooded young Irishman of his time, but not so for Thomas. Not with Paula. That day on Puffin Island, the tide turned from passing fancy to commitment. He decided what path his life would take, and he wanted Paula with him. On a subsequent meeting in Rome, he took her hands in his and proposed that they wed and spend their lives together. When he let go, she disappeared. Their separate paths converged again in Rome last summer, some forty years later, and this time he vowed not to let go of her hand.

To that end, he invited Paula's two adult children to spend the holidays with them and his five children and grandchildren in Dublin. Emily and her young family moved back to the city from the North, and his younger son Michael returned from an assignment in the Middle East, so all O'Connells would be present for festivities. His house would fill clear up through its third floor again with the laughter of grandchildren, the chattering of children, and the warmth of family. Imagine, all of those he loved most in the world under one roof and around one table! The stage was set for a perfect blending of the Koyles and O'Connells into one loving unit.

Thomas chuckled at Paula's assertion that he had grown senile before his time when he proposed that they choose alternate cohabitation over occasional visitation. They hardly knew one another, she reminded him when he visited Colorado in July. He countered that he was merely being sensible. Since she refused to marry him on the spot, they should at least be open about their relationship, especially in front of the family. "I refuse to live a lie," he told her. He would settle his personal accounts with his Higher Power daily, as was his habit.

He thrilled Paula with the suite he remodeled for her on the second floor. "A perfect sanctuary," she said. But when she inspected the rest of the premises and inquired about the dark, formal rooms on the first floor, she informed Thomas that she could not "parlor" or "withdraw to the drawing room" for more than a few days at a time. She required light and space. That was all the impetus he needed to knock down a wall and create an open living area for her. Delighted, she promised not to change the paint, furniture, pictures or knick-knacks to upset his family, but she would reserve the right to tuck her feet up under her on a sofa when reading by the fire.

His daughters resisted the freshness Paula brought to their father's life. They objected to any change in *their* house or his routine. "Maybe the time has come to tear down a few walls and let the light into your own lives," he suggested smugly. The girls were not amused.

Thomas regarded the spacious, open room in holiday dress. Evidence of Paula's hand adorned the living room end with evergreen boughs, pinecones and seasonal plants—natural and serene like she was. He took charge of the den area at the far end—his media mecca—and she encouraged him to add pillows and throws in holiday colors and bowls of nuts and fresh fruit of his choosing. The two social areas shared one huge gas fireplace. She insisted that real logs be stacked on its hearth and that woodsy fragrances of fresh pine fill the air. He transitioned from formal to casual uneasily, but keeping her content was worth every effort, the white-haired, bearded patriarch confirmed.

He bypassed their suite on the second floor and climbed to the third to find Paula, the free-spirited, green-eyed hitchhiker with the never-ending smile that splashed across her face even in the pouring rain. No, he nodded, in all significant aspects, she had not changed in forty years.

* * *

Paula Koyle made a final inspection of the third floor living quarters: a guestroom for her mild-mannered son Kurt, a nursery for napping little ones, a playroom for entertaining little ones, and a guestroom for her strong-willed daughter Kiri, along one side of the hall. On the other side, two additional bedrooms did not need tidying for they would remain empty, she hoped. The two bathrooms, now clean and well stocked, completed her chores here. The kitchen demanded her attention next. She wanted two days' meals ready to pop into the oven before her children arrived, for once they did she would not have one spare minute to relax. This holiday would be nothing like the last several—feet up in front of a fire, a stack of books on one side of her favorite chair, a plate of baked goodies on the other, and her two children collapsed at her feet after a day on the ski slopes.

She turned to find Tom gazing at her from the top of the stairs. She could only call him Tom when alone now. In company—even family—he preferred the formal Thomas. Sometimes she slipped up, but not often anymore. She returned his gaze and wondered what madness lay behind his bewitching slate blue eyes that still danced when he twirled her around in their suite to the music of those days they had so enjoyed together. Surely lunacy drove Tom to believe he could accomplish the impossible with so many variables. The two of them experienced four days of togetherness and forty years of separation—not much of a foundation on which to build a future. Yet Tom was determined that not only they, but their respective children, would forge the familial bonds denied them those many years ago.

Once he had it in his mind that the holidays presented the perfect opportunity to set his plan in motion, he did not waver.

Blind, stubborn, age-challenged man, she thought. But she loved him, so she would support him with her calm, steady presence and would stand beside him to pick up the pieces when his illusion crumbled, just as she had at his near breakdown during Emily's episode last fall. Someone had to maintain sanity and reason in this fanciful family of his.

Paula was determined, too. She understood that the Koyles would invade O'Connell territory, but she would not let it be said that a Koyle— any Koyle—foiled Tom's plans for their future. She could count on *her* children to perform admirably and live up to Tom's expectations, but *his* children were another matter. "I don't know if I'm ready for this," she muttered to herself; then she smiled and took his hand.

As they descended the stairs and passed the second floor landing— Paula's reminder that they had crossed the border from their private life— she leaned against his shoulder and he nuzzled the top of her head. "Imagine, Thomas," she said. "I'm a retired, independent woman in my mid-sixties, and I still tingle at your touch. How long do you think this feeling will last?"

"Until death do us part, if it's up to me," he smiled. "I say we spread some of that festive feeling around to our children and make this the merriest Christmas ever."

*   *   *

Their heavy coats, boots, mufflers and stocking caps gave them away. The Koyle kids appeared bound for the North Pole. They should be prepared with raincoats and umbrellas, but what would they know of Dublin's moderate climate, Michael asked himself when he spotted the duo. The two travelers looked drawn and tired. Apparently they did not know how to chill out and sleep in the first class seats his father provided so they would not arrive feeling as they looked right now.

"God, give me strength," Michael sighed. "Here goes. Kurt? Kiri Koyle? Hi. I'm Michael, here to welcome you to Dublin on behalf of the O'Connell family. Let me help you with your bag," and he reached for Kiri's hefty shoulder carryon.

"I've got it, thanks," she mumbled as she shrugged it away from him, her hat pulled clear down to her nose.

Hmmm. A frosty independent little snit. I'll try to remember not to cross her path. This will be one delightful holiday, Michael thought to himself. He shook hands with Kurt who seemed friendly enough and guided them toward customs. "Luggage? I'll get a taxi to deliver."

"Nope. Whatever wouldn't fit in the carryons, we're wearing. Can't you tell?" Kurt smiled in reply.

"We'll only be here four days," Kiri added, "hardly enough time for a wardrobe change."

She was definitely the one to keep at arm's length, Michael concluded, but Kurt seemed easy to converse with, so the two men chatted while making their way back up the concourse, letting Kiri trail along behind.

The Koyles flew through customs in record time. Michael was a regular returnee from his assignments abroad and on a first name basis with most of the officers. They liked his friendly, easy-going demeanor and passed his guests on through with a wink, a smile and a lilting "Welcome to Ireland."

Kiri's eyes rolled with an "oh, no" sigh as Michael pulled up to the arrivals door in his showy silver sports car. As if scruffy and self-important were not bad enough, now he added flashy to his resumé... and he smiled too much... and his wiry hair was too long and unkempt. She climbed into the nonexistent back seat and dragged her bag in behind her, more than happy to stay separate from the conversation. She just wanted to sleep.

The guys jabbered on about cars, models, and high speeds. Kurt admitted envy of the custom speedster, so Michael offered to take him for a fast drive later during the holiday. Then Kiri heard a slaughter of her name. "Kari, what do you drive?"

"It's **Ki**ri, and I drive a Subaru. Just the right size for all my gear and my body if I need to sleep inside."

Ooh, and sensitive too, Michael thought. "Right. What gear does a girl carry along?"

"Bikes and boats in summer and skis in winter. As a matter of fact, this is supposed to be a great weekend for hitting the slopes. Do you ski here?"

"Nope. Never done it. Most go over to the continent for that sort of thing," he answered.

OK, Kiri thought. No common ground there. Just as I expected, it will be a long weekend.

Kurt and Michael turned from cars to football. Yes, the American version would be broadcast—satellites, you know. That was a relief to Kurt. He hated to miss those holiday bowl games. If he could just get his hands on some of the famous Irish dark ale, he would be set for the weekend. Michael assured him that would not be a problem; his father kept plenty on hand. Their guest could not contain his elation at that news.

*   *   *

Thomas' four-story Georgian mansion, larger than anything Kiri frequented, loomed like a prison with its stone face and large double doors. The travelers entered, and Michael called to Thomas and Paula who came from different parts of the house for kisses, hugs and welcomes. Thomas reached the trio first and flung his arms open to envelop Kiri in one of his signature bear hugs. "Welcome, welcome, my dear child!" he greeted and kissed her on the forehead.

Kiri pushed him away immediately. "I'm not yours. I don't feel at all dear at this moment. And I am not a child," she announced from under her hat, shocking him. She fell into her mother's arms and clung to her with a death grip. Kiri's hat fell to the ground letting her long brown curls fall free to reveal an attractive, real person underneath, Michael noticed.

Kurt stepped in to relieve the tension. He reached out to shake his host's hand. "Thanks so much, Thomas. We're glad to be here. Just give us a while to rest up after the long flight, and we'll be ready to celebrate." He picked up his sister's hat, pulled it down roughly over her head, smacked her on the rear and pointed her toward the stairs. "Get to bed until you feel human again."

"Two flights up, turn right, room on the left. Second floor is ours, exclusively. No visitors. Sleep as long as you need," Paula called after her daughter, embarrassed by her behavior for the first time in years. She smiled apologetically at Thomas who opened his mouth to extend another greeting, when a loud slam reverberated throughout the stately home.

Michael jumped. No one... make that NO ONE—not partner, not child, not grandchild, not a gust of wind—dared slam a door in the house of Thomas O'Connell.

The elderly man reddened and his eyes bulged wide. Before Michael could stop him, he stormed up the stairs, huffed to Kiri's bedroom and barged through the door nearly toppling her from behind it. "What do you think you are doing, young lady?" he demanded.

Surprised and confused, Kiri rose to her feet holding a damp cloth in her hand. "Cleaning mud off the door where I closed it with my boot."

"You did not close the door; you slammed it. No one slams a door in *my* house!"

"Sorry. My arms were full. I guess I shoved a little too hard. It won't happen again."

"See that it doesn't," Thomas ordered as he left.

"Welcome to Dublin, my word," Kiri muttered as she flopped onto the bed. "What's the next level beyond worst?"

"Is there a problem?" Paula asked when he returned to the group at the bottom of the stairs.

Embarrassed by his overreaction, Thomas ran his fingers through his thinning hair and shook his head. "Just a slight misunderstanding. Let's get this holiday started. Kurt, you are up top, turn left, last room on the right. Welcome." He took Paula's hand and led her toward the kitchen.

"What an awkward beginning," Kurt admitted. "I can't wait to see what's next," he laughed nervously. "What's with the second floor?"

"That is the suite Father designed for your mother—where they live their private lives. No one breaches a closed door on that floor. Keypad entry only. The one exception is the emergency room. If someone shows up sick and needs to be close by, like my sister Emily last September, a room is available at the end of the hall."

Kurt remembered his mother's planned visit home to Colorado that never happened—part of the six weeks here/six weeks there scheme for the Thomas/Paula relationship. "That's weird. Mom is not usually like that."

"Maybe so, but that is the policy now. And believe me, they spend way too much time alone in there," Michael raised an eyebrow. "Drop your bag and let me show you where Father stashes the brew. You'll have to put what you want in the fridge yourself. None of us will touch cold stuff," he joked. "Then I'll show you the media setup before I leave."

Kurt did not have to be told twice. The two young men looped down the long, dark hallway through to the kitchen, inched past the adults to stock the fridge, and entered the den from the rear service hall. Michael explained that his father's system had access to international programming capable of recording and/or viewing as many as four broadcasts at a time. He showed Kurt how to juxtapose multiple schedules on the same screen to select what he wanted for the next day. Then he could time them for taping and playing whenever he wanted.

"Wow," was all Kurt could think of to say. "Isn't this system a little ahead of its time?"

"For commercial purposes, yes. But the technology has been available for a long time, mostly for governmental and defense purposes," Michael explained.

"So how did Thomas get his hands on it?"

"Father may seem rather simple and laid back, but when he wants something, he generally knows which strings to pull to get it... and he usually gets what he wants sooner rather than later," Michael clarified. "I have to be on my way now, but I'll stop by tomorrow afternoon to see how you are managing. If there is a good game on, I might like to join you."

"That would be great. You'll find me planted right here. Thanks for the ride and the tech lesson." He shook Michael's hand heartily and flashed a broad smile.

"My pleasure. Relax and enjoy—as much as you can under the circumstances." The two young men exchanged understanding glances. "I'm glad you agreed to come. It means so much to Father and Paula. See you tomorrow."

As the door closed behind him, Michael sighed, "At least Kurt is capable of decent conversation. This might not be as bad as I anticipated." He stopped by his pub on the way home to fortify himself for the upcoming events before returning to his empty flat.

* * *

Kirin awoke sometime mid-afternoon—she thought. She could not tell, with the sky the same gray as morning when they arrived. A gentle rain misted her window. If she wanted gray rain for Christmas, she could have gone to Seattle. At least she had friends there, she grumbled.

On her way downstairs, she paused on the second floor landing. She was tempted to try to open doors and peek where she should not. After Paula's warning, she decided against it. It was very unlike her mother to set boundaries, but Kiri would wait for an invitation. If she did not get one, she would revisit the break-in option.

Smells from the kitchen welcomed her. The spicy scent reminded Kiri of Paula's house at Christmastime. Her mother must be getting a head start on some of their favorite holiday dishes so the load would not be too heavy tomorrow on Christmas Eve. Kiri wandered into the den drawn by the sounds of Kurt and Thomas cheering. They were engrossed in some sporting event or other from a faraway corner of the world, but Kurt paused it long enough to show her some of the capabilities of the system. She had to admit she was impressed and told Thomas. He gave no sign of their previous confrontation. He really was a very nice man... sometimes... and genuinely seemed to enjoy their company. He wanted the Koyle kids to feel welcome and comfortable in his home, she realized.

Kiri found her way to the kitchen where Paula finished the egg dish for Christmas breakfast and dough for dinner rolls—whole grain, of course. Then her mother started on something else—cookie dough, she explained, for the next day's cookie decorating party for the grandkids, just like the ones they used to host at home.

"Yeah, but not on Christmas Eve!"

"You and your friends used to have such fun making a mess and eating it too; I thought these grandchildren should have the same experience," Paula said. "I asked to make sure I wasn't duplicating something they did at home with their families, but they all said no; they didn't usually go into their kitchens. Cookies came on plates at tea time. Well, we need to fix that, I thought, so I'm glad you're here to help me out tomorrow. We'll have ten little ones from eighteen months to eight years."

Kirin's eyes rolled, but she had to give her mother a loving pat on the back. "You'll be too exhausted to enjoy the big day. Why put yourself through all the stress?"

"Thomas loves having his grandchildren around, but he doesn't quite know how to interact with them. He doesn't do chaos well, so I'll keep him away from most of the mess but engage him in frosting and sprinkles—the creative process."

"Why go to all the trouble?"

"To honor Thomas' love for his family. I know his daughters fear me, but I will not allow myself to be cast in the role of wicked step-person who severs all his connections with the past." Paula's lips tightened as she continued seriously, "I will not permit his girls—or any of you children—to sabotage our relationship. If we go under, it will be our own doing." Then her demeanor softened as slyness crept into her smile. "If I establish bonds with the grandchildren, they may help me crack their mothers' shells."

"I still don't understand why—why try so hard if you're not appreciated."

"But I am... by Thomas. I know that when the time comes, he will push my wheelchair with patience and loving care."

"Can't you find that at home?"

"I haven't yet. When we do go home to Colorado, I have Thomas all to myself. Every day I've kept my mouth shut and tolerated insults until then is worth the wait. He satisfies a longing in me that has been still for many years. Can you understand that?"

"I'll try."

"Good girl. Who knows? You may even find one of his children companionable."

"Sure, Mom. Whatever you say." Kiri nosed around the cupboards to see what sorts of decorations were planned and poked her fingers where they were not wanted. That they would eat in the kitchen surprised her. The nook could accommodate six or eight nicely, but she kept passing a formal dining room that looked like it had not been used in years. With Thomas out of earshot, she asked her mother what that was all about.

"The family used to dine formally almost every night," she said. "The girls seemed to have such an attachment to memories there, I thought it best not to tread on those. I'd already caused quite a stir. I'm happy being casual right here. In fact, I prefer it. The two of us at that long table in that big room with heavy, antique furniture is way too fancy for my taste. I'm much happier here where it's cozy and friendly. When Michael eats with us, which is fairly often, he automatically heads for the nook now. I think he feels the same way—that all the fuss and fancy aren't really necessary—except on special occasions, of course."

"But, Mom, you don't like to eat in kitchens."

"We don't usually. You'll see tomorrow."

Thomas and the three Koyles supped on one of Paula's famous stews—at least she had become famous with the O'Connells for her stews. When he sat down, he found a note on his plate.

> *Thomas O'Connell,*
>
> *Please accept my apology for the lack of courtesy I displayed at your welcome this morning. You are very kind to open your arms to our family for the Christmas holiday. In the future I will pay better attention to where I place my feet, and how, in your lovely home.*
>
> *Kirin Koyle*

He refolded the missive and tucked it into his cardigan pocket.

"What is that all about?" Paula asked.

Thomas smiled discreetly across the table at Kiri. "Mending family fences," he replied.

Chapter 2

Paula scheduled the grandkids from noon until five. She offered to take them for the afternoon so Thomas' girls would have some freedom to prepare for their O'Connell family Christmas Eve dinner without the bother of children underfoot. The mothers redirected their nannies to help the adults with arrangements. Paula would feed the little ones a light lunch, and they would bake and decorate cookies. By five, the kids would have full tummies and be ready for naps when they returned to their homes. Then they should last until late dinner and Midnight Mass. All the young ones were expected to attend and be in good spirits. Paula could not believe they all would be, but she agreed to do her part to help bring about a miracle.

Michael dropped in around two o'clock to see what events Kurt had lined up for the afternoon. Squeals and giggles drew him to the kitchen where cookie decorating was in full swing. Paula and Kiri commanded the party, sort of, with flour and sticky fingers everywhere. Organized chaos was more like it. All ten little ones, dressed in old T-shirts usually used for finger painting, crowded into the nook and sat on phone books piled up—a menagerie of wigglers and gigglers.

Paula popped a tray of twisted pink and white candy cane cookies into the oven to bake while the children took turns cutting stockings. Bell and tree cutters lay on the counter. On the other side of the oven, bowls of frosting and decorations—chocolate chips, red and green sprinkles, cinnamon drops and tubes of colored gel awaited those little fingers.

He sidled in and reached for some chocolate chips. A spatula whapped his hand quick as a whip. "Get your fingers out of the candy," Kiri scolded. She was ponytailed and aproned and had flour clear up her arms from rolling dough.

"But it all looks so good. I want to play too," Michael pouted.

"Well, you can't," she stated with a smile. "You're too old. This kitchen is for kids only today. Beer and snacks are in the den, along with adult amusement."

"Can't I have just one bite?" the big boy whined.

"Nothing is finished baking yet, but here," and Kiri scooped out a spoonful of dough from the mixing bowl. She dipped it in each of the decorations and presented the glob to him.

"This is raw!"

"That's when it's best," she declared. "Check back later. We might have a few crumbs left over for the big pouty kids." Michael had to admit that the crazy concoction did taste pretty good.

Pattering footsteps dashed into the living room and interrupted the football game. A wee one in an oversized T-shirt about to trip him up raced for the Christmas tree with a cookie cane in each hand. Kiri ran right behind and scooped him up just before he fell nose-first into the pine needles. "Oh no you don't, you little rascal," she warned. "You have to keep your mess in the kitchen until we're all finished."

"But I think the tree wants a cookie," a tiny voice explained.

"OK, but we don't want the tree to get fat, so you put one on a branch and give the other to Uncle Michael. Where would you like this one to go?"

"On this branch right here by the Rudolph so he won't get hungry." He hung the cookie carefully; then Kiri carried the boy over to Michael.

"Where do you think this one should go?"

"Right here on his ear cuz his tongue can almost reach," and he appended a sticky, crumby cane to his uncle's left ear. Michael gave it a try, screwing up his face and twisting his tongue across his cheek. He hoped the treat would not topple off with his laughter.

Away flew Kiri with a kid under her arm and a shake of her head. She returned in a flash to wipe the floury footprints from the floor and give Michael's ear and face a swipe at the same time. She brought a cookie and a swipe for Kurt as well.

"Yuck! You know cookies and beer don't mix," Kurt complained.

"It's always the right time for a cookie," she teased.

"The right time for a noogie, you mean." Kurt grabbed his sister, pulled her onto his lap, and gave her a good one on the top of her head.

"Ow!" she protested as she whacked her brother on the chest and wrestled off his lap to return to the kitchen.

That ill-mannered American girl did have a sense of humor underneath her hard exterior after all, Michael mused.

Much later Michael heard pitters, patters and mutterings back and forth from kitchen to console by the stairs, to the kitchen and back again. The thunder of thumps on the stairs as the bakery crew headed for the bathroom signaled clean-up time. From past experience with Paula's taking the hoard of grandchildren for an afternoon a month, Michael knew the cherubs would be lined up, alternate short and tall, disrobing from dirty shirts. The big kids helped the small ones, while Paula sat by the sink with washcloth and towel, scrubbing chubby cheeks and fingers and smoothing hair until they looked as if they had done nothing all afternoon but sit on their hands waiting for their parents to retrieve them. She quickly learned that as long as the little ones were returned looking as they had been delivered, it did not much matter how messy, muddy, wet, painty, or giggly they were in the meantime.

Then the thumps headed back down the stairs, and Michael knew if he peeked around the corner, which he did, he would find all those perky noses and downy curls on the stairs by family, calm and clean, ready for return. Paula would usually read them a story while they waited. Today Kiri taught them some song about Christmas cookies and holiday treats as they chorused "munch, crunch, yum" and rubbed their tummies. The parents arrived on time, as they learned to do. Each child picked up his plate of cookies secured by plastic wrap and a ribbon, some balancing their plates carefully before them and others squishing them securely to their chests, as they gave their friendly hostess a kiss on the cheek and marched out the door.

Paula and Kiri collapsed into a big back-and-forth hug with a "thank you so much for helping" and a "not as bad as I thought; kinda fun." The mother headed upstairs to clean the bathroom and bring dirty shirts and towels to the laundry while the daughter aimed for the kitchen. Curious Michael sneaked up on Kiri and found her on hands and knees scrubbing the floor to leave no crumbs lurking. She backed up against his shoes and scrubbed right across them.

"You can stop now. This kitchen is spotless, but you are a mess."

"And you aren't very nice to say a thing like that to a girl," she retorted and started for the stairs.

Thomas and Paula, already halfway up, ascended together. They disappeared into their sanctuary, leaving Michael and Kiri to wonder what two old people do behind closed doors late in an afternoon. Her duty done, Kiri took the rest of the stairs two at a time to the third floor and vanished into the bathroom to clean up her sticky self.

The young reporter returned to the den. At the end of the current game he asked Kurt to let the folks know he would be back about eight to pick up Thomas for the O'Connell family Christmas Eve dinner.

*   *   *

Michael let himself in about 7:30 and found the den dark with no one around. All must be upstairs getting ready for the evening, he assumed. He passed the dining room and noticed nothing readied for the Koyle meal. Lights in the kitchen caught his eye, and he spotted Kiri working at the sink. The wonderful aroma of clove-studded baked ham drifted from the oven.

"Wow!" he exclaimed, startling her.

"Oh, Michael! I didn't recognize you without your crumb-catcher." He shyly touched his cleanly shaved chin. "You look very nice this evening. Your sisters are sure to approve."

"You look very nice yourself," he replied, noticing Kiri's skirt and designer v-neck sweater which accentuated cleavage and curves he had not imagined were there. Her long hazelnut brown hair tumbled over her shoulders in soft curls. The toes of her bare feet flexed and released onto the tile floor with each cut she made to a fresh pineapple.

Michael's fingers were almost as speedy snatching a chunk as the spatula Kiri brought down on them. "You don't learn very fast, do you?" she accused.

"Just one piece, please. I love fresh pineapple and this looks so good. Did you do all this?"

Kiri looked around from side to side and behind her. "Do you see Cinderella somewhere? Of course, I did. It's not that big a deal to pare and cut up a fresh pineapple."

"I wouldn't know where to begin," he said and enjoyed his morsel immensely.

She slid the bowl into the fridge and cleaned up the sink.

"That 'Wow' was for the dining nook," Michael explained. "What happened here? I've never seen these screens before."

"Apparently they are attached to the walls on either side and slide on a track in the ceiling hidden by the lights. Come in here," Kiri beckoned him secretively. She closed the five-foot screens behind them creating a cozy private booth. Evergreens and poinsettias decorated the window sills, and a mural—a stone flower box brimming with bright colored bougainvillea, hibiscus and petunias, with vines trailing over the edges—adorned the screens.

"This looks like a quaint romantic *ristorante* from an Italian film," Michael observed. "I really admire how your mother has made this house her own without intruding on our family memories. No wonder the parents never eat in the dining room. Who would want to sit at that long table in those stiff chairs when they could be here in this secluded little hideaway? How did you discover this?"

"I didn't. Mom pulled out the screens and set the table, including candles and wine, for our dinner tonight. See, three places," she pointed.

"I'm envious. We O'Connells have gathered around this table many times these past few months and never received an invitation. You Koyles have been in town barely twenty-four hours, and you are already privileged."

"What do you think these are for?" Kiri asked as she coyly lifted her eyebrows and pointed to small hooks on the walls."

"Don't have a clue."

"Well, look here," and she turned up one of the bench seats revealing a storage space for accessories. She pulled out three wall sconces with glass bowls, slid them onto hooks and lit the candles inside.

"Wow, and wow again. This is really great. How did you find this?"

"Oh, I am one expert snoop," she said as she lifted the bottle to a glass. "Would you care for some wine, Signore?"

"I'd love some, but do we dare? Won't our parents be coming down any minute?" he asked cautiously.

"I highly doubt that, judging from the sounds I heard coming from their room on my way here. Reciting poetry?" Kiri and Michael raised eyebrows at each other, poured a couple of fingers of wine each, and clinked glasses as they slid into the booth. "Merry Christmas," they toasted.

"Does it bother you that our parents don't keep their displays of affection to themselves?" Michael asked.

"A little bit. It's hard to think of my mother as... you know... sexual. All that fun is supposed to be for people our age."

"Yeah, not old people."

"Oh! Don't ever let my mother hear you call the two of them old! They are simply mastering maturity." They both laughed. "Do you think most older couples behave the way they do?" she asked.

"I don't know. Judging from my sisters and brother, I doubt that they do even now."

"That's sad. I would hope for the magic to last a little longer... like forever," Kiri wished aloud.

"Me too," Michael added. They both sipped their wine thoughtfully.

Thomas' and Paula's footsteps approached and their voices discussed in serious tones. He pleaded, "Please won't you come with me tonight. I don't want for us to be apart when this should be a festive time."

"We've had this conversation for days, and we settled it. Both families need their own time with each of us. We can't go yanking *all* of their holiday traditions out from under them. This time of year is emotional anyway, and to force too much on our children at once is disaster in the making. You go and be with your children tonight. Enjoy them as you usually do. Go to Mass with them as they expect. We'll have our time together tomorrow," Paula insisted, putting her hands forcefully on his chest. "You can do this."

"Share a drink and a toast with me, then, before I leave."

The hide-aways exchanged petrified stares as the screen opened to reveal the two of them. They smiled and chimed in unison. "Ho Ho Ho, Merry Christmas!"

"Kirin Koyle! What are you doing in there? Eavesdropping on us?" Paula asked.

Thomas' accompanying glower was particularly disapproving.

"We were here first, Mom. Sorry. Didn't know you two planned to use it. The nook looks really great."

"Well, scram you two... and leave that bottle of wine right where it is."

Michael and Kiri slid out, leaving their glasses behind. "I'll wait for you by the front door, Father." With a smug grin, Michael added, "Take your time."

Paula and Thomas scowled after the two, then closed the screens and slid into the booth themselves, chuckling.

Kiri walked Michael down the long, narrow hall toward the front door. "I knew you were trouble the minute I saw you," he said, "but I didn't think you would drag me in with you. Thanks a lot!" He grabbed her gently, raised his knuckles and rubbed them lightly on her head. She whacked his chest and ran up the stairs before Michael could snatch her.

Chapter 3

The Koyle family returned to the house first following Christmas Eve services. The sounds of church bells from all over Dublin escorted them in. They mounted the stairs and parted calling "goodnight" and "Merry Christmas." Morning would come soon enough. After a short time Kiri heard Thomas enter and ascend the stairs. The door to the suite closed on Paula's voice welcoming him.

Kiri washed up and put on her pjs—light flannel pajama pants and T-shirt—pulled her hair up into a ponytail again, and tip-toed her way down the stairs and through the dark house to the kitchen. On a mission to raid the fridge, she took the bowl of leftover fruit salad and put it on the counter. She dipped her head to look for more tidbits when Michael entered through the back. He had changed into casual clothes and had a small duffel with him. He could not resist the ponytail peeking up above the door.

She felt a jerk on her hair, a shhhh in her ear, and a hand clasp her mouth as she let out a scream of surprise. "Aahhh! I knew this creaky old house was haunted!" When Michael sensed her relax, he loosened his holds. "What are you doing here? Is something wrong?"

"Nothing friendly company can't fix. I couldn't face staying alone in my flat on Christmas Eve and waking to rattling steam pipes and an empty cupboard. I had such a good time over here today with all of you—the gaiety and the festive atmosphere—that I invited myself to sleep over. You don't think your mother will mind, do you?"

"I doubt it. She's used to taking in strays, and she said herself that you join them often for dinner."

"I've even stayed over a time or two. I've sort of claimed the room across from yours. My old digs. You don't mind, do you?"

"It's your house; you do whatever makes you feel comfortable."

"I see you're having a snack. Mind if I join you?" He poked his head into the fridge without waiting for an answer. "This pie looks yummy. Do you think I can have some?"

"It is heavenly. One of the Mom's best—holly berry."

"Holly berries are poisonous. Does she know that?" Michael asked cautiously.

"Duh! She uses whatever fresh berries she can find and calls it holly berry because it's Christmas. You will not die from eating her pie unless you take more than a sliver. I think she's saving the rest for a snack tomorrow."

"I can cut a sliver so she'll never know I touched it." Michael found a knife and a plate and began to slice ever so carefully when Kiri jostled him with a "Boo!" He cut a jagged hunk right out of the middle. "S**t! That's not fair. I'll tell your mother it was your fault."

Kiri laughed. "She won't care. Go ahead and take what you want."

Michael did just that. He straightened up the cut and began eating. "Oooh, this *is* wonderful. What are you having?"

"Right now I'm tearing off a hunk of ham to chew on."

"Tearing off? Don't you know how to use a knife?"

"Of course, but this is more fun. You pick at the edge of the crust, like this…" She used her fingernail. "… until it begins to separate. Then you pull it down just like string cheese and put it in your mouth and chew. Boy is it good!"

"I think you're very primitive." He crinkled his nose to show his disgust.

"Go on. Try it."

Michael did and nodded an assent as he chomped. "I see you've got the bowl of fruit out. Are you willing to share?"

"Sure."

"You get the forks; I'll get the bowls."

"No bowls necessary."

"You don't mean to eat right out of the serving dish, do you?" he asked, aghast.

"I promise not to put my fork all the way into my mouth if you don't."

"You can't put the dish back in the fridge after eating from it."

"There won't be anything left to put back," she stated.

"You don't intend on eating the whole thing, surely?"

She nodded as she got a glass of water, balanced a couple of reject cookies on top and headed out of the kitchen.

"Aren't you going to eat here in the nook?"

"No. I'm going for the fireplace and the tree."

"Can I come too?" Without waiting for an answer, Michael followed after her with the fruit bowl.

"Suit yourself. It *is* your house. You can show me how to turn the fireplace on and off." They edged into the dark room carefully so as not to spill. Michael started to turn on the lights, but Kiri stopped him. " Just the tree." She got down on her hands and knees.

"What are you doing on the floor?"

"Looking for the tree's cord and plug."

He flipped a switch, and the tree came to life.

"Oh! That's nice!"

He turned on the fireplace and adjusted its flame to her liking. "How about music too?"

"Something soft and seasonal would be great." Kiri folded up a throw for each of them to sit on in front of the fire, facing the tree. They took turns jabbing into the fruit bowl.

"What do you think of the tree?" he asked rather disparagingly.

"It's nice. Thank goodness it's fresh."

"That caused quite a stir around the house when your mother decided to start decorating. Father went to the attic to get the old artificial one down; he hasn't used it since Mother passed. When he tried to bring it in the house, your mother would have none of that. She wanted a *real* tree; 'a fresh one that smelled,' as she put it. So here we have a modest, fresh tree that smells and is decorated in the most appalling manner possible with all sorts of papery, glittery creations hanging around the bottom and nothing above four feet, except that horsy one near the top. I like the lights, though.

"When he saw it," Michael continued, "Father rolled his eyes and sighed, 'whatever Paula wants.' The decorations are courtesy of another one of your mother's famous grandchildren parties. The greenery, flowers, cones and candles along the mantle and around the windows are very nice; Paula didn't let the children touch any of those. I think Father is having his sensibilities sorely tested by your mother's casual way, but in the end most of her schemes are fairly successful."

"Don't knock that horsy thing near the top. That one's mine, I'm sure. See..." Kiri stood up next to the tree. "It is exactly my eye-height. Mom remembered."

"Do you like horses or something?"

"No, not a horse. It's a unicorn, the symbol for my name."

"Kiri?"

"Kirin is the..."

"Isn't Kirin a boy's name?"

"No more so than Stacey, Robin, Kerry, or Taylor, for that matter," she replied defensively. "Kirin is the derivation of the Japanese name for unicorn. You know, the mythical beast that has the head and body of a horse, the legs of a deer and the tail of a lion. And of course, one horn grows out of its forehead. Don't I look just like that?" She giggled. "Long hair...." She unfastened her ponytail and laced her fingers through her rich brown strands to pull her hair back and up from her face imitating a horse's bouncy mane. "I have nice long legs, which you can't see right now, and I'm very fleet of foot when racing. I was born under the sign of Leo, so there's the lion, plus I can be very fierce and fight hard for what I want if I'm pushed to it."

"What about the horn? I don't see one of those," he challenged.

"Feel. Right here." She took his hand and guided his fingers just beyond the hairline near the center of her forehead.

"That bump? That can't be. Are you sure?" Michael drew his hand away in disbelief. "Can't be. You must have fallen on your head as a kid."

Kiri tossed that head with a tease and continued the lesson. "A unicorn's symbols are chastity, purity, and meekness."

Michael's eyebrows shot up at that declaration.

"When I picture a unicorn, it stands alone at the edge of a forest, the fringes, as a sentry of sorts. It observes from there, ready to help or support when necessary—protect, even. When challenged, I can call on all of those animals' strengths to help me."

"I see the quiet and contemplative in you, unattached and watchful. I thought you were just unhappy and resentful of being here—for which I don't blame you—until later today when you started to open up. I think there is a bit of mischief sprinkled in there too," he observed. "What I want to know about are the chastity and purity. Are you... chaste and pure?" he asked sarcastically.

"Aren't we all... at some point?" Kiri asked coyly as she plunged the last piece of pineapple into his mouth.

Since more specific information was not forthcoming, Michael changed the subject. "How was your intimate family Christmas Eve?"

"Once Mom stopped glaring at me for our eavesdropping in the dining nook, it was lovely. We closeted ourselves in and enjoyed traditional holiday dinner fare—long and casual, as usual—and reminisced. Then we walked to church, a first for us kids. Walking instead of driving, that is—not church. We saw lots of families doing the same. Their weavings past and through one another on the paths through the Green performed a ballet of sorts. We did light candles and sing "Silent Night," as I hoped. But the best part of all was leaving the church and hearing bells ring all across the city. It was so beautiful; the peals followed us every step of the way back here."

Kiri grew thoughtful as she continued, "I'm old enough to understand that times change, people change, situations change. Mom is not home with us this year; Kurt or I might be gone next year. The grown-up in me accepts that I can't hold back time, but the kid in me just wants to curl up on Mom's sofa by a fire with her arm around me to gaze at her mountains and to talk like we used to. No phones, no TV, no chores, no bustling, no distractions, no interruptions and no one else but the two of us—the only two people in the world." She sat with knees up and her forearms resting across them to form a shelf for her chin. She gazed dreamily at the tree, then she turned toward Michael, her head still settled on her arms. "How was *your* evening?"

"We were at Anne's, since her house is largest and can accommodate all of us easily. That's where we're going tomorrow night too. The food was good... the usual. The kids made it through the long meal just fine, until dessert. They didn't want the pudding; they wanted their cookies. I could see in my sisters' glances at one another that they blamed Paula. 'We knew it! No good could come from spending all day in *her* kitchen,'" Michael mimicked dramatically.

"I intervened and told the nieces and nephews that if they finished all of their dinner *and* their dessert, maybe they could each take a cookie in by the fireplace and nibble and munch it very slowly until time for church. Dinner proceeded without cranky interruption. I led a trail of children in by the tree and seated them on the floor like your mother does. I handed each one a cookie and demonstrated how to nibble and munch very, very slowly with teeny bites."

Michael snatched a burnt bit of cookie to model his expertise causing Kiri to laugh and test the technique herself. Crumbs scattered everywhere.

"They got so good at it," he continued, "that I fear they will drag their parents slowly through meals for the next little while. Then they tried to sing 'Christmas cookies' that you taught them. They couldn't remember most of the words, so they sang several choruses of 'goody, zoody, munch, crunch, yum!' The volume grew louder and louder... until finally it was time to leave for church."

"That sounds like fun," Kiri grinned.

"It was, rather. Except for a couple of things."

"Such as?"

"Father, for one. He was absolutely glum all evening. I knew he would be. He cannot be away from your mother for very long, except to go to Mass. He becomes nervous and despondent when they are not together."

"Why do you think that is?"

"He hasn't felt relaxed and comfortable for so long," Michael revealed. "He went through quite an ordeal with my mother. He's afraid if he leaves Paula alone, when he returns she won't be there. That's what happened with Mother. She was very ill, but death was not yet imminent. He left the house one night for a short while, and when he returned she had passed. He blamed himself for leaving her alone, convinced that if he'd been with her she would have lasted longer."

"How terrible. Do you kids believe that?" Kiri leaned back on her elbows and stretched out her legs until her toes grasped a low branch.

"Not really. We were all old enough to know that God takes you when it is your time. But Father kept trying to rewrite history... until he met your mother again last summer. Then his whole demeanor changed. He recouped his loving and energized nature, but he still fears to let her out of his sight. He feels so blessed right now. I can see the peace in his face. He may seem weak and clingy, but he is not. He is just trying to protect Paula from the demons that lurk around us all."

"That's sweet," Kiri reflected.

"I think so too, but my sisters see his glumness as torment over Mother. They don't realize they themselves cause his anxiety by separating him from Paula from time to time. They really do like your mother, and she has been more than kind and welcoming to them, but you know... girls and their mothers." Michael lay down and stretched out too.

"That I do! Kurt is so easygoing that Thomas and Mother's relationship doesn't bother him at all. But I'm like your sisters," said Kiri. "I'm very protective of my mother. I see your father as taking her away from us, even though intellectually I know she has gone her own way willingly. I notice change in her too, for the better, and your father is just great… to her. I can tell they care for one another very much. Mom is lucky to have found him. I have to grow up and allow her to live her life."

Michael turned his head toward Kiri. "That sounds like what Paula would say about you, 'allow her to live her life.'"

"It does, doesn't it?" She smiled and met his glance. "I am concerned, though, about what she gave up to be here in Dublin with your father."

"Like what?"

"Well, her level of physical activity for one," Kiri admitted. "Mom used to bike and swim, jog and practice yoga, one or more daily. I haven't seen any indication that she maintains a regular exercise program, other than running up and down stairs all day. Both she and your father should be more active than I've witnessed. Also, she grew most of her own food so she could regulate its quality. I don't see any garden plot in the back."

She sat up and continued to enumerate. "I don't know how she keeps up with her work, and she has to miss her home. Mom has the most wonderful house on a hill facing the mountains. Here, she doesn't seem to have any of her own things around that would remind her of home. And if there are mountains out there, they are obscured by your incessant rain. I don't see how she maintains her sanity through all that dripping, but I can see that she is very, very happy. She just needs to get her healthful living style back on track."

"Do you maintain a healthy life-style?"

"I try to, although you wouldn't know it by all the gooey stuff I've been consuming here. Mom raised Kurt and me that way—diet and exercise. Healthy bodies breed healthy minds. How about you?"

"Of all the siblings, I'm probably the most fit, even though I am a single man living alone… or maybe because I'm a single man living alone. Tommy spends most of his time behind a desk, and my sisters spend too many hours being uptight. Their latest concern is seating at tomorrow's big Christmas dinner. Where are they going to place all you foreigners?" Michael pretended worry.

"Does it matter who is next to whom? Surely you don't have assigned seating."

"Oh, yes! The girls don't want to offend any of you, but at the same time tradition is tradition. It will be interesting to see how they work it out."

"They don't understand my mother very well, then, do they?" Kiri guessed. "My family will be perfectly happy sharing a chair and a plate in the corner. We don't hold with much formality, as you know from scooting yourself in around the nook. If the food is good and the company amiable, the party will be a success."

"Just go with the flow for you, is it?" Michael asked. She nodded. "So, what's the plan for tomorrow?" he wondered.

"For our side of the family, it will be breakfast and stockings as usual. You will join us, of course, so if you expect something formal and proper, you will be sorely disappointed. We're very casual, but we do have a lot of fun," Kiri stated.

"Do you do presents? I don't see any here under the tree?"

"Not anymore. We just do stockings. See them pinned up by the fireplace? I'm sure Mom hung them there before she went to bed."

"What do you do with your stockings? They are so small," Michael observed.

"They don't need to be any larger to hold our 'symbolic gestures.'"

"What in the world is a 'symbolic gesture?'" he asked skeptically, scratching through his thick head of hair.

"Instead of material things," she began, "we trade symbolic gestures—promises or pledges to do something nice for one another or treat them to an experience."

"Very interesting. What have some of these 'symbolic gestures' been?" he asked curiously.

"Well, Kurt teaches junior high school. One year I pledged to make him a bulletin board for each month of school. I didn't make the boards and give them to him on Christmas; I gave him a slip of paper saying I would. When I saw how disorganized he was, the next year I promised to come in at the end of spring term to clean up and organize his files. He loved that one. He asks for a repeat every now and then."

Michael still seemed interested, so she continued. "One year Kurt arranged for a truck to carry ladders and scaffolding out to Mom's, so he and his friends could wash her many tall windows. Stuff like that."

"How did this unusual tradition get started? When did you grow up and leave the material world behind?"

Kiri sat up and pulled her legs into *baddha konasana* to play with her toes. "When I was about nine or ten, I wanted to redecorate my bedroom. It was the late 80's, so Mom thought that might be dangerous what with all the flashy colors. She also deemed it unnecessary. I begged and begged. On Christmas—among other things—I got a small box with a paint brush and a note that said I could paint my bedroom any colors I wanted so long as I was willing to live with my choices for at least two years. I was in heaven! All the other 'stuff' was set aside while I dreamed of all the possibilities—the marvelous environment *I* had the power to create—my sanctuary.

"The idea stuck. The next year Kurt thought of something similar that he wanted, and a tradition was born. Objects bring temporary gratification, but a secret surprise is the greatest! There's no expectation, so there's no disappointment. Ideas for such gifts are very hard to hatch. A lot of thought and understanding is needed to determine what might bring pleasure to another person, but seeing the delight on someone else's face and knowing your gift will be long remembered—that's priceless," Kiri finished.

"What have you cooked up for your family this year?"

"I can't tell! Then it wouldn't be a secret! But all will be small enough to fit in a stocking," Kiri hinted.

"Does Father know about this?" Michael looked a bit doubtful.

"I'm sure Mom has clued him in. Tomorrow will be a test for him of sorts… to see if he grasped the message."

"I hope he passes. I hope he understands that his future with your family is on the line here." He seemed concerned. "Then what do we do? What's next?"

"That's up to your father. He is in command of the day starting about one or two. The parents divided the day in order to be fair. He can take us for a walk in the rain, allow us to nap, tell us interminable stories of his past exploits, or lecture me on proper Irish etiquette—whatever he wants," Kiri explained sarcastically. "What can we expect?"

"The big family dinner is all I know about. But it is BIG, and it lasts forever. Traditional Irish fare—course after course. My sisters have had their staffs cooking and freezing for weeks, so remember to be impressed. Unfortunately they must serve and clean up themselves; they gave their people the holiday off, of course."

Kiri rolled her eyes. "Of course. After the grand meal?"

"Home to bed after an exhausting twenty-four hours, I expect."

"Ah, then comes the best part!" She started to imagine, her body wiggling with anticipation.

"What's that?"

"Sleeping under the Christmas tree!"

"You don't really do that, do you? I've never heard of such a thing!" Michael exclaimed in disbelief.

"Of course I do! Wouldn't miss it." She pulled the throw out from under him and motioned for him to lie down with his shoulders on it. She did the same. Then she used her bare feet to slide herself under the tree, urging him to follow. She looked up through the branches and prodded him to do likewise. "The tree is where Christmas magic resides," Kiri whispered as if imparting a secret.

"I thought that was Santa Claus," Michael whispered back.

"Oh, no. The magic is within the tree," she stated seriously. "Santa Claus is just a make-believe delivery system. A tree is an everpresent living entity with a strength all its own to stand against the wind and, here in Ireland, the rain."

He chuckled at her description. This girl who seemed so reasonable was getting carried away—maybe from the late hour, or maybe she was a ding-a-ling.

"You don't believe me, do you?" she accused.

"Yes. Yes, I do," he replied defensively. "You make a lot of sense for someone who's talking nonsense."

"A tree's branches are pathways to opportunities, to realizing your dreams," Kiri persisted. "Each branch represents a choice you must make that will lead you forward. Watch how the flames from the fire make the lights dance on the ceiling, like stars in the sky—the Aurora Borealis of Christmas—inviting you to dream without boundary."

Apparently there was no stopping her discourse, so Michael let her ramble on while he studied light patterns on the ceiling.

"Mom understands the importance of allowing grandchildren to select branches to hang their ornaments, and then to leave them there whether the decoration is pleasing or not. Those little people are beginning to reason... to make decisions on their own... to chart their own courses toward who they will become." Kiri caught Michael trying to stifle a laugh with his fist. "Are you mocking me?"

"No. No. I find this very enlightening. Entertaining, even," he responded smugly. "Please go on. Your unicorn is nearer the top and on a very short branch, I might say. What do you suppose that means?"

"Maybe I don't have so many choices left. I'm supposed to be an adult now and to know what I'm doing with my life, but I'm still dreaming. Or maybe my choices have narrowed down to a more specific goal. Maybe the shortness of the branch indicates there will soon be a change that will require taking a different turn. I'll just have to wait and see what life hands me to deal with in the next little while," she decided with a sigh.

"You're all alone up there. Does that mean you're lonely?"

"Not really. I'm the unicorn, standing on the fringe, observing and strategizing before I spring into action. I don't want to waste my energy on too many dead ends—or dead *beats*!" Kiri intended to emphasize that last with a punch of her fist to Michael's ribs, but his hand caught her wrist before the blow landed.

"So, where does Santa come into all of this? Surely you believed in Santa Claus once." He egged her on as he released his hold.

"Still do. Santa is a symbolic representation, too, of the possibility that dreams can come true. My paintbrush? That was from Santa, but I had to put in the thought, creativity and sweat to realize my dream," she said.

"If the life in a tree is so important, how do you justify cutting one down to bring home and decorate? Answer me that one," Michael challenged.

"I can't justify cutting down a tree for decoration or profit. But if someone else has done the dirty deed, why not bring the tree home and try to save it even if only for a few more days? Give it a chance to infuse you with its strength and possibilities. Just think. If we each had our own special tree, we could go there to sort things out, to find solace, and to continue dreaming as if there were no limitations," Kiri imagined.

"How long have you had this strange condition—this aligning yourself with evergreens?" Michael joked, sensing another jab to the ribs which he easily deflected.

"Oh, gosh. For as long as I can remember," Kiri answered, massaging her wrist. "I was about three and Kurt six, I guess, when we were still young enough to believe that Christmas was only on the 25th of December, and its magic lasted for a mere twenty-four hours. We decided the charm would endure as long as our eyes were open, so we cozied up under the tree together among the tinsel and the toys to hold onto the magic as long as possible. Of course we fell asleep, but a tradition was born. Our friends called us crazy; secretly, I think they wanted to do it too—sleep under a Christmas tree, even just one time." Kiri looked over at the disbelieving guy who remained very still. "Michael?"

"Hmm?"

"Are you asleep?"

"No. Just thinking."

"About?"

"About... *how crazy you are!*" He started to sit up and tussle with her when his head bumped the lower branches of the tree, causing it to rock and topple. "Yeow!"

Kiri rolled out from beneath and to her knees in time to catch the tree before it reached horizontal, but not before it dumped pine needles and dirt all over Michael and the floor. "What were you thinking... sitting up like that!"

"That I should pull your leg for the tall tales you've been putting over on me tonight. You don't really believe all you've said, do you?"

"Oh, Ye of little faith..." Kiri said as she used the bottom of her T-shirt to wipe dirt and needles out of his hair, off his face and from behind his ears. "...to doubt the magic of a Christmas tree."

Michael was embarrassed at the near disaster. "I do doubt that Santa will come tonight if we don't get to bed soon. I'll clean up the mess in the morning. I'm sure he'll understand."

The two overgrown kids trundled off to bed like sleepy children, turning off the lights and music, and leaving a mess of pine needles, cookie crumbs and dirty dishes behind with their dreams.

*　　*　　*

"How was your evening, my dear?" Tom asked once they turned out the bedroom light.

"Fabulous. The music... and the bells.... They were moving and festive at the same time. Dublin is an enchanting city, as you say. I am exhausted, though, from corralling your grandchildren all afternoon. I'm thankful Kiri was here to help. I suppose I should have warned her what to expect with your brood. Your day?"

"Near perfect. Kurt and Michael got on so well, and Kiri was great with the kids. The laughter of little voices throughout the house delighted me no end. I know my girls appreciate your help with their children. The meal and Mass were lovely too. I can't wait until tomorrow evening when we are all together. Despite your warnings, I think we have a success on our hands."

"Why only near perfect, then?"

"You weren't there with me."

"When will you believe I won't disappear if we are apart?"

"When we are bound together forever."

Chapter 4

Thomas was the first one down Christmas morning, sporting a bright red, woolen cardigan and rosy cheeks to match. His eyes "how they twinkled" as he bounced down the stairs as jauntily as his sixty-five-year-old knees would allow him. He headed toward the kitchen for his assignment. He had never had an assignment on Christmas morning before, other than to be present and in good humor, so the idea of being an important part of the morning's festivities appealed to him. Paula gave him a list: take the egg dish out of the fridge and put it on the stove top to lose its chill; turn the oven on to 350 degrees; start the water for the tea; and turn on the fireplace to warm the living room. His own list included one more duty to accomplish. He hummed to himself, completing the first three tasks carefully. Then he went into the living room to turn on the fire.

A mess at the base of the tree caused him to mutter, "Clumsy American Santa. He needs to learn to pick up after himself." Thomas would clean after he had the fire going. He turned on the gas valve and started to leave when he spied a sticky notepad and pencil on the hearth. He lifted his eyes to the mantle above and, for heaven's sake… where did *that* come from, he wondered. He emptied his pockets of their carefully thought out treasures, then sat down in a chair to ponder a moment. He returned to the pad, wrote on it, stripped the top note off, folded it and tucked it in above. He smiled to himself, his eyes still twinkling, as he left the room with a handful of dirty dishes.

Thomas ran into Michael at the foot of the stairs. "Good morning, Father. Merry Christmas!"

"Michael! Where did you come from? And, yes. Merry Christmas!"

His son, hair mussed every which way, wore baggy sweat pants and T-shirt. "I stayed the night. Couldn't face my abysmal flat. Hope you don't mind. Kiri and I made a bit of a mess last night. I meant to have it all cleaned before anyone else got up, but I see you've beaten me to it. I'll take those and finish the rest. Sorry about that."

"No need to be sorry. I'm just glad the culprit has fessed up to his mischief. Anyone else awake yet?"

"No one from the third floor. Paula?"

"She'll be down any minute to fix the tea and get the rest of our breakfast on. I'll go up and see how she's doing. After cleaning, you'd better go warm yourself by the fire," Thomas hinted with elfishness in his voice.

"Sure thing." After he finished the sweeping, Michael dumped all the dirty bits into the tub holding the tree and its water. He folded the throws and lay them across the back of a sofa, then sat on the floor in front of the fire stretching out to warm his bare feet. His eyes drifted to the mantle, did a double-take, and then blinked. He rose to investigate more closely, then took the stairs two and three at a time until he had his nose pressed against Kiri's door.

He pounded frantically. "Kiri! Kiri! Wake up and come out here right now... please!"

Kurt shouted from down the hallway, "What's going on out here? Anything wrong?"

"Nothing that a little explaining won't fix. Elves at work, you know."

"OK. Down in a few," Kurt said and headed across the hall to the shower.

Kiri peered out her door cautiously. "What's up?"

"You, you little scamp. Did you do that?"

"Do what?"

"You know what. Down by the fire."

"I haven't a clue what you're talking about," she mumbled while glancing at her watch. "And it's way too early to be talking at all. Go back to bed." She started to close her door.

"No you don't. You're coming with me." Michael pulled Kiri down the stairs, too fast for her to keep steady footing. He planted her firmly in front of the fireplace. "Did you do that?" He pointed at the mantle from which hung *five* small stockings. The footie on the end was fashioned from construction paper, laced up with yarn, and bore his name in candy sprinkles glued to one side. "*I* have a stocking and it wasn't there last night... and there are already *two* things in it!" The little boy in him shivered with anticipation.

"You saw me go to bed, and I was asleep before my head hit the pillow. Must be Santa's elves," she replied innocently.

"Not likely. What do I do now?"

"I'd say you've got some deep thinking to do," she said as she seated him by the fire and handed him the notepad and pencil. "I'm going back to bed."

"No you don't! Stay here and help me," he pleaded.

"Sorry, big guy," she said as she tousled his hair. "You're on your own for this one. Call it a test, of sorts. Don't be nervous. It's only *your* future with our family that's on the line here." She laughed as she tripped back up the stairs leaving Michael in front of the fire in furious contemplation.

*　*　*

Paula roused Kiri—her second intrusion that morning—and urged her gently to make herself decent and come join the party. For Kiri, decent meant brushing her hair and donning a sweatshirt over her pajamas and warm woolen socks on her feet. She made a quick trip to the living room first and then found everyone in the kitchen. Thomas had pulled the screens around halfway so Paula could still get in and out of the nook easily with plates of food, while the rest of them enjoyed the coziness within. The table was festively decorated, and tantalizing smells filled the air. Paula could pull a party together in no time.

The rest of the family sipped tea and nibbled fruit bread while waiting for Kiri, it appeared. Kurt moved out of the nook and disappeared, so she slipped in and slid around to the vacant place next to Michael.

"You seem nervous. Don't be. This is our half of the day, so you are commanded to be merry." And she gave his thigh a pat.

He laughed nervously. "I'll manage."

Kurt returned looking silently smug, and Paula took her turn at disappearance. Then they all enjoyed another one of her fabulous meals, her gift to everyone.

Next came the stockings. Kurt and Michael shifted some of the furniture to form a small semicircle in front of the fire and the tree. Each unhooked his stocking from the mantle and found a comfy seat. Paula explained the rules to the new members, that they would each remove one thing at a time and read/show it unless there was a particular reason for simultaneity. This year there was, so to get things started she asked Kurt and Kiri to feel their stockings for the hard egg-shape and both start with that.

Their mouths opened in amazement; their eyes grew wide and then moistened as they withdrew their objects and recognized their mother's handiwork. Both children received a personalized ornament. Each egg was divided in three sections with an old oval photo lacquered onto every one. Hand-painted decorations in holiday colors framed the pictures. In one, each child sat with his/her father; and in another each was pictured with Paula. In the third, they had the same photo with themselves together in front of a Christmas tree, their arms across one another's shoulders. They had to be young... about six and three.

An orb near the top of each ornament held the words "Christmas is..." and a matching one near the bottom read, "... whenever we're together" in Paula's delicate gold calligraphy. Kiri's had a unicorn charm attached at the very top of hers, and Kurt's, an ornate writing pen. They both laughed, and then cried, when they beheld these hints of future separation. Her children ran their fingers over the old photos, then rushed to embrace Paula. "Thank you, Mom, sooo much. These are beautiful," they choroused.

In a quiet moment Michael asked Kiri what was with the writing pen.

"Kurt E*von* Koyle was named for Kurt *Von*negut, an irreverent American author. Fits, don't you think?" she asked. He chuckled.

Next came Paula's gift from Kurt: *to split a cord of wood for your fireplace.* "Why, thank you, Son," she smiled. "We'll be needing that when we come home... late January or early February, Thomas?" He nodded and smiled a yes. "Hooray!" her kids both shouted.

Thomas withdrew his promise from Kiri for *a personal guided tour of an authentic buffalo ranch to be followed by an authentic buffalo BBQ.* "Do they do these in winter? Can we go when we visit next month?"

"Of course," laughed Kiri. "Buffalo don't hibernate like bears. A friend's uncle owns the ranch and is available most any time we can come, so you give me a date, and I'll arrange it."

"Thank you, Kirin. I can't wait to tell the men at my Club. They will be so envious!"

Michael went next. He removed Kurt's note from his makeshift stocking: *a six-pack of award-winning American brew chilled to the proper temperature, of course, and control of the remote all day tomorrow.* "Great!" he said. "I know right where we can pick up the brew, but I may chain the fridge shut on you. It will be nice, however, to get to play with my own toy, for a change. Thanks, Kurt."

Kurt drew Michael's gift next: *a test drive in my racecar at speeds you've never attained before.* Kurt fist-pumped the air three times accompanied by "Yes! Yes! Yes! This is super! Can we go now?"

After catching Paula's glance that said "Not on your life," Michael answered with, "Better save it for tomorrow. We'll have more time." The pressure was off; Michael survived the first hit and thought he might fit in after all.

Kiri opened hers from Kurt: *chauffeuring Kiri and a friend to the ski slopes. Their choice.* "Thanks, Bro. You know how I hate to drive those mountain roads in winter. Just wait until you see what I'm giving you."

"Can I have it now?"

"Nope. You have to wait your turn."

Paula opened hers from Michael: *help with grandchild care on a Kids Day.* "Hmmm. This is very nice. I'll plan an especially rough and messy one for you. Maybe something like mud volleyball with water balloons. That ought to be your style. Thank you." Michael blushed.

At Thomas' turn, he drew Kurt's: *a visit to one of our famous Colorado breweries with taste-testing to include beverages at the proper temperature.* "Can we do this too when we visit next month? I'm anxious to see what makes you think your processes are better than ours. I don't understand your aversion to warm beer. Who wants to drink something cold when the weather's so bad? Thank you. I'll look forward to it."

Michael drew Kiri's: *a lesson in how to cut up a pineapple... and a box of bandaids in case you're a slow learner.* "Very funny, miss. Very funny. You have no idea the extent of my skills, but I intend to teach *you* very soon," he said with a threatening gleam in his eye. Kiri pulled her knees up in front of her in feigned fear.

"Kirin and Kurt need to open mine simultaneously also, so let's do that next," Thomas suggested. "Feel around in your stockings for something that is not a piece of paper." They did, and both discovered a key with a ribbon tied through its hole.

"These are keys to my home which I hope you will think of as yours too. They may be used any time of the day, any day of the year, no warning or invitation necessary. I hope you will use them often and bring your friends who are equally as welcome here."

Both children were aghast. "That's mighty generous, Thomas. Thank you." Kurt shook his hand and Kiri gave him an unexpected hug.

Paula drew Kiri's: *personal packing and shipping service on demand, whenever you remember something you forgot to bring.* "That's very nice of you my dear, but more than that... it's very understanding. Thank you." She kissed her daughter's cheek.

Michael opened Paula's: *a coupon good for one catered party for you and your friends at a time and location of your choosing.* "You really mean this? Anything I want? Anytime I want? Anywhere I want?"

"Until you said that, I did. But now you have me worried. Let me revise. No naked ladies... and no naked men. Anything else I can handle." They all had a good laugh at that clarification.

Kurt opened Kiri's next: *two weekend ski packages for two at Vail. The catch is, I get one of them and you have to drive!* "Well, I guess I know where we'll be having a party soon. Funny how we seem to give things that go together. Great minds think alike? Thanks, Sis. We'll have a good time."

Kiri reached into her stocking for the last, knowing it was Michael's. His scrawl read: *a secret surprise to be revealed tomorrow morning. Be prepared.* "This is mysterious, but how can I be prepared if I don't know what it is?"

He shrugged.

"Besides, that's not fair. Everyone else will have four things and I'll only have three," she pretended to pout. "You couldn't think of anything for me, so you're buying more time," she teased further, trying to force him to confess the secret.

Michael started to blush and looked to Paula for help.

"You'll be surprised well enough, soon enough. I guarantee it. Just be patient," her mother offered.

Michael drew his last from his father: *a promise not to criticize you about the length of your hair for the next six months.* "Father, you don't mean it? You won't bug me about getting a haircut for the next six months?"

"That's right. As much as it annoys me, I will not open my mouth about your hair. Sorry it wasn't for a year, but I knew I couldn't stand it that long."

"Thank you, Father! Now... could I see your stocking... just for a minute?"

Thomas started to oblige and then thought better of it. "Why would you be needing to see my stocking?"

"Just want to check something. Won't take but a minute. Please?" and Michael reached for the small sock.

Thomas held on tightly. "I think I'd better check and see what's so alluring about my stocking." Michael lowered his head and screwed up his face as Thomas felt around inside. The three Koyles were curious to know what was going on between the two men. Thomas removed a sticky note, read it, and smiled at his son as he shouted, "Busted!"

Kurt and Kiri cried, "What is it? What is it?" as Michael shook his head.

Paula took the note from Thomas and read it aloud: *I promise to get my hair cut for the New Year's Ball.* Everyone broke into uproarious laughter, except Michael that is.

"Oh, Paula. I like this game! Even by giving in, I win!" Thomas slapped her on the knee.

Michael tried to regain his composure by taking a deep breath and sitting up straight. "Father... I think I need to argue this point. If you're not going to complain about my hair, why should I get it cut?"

"Because you promised, my son. My feeling one way or another has nothing to do with a promise made. Surely you're a man of your word. I know I intend to be. I will not complain about the length of your hair for another six months." In an aside to Paula, he admitted, "Of course, it will take that long to grow out again!" The laughter continued as Michael took his licks in silence.

Only two gifts remained—Paula's to Thomas and Thomas' to Paula. They each insisted that the other go first, until the kids decided for them that they should open together. They slowly withdrew small rolls of paper tied with ribbon. They pulled on the ribbons and scrolls fell open. The couple examined them, smiled at one another and fell into an embrace, whispering.

"All right already, folks. Not in front of the kids," Kurt demanded. "This is a G-rated celebration here. Break it up and let the rest of us in on your secrets."

They separated but continued to hold hands as Thomas showed what he had received: a small coupon book with a page for each month on which was neatly written: *I will accompany you to Mass on any one day you choose in the month of _____.* Thomas recognized that even baby steps were a sign of progress toward this most important aspect of his life.

Michael agreed, "That's a big one, Father." Thomas nodded back with a knowing smile

"Mother..." Kiri urged, and Paula showed hers: an open-ended round-trip air ticket to Colorado on which Thomas had written, *Anytime you wish. I promise not to think of a reason why you should not go when you want to. I pray you will choose to return.* He had loosened his hold and given her freedom. Thomas finally realized that once Paula knew he trusted her to return, she would not feel the intense desire to leave.

"Wow!" Kurt and Kiri chorused. Then Kurt stood up again. "Thanks, everybody, for a great holiday celebration! I say we have a group hug." They did. And did again. And again, with more thanks and pats on the back thrown in for good measure.

Michael whispered to Kiri, "You were right. Very casual, but a lot of fun. We haven't had this super a family party in… well… in a really long time."

"Our pleasure," Kiri smiled. "Be sure to remember what you just said when you're sitting in the barber's chair!"

*　　*　　*

"Five minutes! You have five minutes to pull yourselves together and get down to the living room. Five minutes!" Thomas shouted throughout the house, enjoying himself immensely.

When all assembled as directed, he announced, "According to my watch, it is now my Christmas half-day. There is no way in the world I could ever orchestrate a repeat of this morning's merriment, so I'm not even going to try. Instead, we will do the exact opposite. We're going to be calm and quiet and simply enjoy being together. You are welcome to do anything you want to… so long as you do not leave this room."

Surprised glances shot from one to another, and Kiri stifled a groan.

"I expect Kirin might nap on the sofa and Paula might read a book, or vice versa. The boys will probably watch a ball game; I notice Kurt has the remote glued to his hand. Old party games are on the writing desk at the far end of this room. You are even allowed to talk to one another or to me. I will join in wherever I want, or maybe I will just enjoy watching all of you 'hang out.' I will ferry the food and beverage back and forth, and there's a WC off the den here, so there's no reason for anyone to sneak out on the rest of us or be fussing in the kitchen. Understand?" Thomas asked.

Sober souls nodded all around.

"Good. We need to be at Anne's by 6:30, so our cars will leave at 6:15. I'll call time at 5:45 to give you half an hour to get ready to go. Michael, are you okay for clothes before I lock the doors?"

"Last night's are in the car."

Kiri wondered what she could do to meet dress code in half an hour. Hair back, necklace and heels—her professional look—she decided, should do the trick.

"Good. Any questions?" They all shook their heads. "Then, let the games begin!" Thomas shouted with a flair.

Kiri's first move was a quiet conference with Kurt. "Thomas is all about scheduling and order, isn't he?"

"Seems so. Heaven help him with Mom. She must drive him crazy with her spontaneous activity. I'm content to 'hang out' for the afternoon after the hectic pace we've kept here. I'm happy to sit and watch football," her brother said.

"I'm surprised Thomas doesn't have us sitting in a circle holding hands. Do you think he would approve if I curled up on the sofa over there by the tree and slept? Without engaging him in conversation first, I mean?" Kiri asked.

"It was his idea. Go for it. Hey, Michael," Kurt called as he pulled the sports schedule up on the screen. "Do you have a preference?"

"Nope. Your choice. The remote is mine tomorrow, remember. I'll get the beverages."

"I don't think so, Son. That's my job," Thomas reminded. "You find a spot, and I'll bring the drinks. What would you two like?"

"The usual."

"Fine. Anyone else want something while I'm up?" Both Kiri and Paula shook their heads.

When Thomas returned, he found the homey scene he desired. The guys pulled up chairs near the big screen in the den. Paula sat on the sofa behind them with her nose in a book, a pencil and notepaper beside her. She always took notes when she read, he observed, except when she read to him in bed. He liked to listen to the sound of her voice; it soothed him.

Kiri appeared to be fast asleep, rolled up in a blanket on one of the living room sofas far across the room with her back to the rest of the group. Poor thing must be absolutely exhausted, Thomas thought. No telling how late Michael kept her up last night… and how long it took her to conjure up the idea for his stocking and the stocking itself. That was very thoughtful of her. She was coming around to his idea of family after all.

Michael's presence that morning really added to his own enjoyment, Thomas felt. He and Kurt seemed to be getting along so well. Despite the misunderstanding with Kiri at her arrival, Thomas realized that Paula raised very nice children—enough fire to make them fun but enough respect for them to be mannerly. He sat down next to her and put his arm around her. She rested her head on his shoulder as she turned a page. Oh, the contentment! Oh, happy day!

*   *   *

"Anyone up for a game of scattered categories?" Kurt asked as he got up from his chair and stretched. "We have time for a couple of rounds during half-time."

Kiri rolled off her sofa and sprang to life. "I'm in!"

"Why not?" Michael chimed as he helped Kurt turn their chairs around to the coffee table in front of the sofa.

"Sounds good to me," Paula said closing her book and squaring herself to the table.

"Looks like I don't have much choice. What is this I'm agreeing to? Anything like the Categories we used to play?" Thomas asked as he leaned forward to pick up a game folder.

Paula shrugged. "You'll see."

Kiri gave a quick overview of the directions with accompanying hand gestures, much as Thomas remembered Paula doing so long ago. When she was finished, she plopped herself down on a cushion on the floor and sat cross-legged between the boys. She explained they would do a quick round, no score, so Thomas could get the hang of the game. Then they would play "for reals." Michael rolled a *D* and they all scribbled away. Once they read their answers, Thomas assured them that he was ready to go. Bring it on! Kiri rolled an *I* and blurted out, "I hate vowels! I'm no good with them. Let me roll again so it will be easier for Thomas."

"Easier for you, you mean," Michael challenged. "I say we play ahead. We're all in the same boat."

"Fine," harrumphed Kiri and took up her pad and pencil. Kurt hit the timer, and away they all went. Or did not. There was more thinking than writing going on as they clenched their eyes, bit their lips, or rubbed their foreheads trying to come up with something. All except for Thomas. He jotted away furiously as if his pencil had a mind of its own. And he smiled! When the timer signaled an end to the agony, they all read what few answers they had. Thomas, however, had answers for every category, and sometimes doubles and triples.

They were truly amazed until Kiri admitted, "I don't recognize any of those words. I think we should challenge." Kurt seemed to agree, but Michael and Paula just laughed.

"These are all legitimate words," Thomas defended. "They just happen to be Irish Gaelic, my native language. Would you like to use my dictionary to check them?"

Kiri shouted, "That's not fair!" as she pounded a fist on the table. "Some of us don't speak your language!"

"But you did not specify in your rules that we had to use 'American' words," Thomas said.

"He's right, Kiri. He takes this round. Thomas, I like your style," Kurt smiled. "Anyway, half-time is over. That was fun, everybody. Let's do it again sometime."

"Yeah. Sometime when we're careful to make the rules very specific according to the competitors!" Kiri shot a stinging look at Thomas.

Kurt grabbed his sister with both arms around her neck and jostled her from side to side. "Spoiled sport!" he charged, smiling.

She tried to break his hold but jabbed his legs in the process. "Ow! Is this how you show your support for your little sister?"

"When she deserves it," Kurt said when he released her.

"Hey, hey, hey there! This was all in good fun, but you are acting like children," Thomas objected.

"Isn't that what you wanted?" Paula asked smugly.

By the end of the afternoon, Thomas sat in a corner of the sofa. Paula snuggled next to him. Kiri scrunched herself onto their sofa and lay with her head in her mother's lap. Michael covered her with a throw and sat on the floor leaning his back against the sofa in front of Kiri's knees. Kurt stretched out on the floor in front of Thomas and Paula, his head on Kiri's cushion. The game ended—no one remembered the score. Empty bottles and popcorn were scattered here and there. Paula did not chase down each kernel as it dropped. Dark descended, so the tree lights and the fire added a warm glow to the room and softened the atmosphere. Thomas looked around him and wanted to freeze the moment. Oh, the contentment! Oh, the family feeling! Oh, happy day!

Chapter 5

Anne could not hide her nervousness as she opened the door to the Koyle-O'Connells. Paula and both her children, all together in force, added to the anticipated tension of the evening. Michael, standing with them, looked as if he were a part of *their* family. Turncoat! She invited them in, took their wraps and handed them off to her husband while she ushered the group into the drawing room to get acquainted with the rest of the siblings and their spouses until dinner was called. She exited before any of the guests had a chance to greet her.

"Hi. I'm Meghan, the middle sister. We're so glad you and your brother could come all this way to be with our family for Christmas. Let me introduce you around." She took Kiri by the hand and presented her to the rest of the gathering; Kurt followed behind.

"This is Tommy, our older brother, and his wife Margaret." Margaret held the smallest cherub from the previous day's cookie party on her lap. "Anne you've met. She's already disappeared back into the kitchen, and her husband Charles took your coats. He bankrolls this fabulous house. Emily is the youngest of the sisters. She and her husband Stephen (he waved acknowledgement) returned from Northern Ireland late last summer and are finally settled in. And Michael, the baby of the family, you have apparently met. Michael and I are currently both without partner, but neither of us intends to make that situation permanent, I hope." Meghan finished the introductions.

"Speak for yourself, Sis," he cautioned.

Kurt and Kiri, overwhelmed by the crowd of O'Connells and the ostentation surrounding them, stood closely together. "You okay, Sis?" he asked, sensing her apprehension. At her reluctant shrug, he offered, "These stuck-ups don't scare me. Stay close."

"Let's get your drinks, and then we'll mingle until Anne calls us. What would you like? Michael, can you help here?" Meghan asked.

Michael headed for the full bar in a corner of the room. He knew what his father and Paula would have. After serving them, he returned for their young guests' orders. "Nothing for me, thanks," came from Kiri.

"You're sure? You won't find a home bar so well stocked as Charles' for a long ways."

She nodded.

"In that case, I'll come with you to see what labels I haven't tried yet," Kurt offered. After receiving an OK nod from his sister, he assured her, "I'll be right back."

On his return, Kiri took his arm, moved into the crowd of O'Connells, and tried to eavesdrop on conversations while pretending a friendly interest in others. She was not particularly excited about sharing the biography of her life again and again and again and again, for each sib. Kurt was the conversationalist in the family. As long as the room steered away from politics, he would remain charming and verbose, leaving her to nod politely. Her ear picked up a snippet of exchange between Michael and Meghan.

"Father looks so good tonight, quite an improvement from last. I thought he would come apart little piece by little piece, but he is holding together well now. He even seems relaxed and cordial," Meghan observed. "And you... you look positively jolly."

"Meghan, we have had the most terrific day. You wouldn't believe... I don't know when I've had such a good time." Michael's eyes lit up with excitement.

"You mean you've been over at Father's all day?"

"And all night too—after church and through the night. If I had a choice, I'd stay there."

"A thirty-year-old man moving back in with a parent? You'd better stick to water for the rest of the evening. You're not thinking straight," Meghan laughed and moved on to chat with her father.

Anne, distraught, came to the doorway and motioned to her sisters. They gathered in the hallway and whispered. "The roast is not cooked through yet. It won't be ready on time, and I haven't finished with the table. What do we do?"

"No bother," Meghan comforted. "No one will notice if we don't sit down exactly on time. Michael and Kurt seem to be entertaining everyone."

"We'll help," offered Emily. "What can we do?"

"Help me with the table, I guess. The meat will finish itself, given time. All the other dishes have been reheated and are ready to go. I can't believe it. The only thing I had to do was get the roast in and out of the oven on my own, and somehow I've managed to botch even that."

"Let's get to the table then. What seems to be the problem?" Meghan asked.

"I have enough chairs. Dishes and silver are ready to be set on. But I don't know where to place everyone," Anne lamented.

"I thought we settled that last week," Meghan reminded her.

"I thought we did too, but I don't feel comfortable with it. Uh oh...." Anne nodded toward the doorway where Paula approached.

"What's up, girls? Anything I can do to help?"

"Everything's under control. Thanks. We're running a bit late. The roast...." Anne replied.

"Ah. Pesky roasts. Never seem to cooperate when you need them to. Not to worry. We're having a good time watching all you children get acquainted. Anything else?" Paula inquired.

"The table..." Emily let slip before her sisters could stop her. Anne was mortified.

"The table? Yes, it would be the table causing all your worry," Paula remarked. "Listen, Anne. My children and I are honored to take part in your Christmas, but we will not take your places. We will be comfortable anywhere you seat us. Put yourselves where you really want to be, and fit us in wherever. We have no preconceived notions of the proper order of things."

Paula looked directly at Anne and spoke softly. "Never mind what your father wants; you do what *you* want. This is *your* home. If you prefer to seat us in the middle with the grandchildren and to put your father at the head, that's where he will be—and he will not say a word, I guarantee. If he seems out of sorts, perhaps you would consider a shuffle before dessert, with the grandchildren too, and he could move to a seat next to me then. Please, do what *you* want. That is my Christmas wish, and you must honor it."

She turned to leave and noticed the table still empty. She stepped across the hall and returned with her daughter. "We are happy to lend a hand here. Kiri, why don't you help with the table while I take a peek at the roast with Anne," she offered.

Kiri grabbed a handful of silver from the sideboard and went to work setting a place in front of every chair. She had just about made her way around the long table when she heard snickers from Meghan and Emily who had not yet begun to help.

Anne returned with Paula right behind. "What in the world have you done! This is no way to lay a proper table. Everyone knows the soupspoon lies to the right of the teaspoon and the oyster fork to the right of soup. Now I'll have to do it all over again," she stated harshly.

Kiri was about to protest when Paula stepped in. "No need for that. Why don't you show us exactly how it should be done, and we'll have it rearranged in no time."

Meghan and Emily nodded to their sister who harrumphed her way through a lesson. The Koyle women did have the settings redone in minutes, then they left the dining room for the sisters to finish the job to their satisfaction. As they walked out, Kiri overheard Anne fuss, "Americans. They don't even know how to lay a proper table!"

"Mom, how can you be so kind to them when they are so critical of you? I wanted to tell Anne right where she could stick her spoons and her forks. If you hadn't been there, I would have. How can you even like them?"

"I don't have to like them... or love them. But I do love Thomas and he loves his daughters, so I must find the good in his girls and do my best to be understanding and compassionate." Paula put her arm around Kiri's shoulders as they walked slowly down the long, dark hallway. "That scene wasn't about spoons and forks; it was about longing and envy. You have your mother to hug you tonight. They don't. You may not be able to set a proper table, but you do know how to help others and to rein in your emotions until a more appropriate time. They don't. You and I are casual and efficient. The girls are all about spoons and show. For us a utensil is to move food to the mouth. For them, presentation is more important than function. We have to accept that we are different.

"I tried to tell Thomas that throwing our two families together for the holidays was a bad idea, but he is stubborn when he sets his mind. You and I understand we don't need proper place setting to make an occasion. We just need each other. I know you and Kurt don't want to be here. But you are, and at least we are together, so we will take the high road and do what is right—most of the time.

"Take a deep cleansing breath with me, Kiri, and we'll return to the others without saying a word about our inhospitable hostess." With a gleam in her eye and a sly smile, Paula shared, "But you can bet, the next time those girls slide into the nook for one of my great meals, I'll put a pile of *sporks* on the table and watch how they deal with that!"

Squeals of "Paula! Paula!" caught her attention as the women returned to the living area. A gaggle of children scampered down the stairs. "You're here. You're here at last." Where were they all hiding, she wondered. They were probably bribed to stay upstairs and out of trouble until dinner, but their patience obviously reached its end. They flooded into the room and found their respective fathers and then their favorite playmate.

Kiri laughed, finally brave enough to stand on her own. She took sanctuary beside the Christmas tree to admire its adornments. The tree was truly exquisite, hung with red, gold and silver balls and ornate decorations, symmetrically placed, and circled with strands of gold and silver beads, each equidistant from the one above. The evergreen was white, artificial, and garlanded with white lights. Not a ball or a needle jutted out of place. The tree made a singular if not stark statement of opulence and refinement. And it did not smell.

Michael approached Kiri from behind. "Beautiful, isn't it?"

"Yes. It is beautiful. Very elegantly done."

He whispered in her ear, "But I think I like Paula's better."

"Me, too," she sighed. After Michael moved away, Kiri heard her name being called, and she felt hands patting her legs. They belonged to the three eldest grandsons, Anne's Ronan, and Meghan's Brendan and Connor, a couple of sixes and an eight-year-old.

"What are you doing? We were waiting forever for you to get here," the boys complained.

Michael watched the quartet in deep discussion across the room, Kiri crouching to talk with the boys on their level. Then he turned back to invite Meghan and Emily to join him in conversation with Kurt. The next thing he knew—it could not have been a half-hour later—Anne came hurriedly into the room and sought them out, obviously upset.

"I can't find the boys anywhere. I can't imagine where they've gone or what they're up to. I've searched upstairs—both floors—and down, and the big boys are gone. I can't find Meggie either. If anything has happened to them... if they've wandered off...."

"Calm down, Anne. They can't have gone far. I'll take a look outside and you girls check the upstairs again. I'm sure no harm has come." Michael tried to be reassuring. He had a good idea where they might be but didn't want to say anything quite yet.

"Hurry, everyone. Please. I don't want to have to tell Father or our husbands that their boys and Meggie are missing. This is supposed to be a happy and festive evening."

"It will be, Sis. Hang on. I'm sure we'll find them in no time," and Michael headed toward the back of the house.

From the deck he could see the group below, the three boys and Kiri in her heels, with her arms wrapped around two-year-old Meggie's tummy allowing her short legs to dangle just above the ground so she could kick the black and white Irish football too. Giggles and happy laughter masked the sound of his footsteps as Michael hurried down the stairs toward them.

"Kiri Koyle! What the hell do you think you're doing with the children out here in the dark! My sisters are frantic! They're worried silly about where their children could have gone. Damn poor judgement on your part, bringing them out here without asking! No one had any idea where they were. Who the hell do you think you are? Some Pied Piper stranger coming into our family and stealing our children away? Get over here and help me clean them up. They need to be back inside before Father gets wind of this. There will be the devil to pay if this ruins Anne's party."

Michael, his face plum red and his brow deeply furrowed, wiped off little shoes as fast as he could with his handkerchief, while Kiri unrolled pant legs. Then the group scampered up the steps toward the house, Meggie in Kiri's arms. As soon as they entered, Kiri handed Meggie off to Michael as he headed toward the living room, while she went in search of his sisters, wiping mud off her own shoes on the way. Deeply hurt by what Michael said and how, she knew what she had to. She meant to bring this second unfortunate misunderstanding to an end immediately.

The young boys stood waiting for Kiri when she returned to the living room, then they disappeared and reappeared just as fast. At first, she was reluctant to talk to them, but no one else in the room seemed to take notice, so she let the boys bombard her with questions. They all huddled around the writing desk at the far end. She took a seat, and the boys ran out of the room and back again with a handful of paper and pencils. They watched intently as she began to write.

Michael wandered over, but Kiri waved him away—and it was not with a smile. After a few minutes, he tried again, but she responded the same. He waited longer and tried the third time that is supposed to be a charm, but Kiri was adamant that he not come one step closer than ten feet away, or else. Then Anne called time for dinner.

All twenty-two of them managed to fit around Anne's miles-long dining table. The table itself was elegantly laid with silver, crystal and china—perfectly arranged, at last—like nothing Kiri had seen before. Everyone had a place card. Thomas, Anne, Charles, Emily and Stephen were at one end. Tommy, Margaret, Meghan and Michael were at the other. Paula, Kurt and Kiri were in the middle along the two sides, interspersed with the grandchildren, the younger ones near their parents and the older ones near the guests. Thomas looked a bit out of sorts until Paula gave him the eye. Thankfully, Anne and her sisters appeared calm. Kiri turned her head from one direction to the other perusing all the celebrants. This is one huge family, she thought with a shudder. Heaven help us Koyles!

Michael was right. The meal was BIG—course after course: oysters, soup, salad, a light fish dish, roast with potatoes and several vegetable dishes, cheese, fruit and light dessert. The "afters"—coffee, cake and brandy—would be served in the drawing room by the fire. During the fruit, Michael caught Kiri's eye and mouthed, "No pineapple," and then faked a glum face. The children behaved, and Thomas resigned himself to his place at the head of the table, content to see all his loved ones surrounding it. Paula lost count of the number of plates each person dirtied. Twelve white tapered candles burned low, not daring to drip a spot of wax on Anne's mother's generations-old Irish linen tablecloth.

The time for "afters" arrived. Thomas' girls carried the last of the dishes to the kitchen, and fussed over them, trying to find more clean plates for cake. Paula followed them, intending to thank the girls for the lovely meal and to tell them how proud they should feel for pulling such a large fête together. She was astonished at the disarray surrounding them.

"My goodness, girls, that was a wonderful meal. Thank you so much! But any good meal makes a good mess. Let me help you with these."

"No bother. Cook will get to them first thing Monday. You join the others in the living room. We'll bring cake and coffee right away," Anne said.

"You can't live around this all weekend. My children and I will take care of it. Won't take us any time at all. I insist," Paula offered.

"But you are our guests, and we've not had cake yet," Anne replied.

"We're all so stuffed, we couldn't manage cake now anyway. Save three slices for us—the biggest ones—and we'll come join you before we're even missed. Tell me where to find the dishtowels and plastic containers." Paula began to organize the chaos in the sink.

"You girls go enjoy your husbands and your children. This will be our family's Christmas gift to you. Kurt. Kiri. Come in here, please. We have some Santa-Clausing to do!" she called to her children. "And girls, you tell your father not to dare poke his head in here, or he won't have me for dessert later!"

Emily slapped her hands over her eyes, Anne clapped one hand across her mouth, and Meghan laughed.

Crystal hit the suds first. Then clean water, clean towels, and silver came next. Then clean water, clean towels, china next. Serving dishes, pots and pans, roaster—all suffered similar treatment. The Koyles accompanied their work with jolly Christmas carols. They rather enjoyed working together—just the three of them—in such a well-appointed kitchen, larger than their own living room. They did not play "catch the wine glass" or "flip the forks" as they might have at home, however. They tried to keep their merriment relatively low-key in case someone spied on them.

As Paula predicted, they rejoined the others in no time. Three nice hunks of cake were set aside for them. Kurt and Paula took theirs to mingle by the fire. Kiri carried hers to the desk at the far end of the room, picked up a pencil and resumed writing. The boys guarded her place; she could tell by the cake crumbs scattered over her work.

Conversation finally ebbed. Thomas indicated that the evening should conclude; he would take his group home. Paula thanked the girls again for a lovely evening. Michael approached Kiri, but she gave him another one of those looks. Kurt then came to get her.

"I'm not quite finished with what I'm doing. You go ahead, and I'll take a taxi home. I assume they have taxis here. Remember, I have a house key. I won't be too much longer," and she returned to her work.

The three sisters gathered in a small group near the tree. Sleepy Meggie was in Emily's arms, and Anne's littlest boy was in hers. They formed an almost perfect end-of-Christmas-Day picture except serious discussion rather than pleasant reflection marred their faces. Emily suddenly broke from the others and rushed to speak to her father before he left. His countenance changed immediately as he hurried out the door.

When Emily returned to her sisters, Anne spoke louder than she intended. "You didn't! How could you tell Father?" Then they whispered too softly for Kiri to hear any more.

She finished her task to the satisfaction and approval of the boys. They gave hugs all around and then folded her papers and took them to show their mothers. Kiri did not wait to see the reaction. She had thanked the girls earlier for the evening's festivities, so she said her goodbyes to the men and started to call a taxi when Michael appeared with her coat.

"The others have gone ahead of us. There's no avoiding me now."

*   *   *

"One of us had to tell Father before he heard it elsewhere," Emily protested. "If Meggie figured this out, the boys won't be far behind. And Kiri may tell Paula, but I don't think she's said anything yet. Anne, I'm surprised at you. Why didn't you even tell *us*? We could have helped you figure something out."

"I can't believe what I have done," Anne said. "Father will be so angry with me, and so disappointed."

"What on earth came over you?" Meghan spoke, aghast. "You're not spiteful and vindictive. Whatever got into you?"

"I don't know. I thought I had everything under control, myself included, until one thing went wrong—and then another and another—and then the doorbell rang. There they all were, standing together on the porch, with Father in his red vest looking happier than I've seen in ages. And Michael too. The whole group looked like one big happy family... only, we weren't in the picture. Then it hit me. Father is finding happiness beyond us," explained Anne.

"At that moment I resented all the Koyles, even Paula, for intruding in our lives, and I snapped. Why should Father and Paula be happy when I'm not? Why don't those... Americans... go back where they came from!"

"Anne, you don't mean that?" Meghan cautioned.

"Oh my word! I can't believe I said that! God forgive me, I did not mean that. How will I ever make this right?"

Chapter 6

"We survived the first meeting of the septs, didn't we? And it went pretty well, I'd say," Michael claimed as he turned his car around and headed for Thomas' house. "Father certainly seemed delighted." Kiri did not comment, so he continued. "For a while there, when Anne was so frantic, I thought the evening would be a bust, but somehow it turned out just fine, don't you think?"

"I think if I hear one more word about tonight, I won't need a plane to get home. I'll scream my way there!"

"What do you mean? It wasn't that horrible, was it?"

"I mean that if I hear another word about tonight, I'll get out of this car and walk home. Please, think of something else to talk about."

"Fine." After considering through a few moments of silence, "Do you want children?"

"What!" Kiri was astonished. "Where did that come from?"

"You've been so good with the nieces and nephews…"

"I said no more talking about tonight."

He continued, "…these last *two days*, (notice I didn't say 'tonight'), I wondered if you were anxious for children of your own."

"I'm obviously not mature enough to be responsible for raising other human beings. I cannot believe how stupid I was. I couldn't stop with doing one stupid thing tonight; it had to be two!"

"Now, now. We're not talking about tonight. Your rules," Michael teased.

"I said I didn't want to *hear* another word about tonight. Apparently I don't listen to myself, so what I *say* doesn't count."

"Then, what two stupid things have you done… recently?"

"The obvious. I took your sisters' children outside without asking first. Second, I let the children design the punishment for my bad behavior. Who does that? What imbecile would let a kid design a punishment? Not a mature adult! I mean, who writes sentences anymore? I thought that went out with the Dark Ages—or at least with the sixties. I'll be horse-whipping myself for a long time over this." Kiri banged her head against the back of the car seat in frustration, causing her hairdo to unravel.

"Don't be so hard on yourself. What did you expect?"

"Going without dessert or no story before bedtime or even a time out. But sentences?"

"How did they come up with that?" Michael chuckled.

"Grace, not even involved in our escapade, butt in and said 'Whenever we do something bad at school, Sister Mary Francis makes us write sentences.' The boys seized on that, perhaps because they've all suffered through the same fate at one time or another."

"What did you have to write? *I will not…*"

"They came up with some great long paragraph about how *I will never, never, never do such a horrid thing again*, describing all my despicable acts. I could see myself writing nonstop for the next three weeks—worse than a term paper. So I talked them down to a short, direct, positive statement. I said it is important to be positive and say what you *will do* to fix something rather than repeat *no, no, no*. That just makes you feel bad about yourself and want to do it again. Empowerment comes from knowing you can change your behavior for the better."

"Very smart. I'm impressed. What did you end up with?"

"*I promise to ask permission to play outside.* I could fit it all on one line, and I thought that if they checked my work and read it enough times, the idea might stick with them too. I know it will with me. I will *never*... I will *always ask permission* before touching another person's child."

"How many of these positive phrases were you condemned to write?"

"One hundred!"

"One hundred? Oh, no!" Michael burst into uproarious laughter, and pretty soon Kiri joined him. Finally, he turned to her and said, "Do you know, you probably gave those kids the most valuable gift they received this Christmas, and for Anne's household, that's saying a lot."

"How's that?"

"You turned what could have been a very ugly, uncomfortable situation into something positive and taught the children a valuable life-lesson in the bargain," he contended.

"To ask permission?"

"That, and to own up to responsibilities and follow through with commitments you make whether you really want to or not. That's probably why they gave you one hundred sentences instead or ten or twenty; they wanted to see if you really would do it. But most important, to empower themselves with positive action instead of moans and groans. You guided them along their 'branches' toward reason and decision-making."

"Those are pretty fancy words," she said.

"Yours were pretty fancy deeds, Santa Claus. But, back to the point. Seriously. Do you want to have children?" Michael asked again.

Kiri thought quietly for a few moments. After all that happened, she was not really in the mood for a serious conversation. She wanted to get home, slide under the tree and let go of the evening. "Someday, maybe. I haven't ruled it out. I have so much left to experience—and to learn, obviously—that right now, children are not in my radar."

"What would change your mind?"

"Besides growing up myself, you mean?" Kiri noticed Michael grin and chuckle to himself. "The right man. I think it's important to find your soul mate first, and if that relationship is strong, children will come along when you're both ready."

Michael's eyebrows raised to indicate his skepticism, so she continued. "Raising kids is a two-person job. I don't intend to go it alone—no offense to my mother or your sister Meghan. One's goal in life shouldn't be children. It should be finding the love that creates them." She noticed Michael's continued doubt. "Too idealistic for you?"

"That is a rather romantic notion. But appealing. You have to realize, however, that perfection is unattainable. No man is perfect."

"I didn't say the *man* has to be perfect; he just has to be perfect for *me*. The right fit. How about you? Children? The little ones seem to enjoy you a lot."

"As an Irish Catholic, that's not really a choice. Marriage and children are one's ultimate goals in life. Witness my father, brother and sisters."

"But which is more important, the partner or the produce?"

"You make marriage sound like a salad," Michael shook his head.

"Well, isn't it? All kinds of random ingredients are thrown together and mixed, hoping for a pleasing compatible combination. Sometimes it works, and sometimes it doesn't." Kiri thought quietly for a moment. "A simple fruit salad always works."

Michael spit out a guffaw which immediately turned to a petrified "Ohhh, nooo!" He turned into Thomas' drive and left the car's motor running as if there were safety in its sound.

"What's the matter, Michael? The thought of being a mere chunk of pineapple too distasteful for you?"

"It's not that. Look. The living room lights are still on—with no other lights in the house. Father is waiting up."

"So?"

"When Father waited up—at least when he used to, when we were teenagers—it meant we had done something wrong, disobeyed, crossed the line... and we were in for a talking to. I can't imagine what I've done to displease him." He counted off on his fingers, "I dressed appropriately. I was friendly and polite to everyone, even Stephen. I engaged in conversation. I didn't drink too much. I paid attention to the kids. I offered to help. I didn't tell any dirty jokes. I can't imagine what I've done, but whatever it is I'd better go face him now." He cut the engine and got out.

"I can't believe your family," said Kiri trailing behind him. "Writing sentences and waiting up for an adult child to give him a talking to. What century do you all think this is?" She shook her head in disbelief.

"Father is rigid, I agree. Only Paula can cause him to bend with her calm persuasiveness." Michael decided they should enter by the front door. No point in trying to sneak up the back stairs like he used to. That had not worked years ago, and it was not likely to now. Just get it over with. Merry Christmas. "You go on upstairs for a while. This shouldn't take too long. I'll let you know the verdict later. See if you can guess what medieval fate I'm in for."

"I'll stay with you, if you want. Be a buffer if you need one," she offered.

"Better not. I don't want you to see Father at his worst. He's been in such a good humor today, I can't imagine... Well, here goes." Michael opened the door and they entered. Kiri headed for the stairs and he, for his father.

Thomas' voice boomed from the living room, "Kirin, will you come in here... please." It did not sound inviting, more like a command. She turned to Michael, horrified. He returned a baffled look and then barged into the room in front of her.

"Father, what do you mean by..."

"Michael, this doesn't concern you. Leave us. Kirin, come over here and sit down on the sofa. Michael, do as I say!"

Michael gave her shoulder a pat. "I'm so sorry, but don't worry. I'll be right outside if you need me. Welcome to the family." He exited the room, leaving the door slightly ajar.

Thomas motioned exactly where Kiri should sit on the sofa. Reluctantly, she did. She knew it was important to be respectful, but it was equally important not to show pride or fear. She straightened herself, folded her hands in her lap and looked directly into the eyes of the man who dared to call her out like his own child.

"Kirin, it has been many years since one of my children has brought me to this, so I am not looking forward to our conversation."

She wanted to cry out, "I am not your child and you are not my father," but she did not. She tried that the first day and came off infantile. A repeat would only make matters worse.

Thomas kept talking. "Something has gone on around me tonight which none of my children saw fit to reveal to me until the moment before we left Anne's. I want you to... I would appreciate it if you would tell me your side of the story."

Uncertain quite what the man meant, Kiri took a deep breath, let it out slowly and waited for him to take the lead. She did not avert her eyes from his.

"Kirin, I understand you took Brendan, Connor, Ronan and Meggie outside to play football before dinner. Is that true?" A wisp of his white hair fell across his forehead.

"That is not quite accurate. I didn't take Meggie. She came out on her own after we were already playing."

"Right." One side of his mouth tightened when he grew thoughtful. "Can you tell me what transpired before you went outside?"

"I admired Anne's beautiful tree until Brendan, Connor, and Ronan shouted my name. They joined me by the tree, and I asked them if they had a nice Christmas. Ronan said he got a new Irish football and asked if I would like to see it."

"And?" Thomas twirled his thumbs in his lap.

"I said 'yes,' and he brought the ball. He asked if I would go outside and play with them. I asked if it would be okay with their parents." Kiri did not blink. "When they said 'yes,' I asked if they were sure. They looked at each other and nodded. So we went outside."

"What did you do then?"

"Ronan turned on the lights in the back, and I rolled up their pant legs so they wouldn't get dirty. Then we started to kick the ball around."

"When did Meggie join you?"

"It couldn't have been more than a couple of minutes later. She came out on the deck and wanted to play. I said 'no' because she might get her dress dirty; she should go back inside. She started to cry and unbutton her dress to take it off, so I relented and said I could probably hold her up off the ground, but we'd give it a try. We passed the ball around some more. Then Michael came out and called us all in."

"What did he say?"

Moment of truth, Kiri thought. "He said Anne and her sisters were worried about us; they had no idea where we had gone. Who was I to be taking the children out in the dark anyway?"

"Is that *exactly* what he said?" Thomas' unruly eyebrows tightened, nearly meeting above his nose.

"Pretty much."

"Did he use profanity with you?"

Kiri did not know what to answer. If she told the truth, Michael would be in trouble too, no doubt. If she lied, which she felt she should not do, the truth would probably come out anyway. Maybe Thomas already knew; he would not have asked if he did not suspect. When in doubt, go with the...

"Come on, girl. Tell me the truth! Did my son use profanity with you in front of my grandchildren?" Thomas was red-faced and visibly flustered.

Kiri did not flinch. "Yes," she replied softly, her eyes still staring into his. "But he was upset and obviously angry with me. I'm sure he spoke without thinking."

"What happened after you went inside?"

"I handed Meggie off to Michael. I went in search of Anne and found your three girls in the kitchen together putting the finishing touches on dinner. I apologized to Anne and the others, and then I left."

Thomas' impatience heightened with each question. He obviously expected Kiri to be more forthcoming with her responses. "What did you say to them?"

"I told your girls that I came to apologize for taking the children outside without asking them first, despite the boys' assuring me it would be okay. I was the adult and should not have trusted their word; they were still too young to say no to temptation. I felt the boys should not bear any of the fault; I should know to ask their mothers first. I regretted any distress I caused if they felt their children were 'lost,' but I hoped an apology would put the matter to rest so we could all enjoy the nice meal they prepared. I knew how much their father and my mother counted on a pleasant evening."

"What happened then? Did my girls say anything else to you?"

"No. I left the kitchen."

Thomas repeatedly stroked his mustache with a thumb and forefinger. "Did the boys talk to you later about any of this?"

Upset now, Kiri tried to maintain a cool control. "Why do you continue asking me these questions? Am I on trial here? I told you what I did wrong; I took the children outside without their parents' permission. I told you that I apologized. If that was not sufficient apology to satisfy you or your girls, then just tell me what you want me to do and I'll do it, so we can put this behind us. I've already done penance for my sin." She stopped herself abruptly. "I'm sorry. That was very rude of me. I didn't mean to disparage..."

Thomas' visage changed instantly. "Kirin, you misunderstand me. *You* are not on trial here." He shook his head. "I'm not handling this very well, am I? I heard something this evening about my girls, and I'm trying to get to the truth of the matter before I confront them. Please bear with me on this."

Kiri's face betrayed her surprise. If she were not on trial here, she would hate to face the harsh old man if she were. Now she understood Michael's fear.

Thomas pressed on, determined to get answers out of her. "Did the boys talk to you later about any of this?"

"Yes. They found me a few minutes later and told me they went to the kitchen to apologize to their mothers for telling a lie—that they could go outside—when they weren't sure. They didn't think I should be punished because they shared in the fault."

"Were they punished, do you think?"

"I don't believe so. At least, not before we left."

"But you mentioned penance."

"I misspoke. I told the boys not to feel guilty. As the adult, I should have known better. They asked me if I would be punished, and I said I didn't know. Did they think I should be? They nodded. I asked what would be appropriate. They meted out the punishment, and I fulfilled it. Can we move on, please?" Kiri's impatience finally won out.

Thomas broke into a crafty smile. "Not until you tell me what you had do."

"I wrote sentences. One hundred of them. *I promise to ask permission to play outside.*"

Now Thomas laughed at her. "Oh, Kiri. I'm so sorry. So that's why all of you gathered around the writing desk for the whole evening. I couldn't imagine what you did to keep those active boys so intensely interested. While you were in the kitchen with your mother, I tried to discover your secret. The boys were very hush, hush and said they needed to guard some papers for you so the 'little' kids would not scribble on them. I heard them whisper, 'That's 72; only 28 to go,' but thought nothing of it."

"I had them number all the sentences for me while I helped in the kitchen. I thought it might speed up the job."

Thomas really roared now. "Oh, Kiri. Kiri. You were sorely mistreated tonight, first by Michael, then by his sisters, then by my grandchildren, and now by me. What can I do to make this up to you, you poor child?"

Kiri bristled at the reference again. "Well, first you can not call me a 'poor child.' I'm not 'poor' and I'm old enough to take what's coming to me. Next, you could tell me what the point of this interrogation is."

He chuckled. "Ah, yes. The point. As we were about to leave Anne's house, Emily rushed over to me with Meggie. Apparently the girls discussed the sordid events of the evening when Meggie protested, 'Auntie Anne is not telling true!' According to Meggie, she was about to follow you outside, when Anne caught her leaving and asked whereto. Meggie said, outside to play with you and the boys. Anne apparently gave her a pat on the head and said, 'Go along, then, but don't stay too late. Dinner will be ready soon.' Meggie went on to say that a few minutes later you both saw Anne watching all of you from the window, that you waved to her and that she waved back. Kirin, is that true?" Thomas stared deep into her.

"Yes, it is," she admitted, finally letting her gaze drop to the hands she still had folded in her lap.

Hearing this, Michael burst through the door. "You mean to tell me that Anne's story about *lost* children was a phony? She knew all along where they were, and she lied to all of us!"

"You are not supposed to be in here, Son. This discussion is between Kirin and me."

"Inquisition is more like it! Have you listened to yourself, Father? You've grilled Kiri as if she were a guilty teenager. And she's managed to keep her cool and stand her ground against you... which is more than your own children could have done, myself included."

"You didn't treat her any too kindly yourself this evening. I think apologies are due all around."

Michael turned to Kiri. "Why didn't you tell me the truth when I railed at you?"

"I tried to, but I couldn't get a word in between all your expletives."

"I am so sorry! I apologize for what I said to you. I promise never, never, *never* to..." He stopped short when he saw her icy glare. "I promise to...." He was fumbling for the words. "I promise to...." He was thinking hard. "I promise to choose appropriate language to express my anger," and he let out a deep sigh.

Kiri laughed. She could not help it.

"Private joke?" Thomas asked. They both nodded. "I don't understand why you didn't tell me about Anne the first time I asked you to recount the events of the evening."

"Because I thought you were angry at *me* for what I had done, and what Anne did or didn't do was irrelevant. When Michael upbraided me, he said something very important. He said that I never should have taken the children without asking first. So true, no matter how he chose to say it. I did something wrong, and I owed the mothers an apology. The fact that Anne did not fess up didn't change a thing," Kiri explained.

"When I walked into the kitchen and saw all three of your girls standing there, and Anne so nervous, I thought... Well, I thought about what we say when encountering an injured or wild animal. You don't challenge it, you don't show fear, and you don't turn your back on it. You face it with strength and confidence. That's how I tried to approach Anne. I learned long ago that you can't control how other people treat you; you can only control your own reaction to them. I apologized for my wrongdoing. What Anne chooses to do is up to her. My conscience is clear; at least, it will be when you finally let me off the hook here."

"Absolutely. You are definitely off the hook," Thomas stated. "Apparently we O'Connells will be writing sentences for you for a very long time!" Michael laughed and Kiri groaned at the mention of more. "But I hope you will indulge me one final question. Why do you think Anne behaved as she did?"

"I don't think I should answer that. I have no idea what went on in her mind. It would be pure speculation on my part, and I don't think I could give an objective opinion," she replied.

"Please. You must have some idea. You are both young women for one thing, and I know she's a well-meaning person most of the time. If you have any notion, it would help me deal with her tomorrow, and I promise not to...." Michael shot Thomas a glance that stopped him abruptly. "I promise to listen calmly with an open mind."

"If you're sure...?"

Thomas nodded.

"Then Michael will be our witness that none of what I say will be repeated."

Thomas nodded again. Michael rested his forearms on the back of the sofa and leaned in to hear what she dared say to his father. Her first words stunned him.

"I don't like you very much, Thomas," Kiri began with hesitation. "You are a nice man, a kind man, a generous man, so I should like you, but I don't. You frighten me. You represent the end of my life as I know it. I resent you for the change you are forcing on me. I'm not ready to accept that change as inevitable, but I *am* trying.

"Every time I see you put your arm around my mother's waist, I see her move closer to you, away from me. Whenever you take her hand and she squeezes yours in return, I see her shift toward you and from me. And when I see you look at her and see her return your glance, she drifts further and further away.

"When we first arrived at Anne's house, I could tell she was nervous and out of sorts—maybe feeling the pressure from last night's dinner, then Christmas morning, and then tonight's. I don't know if simple fatigue was the villain, but I suspect not. I think it went deeper than that."

Kiri searched Thomas' face for a clue to his reaction. "I think that she, and actually all of your girls, are confused and agitated about your relationship with my mother, just as my brother and I are. Deep down they want what's best for you. They want for you to be happy again, but they don't quite know how to reconcile this new reality.

"When Anne saw all of us standing there, together, it tipped her over the edge and she couldn't accept the present situation. I felt the same way. When I saw your whole family gathered there in the drawing room, I felt outnumbered. If there were a battle, we Koyles definitely would not be on the winning side. As it turned out, there was a battle of sorts… and it won't be the last.

"I love my mother so much, and she deserves to be happy. But I'm finding it hard to admit that all the joy and love she derives from me and Kurt, her children, are not enough to fill the void in her heart that yearns for the love and companionship of a good man. I suspect your girls have not come to that understanding either. They are trying their best to fill your life with their love and their children's and to make you a part of everything they do so you will not miss their mother so much. They don't understand that even though you will always love their mother—for I know you do— you still have a present need for the love and companionship of a good woman."

Thomas lifted his handkerchief to his forehead and let it pass over his moist eyes on the way back to his pocket.

"For the moment they are filled with resentment for our family, just as I am for yours. Neither you, nor my mother, nor any of us can change that feeling by wishing. Your children need to come to that realization themselves," Kiri continued.

"You're a nice man and I know my mother is happy and safe with you, but I want to pack her up in my suitcase and take her home with me and never see Dublin again. However, at least I understand that feeling inside me, and I try to keep it under control. I'm trying to accept that Mom is not replacing me with you; she's enlarging her heart to encompass us both. She expects me to do the same. I ask for your patience." Her eyes appealed to him.

"For Anne tonight, her emotions won. She lashed out at me because she doesn't know how to tell you or my mother how she feels and because I was there. To add to her discomfort, Mom really helped her out with dinner, and Anne felt conflicted and guilty. If it hadn't been children playing outside, it would have been something else. She had no control over how she acted."

Kiri offered, "If I can give you my advice as well as my opinion, you shouldn't 'deal with her' tomorrow. You should let Anne come to you after she has time to reassess the evening. Eventually, she will."

"Oh my dear Kirin. Will you stand up and let me hug you close?" Thomas approached her more gently this time. "You are wise beyond your years and the strongest of all my children. I see that clearly. You have an ancient inner strength. Through all the years your mother and I may share, I know it will be you who will hold this family together... or allow us to break apart. Thank you so much for giving up your own plans and coming such a great distance to make this holiday a very special and important one for all of us. I hope I haven't completely spoiled your Christmas; mine has been more than I ever could imagine." He conveyed his appreciation with a kindly smile.

"For heaven's sake, Father. Don't place the whole weight of our two families' survival on Kiri's shoulders," Michael interjected. "Surely you have faith enough in your own children to come through for you and carry some of the load."

"Then let it start with you, my son. You have a surprise to produce, and it better be a good one. As for me, I'm going to bed. Paula has dessert waiting for me!"

"Father! Yew! Children present!"

Thomas disregarded his son's impudence. He was long gone, taking the stairs two at a time, until he stumbled and had to settle for a jaunty one-step.

When they heard the bedroom door close, Michael turned to Kiri and asked, "Don't you find that disgusting?"

"What? Our parents sleeping together? The way I've been treated tonight? Your foul language? That Christmas is almost over, and I'm not yet bedded down under the tree?"

"Oh my gosh, I almost forgot. The tree! But really, what do you think of Father, now that you've seen all his sides—best to worst?"

"Really?" Kiri wanted to be very careful here. "I think your father is an aging... Alpha-male... who gives a great bear hug."

Michael laughed at her fitting description. "That is so true. Very perceptive. Wanna hit the fridge?"

"Nope. I'm going to jump straight into the shower. I plan to use every last drop of hot water to wash all the negative emotion, distress and frustration right down the drain so I can come to the tree feeling nothing but 'peace on earth, good will to men.' All men—including your father."

Michael hollered after her as she climbed the stairs, "Remember to take off your clothes first!"

Kiri hollered back over her shoulder, "Ha. Ha. Very funny. I hope you choke on a hunk of pineapple!"

* * *

Tom turned on the light in their room to find Paula on the floor at the foot of their bed resting in a supported child's pose. An open cedar chest released its soothing aroma to further relax her. She turned her head from left to right and snugged the bolster closer to her chest. "Did you get lost in your own house? I've been waiting here in the dark for you forever."

"No. I had a sense that there was some friction between our girls this evening, and I wanted to chat with Kirin." He knelt to massage her shoulders. "I'm sure it will work itself out. They are all adults."

"You do know that when we are together as family, our adult children slip into their old roles and become children again."

"Not ours," he was certain.

"In your dreams. I'm sure we don't know the half of it." Paula wondered if her daughter apprised him of the dining room episode.

"I'm sure we don't," Tom agreed, hoping Kiri had not shared the incident over the grandchildren with her mother. "How are you feeling after our long day?"

"I've never seen so much food on one table, nor eaten so much. I'll pay for my gluttony for weeks."

"You don't have to eat everything that is set in front of you, you know."

"I wanted to try it all, and I didn't want to offend your girls."

"My girls? You couldn't possibly offend them." Tom gave her a peck on the cheek. "Now that I've had my turn with Kurt and Kiri, what would you like to do on your children's last day—beyond Michael's surprise, that is? A tour? A concert?"

"I would love to sit with an arm around each one all day long, but I think we should leave them be—not force them into more activity—if you want to foster that elusive family feeling you keep talking about. They need some time to digest—both the meal and our situation."

"Wisely thought out, as usual." Tom helped her up from the floor and put out the light.

She crawled under the covers. He climbed in beside her and pulled her close. "I miss being near my children, Tom. I'm not sure I can wait a whole month to see them again. You... We have to be more serious about alternating time between here and my home. I want you to know them as the adults they are, not as the roughhousing adolescents they've been these last couple of days. I hope our brand of family hasn't been too wild for you."

"Not at all. I've secretly enjoyed their antics, but I don't know how to show it. My children must have behaved that way too."

"You mean, you don't remember?"

"No one dared challenge Tommy, him being the oldest and reluctant to initiate childish tomfoolery. Anne thought she was above such silliness and scolded anyone who stepped out of line. Emily giggled a lot. She yearned to join in, I know, but would never cross her sister. That leaves Meghan and Michael—the firebrands. Yes, they did keep things lively around here. I do remember now."

Tom squeezed her tightly. "Thank you, Paula, for a wonderful day—exactly what I wanted for Christmas. Near perfect."

"Only near perfect? What was missing?"

"That dessert you promised me!"

Chapter 7

Kiri did... take her clothes off before stepping into the shower. She had no idea how long she remained there. She let the hot water hit her head and then ripple down her body until it pooled at her feet and was sucked down through the vortex in the drain. She thought about Christmas morning and how extraordinary it turned out to be—a really wonderful time. She thought about the afternoon and how something that sounded so simple and so mundane turned out to be rather extraordinary—a really wonderful time. She thought about the evening and how out-of-the-ordinary it was. Not so wonderful, but revealing. Life was like that—some wonderful and some not so great all mixed together, like a salad. Not every hour of every day could be extraordinary, she knew, but today so much emotion was compressed into such a short time. Now was her time, finally, to decompress and she intended to do exactly that, to let all her feelings neutralize and to find a harmony with the spirit of the tree.

The bathroom door creaked open. She called out in a loud whisper, "Ghosts? Norman Bates? Whoever you are, you better get out of here before I scream!" The door closed. She watched the wall for shadows and listened for any signs of movement. Satisfied that she was alone again, she resumed enjoying the play of the water.

When the water turned cold, she shut it off and pulled back the curtain to reach for a towel. A stack of fresh bath towels and her neatly folded pajamas waited for her on a stool. Nice ghost, she thought. She dried herself off, slipped into her pjs and wrapped a towel around her wet head. She opened the door to cross the hall to her room and almost tripped over a body, leaning against the jamb, nearly asleep.

"Michael! Why haven't you gone to bed?"

"I wanted to make sure you didn't drown." He straightened himself and lifted his head to look at her. "My word, we have a lot of hot water in this place. You took forever in there."

"Thank you for the towels and clothes. I didn't think about them, I was so anxious to get into the water."

"Don't thank me. I didn't do anything. Must have been Christmas elves," he replied innocently.

"Well, then. 'Thank you, elves,'" she chuckled. "You'd better get to bed. It's really late."

"Are you still going to sleep downstairs?"

"Of course."

"Is Kurt going to sleep down there with you?"

She laughed. "No. He gave up the tree thing long ago. I'm the only infant left in our family."

"Then can I come down and sleep with you? I mean, under the tree with you? I mean, under the tree with you on one side and me, the other?"

Kiri laughed again at his deep-seeded sense of propriety. "Suit yourself. It *is* your father's house. Do you think I should ask permission first to take you with me?"

Now Michael had to laugh. "No. Best not to disturb him. I'll help you write sentences, if it should come to that. What do I need?"

"Something to roll up in. The blankets off your bed, I suppose. I doubt you're the sleeping bag type."

"You have no idea of all the places I've slept," he stated.

"Do I want to?" she asked suggestively.

Michael flushed at the inference.

*   *   *

Kiri took her time drying her hair and gathering blankets and pillow. She tip-toed quietly down the stairs and into the living room expecting to find Michael asleep. She found his bedding rolled out on the left side of the tree, but he was not in it. He probably chickened out, she guessed. The tree lights, the fire and the music were on the same as the previous night. She folded one blanket onto the floor on the tree's right side, lay down and covered herself with the other. A few deep relaxing breaths, then she would take a final look at the tree and drift off quickly, she hoped.

She closed her eyes, inhaled the exhilarating scent of pine, absorbed the warmth of the fire and thought to herself, a light skiff of snow would make this a near perfect holiday. She opened her eyes to drink in the last twinkling of lights... and saw Michael standing over her, staring hard.

"Oh, good. You're awake. I made us a pot of tea."

"You?

"Why not me? I may be single, but I'm not helpless. Here. I brought mugs. Hope you don't mind." She nodded a thank you as he set one in front of her. "You're wrong way 'round. Your feet are under the tree."

"Safety precaution," Kiri said as she sipped her tea and let its warmth flow through her insides. "I was afraid you might wake up in the night and topple this live needle factory over on me again."

"Good point." He turned his bedroll around and sat cross-legged on it. "Ah, this *is* nice." He took a long sip from his mug and gazed at the tree.

Kiri sat up to face him. "Where have you slept, Michael, that makes bedding down on the floor second nature?"

"Lots of places on assignment, none of them very glamorous. In Iraq I had an army cot, but in Pakistan I rolled in a blanket on the floor of a hut, and under the stars in Afghanistan. I didn't enjoy that one much—more stones than dirt and too cold. If I have to sleep outside, I'd rather it be the Sudan where at least it's warm. You name a Middle Eastern or African country that has been a hot spot in the last eight years, and I've probably slept there."

"I thought foreign correspondents stayed in hotels or company flats."

59

"In many of the larger cities, that's true. But not all the news takes place in the cities. As a single man with no young family, I go where they tell me to go. I'm not usually in the field for long. I know I'll be back for a hot shower and a clean bed within a few days, so I don't mind roughing it."

"Do you have any say in where you're sent? Why don't you ask for Paris or Amsterdam?"

"That's not where the help is needed right now. I go where I can do the most good." He diverted his eyes from hers and studied his mug.

Kiri sensed there was more to his story. "What exactly do you do?"

He took a deep breath. "I don't mean to be evasive or smart-alecky about this, but I really can't tell you. Not even Father knows for sure. I follow the news. Can we just leave it at that?" He wiggled under his blanket. "I will say that if I have to sleep on a floor tonight, I'm glad it's a clean floor, under a clean blanket with a clean companion."

She chuckled as she finished the last of her tea, set it aside and slipped back under her own covers. She took another relaxing breath and closed her eyes. "Do you think I hurt your father tonight with what I said?"

"I don't think so. He asked. You answered. You were respectful, just blunt. Why?"

"Do you think I should return his house key after what I said about never wanting to come back?"

"Now, that would hurt his feelings. He means for you to keep it and use it. He wants you to know you are welcome as family whether you choose to take advantage of the offer or not. If he changes his mind, he'll probably just change the locks," he teased.

They lay quietly and lost in thought as the music played on, the fire kept them warm and the lights danced on the ceiling.

"Kiri?"

"Yes, Michael."

"Did you mean what you said tonight? About never wanting to see Dublin again?" He turned toward her now and propped up his head.

She turned toward him and propped her head up as well. "When I said it, I did. From what I've seen, Dublin is gray, drizzly and stone cold. I know nothing that would entice me back here."

"What about your mother... or me?"

"Last time I checked, you were people, not things."

He chuckled. "Well then, we'll tour around tomorrow, and I'll show you some more *things*. Maybe you'll change your mind."

"Maybe I will. Ask me again tomorrow night. You're going to be one very busy elf tomorrow, aren't you? There's my surprise and Kurt's test drive and now a city tour. When will you ever find time to touch the remote?"

"Hmmm. We may have to give up your surprise to make time."

"I knew it! You don't know what you're going to do yet, do you? Admit it!"

"Of course, I know what I'm going to do. I'm going to sleep right now so I will have energy enough to live up to all my obligations. Good night." Michael lay back down with his face toward the ceiling and his eyes closed.

Kiri did the same. "Good night." She took another relaxing breath and almost closed her eyes. "Michael?"

"Hmmmm."

"Do you know when or where our folks met?"

"You mean, last June or long ago?"

"Both, actually.

"June is a mystery. It wasn't here in Dublin or in Colorado, apparently. As for long ago, that's just as much of a puzzle and likely to remain so. We can try to figure it out. I heard reference to 'forty years ago.' Even if that is not exact and it is now December 2008, that puts them together in the late sixties. Any ideas?" he inquired.

"Mom backpacked through Europe in the late sixties—you know, the 'Summer of Love'—so possibly then, though looking at how different they are—backgrounds, I mean—I can't imagine where it might have been."

"When Father was away from the city, he either sailed along the east coast or visited relatives in the west. My vote is for the west, I guess, since I know he went back there this past June."

"I can't imagine my mother spending much time alone along the sparsely populated west coast."

"Your mother was alone?" he asked, surprised.

"That she was. She hitchhiked most of the time. Think we'll ever find out for sure?"

"Probably not. Now, go to sleep."

"Michael?"

"Hmmm?"

"Will I really get a surprise tomorrow?"

"Of course. I promised."

"If you won't tell me what it is, will you at least give me a hint?"

A cunning grin crept across his face. "I'm going to prove to you that Christmas *is* whenever you're together no matter what the date on the calendar. Anything else you'd like?"

"I'd like to see Mom's inner sanctum, of course, but she hasn't offered yet. As for Dublin, maybe see something that isn't stone and maybe one of the singing pubs I've heard about. I'm really not that hard to please. Despite this evening's events, I've actually had a very satisfying, pleasant holiday. I think I'm ready to go to sleep now. Good night, Michael."

"Night, night, Kiri. May all your Christmas dreams come true."

Chapter 8

"Michael, what do you think you are doing!" Thomas' voice boomed as he opened the French doors and entered the living room, surprised to spy two bodies on the floor. Paula warned him he might find Kiri, and even Kurt, there… but Michael?

Kiri's head disappeared under her pillow. His son rubbed the sleep from his eyes as he looked up at his father and replied, "Sleeping under the Christmas tree—an old family tradition. Koyle family, that is. Problem?"

"Paula has breakfast started for all of us. Better get up. And when you're finished being embarrassed, Kirin, you should be getting up too. You can nap later. Tea is ready." Thomas left the room shaking his head and chuckling.

Kiri could not imagine why they had to rush on the day after Christmas, but the looks on Thomas' and Paula's faces hinted that something was afoot. Maybe they expected company and needed to have the living room mess cleaned up. Whatever. She could not believe she was so hungry after last night's meal. Must have stretched her stomach. "Thanks, Mom. Yummy, as usual. Need any help?" she tossed over her shoulder on the way to her bedroom upstairs before Paula could answer.

"Hold on there, Kiri," Michael said mysteriously. "It's time for your secret surprise." That stopped her cold in her tracks. "You should be dressed in warm comfortable clothes, and you need shoes, hat and coat. Hurry, now. We don't want to be late."

"Where are we going?" she asked with a big smile and expectant eyes.

"You'll know when we get there. Hurry."

She did not have to be told twice and ran for the stairs.

"What's up?" Kurt asked, unable to imagine what was in store for his sister. The other three let him in on the secret. "I can't wait to see this. Good one, Michael."

Kiri reappeared wearing everything he ordered. "Ready!"

"I don't think so. No jeans. They're not comfortable enough. Go change."

With a harrumph, she ran upstairs again and soon returned in her pajama pants.

"What part of '*warm* and comfortable' do you not understand?"

"The part where these are the only two things I brought that aren't a skirt."

"My word, woman. Come with me." Michael grasped her hand and dragged her upstairs. He brought his sweats from the bedroom and motioned for Kiri to put them on over her pjs.

"I can't wear these. They're yours," she protested.

"I trust you won't have an accident in them, then. Jump in and let's go." He led her back downstairs to the front door. "Oops! Forgot the most important thing." He took a camouflage bandana from his pocket and blindfolded her. "Now we're ready to go."

"Kurt? Mother? Help. I'm being kidnapped!" Kiri shouted good-naturedly as she stumbled out the door behind Michael, headed in the direction of his car. He buckled her in, still protesting, backed down the drive, and squealed away toward the city.

He sped for a couple of blocks, then made a sharp right and really gunned the motor. Then a sharp left. When Michael did a 180, Kiri was afraid for her clothes—and his. He swerved again, and then did a 360, she thought. She could not be sure, but she knew her stomach turned at least that much.

"Michael, is this some kind of a joke? If you are trying to make me sick, you are about to succeed."

"Hang on. Just a bit further. You don't want them to catch us, do you?"

"Who is 'them'?" she asked between gasps, but did not hear an answer, as the car swerved and spun again. On a blazing straightaway, she managed to blurt out. "Michael, stop! This isn't funny."

"It's not supposed to be funny. It's supposed to be a surprise." He moderated his speed and turned onto a gravel road, Kiri thought. The car bumped along, turned and came to a stop. He jumped out quickly and came around for her. Then he took her up a pathway, through a gate, along more pathway, through a door and up some stairs...

"Be careful, duck your head. Through here. Stay close so you won't fall off. Closer!"

...then down some stairs.

"Jump. Now, this way. Step over that. Good. Just a few more steps. In here. Sit down and wait until someone comes. No peeking. You have to promise."

"I don't think I like this."

"You will."

Kiri heard his footsteps walk away. Then footsteps returned, a door closed, and someone sat next to her. The blindfold began to loosen and then fall from her face.

"Welcome home, Sweetie."

*   *   *

Kiri opened her eyes... and could not believe them. Her mother sat near her in Paula's Colorado library... or at least a near replica. An identical fireplace nestled between tall windows and burned with a nice warm fire. A similar desk held her computer station with writing pads stacked just so, pictures of her children and souvenirs. Books filled duplicate bookshelves. Same carpet, same couch and chaise, and same coffee table, grouped in the center of this expansive room, faced the fireplace. Even comparable wood paneling extended half-way up the walls to meet a soft wheat color.

The only difference was where other windows should be. Instead of vistas of her mountains, giant-sized 6 ft X 12 ft photographs graced the walls—pictures of Paula's beautiful summer mountains as seen from her library. The last winter snow clung to the high reaches of deep purple peaks giving way to fingers of treed valleys pointing to variegated green foothills below. Patches of multi-colored wildflowers dotted the landscape until it turned to cultivated fields alive with new growth.

The other side of the large room, opposite that which was indisputably Paula's, housed a media center similar to the one in the den and easily visible from the central lounging area. In the far corner diagonal to Paula's desk, a second one, exactly set-up with computer and papers, displayed photos of Thomas' family.

"Mother, what is this? Where are we?"

"We're home, Kiri. *My* home. Thomas created this suite for me last summer when we visited Colorado. This was *my* surprise... my special surprise when we arrived here. He wanted me to be comfortable. He wanted me to feel 'at home' while far away. Welcome to my 'inner sanctum.'"

Paula confided, "I haven't shared this with anyone except Thomas... and now you. For the rest of the morning, it's just you and me." She put her arm around her astounded daughter. "No phones, no TV, no chores, no bustling, no distractions, no interruptions and no one else but the two of us—the only two people in the world." They curled up together on the couch in front of the fire, gazing at Paula's mountains, and began to talk.

*   *   *

"Do you think you surprised my sister?" Kurt asked Michael as he came into the den.

"I think so. Her sense of direction was all messed up by the way I swerved her around. I feared I might make her sick, but she survived. Kiri's got a strong constitution. How long do you think your two women will be? An hour or so?"

"Knowing those two, it could be a day or so."

"Why don't we take your test drive, then?" Michael suggested. "You'll need coat, hat and shoes. I've got extra gloves."

"Now?" Kurt asked excitedly. When Michael nodded, he bounded up the stairs and reappeared seconds later, ready to go. "Can we put the top down?"

"It is freezing."

"Who cares? Let's go!"

"Out the back. The car is in the alley. All part of the ruse," Michael revealed. "I'll drive us out of the city. Then you can take over—to get you used to driving on the left before we get to the track"

"The track?"

"You'll see."

While Michael drove, Kurt asked how Thomas accomplished such a feat—a virtual facsimile of his mother's beloved library—without being in Dublin to oversee its construction.

"Father created the scheme, that's true," Michael said. "But I managed his project, and I hope never to have such a task again. I hired a contractor willing to work crews 'round the clock until complete. We only had about three weeks, you know."

He explained that to guide the design, his father took pictures of every detail of Paula's library and, from the deck outside, a 180-degree perspective of her mountains. He also wanted the bathroom tub duplicated. He sent Michael a photo file with instructions about knocking down walls to make adequate room in order to create what he called a "suite" of rooms where he and Paula would spend most of their time. He wanted Michael's mother's furniture moved to an "emergency room" so that the girls would not be offended, but he needed to feel free to begin a new life with a new partner.

When Michael questioned the cost, Thomas said, "Think of this as an investment... an investment in my future happiness. When it becomes the family's, you can sell the house and make a bundle, for there will be nothing else like it in Dublin." So his son complied.

"Why wasn't your brother asked to help? Or your sisters?"

"Father wanted it to be a secret meant only for Paula. Tommy would tell his wife, and she can't keep anything from my sisters. Pretty soon the whole city would know, 'Thomas O'Connell is building a palace for his live-in... special friend.' All of us would want to see it, of course, and would make critical comments. Father couldn't stand the thought. He wanted the two of them to start their relationship here anew, 'no ghosts or shadows lurking,' as he put it."

"I can't believe it," Kurt said. "Even down to the bathtub. That's almost a custom design, you know."

"I know. Father and I both did some fancy talking to convince the manufacturer it was for the same customer. Father can be very persuasive," he said.

"The tub looks like it has the same jets and about the same dimensions, but does it have the temperature sensor?"

Michael nodded.

"And the sea simulator?"

Michael nodded again.

"Kiri and I love to go out to Mom's house just to use the tub sometimes. Who needs a whirlpool when you can experience the whole ocean! I don't suppose you've had a chance to try it out," Kurt wondered.

"Not on your life. From the moment my father and your mother walked into that house together until today, no one else has set foot in that suite. I, of course, got to see the finished product but never how they fixed it up to be 'theirs.' My sisters would be so jealous if they knew I got a peek today."

"There's much more to your father than appears," Kurt admitted.

"That there is. And let's hope today he has it together enough to remember his part in this surprise: no interruptions nor intrusions; the women will be out when they are good and ready!" The two young men laughed, imagining Thomas sitting at the top of the stairs waiting for the slightest indication that the females had talked themselves out.

"Here's where we switch," Michael said, pulling over to the side of the road. "You can drive from here on. We'll go about fifteen km in this two-way traffic until you're comfortable with it. Then we'll turn off toward the track. Keep your speed under 100kph here and under fifty on the side road. We'll hit super-speed later."

Kurt knew enough to follow directions. The icy wind whipping past his face felt so good, almost like flying down a ski slope. They pulled up several minutes later in front of a massive chain link gate with the name "Raceleigh" welded on it, accompanied by "Private Property—Under Surveillance." Every direction Kurt looked along the fences, he noticed electronic monitoring just like a military installation. "What is this place?" he asked.

"Tell you in a minute. I'll need to take over the driver's seat until we're well in," he replied. He and Kurt switched seats, and Michael idled the car at the first station until retinal and fingerprint matches confirmed his identification. The second station confirmed his car's ID, and then the gate slowly opened allowing them a speed-controlled entry.

Michael explained, "A few years ago, some mates and I got together at our favorite pub and compared our lives as single young men with very few responsibilities. Besides marital status, our common interest seemed to be speed—the thrill of driving fast—which we couldn't do legally anywhere near the city. So we pooled our money and bought this piece of property— about four square miles, in your terms—out in the middle of the boonies where we could do just about anything we wanted with it. No restrictions.

"We designed a track with curves of all degrees, even hairpin, a few slopes and dips, that sort of thing. We saved the woods and shrubbery to maintain a private feel, but we paved two lanes wide so we could race. When we needed more capital, we let a few more in on the deal. There are about twenty of us now, and others begging. Even that is too crowded if we all want to use the track at the same time, so we tell others to go build their own playground."

Michael directed Kurt to push a button on the dash, and a whole section turned into a screen displaying the complete track—twelve miles within the boundary, twisting and turning back on itself many times. "Our cars all have custom electronics that exchange information with the sensors planted along the raceway. Once we're on and our system is activated (which you just did, by the way), the screen will show any obstruction—other vehicle or deer, for instance—within a half a kilometer in either direction by a yellow line which shortens as the distance does. That allows us to take a curve without worrying about running into something we can't see. When these arrows along the top of the screen start to blink, they warn that the traffic direction will change in about five minutes. We can judge where we are on the track and how long we have to make the exit or a pullout before that happens. Those are the basics."

"Wow!" exclaimed Kurt, shaking his head. "Where did you get all this stuff?"

"Most of the technology has been around awhile for government and military use, but it is available to the public. You just have to know where to look for it, how to acquire it, and be able to pay for it."

"What kind of a job do you have that makes this possible?"

"Let's just say it pays well enough to allow me to work off my frustrations with speed. Shall we give it a try?"

"You bet! I'm ready."

"Two more things, actually. Helmets are required, although car tops are optional since a roll bar frames the windshield, and you must blow into the breathalyzer. No helmet or too much alcohol... no ride. The car will completely shut down before it hits the track. This is safe and sane recreation we created." Kurt complied. "Touch the screen here, and we can talk to each other. Here, other drivers. Let's go!"

Michael wanted Kurt to take the first circuit at between 80 and 100 kph to get a feel for the car and track. "Second go 'round, you can travel 100 to 120 kph, and third time around, 150 kph. Then we'll see if you're up for more."

Since Michael's racer was the lone car on the track at the early hour, Kurt felt safe in going slow enough to try all the controls and gears. Then he stepped on the accelerator, and away they flew. Kurt was in heaven!

Heaven was interrupted more than an hour later when their radio flashed and Michael connected with #142. "Hey, there, Mighty Mike. You drivin' today?"

"Negative. I've got family in for the holidays."

"Thought something like that. You'd never let me pass you on that last straightaway."

"Enjoy it now. You won't get past me next time!"

"You up for a race?"

"No can do now. We're about to leave. Family stuff this afternoon."

"How about tonight? A bunch of the lads are meeting at Monahan's. Wanna come?"

"Might do. Gotta see what else is in the plan. Later. Out."

Michael turned to Kurt. "We need to finish up here. Dodging six other cars on the track is a bit much for a newbie. Pull off at the exit, and I'll drive us outside. Then you can drive home. You'll have to mind the speed limits, though. If we get pulled over for speeding or any other moving violation, the car is automatically kicked out of the system for a thirty-day time-out. You wouldn't do that to me, would you?"

"Not on your life."

"Have fun?" Michael asked as he removed his helmet and threw it in the back of the car.

"God, yes! Greatest drive ever!" Kurt freed himself as well.

"Do you know your fastest speed?"

"About 180?"

"You hit 200 once. That's about 125 mph. Pretty good for your first time out."

"Wow! I had no idea. Once you hit 'fast,' you can't tell what 'faster' is. Will there really be a second time?"

"If you can get your sister to come back over here with you next summer, I'll bet we could arrange another drive."

"Say no more. We'll be here. What does your dad think about all this?"

"Father? Not much. He threatened to put a lock on my trust funds if I intended to squander money this way. I showed him how I paid my share from my earnings without touching the funds. I told him it was an investment; my shares could easily be sold at a profit. He dropped the issue and hasn't discussed it with me since. I live a simple life, have a small flat in a modest section of town, and have no other financial responsibilities, so my car and the track are my children. As long as I don't dip into the funds, Father can't object."

They made one quick stop on the way home—for 'good American brew'—and found Thomas waiting eagerly for them in the den. Almost noon, he tapped his watch, and the women were not down yet. "Could something be wrong?" he asked Kurt.

"No," he assured him. "They are just enjoying themselves." He handed Michael a bottle and the remote with a deep bow, and the two young men settled in for a pleasant afternoon of football, while Thomas continued to fret.

*   *   *

The women appeared some time later, both faces aglow. Kiri obviously enjoyed her private time with her mother, and Paula seemed more relaxed too. Kiri tiptoed up behind Michael and wrapped her arms around his neck. "You rascal! You tricked me!"

"Surprised?"

"Absolutely. That was the best special surprise ever! Exactly what I needed." She kissed him on the cheek. "Thank you so much," she said as she rocked him from side to side. "What did you have to negotiate to arrange it?"

"I'll be your mother's slave to the grandkids for the next year."

"Way to go, Mom!" Then she tousled his hair and left.

Michael followed her and grabbed her by the hand just before she reached the stairs. "No you don't. No nap for you. Now it's my turn." He led her into the kitchen and directed her attention to two paper bags twisted closed at the tops.

"I don't drink, you know—just two fingers on special occasions. That is definitely more than two fingers."

"No booze there. Open them."

Kiri untwisted the bags and peeked inside... at two fresh pineapples. "You want your lesson now? Today?"

"Why not?"

"Because I'm supposed to get the pineapple for you, along with the bandaids."

"No. You are supposed to give me a lesson. There was no stipulation as to the source of the pineapple. I won't need bandaids; I'm a pro with a knife."

"But there are two of them."

"I may need lots of practice."

"Fine. Wear comfortable clothes that can get dirty. Find an apron, towel, sharp knife, cutting board, plate and bowl," she said smartly. Michael complied and returned for his lesson. Kiri was very precise and specific in her directions. She took her job as teacher seriously and expected him to be a good student.

She complimented Michael on his selection of fruit—well ripened with a small crown, protruding eyes and sharp tropical aroma. He admitted the grocer selected them. She showed him how to jerk on an inner leaf to see if it pulled out easily. She talked him through peeling and coring a pineapple, then cutting it into chunks. With the second one, she had him slice off the bottom, core the fruit, and slice it into eight lengthwise wedges. He arranged them on a plate like spokes, little boats with a piece of crown for the rudder. He sliced the pulp into half a dozen sections and put berry passengers on each piece with toothpicks.

Then Michael proudly shared his creation with the rest of the family, one boat for each and a few to spare. Cleaning up the kitchen was part of the lesson; cleaning up himself was his choice. Kiri seemed delighted with the aptitude of her pupil. She reminded him, however, that consuming too much pineapple at once could result in hives, trots, or stomachache. He took her warning seriously and promised to eat only one boat for now.

* * *

Toward the end of the afternoon, Michael informed Paula they would not be home for dinner. He wanted to take Kurt and Kiri for a short tour around Dublin with a stop at a pub or two. Kurt seemed surprised; Kiri was happy he had not forgotten. They piled into his car (Michael drove) and headed first for the harbor before it grew too dark. He wanted Kiri to see the water, which was definitely not as unyielding as stone, and to feel the soothing motion of Thomas' sailboat on the swells of an incoming tide. Then he drove a circuit that encompassed all major points of interest. Kiri's favorite was the zodiac mosaic at the entrance to the National Museum, and Kurt's was Abbey Theater. "Maybe we could go sometime," he suggested.

The Country Boy, a singing pub, was their next stop. A small but lively group of vocalists crowded around a large table. The three squeezed in and ordered the house brew. Kiri joined in the singing while the two guys enjoyed the drinking games. Michael remarked that she had quite a nice voice and did not seem at all shy about using it. Kurt told him they frequently engaged in an evening of karaoke at the bars at home where his sister was quite a favorite.

Michael planned dinner at Monahan's to meet up with his mates. Kiri was sorry to leave the gaiety of the singing pub, but a hot meal sounded good. Kurt, always game for food, relished the thought of more "car talk." They entered to shouts of "Mighty Mike!" which seemed to embarrass their host. He explained that the nickname was due to his shorter but stockier stature than most of the others and to his physical strength, a job requirement that his deskbound friends did not have to endure. They ordered typical pub grub and drinks; Kiri had water with lemon.

After the Koyles were introduced as distant family from a distant land—America—the guys caroused with some of the other drivers from Raceleigh. Kiri listened to their tales contentedly. Friendly games of darts sprang up around the room. Kurt joined in and was soundly beaten most of the time; he did manage to pull out one win; "foreigner's luck," they called it. Michael seemed to be a winner most of the time; when he did lose he claimed loss of focus, not talent. "Yeah, sure," his friends taunted.

Asked if she wanted to give the game a try, Kiri declined until the end of the evening. The rowdy friends thought it only fair that she at least attempt to beat her brother, and Michael would compete just to keep the match honest. She cheerfully agreed to join in the final game but after a couple of throws, she complained that she kept aiming for the inner bull, but her darts seemed to drop. "Could I use different ones?" she asked.

"Sorry, Kiddo. Deal with it. This is only a game, you know," Michael teased.

No one paid much attention to her as she crept up on the two young men battling it out for top dog. Both of them stalled, unable to zero out. Kiri stepped forward—last dart, deep breath, let fly—and scored a double 19 for zero. Her competitors were astounded. How did that happen? As the room erupted in cheers for her and jeers for the other two, she taunted, "Sorry, guys. Deal with it. This is only a game, you know!"

The trio headed for home as soon as the crowd had its fun at Michael's expense. A girl bested him, and the throng did not let him forget it. Once in the drive, Kurt got out and started to pull his seat forward so Kiri could too. Michael stopped him. "You go ahead. We'll be in shortly." Kurt shut the door with a shrug and left.

Michael's serious eyes stared straight ahead. "Why did you win?"

"What?" Kiri asked, confused.

"Why did you beat me at darts tonight?"

Kiri laid her forearms along the top of the passenger seat and rested her chin on her hands, also staring straight ahead. Was she doomed for a "like father, like son" interrogation? "I didn't know I would, but I had to give it my best shot. You would be insulted if I feigned weakness and threw the match just to puff you up in front of your friends. They wouldn't buy it."

He did not react, so she continued. "You don't admire weakness, even in women. It takes a strong man to win but an even stronger one to lose. I suspect you have strengths you haven't even begun to reveal. You should have confidence enough in your Irish manhood, Mighty Mike, that you can accept defeat at the hands of a woman once in a while—so long as it doesn't become a habit!"

"You're free to go now," Michael chuckled.

Kiri let herself out of the car and made her way into the house, shaking her head at O'Connell men and their need for dominance.

Chapter 9

Paula and Thomas were just going up to their suite when Michael and Kiri entered. "You'll be staying here with us again tonight, Michael?" she asked with a smile.

"Yes, Ma'am, if it's okay."

"You know you're always welcome. See you in the morning." With that, she and Thomas disappeared and left the younger ones to ponder their next step.

"Are you going to sleep under the tree again?" he asked.

"I hadn't thought about it. Why? Christmas is over now, you know."

"It doesn't have to be."

Kiri seemed reluctant.

"Let's. This is the best holiday I've had in years, and I'm really not ready for it to end," he appealed.

"You're not still mad at me for the dart thing?"

"Never was. Come on. It will be fun. All the pressure's off now. We can relax."

"Give me five," she said as she headed for the third floor. She pulled on her pjs realizing she was barely out of them. She brushed her hair, gathered blankets, and headed downstairs for one more night on the floor.

Michael had the tree lights, fire and music on as before and sat atop his pile of bedding, tea and snacks nearby. "Well, what's the verdict? Is Dublin really so terrible after all?"

"Your tour today helped. The whole day helped—having time to put things in perspective and let the tension subside. I arrived thinking 'It's going to be a long weekend,' and now I feel it wasn't near long enough. Yes, I think Dublin deserves a return visit."

"When?"

"When? I haven't even gone home yet," Kiri laughed. "How can I think about coming back? Summer maybe?"

"That would be good. We could go sailing then. I suggested it to Kurt today, and he seemed agreeable. Said it might depend on your vacation time." Michael alternated bites of pineapple boat with cookie.

"I swear I'm the only one who has a real job. I can't just leave on a whim. I'll need to build up days for summer if I want to make another trip over here... but it is doable. Won't you be away between now and summer?"

"I'll be gone most of April and May, I think, but other than that, I should have short three-day trips which I imagine we could work around. Let's make it a promise."

"Promise... I'll try." She sipped her tea and nibbled at a cookie.

"What's your plan for New Year's?" he asked between bites.

"Oh, that's an easy one. Kurt and I and a whole gang of friends will be up at the condo west of Denver. Every winter, a bunch of us lease a place for the season—about a dozen of us in all. We can sleep eight, plus we store a couple of blow up mattresses. We're usually not all there on the same weekends, so it works out great. We even bring friends, but there's no guarantee everyone will have a bed. We'll have a great time next weekend—skiing all day, then dinner and karaoke bars in the evening, maybe some dancing, and board games. Dare I say darts? I can't wait! That's where we would be this weekend too, if we were home."

"Does 'we' include a special guy?"

"Not this year. What about you? Have you got big plans for ringing in the New Year with a special gal?"

"Not likely. I'm out of town so much for work that it's hard to maintain a relationship. I'm promised to Father for a special 'do' at his Club. I can't wait—Ha Ha."

Kiri put her food aside and rolled out her bedding. Michael finished the last of his tea and then placed his bedroll next to hers and climbed in.

"What do you think you're doing?"

"I thought I'd sleep next to you tonight."

"Because...." Her eyes widened.

"Because... it would be a cozy, pleasant end to the holiday. I feel safe here now, enveloped in the magic of the tree," he said dramatically.

Kiri replied with a frown, then gathered a couple of throws from the sofas. She rolled them together lengthwise and placed the bundle between their two beds.

"What is that?" Michael laughed.

"This is a chastity bolster—forced abstinence frontier-style, if you will. This is what we do at the condo if we end up with more people than mattresses and have to share with a stranger."

"You're not serious?"

"Try me. This *is* your father's house, and we may be brother and sister soon. My rules, or you can sleep upstairs by yourself." She slid into her make-shift bed and gazed up at the tree.

"Kiri?"

"Hmmmm?"

"What do you think of me?"

"I think you are much different from my first impression. I thought you were arrogant and self-important, flashing your badge at customs, screeching up in your fancy car, showing off your big house and state-of-the-art media equipment."

"You weren't exactly Miss Friendly, more of a frosty ice princess. Didn't want to talk, didn't want to do, just headed for your room to stuff your face under a pillow. I wondered why you even bothered to come if you were going to be in ill humor the whole time."

"You had this wild hair that darted every which way," she flailed her arms to demonstrate, "and you smiled too much. You had a hole in your shoe, for heaven's sake."

"You were hairless, for all I could tell with your stocking cap pulled clear down to your nose. Your smile must have taken a different flight, for it didn't show up 'til twenty-four hours later. And I don't have a hole in my shoe; the leather is merely separated from the sole. It can easily be stitched back together." Michael tried to defend himself.

"I like your comfy, casual look now that I know you clean up well when it's important, but decent footwear shows that you care. You do care about your appearance, don't you?"

"As much as any single man out for a good time. Besides, my sorry loafer lures the young ladies who think I need looking after. You should talk. You practically lived in your pajamas your whole time here," he accused.

"You only know that because you keep barging in on my alone time. Besides, I can't get much variety into a carryon."

"Actually you've done very well for an unrefined country girl—very appropriate, very trendy, and very nice looking when we've gone out in public. No complaints, although I haven't seen enough of your legs," he joshed.

"And you won't in this cold, wet weather. I have reassessed my original opinion, and I now think you're a good-looking guy in a rugged sort of way. Your smile is impish, and your hair is not wild—it just has a mind of its own, like you do. I side with you against your father; its length is perfect. I especially like the curl that hangs over your right eye. This one here." Kiri pulled on a lock and tried to make it stay low on Michael's forehead, but to no avail.

"Seriously, what do you think of me? What kind of man do you think I am?"

Kiri considered her reply carefully. "I think you are... a true 'fighting Irishman.'"

"I'll take that." Michael seemed pleased.

"I feel safe with you—not the 'you wouldn't dare try' kind of safe. The kind of safe where I know you would do anything to protect those you love from harm... and from sadness or adversity if you could. You would raise your sword against all aggressors." She flailed around to mimic this drama.

"Funny you should say that. My namesake—my symbol if you will— is Saint Michael, the protector of soldiers and souls."

"That image fits you. You are a good man, Michael. You have no reason to doubt your worth as you are doing now. You don't need to seek affirmation. Your parents are proud of you." Kiri turned to face him. "Why did you come back here Christmas Eve and move in with the rest of us?"

"I told you the other night. I needed some friendly company. I didn't want to stay alone when it was so festive over here. In truth, this wonderful old house experienced a love and gaiety I haven't seen here in a long time, and I wanted to reclaim just a piece of it if I could. I wanted to feel like a kid again, like I used to in the good old days when we were one big happy family... when we were living our own brand of Christmas magic."

Both were silent for a time. Kiri asked herself why there were not guys like this in Denver. She could go for someone like Michael. He reflected on how easy she was to talk to.

"I can't believe how thoughtless I am," Kiri said in disgust. "My mother this and my mother that, bemoaning the fact that I can't be with her when I want, acting the wounded party. I sympathized with your sisters and how they must feel at a time like this, but I completely overlooked your feelings. This can't be an easy time for you either, yet I've given you no consideration as I talk on and on about my family and myself. I'm sorry, Michael. I am so thoughtless."

"Don't be sorry. I'm resigned to being the forgotten soul in the O'Connell saga. Besides, I enjoyed every minute, even these less than comfortable ones under the Christmas tree. I like feeling close to someone, and I like your idea that the tree is where Christmas magic resides—not with people but with possibilities. That is something I can take with me wherever...."

Both Kiri and Michael rolled to the right. She snuggled against his back, at least as close as the bolster would allow. She slid her right arm between his neck and pillow, then flopped it up across his chest toward his shoulder. He clutched her right hand with his left, holding it tight against him. His hand was broad and strong, dwarfing her long slender fingers. With her left hand, she stroked his forehead and ran her fingers into his hair like a mother would for a fevered child. "I can't change your reality, Michael, but I can listen. Do you want to tell me about past Christmases... your family... your mother?"

He nodded ever so slightly, gripped Kiri's hand more firmly, and began to share his story.

Chapter 10

"Michael, what do you think you're doing down there with our guest?" Thomas and his booming voice burst through the French doors and awakened them once more, and once more Kiri pulled her pillow over her head.

Exposing the bolster when he threw back his blanket, Michael retorted, "Nothing, Father. I am every inch a gentleman, and the lady is still pure as the driven snow."

Thomas had to laugh at how ridiculous their set-up looked, recalling a similar blanket on a beach long ago. "Don't you have your phone on? Your sisters tell me that they tried to get hold of you all day yesterday and again this morning, and you are not responding to their messages."

"I didn't want my day with Kurt and Kiri to be interrupted with family 'business.' You know what they're all tight about. I made my peace with her, and I just wanted to enjoy our time together. After all, they are leaving today."

"I'm well aware of that. Your brother and sisters will be here later this morning to say goodbye. You'd better give them a call; they want your input."

"They don't need my advice on how to conduct their lives. They've never asked for it up to now."

"I told them not a minute before eleven. Knowing them, they'll be here on the dot. You'll need time to get this place cleaned up. When you're finished being embarrassed, Kirin, your mother has breakfast just about ready." Thomas left the room, closing the French doors behind him, chuckling and shaking his head at the children.

"You sleep okay?" Michael asked.

"Once you finally fell asleep, I did. A fitful sleep is the best you could have had. You okay now?" she asked. He nodded.

Kiri and Michael made quick work of their mess, dirty dishes in one pile, blankets and pillows in another, and crumbs whisked under the tree. As they were about to stand up and leave, he put his arms around her shoulders, resting his chin on the top of her head. She clasped her hands around his waist.

He rocked her from side to side. "I really don't want this holiday to end. In case we don't get another chance to speak privately today, I want you to know how wonderful you were last night... to listen to me drone on and on without dropping off to sleep. I feel so much better today, and I'm really going to miss having you around."

"My pleasure. Even Mighty Mikes need a little comfort now and then."

* * *

Eleven o'clock on the dot, Tommy, Anne, Meghan and Emily burst through the front door, sans spouses and children. When she did not find Michael in the living room, Anne aimed for the kitchen. "Michael. Living room. Family conference. Now," she summoned. He gave Kiri a wink and followed his sister dutifully.

Several minutes later, Michael asked Kurt and Kiri politely if they would join the group in the living room. Paula and Thomas were not yet invited. "I would love to hear what's going on in there," he said. "My girls are beside themselves with embarrassment over their behavior the other evening. I would love to listen to them try to dig themselves out."

Paula gave his arm a pat. "Children. They'll work it out."

Emily, Anne, and Meghan sat on the sofa near the Christmas tree. Tommy stood behind Anne with his hands on her shoulders. Michael brought Kurt and Kiri into the room where chairs were repositioned for them to sit facing the others. She thought this a rather strange arrangement for a friendly family conversation but agreed to play along. Michael stood between the Koyles, facing Tommy.

"My sister Anne has something to say to you, Kiri." Tommy began the conversation.

Anne looked at her hands and then across to the Koyles. She apologized for her lack of honesty on Christmas and for her unkind remarks about table setting. She tried to explain what led her to do that, but her words did not come out easily.

Kiri did not interrupt; she waited until Anne was through and both Emily and Meghan had added a phrase or two of their own. "Apology accepted," Kiri began. "This has been a difficult time for all of us, and with added excitement and responsibilities, none of us has really had an opportunity to search the truth of our emotions. We're all feeling the same, I think—confused and threatened by our parents' relationship. I hope we'll be able to speak frankly with one another in the future and avoid unfortunate misunderstandings. No hard feelings here. We're leaving soon, so that should relieve some of the pressure—give us all a chance to calm down." She turned to her brother. "Kurt?"

"I concur. Not until now did I have any idea there was a problem. I enjoyed myself immensely, both here and at your home, Anne, so I think you who are frustrating over this should put it behind you. Let's move forward and let the parents get on with their lives."

"That's the other thing we wanted to talk to you about," said Tommy. "Our parents. How do you feel about their... arrangement?"

"To be honest, I'm upset that Mom is away from Denver more than she is there, but that may change soon. They may work out a routine that includes more time in her own home," Kiri replied.

"I've been thinking that our children will never know their real grandmother, and Paula is so good with them. I appreciate the affection she shows," Anne offered.

"I know she has been a great help to me personally," Emily said.

"Thomas makes my mother very happy," Kiri added.

"And Father seems so happy now too," Meghan said.

"We were wondering," Tommy interjected. "We were wondering if we should say something; let them know that we approve of their... liaison?"

Michael's fist went to his mouth to stifle a smile. He looked at Kurt who was in the process of the same. "Kurt, you've not weighed in on this. What do you think?"

In his devil-may-care attitude, he responded. "I think this conversation is the biggest load of crap I've heard this holiday!"

Michael could not muffle his laugh any longer, but everyone else was in shock at his remark.

"I apologize. Apology accepted. I understand how you feel. I understand how you feel," Kurt mimicked the girls. "End of conversation! Everything else is irrelevant. It doesn't matter what *we* think about their arrangement. They are the only two involved in their decisions. To suggest that they might need our approval is ludicrous.

"Thomas and Mom have problems enough as it is without worrying whether we children approve," Kurt continued. "Your father is ensconced here; my mother is trying to live between two worlds. Your father is a Catholic; my mother is not. Your father has a flock he feels responsible for; my mother has a divorce to reconcile. They don't need our approval; they need our support and they need us to leave them alone to find their own way through what could be one more week or one more month or one more year. Who's to say?"

All O'Connells except Michael stared open-mouthed as Kurt pressed on. "There are two things we can do here. We can get out of the way or we can throw obstacles in front of them. We can make it easier for them or more painful, but what *we* feel inside shouldn't make a bit of difference to Thomas and Paula. What they feel for each other should be the only thing that matters."

"Hear! Hear! My sentiments exactly," exclaimed Michael. "Let the parents *liaise* as they see fit, and never mind what's proper."

"Don't you agree that they are concerned about us... about how we're reacting?" Tommy reasoned.

"Of course they are," returned Michael. "They want us to become one big happy family, but they shouldn't worry about us. Who knows if we'll ever get along? All of their energies should go into dealing with their own problems, not with how their choices affect us. We're grownups, for heaven's sake. Let's act like it."

"I still think something should be said to them about where we children stand on this. We're all gathered here. They know we're up to something. We'd better produce some sort of resolution," Tommy responded.

"But there is nothing to resolve. There isn't—or shouldn't be—any conflict among us or between us and them," Michael countered.

"At most, we should give them both a hug and wish them well," admitted Kurt.

"Who shall speak for us, then?" Tommy asked. "Should I, being the oldest?"

Kiri rolled her eyes. Are we really going to take a vote on this, she wondered.

Kurt ran his fingers through his hair and shook his head in disbelief. Michael started to say something, but was interrupted by Anne.

"I think I should speak. I started all this discord in the first place."

"But, Anne," Michael reminded. "Theoretically they know nothing of it. Kurt was kept out of the loop, and Paula may have been as well."

"I will," said Emily. "This whole thing is about our feeling uncomfortable with Paula taking Mother's place, so I think I should speak. I'm the most resistant. I was closest to Mother, her favorite you'll agree, so if it comes from me, at least Father will know we mean it."

Kiri caught the hurt in Michael's eyes. She wanted to pat him on the shoulder and say, "Not true. Not true," but he was too far away.

He recovered and addressed Emily. "If you're going to speak, be careful what you say. Mean what you say, and know what you mean."

Kiri and Kurt stared at one another, shocked. They used that phrase regularly in their own home. "I'll speak for the two of us, then," Kurt decided. He was not about to let the O'Connells speak for the Koyles.

Michael left the room and returned with the parents in tow. He motioned for them to take the sofa across from the wall of O'Connells. Thomas recognized by their demeanor that his children were preparing for a pronouncement. Paula was as amazed as Kiri at the unfolding of a drama; she was preparing to say goodbye to her own children for their return trip.

"Father," Emily began as she stood up and crossed the room toward him. "I know you have some concern about how we are all handling this… situation. Please have none. We are in accord. You have our support. We wish you and Paula well." She smiled and bent to hug her father and then Paula.

"Yeah, Mom," Kurt broke in. "You've told Kiri and me more than once that you would be happy when we found our happiness. Well, turnabout is fair play. We'll be happy when you are, so go for it!" He gave his mother a hug and shook Thomas' hand. The rest of the children followed in like fashion, and the tension in the room subsided.

With all the children gathered around them, Thomas took Paula's hand in his two, looked into her eyes, and kissed her hand tenderly. "Well, my dear," he said. "It seems the children have spoken. I propose we take formal steps toward this happiness they wish for us." He lifted himself from the sofa and got down on one knee in front of her, still holding her hand.

"Paula, I love you. I try to show you every day how much. If loving you means I must ask daily forgiveness from God for loving you, then that is what I will continue to do. But if we were to sanctify our union in front of God and these children, think how blessed our lives would be. You know how much I need you, and I want for us to spend the rest of our lives together, however many days the Lord may choose to grant us. Will you marry me and join me in that journey?"

"Yes, Tom," she answered without hesitation. "Yes, I will."

Shocked, the youngsters broke into claps and hugs again. Kiri rolled her eyes. "What century are these people living in?" she whispered to herself. "Down on his knees? No one does that anymore."

Michael put his arm around her shoulder. "Guess we'll be brother and sister sooner than we thought," he said with a glint in his eyes.

Excitement erupted in the room. "When will you do it? Large or small? When can we get together again? Make plans! What are you doing next weekend? Could you come for the Ball? Father could announce then; it would be grand! Maybe we could all go to Copley Castle; it is the greatest for a New Year's celebration. Please say you'll come."

Kiri stood her ground among them. "These wedding 'plans' are not ours to make. You can't expect us to fly across the ocean on a whim. I have a job. Kurt and I have our own plans for a 'grand' weekend. Do your own thing and we'll...."

Chapter 11

As firmly as he vowed to Paula never to mention him again, Thomas could not help imagining what this same scene would be with their lost son at the center of it. Where would *their* boy have fit in this gaggle of beautiful, healthy children from two disparate families?

When they reacquainted in Rome in June, Paula gave him the sense that she had a story to tell, but she was reluctant, and he did not want to hear it. He was too ecstatic at finding her again after forty years to listen to any reason why they should not be together at present. Tom took her back to Dublin and put her up in a hotel. He did not want to rush her, to presume. She insisted they return to her home in Colorado for the Fourth of July; she had obligations, she said. Her home was just as she described, a beautiful house on a hill with prospects in the four directions, alternate purple mountains and green valleys, each one enchanting and distinct from the others.

Paula staged her annual BBQ with neighbors from all around. They were a nice bunch, and lots of them, friendly good people who included him in their conversations easily. Tom met her children. Kurt was a handsome young man, tall and lanky, with an engaging personality and never-ending discourse. Kiri was a striking young woman, all business, with a friendly nature and a tendency to observe and remark rather than be the center of interest.

At dusk, fireworks began in the valleys below, and all the guests staked out their favorite viewing spots. Tom and Paula strolled arm-in-arm the full perimeter of her house along the wooden planks of its deck, leaning on the railing here and there as she told him of this place and that, this experience and that. He recognized the same exuberance she displayed as a twenty-something on a beach on Ireland's west coast, regaling him with her stories. They had not been intimate yet, then or on this trip, but he was falling for her again as deeply as before.

A couple of mornings later, after breakfast, Tom found Paula on the east deck, drinking in the warm July sun as if she were a cat. She rested her elbows on the rail with her hands molded around a coffee mug. He took the cup of tea she indicated and joined her at the siding. Her eyes were fixed on some distant point on the horizon, an object he could not discern.

She spoke without looking at him. "There is something you must know, Tom... before this... before we go any further."

Please, no, he thought. Not before we give ourselves a second chance. He turned her face to his with a hand and stared into her eyes. "I told you in Rome it didn't matter. I told you I would never ask why you did not contact me to join you in Paris. I do not need to know."

A deep sadness filled Paula's eyes. "But I need to tell you. We cannot have ghosts or shadows between us. I can't carry this alone, now that you are back in my life."

"I don't want to hear it. I won't listen," he contended, shaking his head.

"You'll hear it, or I'll send you away… my choice. If you want to have any input, you'll listen and the outcome will be up to you… your choice."

"But I don't need to know if you realized two days later that you found me repugnant, or not good enough for you. I don't need to know if you couldn't see yourself as part of my life in Dublin. I don't need to know if you fell in love with another man who eventually became your husband. I don't need to know…"

"…if I were pregnant?"

Stunned, Tom let his cup shatter on the ground. "What?"

"I didn't contact you, Tom, because I was pregnant… with your child."

"But where… ? Is Kurt…?"

"No. Kurt is not yours. He is only thirty-three."

"Why didn't you tell me *then*? Why did you stay silent? Where is…?"

"What would you have me do? Send you a postcard that read, *T. Pregnant. P.* What would you have done? Or better yet: *T. Can't make our date in Paris. Am in London having an abortion. P.* Or how about, *T. Need to postpone our rendezvous. Just had miscarriage. Am not in shape, physically or emotionally, to receive you. More later. P.* What would you…what *could* you have done? No. To walk away seemed the only choice at the time."

Tom drew back and shot at her fiercely, "You had no right to deny me knowledge of *my* child. Abortion! You seriously considered *abortion*? One of man's gravest sins… the taking of a human life! Unforgivable!" He backed further away and shook a finger at her. "God will judge you harshly for your actions, Paula."

"But I didn't act. I didn't have an abortion. I considered it, but I didn't do it. Our son miscarried before I could abort him."

"My son. My first son! You intended to kill *my first son*? May God have mercy…" The rest of his words were lost as he tried to find his way out of her presence and onto the gravel path leading to the valley below.

His pounding steps crunched the ground as he hurried from Paula as fast as he could. Gouging him in the chest and cutting out his heart could not have pained him more. Hell's fire could not match his anger. The world's greatest mystery had nothing on his disbelief. Tom headed for the creek at the bottom of her hill. He awakened to such a beautiful summer morning, bright with possibilities, and now phantom cumulonimbus—black, forbidding clouds—seemed to descend on him, their icy particles surrounding and stabbing him with questions and condemnations.

Damn Paula! She had no right! How did this happen? Why did she not tell him? What drove her to consider such an option? Was intent as sinful as the act? What would he have done? What could he have done? Why did she tell him now, after all these years? What purpose did it serve? Had he not suffered enough tragedy in his life?

Tom stumbled along the edge of the creek, knowing that if he followed it, he would not lose his way. He puzzled the questions, even as their answers became apparent. Who was *he* to condemn and judge her? His God was the ultimate judge. Had she sought and received His forgiveness? Of course she had a right—her body, her choice—so long as she was willing to suffer the consequence of her actions... and she had.

Paula and Tom bore equal responsibility for the creation of the child. They both knew what to do to prevent its happening, but they did not take precautions, even after discussing contraception that day on western Ireland's Puffin Island at a time when inappropriate conversation between the sexes defied the conventions of that day. Paula did not tell him because she already knew what his response would be. Tom revealed that too on the island. Bastard children would never be recognized by the family; illegitimates could not inherit. Marriage was out of the question. His traditional Irish family would never approve his union with a pregnant, American, non-Catholic of no family background. They would insist he write her a check and ship her off to London—same intent, same end. So, Paula had two options: to become a single mother in a foreign country in the sixties with no means of support... or to end it, knowing how abhorrent abortion was to him. Either way, Tom would not, or could not, be part of the solution. Her body, her choice.

She told him now because she felt compelled to. Paula could not allow them to move forward in a relationship without revealing the consequences of their previous one. Any hopes for a future together could just as easily be dashed now by some unimagined event or other. There would be challenges and consequences along any path they chose to walk together. And she was weary of holding this secret deep inside her, letting it slowly eat at her soul.

Yes, Tom suffered tragedy in his life: the death of his beloved wife, his sister, his mother and father, aunts and uncles, and his dear Aunt Moira who started it all. "Let Paula be the 'little sin' in your life," she said, "and then be strong enough to let her go." He had. Now this, the tragedy of a beautiful soul never loved. Who is to say how much calamity is enough for one man? Or one woman—and Paula suffered theirs alone. She suppressed the memory and harbored the guilt—not only hers, but theirs.

So it came down to this: Was intent as sinful as the act? His family's vs. Paula's? If one plans to do a bad thing and does not, is she still guilty of the crime? Has a crime really been committed? No, thought Tom, he could not reconcile the same punishment for intent as for action, and he played an equal part in the decision whether he knew it at the time or not. He recalled their last words—was it minutes or hours ago, he could not tell—and heard selfishness. "*My* son. *Your* guilt. Unforgivable!" Tom saw a hard, unbending face reflected in the creek's rippling waters, and it was ugly. When he turned for the walk back to Paula's house, he could no longer see it. He went farther than he realized. Only days ago he felt forty years younger. Now he was ancient. "I am too old for this," he sighed, trudging upward.

Paula's car in the garage was a good sign. But he could not find her anywhere outside, not on the deck, not in her garden. He entered the house without knocking and found his suitcase by the door. A sticky note on top had the number of a shuttle service and times for the next two departing flights for Dublin. Tom cursed himself for leaving in anger. She assumed his choice.

He walked quietly through the rooms on the first floor, calling her name softly. Then he went upstairs. She was not in her bedroom. He heard a low hum coming from her bathroom. He opened the door and found her sitting in her tub, a slight movement of waves soothing her body. Steam rose from the surface carrying a hint of lavendar with it. Her back was to him.

"Paula?" he tendered.

"Your choice," she said as she filled a cloth with hot water and squeezed it over her right shoulder. She filled it again and squeezed it over her left without turning her head.

Tom shed his clothes and slipped into the tub behind her just as he had those many years ago. He folded his arms around her shoulders and chest and whispered at the nape of her neck. "I will never allow you to turn your back and walk away from me again—not on a lonely road to Galway, a cobbled street in Rome, a sandy beach or rocky coast, a tree-lined avenue in Paris or a gravel path surrounding your home."

Paula leaned back and laid her head in the crook of his neck. He kissed her forehead and she began to weep, softly at first, then harder and harder, spewing phrases between her sobs, lamenting her sins and asking his forgiveness. When she was exhausted and he wiped the last of the tears from her red, puffy eyes, they shifted. Paula held him while he confessed his every transgression. He had not felt free to spill such emotion in all the years they were apart. He spoke of his wife, children, hopes realized and dreams dashed. He cried for the son they had never known.

When they were both spent, Tom took her to her bed, and they lay together as they had that fateful night in Rome. He found all her familiar places—the scar beneath her chin, the dimple at the base of her spine—and wondered that he still remembered. Paula did the same, knowing that she had never forgotten.

A bright July sunrise blazing through the window awakened them to a new reality. "You are even more beautiful to me now than you were before.

I feel the same safety and comfort and completeness that I remember." Tom took her hand and held it to his chest. "Where do we go from here?"

"Downstairs to breakfast."

"I'm not joking, Paula. We have some heady issues in front of us."

"I'm not joking either. I'm trying to be sensible. We're both exhausted, emotionally and physically. Yesterday's confrontation sucked the energy right out of us. We've not eaten in more than a day. We're in no condition to think rationally. We're not going anywhere, literally or figuratively, until we're in an adequate state to do so." She patted his chest softly, slipped out of bed and into her robe, and headed for the stairs.

Tom's suitcase was where he had left it by the front door. "May I take this back upstairs?"

"Suit yourself."

"…to your room?"

"Your choice."

Tom returned to breakfast on the east deck. Paula was soaking up the sun again with another mug of coffee in her hands. She prepared tea for him. They ate without speaking. Finally, he dared to ask, "Paula, will you…."

"I need time, Tom. I need time to rest and relax… to clear my head. Will you give me that, please?"

"Of course. Take what you need. I'll just sit here in the sun until you are ready."

She left with the dishes and returned with books, one for each of them. She handed Tom a small volume, then eased herself into a deck chair and opened hers. She watched his face carefully and smiled to herself when his eyebrows raised in incredulity. She kept her nose poked in her book but noticed every time he got up to pace, to start to say something then think better of it and sit down again, from chair to chair along the deck. Finally she laid her book on her chest and closed her eyes just for a minute, a quick snooze.

The sun was at eleven o'clock when Paula opened her eyes again and found Tom in a chair facing her, staring intently as if willing her awake. "I had no idea. None. Did you really write this?"

"It has my name on it," she laughed.

"There is so much we don't know about one another, Paula. So much for us to learn. Could we start now?" He smiled hopefully.

She smiled back as she aimed for the kitchen. "Grab a hat and those cushions. Let's go for a walk." She packed a snack of fresh pickings from her garden and bottled water into a shoulder bag and led the way down to the creek.

He followed after her but did not take her hand. "How many times a day do you descend this hill?"

"As many as I need to maintain my sanity." She headed them in the direction opposite Tom's route of the previous day and found a place to sit beneath trees, on her thinking log.

"We had a child together, Paula. I can't believe we had a child. In the light of a new day, that has become a beautiful thing."

"We didn't *have* a child, Tom. We *lost* a child, and that is a sorrowful thing."

"But we have a chance now to imagine... to imagine what our lives might have been... what *he* might have been. We can find comfort in those thoughts."

"I'm not convinced that more thinking or talking will bring comfort. I'm thought out and I have no more tears left for weeping. If you need more time, I'll give you that. I'll give you the rest of this day to ask your questions and shed your tears. But there must be a limit to our grief. Sundown. Once the sun sets on this day, we'll never speak of our child again. Promise me that."

"I promise never to mention him again after this day." Tom moved his cushion next to hers on the log. He removed his hat, wiped his brow with a handkerchief, and re-covered his head. He had no idea how to speak to a woman of such personal matters. He had not with his wife until late into her final illness. He grasped Paula's soft left hand gingerly in his arthritic ones and pulled it with him as he leaned forward with his forearms on his thighs. "When did it happen?"

"I can't remember—late January, early February sometime. It hardly matters now."

"Don't tell me you don't know. Women remember. Mothers remember! I need to know what I was doing the day I lost my... the day *we* lost our son," Tom insisted.

"February 3, 6:27 p.m."

"How old was... how far along were you?

"Eighteen weeks."

"Isn't that rather late?"

"Yes. At first, I couldn't believe I was pregnant. Then I couldn't accept it. I was conflicted about what I should do. There were no safe options in France in those days, so I was trying to get to London."

"Where did it happen?"

"A Catholic hospital on the Left Bank."

Tom wondered how a man could show a woman he barely knew that he ached to share her suffering. He gripped her hand more tightly. "Were you in much pain?"

"Some. When the vomiting and contractions didn't stop, I went for help. Funny how a Catholic hospital wouldn't perform an abortion but attended very well to a spontaneous one. They stayed right with me until... it was over."

"Did you… see him?"

Paula closed her eyes, remembering that heart-rending night. "Yes."

Tom massaged her fingers. "Did you… hold him?"

"Yes. I pleaded to. The nurse rinsed him and placed him gently in my cupped hands. He was only about five inches from his head to his rump—a tiny bit of a thing curled into my palms, barely human—but he had arms and fingers, legs and toes, eyelids and ears, a slit of a mouth, a wee nose and a nice little butt. When I discovered his manhood, I looked for the hint of a cleft in his chin like yours, but it was imperceptible. There was no way of knowing if his eyes were the color of the sea, as you had predicted for our future children."

Tom drew her fingers to his lips and blew on them. "Was he alive? Did you ever feel his heart beat?"

"He had been active for a couple of weeks. Then his movement stopped, and… No. I never felt his heart beat in my hands. I held him for only a moment, kissed him on his precious head, and then they took him away."

"Where did they take him?"

"I don't know. Wherever good Catholics take…." she replied impatiently.

"Was he blessed?" Tom asked with some urgency.

"I don't understand."

"You were in a Catholic hospital. Did a priest come to bless him before he was removed?"

Paula nodded faintly. "Yes, a priest was there."

"Thank God. His soul is in the hands of St. Michael." Tom dropped her hand, put his arms around her and kissed her on the cheek. She could feel the dampness of his mourning. "Thank you, Paula. Thank you for reliving your woeful memories for me."

They rose together and walked opposite directions along the creek. Tom used his handkerchief again to wipe his eyes and nose. Paula used the back of her hand. He leaned against a gnarled tree and watched the water in the stream skitter over stones. Then he surveyed the distant mountains. She studied her sanctuary on the hill and finally returned to the log to set out food for them.

"I can't eat a thing. Not now," Tom said when he joined her.

"You must. Healthy body; healthy mind," she insisted.

They nibbled at the snack. Their seriousness left them and ease returned. They started to imagine. Would their boy have been tall and lean as Paula was or short and stocky like Tom? Would his hair have been straight or wavy? Light or dark? Would he have been a scholar or a sailor? Serious or ribald? Would he have been all-American or every inch an Irishman? There were two things on which they agreed: he would drive a sports car and have eyes the color of the sea.

When they exhausted their fancies, they packed up and hiked the hill to her octagonal house. Paula leaned down periodically to pick fireweed, monkey-flower and bitter-root here, blue bell and columbine there. She put the blossoms in water in a handmade vase and placed the multihued, aromatic arrangement on the west deck.

"Wildflowers don't last long once picked, you know," he observed.

"I know. But these will last until sundown," she replied wistfully, fingering the blooms.

Paula admired nature's beauty for a few moments and then turned to him. "I think it's time for a ride." She drove them down the hill and into a small town near the base of the foothills. They wove its narrow streets until she found what she was seeking—a Catholic church. The modest brick structure was hardly the cathedral he was used to, but all Tom needed now was a candle and a priest.

She would wait for him, Paula indicated, and took a seat. Her faith tradition, if one could call it that, had not changed in the last four decades he gathered, but Tom knew she would be there for him when he was done. He felt comfortable to take all the time he needed. In the car on the way back up the grade he said, "Thank you again, Paula. I think you understand me better than I do myself. Now... I am at peace. And you?"

"Soon," she said and patted his hand.

Supper was simple and subdued—no wine, no music. The two of them sat, lost in thought, gazing at the mountains to the west taking on their shadows and the creek darkening at the base of her hill. When the last gilded ray of sunlight sequestered itself behind a peak, Paula lifted the small bouquet from its vase and cast it from the deck. The brilliant reds, oranges and yellows, blues and purples were caught by the evening breeze and carried gently to the valley below. The sun was down and their lips were sealed. Paula was at peace.

Chapter 12

Thomas knew what he had to do. As firmly as he vowed never to speak of their son again, he could tell by the look in Paula's eyes that she was imagining, too, how *their* son would have fit in this menagerie of children. Would he have had the seriousness of Tommy, the assertiveness of Anne, the sensibility of Meghan or the fragility of Emily, Kurt's congeniality, Kirin's strength or Michael's good-natured spirit... or all of these qualities rolled into one perfect package? Thomas knew what he had to do. He raised his fingers to his lips and whistled, driven to bind these *two families* into *one*.

No response. He whistled again, and the room began to quiet. On the third shrill sound, Emily responded. "Father, you can't mean it. You haven't done this to us in ages."

A crafty smile crossed his lips.

Emily turned to the others. "He wants us to line up like we used to, you know, Von Trapp-style like *The Sound of Music*."

The others moaned. Kurt and Kiri looked puzzled, but as a line began to form—by age, apparently—the two Koyles tried to discover their places. Kurt's was between Meghan and Emily, but Kiri and Michael were fighting it out at the end of the line.

"What is going on with you two?" Thomas inquired. "Don't know how to count backwards?"

"It's not that, Father. We're both thirty, but we can't agree on who is older. Kiri insists she is because her birthday is late July. Mine is early August, but I know I'm older. I can feel it," the youngest son protested.

"That's ridiculous," Kiri laughed. "By virtue of my birthday—July comes before August—I'm older, and you are on the end." She pushed him aside and wriggled in beside Emily.

"No. I won't agree. I cannot possibly be the baby in such a large family. I say we pursue this further—last throw, best shot, win or lose. What do you say to that?" he asked Kiri who shrugged her shoulders.

Michael continued, "Good. Catholics, raise your hands." He counted. "Protestants, raise your hands." He counted. "You will all observe, there is a Catholic majority here."

"You're not going to pull a 'majority rules' on me, are you?" Kiri challenged. "That is definitely not fair."

"No. But I will not relinquish my claim to being older until we take this one step further." He turned to face his siblings. "Catholics, when does life begin?"

The O'Connells answered in unison, without hesitation, "At conception."

"Protestants, when does life begin?" he asked the others.

The Koyles eyed each other until Paula answered, "At viable birth."

"So," Michael pronounced, "by birth *date*, Protestant definition, Kiri wins. But I say that since Catholics are in the majority here we use the Catholic definition, 'life begins at conception,' and determine which of us was first *conceived*." All eyes in the group widened with this bizarre proposition. "Win or lose, I will be satisfied and forever hold my peace and that place in the family. Kiri, can you live with that?"

Kirin, knowing she had the earlier birth date and trusting that no one could possibly pinpoint conception by remembering one specific night some thirty years earlier, felt safe to agree. "Sure. Why not? If it will make you feel better, we'll play your little game."

"Good. Paula, can you remember when your daughter was conceived?" Michael asked seriously.

Paula glanced at her female offspring and wavered before replying, "Thursday, November 26, about six in the morning. I remember because I planned to get up early to get the Thanksgiving turkey ready for the oven. I awoke earlier than intended and felt... aroused... and knew it was 'the right time' so to speak, so I nudged your father and... the rest is history as they say. Sorry dear, you were born two weeks before your due date."

Kiri was horrified. "Mother! How embarrassing! How can you talk like that? How can you know *that* one was the time?"

"Given the frequency your father and I... Let's just say, mothers know these things."

"Father, do you have any idea when I was conceived?" Michael waited hopefully, buoyed by the response thus far.

Thomas scratched his bearded chin thoughtfully. "If we're talking about the same time period—late November of the same year—I would have to say... Well, the last Wednesday in November was always the Harvest Social at the Club. Your mother and I would have left near the end... about midnight. By the time we got home and to bed... place it between one and two at the latest. It really doesn't take very long you know."

His children were aghast. Paula patted him on the chest. "Hmmm. You've improved with age. You were a busy young man."

Thomas flushed, "It may take us O'Connells a while to get started, but we've proven to be prolific in our thirties."

"Father! This is absolutely mortifying!" cried Anne. "How can you discuss such things so openly in front of your children... and strangers?"

"Because I am not ashamed of them. You are adults now and know *intimately* what we're saying."

Anne turned to Tommy. "Do something! Stop him from embarrassing us like this."

"I am absolutely speechless," and Tommy turned away shaking his head.

Kiri appealed to her brother. "Kurt, say something. Save *us* from humiliation."

He shrugged and blurted out with a chuckle, "This is the best game I've seen all weekend. Saints vs. Sinners. Bring it on!" He gave Michael a high-five.

Emily hid behind her hands and did not want to hear any more of it, so even-tempered Meghan took command. "I say we get this settled as quickly as possible and move on. Given that… 'the act' and 'conception' are not instantaneous… for the sake of argument let's say Kiri's creation began around 6a.m. at the earliest. That's *1p.m.* Dublin time. So if Michael's began at *2a.m.* at the latest, that is an eleven hour difference. Given also the evidence of all these stair-step O'Connells standing before you, it is highly unlikely that the swimmer that created Kiri could overtake Father's lead.

"I'm sorry, Kiri. I really wanted you to win. It would serve my brother right for being so brazen. But I think even you will have to agree that Michael is revealed most likely the older, and therefore the winner. At most you are twins," Meghan pronounced, putting an end to the contest.

Kiri startled the room by bursting into loud sobs. Everyone was visibly disturbed, but no one knew what to do, not even her mother. Michael grabbed her and squeezed her tight saying, "I'm sorry. It's not that important. You can have it."

Jerking herself free, Kiri took her hands from her face revealing a broad smile and laughter. "Gotcha! Oh, for heaven's sake, people. Lighten up. This is not that big a deal. I will play the 'baby' if it will keep peace in the family. But, Michael O'Connell, know this. If you are my older twin I expect you to behave like one—protective, more responsible, more mature and definitely more generous toward *all* your sisters with your time and treasure."

She turned to face the gathering. "Now, can we get on with this, please? That ridiculous exercise started with a whistle. Thomas, you must have something you want to say."

The buoyant elder inhaled deeply and pondered while the children took their places back in line. "Well, I never expected all of *this*. I meant to say… that is, Paula and I want to say… that we will take all of the grandchildren from noon New Year's Eve until 6p.m. on New Year's Day, so *all* you *children* can go to Copley Castle and have a wonderful time together. In return, you will agree to go to the New Year's Ball at the Club with us on Saturday where Paula and *her* family will be officially presented to our friends as part of *ours*. You are expected to be in good humor and fancy dress, no complaints. Is it a deal?"

Each O'Connell replied in turn as Thomas stared down the line. "Yes, agreed. Yes, Father. Of course. Yes, sir." A shy "Yes, Father" from Emily completed the roll call. Thomas then returned to Kiri and Kurt, waiting for their responses.

Kiri looked past Emily at Kurt, and then to Thomas. "Since we don't have any children for you to watch," she tendered, "does that mean we don't *have* to participate?

"That's not what it means," Thomas replied. "By that reasoning, if Emily has one child and Anne, three, does Emily only come to the Ball for one hour and Anne for three? I don't think so."

"Is this what you call Irish extortion?" Kiri challenged, trying to remain respectful.

Disbelieving, the O'Connell children whispered to one another, "No one... make that NO ONE... dared to defy Father like this!"

"Call it what you will," Thomas responded. "I prefer to think of it as Irish persuasion."

"Is manipulation what Kurt and I can expect from you, as Mother's husband, in the future?"

"I pray I may never stoop so low again, but this event is important for the two of us... for all of us," he replied calmly.

"Could we fly in Saturday afternoon, in time to make your party?" Kiri bargained.

"No. That won't do." The man remained steadfast.

"I need to understand your reasoning, Thomas, if I'm to abide by your edict," Kiri stated firmly.

"I planned to take your mother to the Ball this year, even though she was reluctant to go saying 'Balls aren't my thing.' It would be the first time for me since... in many years. Michael and Meghan agreed to accompany us, while the others were making separate plans. You two came all this distance to share our holiday and added so much to it, and my children behaved more as children than as adults until today. With their apologies and your conversations earlier, it seems you were just beginning to know and accept one another."

Thomas continued reflectively, staring straight into Kiri's eyes. "You need an opportunity... on neutral ground... to continue that familiarity. If not, the only times you will all be together will be at our wedding and our funerals. What a sad loss for everyone. So, fair or not, if we are going to be family, it's all or nothing for the whole lot of you. Copley Castle and Club Ball or no castle, no ball from the eldest to the baby. What do you say?"

"What world do you live in, Thomas, where you think that you can mold familial love from disparate pieces of human flesh?"

"A world of faith in the people I love."

Kiri turned and mouthed to the O'Connells, "He can't really keep you from going to this castle, can he? At your ages?"

They nodded, "Yes he definitely can, even at our ages."

Incredulous at Thomas' apparent power over his children, Kiri implored Kurt, "What about our ski weekend?" Michael cringed, knowing how much this meant to her.

"I guess we're expected to put it off until another time... to show family solidarity or something," her brother answered.

"Why are you putting all this on *our* shoulders? This is some kind of a test, isn't it?" Kiri shot at Thomas, refusing to be the wounded animal backed into a corner.

"You could say that, yes. This is our first major challenge. If we're going to function as a family, even though separated by miles and lack of common history, we need to be cognizant of what is important to each and every other member here. So, yes, this is a test."

Thomas was not so easy-going and laid-back as he appeared. He could be very forceful and take charge like he did in their confrontation two days ago. Kiri appealed to her mother for help. "Mother?"

"I must defer to Thomas in matters of his family. I guess it's up to you and Kurt to decide if you want to be a part of his ideal or not. I have accepted his proposal, so my place is beside him. I will be where he wants me to be even though you know I'm not the 'Ball' type. I can't pretend class or sophistication. I'm the braless, woolen shawl and sandals by the fire type. But I will be by his side this time because it is important to my partner.

"You could put your personal preferences aside, too, if this is important enough to you. I will support you in whatever you decide," Paula answered with compassion for her children's dilemma. "If you do come, however, you must be in good humor, no complaints. You will not come as petulant teenagers, tokens or spoilers. Come as full participants, or stay home."

"Kurt, be a big brother and help me out here," Kiri pleaded.

Kurt searched her face and then stated resolutely, "There are only two of us standing against the rest. Despite that, we hearty Westerners could take you easily. Thomas, we won't let your foolish ship of dreams sink on our account. We'll say 'aye' to your noble experiment. Yes, it's a deal. We'll be here in good humor and fancy dress, no complaints." He turned to his sister without apology. "We're her family, Kiri. Mom needs us to be here."

Crestfallen that her brother caved, she understood he was right. This was a time for kinship. They owed it to their mother, even if she did not approve of Thomas' tactics.

"It means wearing patent leather shoes and a cummerbund," Michael joshed in an attempt to lighten the mood.

Emily giggled at the thought.

"You're kidding. Is it too late to rescind my vote?" Kurt asked.

Michael laughed, shook his head, and pumped the air with his fist. "Yes! I have a twin!" He grabbed Kiri and hugged her.

With the tension broken, the children started making plans again for the upcoming weekend. There will be an "entertainment." They will do a Von

93

Trapp simulation. It will be super! And clever! They will exchange emails. Hugs and backslaps abound.

Michael sensed Kiri's discomfort during the hectic family planning. He led her to the Christmas tree, placed her next to it and moved her back a little, behind a branch. "While Anne's got her captain's hat on, you'll feel safer on the fringe of the forest. I'll rescue you with my trusty sword in a bit." Then he returned to the fray to see how Kurt was holding up.

When Thomas had had enough, he directed, "OK, you O'Connells. Get out of here. You've taken up too much of our morning as it is, and these two have a plane to catch... so they can turn right around and come back! We'll welcome 2009 together—as one united family."

Everyone but Kurt and Kiri found humor in his remarks.

Michael said goodbye to his siblings, waving them out the door. He returned to the tree to retrieve Kiri. She did not smile, but she did not pout either. She was resigned—deflated, even. Her sparkle and her spirit ebbed. He took her by the hand and turned her to face the tree. "The magic of Christmas resides in that tree, you know," he whispered in her ear. "I learned that from a very beautiful young woman. She also taught me last night that hard times pass, but memories of good times last forever."

A weak smile crossed her face.

"I know how much your ski weekend means to you, Kiri," Michael said as he turned to face her and study her distant, hazel-flecked blue eyes. "...and I appreciate your giving it up for us. I know the logistics are terrible, but you'll make it work. You are disappointed, but I am overjoyed. If I'm to have another sister in my life, I couldn't ask for a more wonderful one than you—a Christmas wish come true. To have you back again so soon will be awesome. As your new big brother, I guarantee the trip will be worth your sacrifice."

Michael wrapped Kiri in a great ursine embrace. "I promise you a New Year of memories that will last forever."

*   *   *

Thomas stood with his arm around Paula's waist, regarding the sorry specimen for a holiday tree that now tilted to the right in front of them. With all the children excitedly moving about the room earlier, he had not noticed its precarious state. "Will you help me take the tree down? I believe it has seen its last good day."

"Not on your life!" Paula replied. "If my children are bound to return next weekend and this tree in not here, Kiri especially will be so disappointed that any good humor she managed to bring along with her will fly right out the window. It is you who must help me straighten it, feed it, and talk to it tenderly to keep this Christmas tree alive until my two are gone for good."

He shook his head at the improbability that they would succeed. "Whatever you say, my dear." He turned to his intended partner, obviously pleased with himself. "I told you I could make this happen. One big happy family coming up!"

"Don't you be touting your cleverness, Thomas O'Connell. I wanted to box your ears for coercing my children the way you did, but I would never cross you in front of yours."

"Oh come now, Paula," he chuckled. "You saw Kurt's eyes light up at the mention of a castle. Your son is so amiable, he is happy to return, and you enjoyed my sparring of wills with Kirin as much as I did. That daughter of yours will never be bullied into anything she does not feel is right for her. She has more than held her own with my girls. I can see your spunk and spirit in her eyes. She would do anything—climb a mountain, cross a desert, pull up roots and move to Dublin—for the ones she loves. Kirin will surprise us, you'll see." He tilted Paula's chin upward until their eyes met, then stroked her under the chin. "Let me claim a small victory here. Hmmm?"

"All right. A wee one. But if you ever challenge my children like that again, I may have to rethink my opinion of you."

"You can't," he said, holding her gaze with his. "You said 'yes.' This time you accepted my proposal without hesitation—no objections, qualifications, or list of obstacles facing us. What changed your mind?"

"I've come to realize that who you are with is more important than where you are... and that you can't foresee obstacles to erase them before they confront you. You face them together, for better or worse."

Thomas squeezed her hand. "I'm off to Mass now, Paula. I'll be a little longer than usual, to add thanks for my many blessings."

"Would you like some company?"

"I would love yours... but I don't have a coupon until January."

"Call this one a bonus... for misguided but well-meaning intent."

Chapter 13

Somewhere over the North Atlantic, Kurt nudged Kiri. "Sis, are you awake?"

"You know I can't sleep on a plane."

"What did you think of the O'Connells?"

"Thomas and I didn't get along at all. Can you believe the con he pulled on us? Next weekend will be the last weekend I will ever spend in that man's house."

"What about the wedding?" Kurt reminded her.

"Fly in. Watch them say 'I do,' say congratulations, and fly out," Kiri stated firmly.

"I thought he was pretty nice for an old guy. He treats Mom well, and he is easy to talk to. I felt like he was trying to make the holiday pleasant for everyone."

"That's because you are so easy to get along with. I couldn't do one thing right—or at least I couldn't perform to his standards. And I don't like the way he cornered me into a confrontation—twice. It is true that he is good to Mom. I haven't seen her so happy in years."

"So give him another chance. Next weekend could be altogether different."

"Oh, please let it be different," Kiri appealed.

"What about his kids?"

"It's no secret that I didn't get along with the girls. Meghan seemed friendly when she wasn't with the others, though."

"Yeah, I liked her best too," Kurt agreed. "How about the guys?"

"I don't think I exchanged more than two words with Tommy. But Michael was a lot of fun. I got to know him pretty well. I wish I knew more guys like him back home."

"I thought he came on too strong—making such a big deal out of being your twin brother."

"Do I detect a hint of jealousy in your voice?"

"Of course not. I just don't understand why I'm not big brother enough for you any more."

"You'll always be my one and only favorite. You know that." Kiri stretched from her seat belt to give him a hug.

* * *

Emails flew furiously between Dublin and Denver for the next three days—so much to do, and so little time. Particularly frantic, Kiri tried to juggle her work responsibilities with everyone else's expectations. She was the reluctant soldier, but she would do her duty as decided by the majority.

To: Tanya, Charlie, Zach, Susan, Lara, Jason, et al.

So sorry. Kurt and I must cancel NY bash at condo. Family obligation across the pond. Harrumph. Details later. We're still on for MLK weekend. See you guys then. Kiri

To: Mom.

Please don't call. I'm turning off my phone. Up to my nose hairs in work. Have to shop tonight. Fancy dress—Yuck! Big presentation tomorrow and annual report due Wed. a.m. Then must pull things together so I can leave by noon. This is crazy! E-mail only, please. K

To: Kiri

OK. Thomas and Michael are setting up a great surprise for the grandkids, but Kurt will love it most. Mom

To: Mom

What is it? K

To: Kiri:

I can't tell. Then it wouldn't be a surprise! You'll have to come see for yourself. Mom

To: Kirin Koyle

Thank you. Thomas O'Connell

To: Thomas O'Connell

My pleasure. Kirin Koyle

To: Kiri

Can you believe what they want me to do? Besides sing and wear my cowboy hat? They asked for my tux size. My TUX size! I don't even own a suit! And my shoe size—so they could reserve a get-up for me at the rental place. Now, if they wanted ski boot or hat size, I could oblige, but tux size? Please advise. Kurt

To: Kurt

Go to a rental place in the city and be measured/try on. Then you'll have sizes to send. Kiri

To: Kiri

When am I supposed to do that? I'm going skiing! Kurt

To: Kurt

Don't even mention skiing! Find time. If I have to be fancy, you do too. I hope the interstate is closed.

To: Kiri

Let me know what you want to have done so I can set your appointment with ours: hair (cut, trim, style, color), manicure, pedicure, facial, other. Meghan

To: Meghan

None of the above. Kiri

To: Kiri

Are you going out with your mother, then? Meghan

To: Meghan

No. I'm sleeping. K.

To: Kiri

Remember, this is fancy dress. Meghan

To: Meghan

The dress *is* fancy. I'm not. K

To: Mom

Pkg coming via international air overnight. Let me know when it arrives. K

To: Kiri

Package arrived this afternoon. Mom

To: Mom

Please open and hang in shower. Dress and blouse (not you, the box, or the shoes). Tkx, K

To: Kiri

Wrinkles have all hung out (of clothes, not me). Dress is beautiful! Mom

To: Mom

Hope it will be OK. Refuse to go long and trip over my own hem. K

To: K

No worries. The men are the ones who will trip all over themselves to dance with you. Maybe you'll meet someone nice. :) Mom

To: Mom

Not looking, Mom. You know that. Besides, once this shindig is over, I plan to leave Dublin far behind. I won't be dancing Irish jigs again till your wedding—if you ever get around to actually having one! K

To: K

HA! HA! HA! Mom

To: Kirin

Anne says I'm to supply you with your lyrics for our skit. She says to wear a mini-skirt and pigtails. She didn't say where you're to attach the tails or how many there should be, however, so use your best judgement. I'll supply the giant lollipop—for "the baby." Lyrics are attached. Yours are emboldened. Michael

To: Michael

Message received. Who wrote this lame thing anyway? I'll have to be emboldened to sing it! Kiri

To: Kiri

Thanks a lot. I did. I'm considered the writer in the family. Michael

To: Michael
     HA! HA! Then, will you write my epitaph—now? I'm going to die of embarrassment. K
To: K
     That will make a dramatic finale. I'll add it in. M

To: Anne and Emily
     Just found out Kiri and Paula are *not* having hair done, etc. Meghan
To: M&E:
     I knew they'd find a way to embarrass us. Don't they know what a Ball is? Do you have anything old that might fit Kiri—just in case? Do you think they know to wear gloves? Anne
     Gloves—don't know. Dress—I'll take a look. Meg
     Me too. I think they're both nice enough, just unrefined. Emily
     We have to give them a chance. They might surprise us. Meg
     Yeah. They might show up in denim and gingham! Anne

To: Kiri
     Don't bother to pack a fancy wrap. We'll rent. What size do you wear and what is your dress like? Meghan
To: Meghan
     Size 8. Blue. K

To: Mom
     Got a message from Thomas. Yes, Mom. I replied. Kiri
To: Kiri
     Thank you. Mom
To Mom
     I bet he's feeling pretty proud of himself now, after the shrewd ploy he pulled. K
To: Kiri
     He's paying dearly. His girls are driving him crazy with daily calls about clothes, hair, transport. Mom
     Good for them. I think they're worried we'll embarrass them. Nothing we do (or don't) could be worse than the crazy skit they've worked up! K
     I have also exacted a concession. We have all Saturday together—your room. Just you and me, babe! Thomas is banned from the third floor all day long! Love, Mom
     Way to go, Mom! Should we paint our toenails purple? K
     I was thinking puce. Much love, Mom

To: Anne and Meghan
     When are you leaving tomorrow? Emily
     Socials begin at five, so we need to be there by four to settle in. Meg

We'll probably show up about four too. But since Father will take the kids at noon, plus we're donating our nanny from noon to six, I'll have them over to Father's by 12:01—to give us extra time on our own. Anne

Think that's okay? I'd like extra time too. Em

That's what Father said. And from noon until six on Friday, Margaret and Tommy are donating their nanny to help, so I plan to use every minute. Anne

Don't you think that's taking advantage? Meg

Not if we're donating nanny help. Well, maybe it is, but we deserve to after Father forced us to bring Paula's kids along. Anne

Don't be so harsh. We're all going to get along just fine. I'm excited. I haven't been since the divorce. Meg

Maybe you'll meet someone new this time out. A nice guy. Em

Maybe I'll remind Tommy and Michael to aim for four. Meg

To Mom

I've done nothing but work and answer e-mail for the last 48 hours. I'm exhausted. Doesn't anyone else have a *real* job? Kiri

To: Kiri

Hang on. This whirlwind will be over soon. Mom

I'm praying for a blizzard. K

You're wasting your time. You'd be snowed in and couldn't go skiing anyway. Give it up, kid. Put on your happy face and come visit your mom. We'll have fun being silly together. M

I'm still praying for a blizzard. I need SLEEEEEP! K

To: Kirin

I'll pick you up at the airport. Michael

To: Michael

I doubt you can lift me. Kiri

To: Kiri

HA! HA! Mighty Mike.

*   *   *

Michael met the Koyles at the airport New Year's Eve morning. He literally picked Kiri up and carried her over his shoulder to customs, despite her protestations. "Don't you ever doubt my strength!" he scolded with a foxy smile she could not see.

"Ah, Mr. O'Connell. I see you have baggage today," the officer laughed as he passed them on through.

Kiri was not amused. Kurt followed along lugging both carryons, while Michael led the way to the parking lot this time. She wriggled away from him with a harrumph and squeezed into the back of his car, muttering. She pulled her stocking cap even further down over her head, closed her eyes, and endured the ride to Thomas' home. On arrival, she preceded the men into the house and targeted the staircase.

"I'm going to show Kurt this great surprise for the grandkids. Wanna see?" Michael asked.

"Later," she replied gruffly, bumping her bag along the stairs. The young men heard the slam of her bedroom door from two floors down. The guys shuddered at the thought of what that sound sparked a week ago. Thomas was outside in the rear, thank goodness.

Back to square one, Michael thought. Was last weekend a figment of his imagination? "What's up with our sis?" he asked Kurt. "Where's the good humor, no complaints?"

"Don't mind Kiri right now," Kurt replied. "She had a bummer of a week. I don't think she's stopped since her feet touched ground in Denver. Major big presentation at work, annual report, shopping for the Ball, answering everyone's emails. She hasn't slept or eaten in days. When it's time for the curtain to go up tonight, however, she will rally and do her best not to disappoint."

"What can we do to help?" Michael worried.

"Leave her alone for as long as possible. She needs sleep, food and water."

"Water? Like a glass or a bottle?" asked Michael confused.

"No," Kurt laughed. "She needs to soak in water—you know, like a shower or bath—to decompress. Give her time. Mind if I run this bag upstairs before you show me the great surprise?"

"Absolutely. Go. No hurry. We have about four hours before we need to take off," Michael said. "I'll meet you in the den in a few."

*   *   *

Kiri unpacked and repacked her small bag—costume on the bottom, skirt and blouse with appropriate undergarments next. Don't forget decent shoes. Where did Mom hide the blouse and shoes? Slacks and sweater for dinner and entertainment. Oops, jewelry for the blouse—slip it into the pocket with toiletries. Makeup. Brush and comb. Jeans and comfy sweater for the drive there and back. And her boots; it would probably rain. Leave airplane clothes here. This was more variety than she used in a week at home!

A soft knock on her door broke her concentration. "Go away!"

"Kiri, please. It's Michael. Please open the door."

"You could be Sir Lancelot and I'd still say go away... so, go away. Not interested."

"Kiri, please. I've fixed something for you."

She flung open the door. "What part of 'Go Away' do you not understand?" she practically shouted.

Her disheveled appearance stunned Michael. Her eyes, void of their color and sparkle, were red and blotchy like the rest of her face. Deep gray circles lay beneath the sunken orbs. Her nose dripped. Her hair, half ponytail and half stringy hanks, flew every which way, and her mouth quivered.

"You look terrible," Michael gasped. "What's wrong? Are you sick?"

"Thank you for reminding me I look terrible. I needed that. You made me feel so much better," she said sarcastically. "I am not sick... not yet, at least. I'm just behind on sleep. I didn't learn in four days' time how to get any on an airplane. If you will excuse me, I'm going to disappear under the covers until you drag me back to your car for the drive to our next social obligation."

Kiri tried to close the door, but Michael persisted. "I didn't mean anything. Here. Take this robe. I've drawn a warm bath for you and left enough hot water for the shower too if you want. Relax before you try to sleep; you'll rest better." He handed the robe in gingerly. "I'll come back in about half an hour to make sure you haven't dozed off in the tub. Anything else I can do?"

"No," Kiri said timidly. She took the robe and lowered her eyes. "Thank you."

Michael joined Kurt in the den. He was already playing with the new big screen the O'Connell men set up for the grandkids' sleepover. "Why another big TV?" he asked.

A click of the remote to enact the DVD player showed exactly why. Colorful animated characters jumped right off the screen and into his lap. Kurt was flabbergasted. "I didn't know 3D TV was available yet!"

"It's not, really. I borrowed it from the network. No one will be there over the holiday, I hope. I rounded up what few movies I could for the kids, but I'm really anxious to get back tomorrow and watch some of your 'football.' There is one outfit from London that will broadcast two or three of your major bowl games in 3D as a practice run. Of course, no one will see that except for a few because the sets aren't out for commercial use yet. That station has half a dozen so they can test their equipment, and I commandeered the one from our office," Michael explained, very satisfied with himself.

"Oh... my... God!" Kurt exclaimed. "Heaven on earth! Can we just stay here all weekend?"

"Not likely. You know Father. But let's set up the schedule to record while we're gone. Isn't there a game on tonight?"

"Sure is!" Kurt replied, and the sports junkies got down to business.

* * *

Michael listened at the bathroom door before he knocked. He heard a violent gushing, sucking sound, and then splashing, like dolphins frolicking. He knocked lightly, somewhat alarmed. "Kiri? Are you okay? It sounds like you're drowning in there."

"I just came up for air. I've been lying on the bottom, making waves. Oh… this feels sooo good. Thank you," she said. "I'm sorry; I've made a mess all over the floor. I'll be out in a few minutes after I clean it up. Thanks for the tea and the snack, too, by the way. The pineapple and cheese crackers hit the spot. I'm almost resurrected."

"Don't worry about the floor. I'll wipe it up. You get yourself into bed. If I wake you a half-hour before we need to leave, will that be enough time?" he asked.

"Perfect. And, Michael…"

"Hmmm…."

"I'm sorry I didn't appreciate your joke at the airport—the 'pick me up' thing. That really was very clever," she offered.

"No worries," he said. "You'll have many more opportunities to exclaim over my wit. Now, get some sleep. Big brother's orders."

*   *   *

A few minutes before departure time, Thomas took a break from playing Candy Land with three of his granddaughters to call Michael, bags in hand, over by the Christmas tree. "On your way, then?" he asked. At his son's nod, Thomas reminded, "Your duty is to make sure that Kurt, and especially Kirin, have a marvelous time tonight so they will not regret coming all this way for a party. Remember, they are not familiar with our social customs, so be on guard for the scoundrel or two who might attempt to take advantage."

"Got it, Father."

With a hand on his son's shoulder, Thomas continued, "I realize you probably gave up plans of your own to accommodate our guests. I appreciate your stepping in this weekend. This means so much to me… to the family."

"No problem, Father. Happy to oblige. Kiri should be down in a minute. Then we'll take off. Don't you make too much whoopee tonight," he joked on his way out the door.

Kurt was next down the stairs with a friendly wave for his host. Finally, Kiri arrived at the landing with her bag in tow. Thomas motioned for her to join him near the tree. "I'm glad to see you looking so rested, Kirin. I hear you've had a few rough days since we saw you last."

"Thanks to Michael, I recuperated quickly. On the surface, I'm ready to go. I shall try to dazzle them all with my pigtails and knee socks tonight," she joked.

"Kirin, before you go, I want to give you this." Thomas removed a small object from the pocket of his cardigan. He unwrapped the thin cord looped through its back and wound around it to reveal a miniature compass no more than a half-inch in diameter.

103

"This is a Celtic compass, Kirin. The Celts revered the circle. They believed rhythms in nature and the divine followed circular patterns. See here," and he ran his finger around the circumference of the ancient object, "how Celtic interlacings form the border of the compass, Celtic trinity knots decorate the face, and the needle resembles the eyes of symbolic animal figures incorporated in Celtic illuminated manuscripts. That eye is meant to remind you not to lose sight of the direction that is right for you," he divulged as he placed the hand-warmed compass in her palm.

Kiri shook her head and attempted to return the well-worn, antique ornament to him. "I can't. This is surely a family heirloom."

The kindly man closed her fingers around it. "Please. I want you to have it now. I see a flash of your mother's spirit in you—a defiance of convention. Do not let my daughters try to mold you into what they think an O'Connell should be. Let this Celtic compass be a reminder to be true to yourself... to find your own direction, your innate inner strength. You must not let the O'Connell women bully you into doing what is not right for you... like I did. I give you my word; I will never put you on the spot like that again. If I attempt to, show me this compass and I will back off. I will let you find your own way as the strong, spirited woman you are."

Kiri shook her head again, but he insisted, so she put the compass carefully in her pants pocket. "Thank you, Thomas. I may need the extra support tonight," she said thoughtfully. He patted her on the back and returned to his grandchildren. Kiri shouldered her bag and followed the young men out the front door.

Michael demonstrated his responsibility for Kiri's good humor by adding a pillow and throw to the cramped back seat of his car. "I thought you might like to rest more on the way to the castle. We'll be on the road for about an hour and a half. Do you want us to take Father's car so you'll be more comfortable?" he asked, trying to accommodate Kiri so she would arrive at the party well prepared for the festivities.

"This will be just fine," she said with a smile. "You've gone out of your way to turn me around today. How can I deny you and Kurt a ride in your prized racer? Let's do this!" and she climbed into the car with enthusiasm. As she cozied up, an unsettling notion crept into her head: *Witty, good-looking and thoughtful, too. I could really go for a guy like Michael. Stop it, Kirin! Do not entertain such ideas. He is your new big brother.*

Chapter 14

Kurt jostled Kiri awake. "We're almost there. Michael says you'll want to see the views along the rest of the road." She yawned and stretched until she could see clearly out a window. Michael was right. An unparalleled vista appeared around every bend. The party turned off a country road, and crossed a one-lane stone bridge over a narrow river with trees lining both banks. As they came out of a curve, the scene revealed Copley Castle dominating a rise, surrounded on two sides by parkland edging on forest-covered hills. A third side opened onto lawn, a walled Victorian garden, and one of the only remaining segments of the original castle wall joining a rounded tower. A circular drive sloped to the entry on the fourth.

Michael drove past the courtyard circle, into a parking lot behind. Speechless, Kurt and Kiri wrested themselves from the car. She reached for her bag, but Michael refused to relinquish it this time. "A gentleman would never allow a lady to carry her own duffel into the entrails of a castle." She laughed and enjoyed her walk to the main entry through the courtyard between stone walls under vine-covered arcades. The path came out near a twenty-foot arched entryway to the ancient inner keep bordered by two five-story towers marked with plunging arrow loops, a part of its ancient defenses.

Two medieval knights in armor guarded the reception area located inside the keep. Rows of skeleton keys attached to palm-sized leather holders lined the wall behind the desk. All keys seemed to be in place, Kiri noticed. As he checked them in, Michael explained that the two Koyles would also be asked to sign the historic guest registry—ladies first. Kiri wrote her name with a flourish, using the gold-handled pen she was offered, but she paused at the column labeled "Sept." "What does this mean?" she asked him.

"Irish for 'clan.' You'll want to write 'O'Connell' or they'll seat you with other unrelated guests. About 200 are expected, so we should probably stick together—unless you're against being an O'Connell for the evening."

"I'm already committed to play the 'baby sister' in your lame skit, so I might as well be an O'Connell for dinner too," she joshed as she finished signing in.

Michael escorted the Koyle-O'Connells up the grand mahogany staircase and pointed out married quarters in front of them, men to the left wing and ladies to the right. He informed them that Kiri would room with Meghan who had probably already arrived. Keys were not handed out for the evening. Numerous rooms in the castle and more in the stables outside made security an impossibility during a large affair, and women had no place to stash them in party dresses. Any valuables should be locked in her bag. Castle etiquette: knock before entering a room. "And don't slam the doors!" Michael added with a grin.

The medieval castle, originally constructed during the 13th century, was nearly destroyed during the Cromwellian Wars, rebuilt in the late 17th century, and expanded and refurbished in the 19th. The exterior walls of the bedrooms displayed the same massive girth as the thick stone walls of the inner castle, but the interiors were recently remodeled and furnished with antique accoutrements. Thankfully, Kiri noticed, electricity was available, and the room had a bath—no padding down the hall with a candle in the middle of the night in search of a garderobe.

Michael indicated that the men would leave her to get settled, hang her clothes, that sort of thing. The social took place in a near section of the Grand Ballroom and would begin at five. Casual. They would come back for her about then.

"Don't bother. I may not be ready right on time. I'll find my way. With a crowd of 200, I'm sure I'll be able to follow the noise. See you there." Kiri thanked him and closed the door to her chamber. Roommates Kurt and Michael backtracked along the long corridor, past the couples' rooms in the main hallway and into the male wing.

True to her word, Kiri was not ready right on time. She hung her clothes, laid out her costume, and investigated. The bathroom was fabulous with an old copper claw-footed tub, an ornate hanging showerhead above and pedestal sink. Meghan had already been and gone as evidenced by toiletries and clothes scattered here and there. Kiri spent some time at the window admiring the view of the woods beyond and sat at the antique dressing table studying her reflection. She wondered how she would have fit in those times. So elegant. Such pampering. But did women exercise minds of their own?

She changed into her slacks and sweater, brushed her hair, pinched her cheeks and headed out the eight-foot, heavy wooden door to find her way to the ballroom. At the top of the staircase, a nice-looking young man who appeared to be heading in the same direction joined her. He was tall, slender, sandy-haired, clean cut… and very friendly.

"Hi. I'm Patrick. And you are…." He extended his hand to shake hers.

"I'm Kiri. Kiri Koyle," she said, and accepted it.

"I don't believe I've seen you before at one of these shindigs. New to Dublin?" he asked.

"I'm visiting fam… for the holidays," she said. He had interesting Arctic ice blue eyes with a strange playfulness about them, she noticed.

"I thought I detected an exotic accent," he said as he slipped his hand behind her back and guided her down the stairs and along a vast corridor toward the noise of a crowd.

"Colorado is hardly exotic," Kiri laughed as she tossed her head.

"Colorado, is it? Rocky Mountains and skiing, I believe."

"Skiing, absolutely," she declared. "That is where I should be this weekend. Do you ski?"

"Slide is more like it. But I love to go whenever I'm over on the continent in winter. Maybe we'll have an opportunity to 'fall into' one another sometime over there." He smiled enticingly at her. "Kiri, is it? Kiri, I'd love to introduce you around." He placed his hand more firmly on her back.

"That would be great... until I can find my party," she replied.

"Your party?"

"I'm here with the O'Connells tonight."

"Ah, the O'Connells. How many of them are here this year?" he asked as his eyes darted quickly around the crowded room.

"*All* of them," she answered. "And that's a lot more than I'm used to."

"Well, let's meet some other folks, then," Patrick said as he led her to a table full of upbeat strangers. He positioned Kiri with her back to the room and began introductions.

Kurt and Michael chatted at a small table at the far side of the room. "What do you think of Copley Castle?"

"I tell you, our two trips to Ireland have been one great surprise after another, and this is right up there with the best. This is one super venue!" Kurt replied.

"Worth giving up a ski weekend?"

"Absolutely! I would love to go a-snooping, but I'm afraid I'd get lost," he answered. "How many rooms are there in this place?"

"I have no idea—one hundred bedrooms for sure, and then drawing rooms, sitting rooms, and other themed rooms on the ground floor here. I'll show you around what I know after we've had another drink. Do you think we ought to take our sister with us? When can we expect her to come down?" Michael asked.

"Kiri? She's right over there... making new friends, it looks like."

Michael jerked his head around in the direction of Kurt's gesture, got up quickly and strode over to Kiri and the young man who was being very familiar with her. He broke in between them and put his own hand to Kiri's back. "Patrick, thank you for bringing Kiri in. Kind of you. Kiri, I have something I want you to see. Come with me. Excuse us folks. Later." Michael took her by the hand and led her swiftly away from Patrick and the confounded others.

"Michael!" she complained. "What do you think you're doing? I was having a very nice time with Patrick and his friends. He was kind enough to..." she protested.

"He was kind enough to get his hands on you, it looked like," Michael said sternly. "Patrick Murphy is not the kind of guy you want to befriend."

"Why is that, Michael?" she challenged. "Why doesn't he meet with your approval? Not that I *need* your approval."

"Do you want to find yourself smashed up against some stone wall trying to fend off his pecker all night?" Michael asked, furious. "You're not to associate with him or anyone of his ilk!"

"You don't seem to mind who Kurt talks to."

"None of the guys are likely to ask him to dance or pin him against a wall for a kiss... or more."

She brushed off his concern. "I know how to defend myself from scumbags. Who do you think you are, telling me whom I may or may not associate with?"

"I'm the brother who is supposed to guard your reputation this weekend."

"You might want to worry about your own, Mighty Mike!" Kiri flung in anger. "Who's going to protect me from *you*!"

She tried to escape his grasp and leave, but he held onto her hand even more firmly. "Look. I'm sorry. I haven't handled this well at all." Michael tried a milder approach; calm reasoning was more her style. "I've known Patrick forever. We were in school together, then university and now we work in the same unit. I know him well, Kiri, and he's always been a spoiler. He capitalizes on a situation whenever he can. He has no compunction in compromising someone inappropriately for his own gain or pleasure."

He sensed her anger subside. "I can already tell by the way you enthralled his table that you will be tonight's prize, the fair young maiden to be won. Please, not Patrick. Half the men here are single and most of them very nice. When you become bored with us O'Connells, let me know and I'll introduce you to some who are trustworthy like Henry Callaghan, for instance, or Jimmy O' or Christopher. But not Patrick, please."

"You're probably right," she admitted. "I'm tired and my defenses are down. I wouldn't have let Patrick become so friendly if I were thinking clearly. You should just lock me in my room until time to sing and dance, then lock me back in again after." She paused. "Oh, but you can't. No key! I'll have to rely on your judgement, then. Damsel in distress? Hide behind her champion big brother."

"Good. Let's find Kurt and go exploring."

"Yes!" Kiri exclaimed excitedly. "I want to see everything!"

The wanderers ducked into a small sitting room dressed in royal red. From there, a series of *ogee* arches through the three-foot thick walls connected one chamber to the next differing only in color, like repeated reflections in opposing mirrors. Each room was themed, papered luxuriantly, and lit by a flickering fire. The snoopers strolled from one to the next regarding themselves in the gilded-framed mirrors above marble-topped sideboards. They tested the lavish furnishings, but Michael warned the other two not to touch the artifacts—hard to tell which ones were authentic. Somewhere between the library and the withdrawing room, the trio ran into Meghan.

"There you are," she cried. "We've been looking for you. Wondered if you were even here yet."

"Just taking a quick tour before dinner. Kurt and Kiri haven't seen a castle from the inside before, so this is as much a history lesson as it is an outing. Care to join us? We're about to see the music room with the gold leaf trimmed piano."

"No thanks. Anne and Emily are waiting at the social. By the way, Alice is looking for you, too."

"Later," Michael said and led his troop hurriedly out into the main corridor, past generations of peering eyes lining the walls.

Dinner was held in the Great Hall, a long room in an early section of the castle that retained its medieval feel. Five wooden, candlelit tables on a side each seated twenty. The ancient walls were lined with tapestries and hung with colorful banners jutting out into the room. A wide aisle down the middle of the stone-floored hall led to a raised platform at the far end where sound equipment and microphones awaited the entertainment. The O'Connell table was at that end, right in front of the stage. Their party consisted of the ten immediate members along with first and second cousins and some spouses from both Thomas' and their mother's sides of the family.

Kiri regarded them all carefully. She could not remember the names and did not try. She noted family resemblance. By comparing the mother's kin and the father's, she decided Tommy, Anne and Emily must favor their mother, while Meghan and Michael revealed more of their father. She wondered if personalities followed suit as well.

The Koyles were smack in the center of the table, with Meghan and Michael to one side of each of them and the relatives to the other. During the meal, Meghan explained how this fête had changed over time.

"In Father's day, it was still a very formal affair—long gowns, tuxes, jewels and manner. Can you imagine walking in heels on this stone floor or dining in a long gown and corset?"

Kiri could not. She would spoil hers with drippings from her meal, for sure.

"A string quintet or some such provided entertainment, and a ball followed until midnight," Meghan continued. "About the eighties, that began to change. I think the wives had a lot to do with it. If they were going to have fun, they wanted to be comfortable. And they wanted to be entertained, not attend a concert. Manner and formality gradually gave way to comfort and gaiety.

"By the time our generation took charge, this 'do' evolved into a casual social, dinner at ease, family skits and traditional Irish music by a folk group with a finale sing-along, and a dance—the kind you can actually move to. Tonight there is even more change in store. The Irish band is out, and karaoke is in. None of us," (Meghan indicated the entire hall) "has done much of that, so no telling what we're in for. Should be fun!"

Michael, sitting next to Kiri, turned to her. "Kurt tells me you're a pro."

"Hardly. He's pretty good himself, once he gets wound up. Keep pouring the mead down him, and he won't be shy."

Time arrived for the family skits. Half the hall disappeared to don costumes and find props. Meghan was in and out of their room before Kiri arrived. She reluctantly put her getup on: black mini skirt and shoes, everything else was eighties neon colors—oranges, greens, and rose pink—knee socks, frilly blouse with polka dots, bows around her two pigtails and on her shoes. She pulled floppy bangs over her eyes, rouged her cheeks and added a few freckles for good measure. She glanced at herself in the staid antique looking glass. "Absolutely humiliating! This cannot be over too soon." She took one last deep breath and left the room. She counted on Michael to remember the giant lollipop and hoped it was not licorice.

Back in the Great Hall, she found Anne, Meghan and Emily in matching frilly white dresses with blue satin sashes and bows in their hair. Tommy and Michael wore knee-high britches and suspenders, white shirts open at the collar with sleeves rolled up, and jaunty caps. Kurt dressed in his cowboy gear—hat, kerchief around his neck, shirtsleeves rolled up and cowboy boots. And Kiri? She looked ridiculous. The sisters had obviously viewed *The Sound of Music* as many times as she, but she was not in their version.

Michael grabbed her hand and pulled her chair closer. "You look adorable! Here. Have a lolly."

"That's not exactly what a thirty-year-old woman longs to hear. I feel ridiculous. This cannot be over soon enough," she moaned. Happily, the lollipop he provided was colorful and still wrapped. "You haven't taste-tested?"

"Nope. I was afraid I might take a whole bite out. Now that would look truly embarrassing!"

The O'Connell skit came midway through the program. Anne introduced them as the Von O'Connell Family Singers and explained briefly the addition of two members to their family. Then they lined up, Tommy at the head and Kiri at the tail. They began with the usual chorus, "Doe… " for Tommy and "Tea… " for Kiri who mimicked her phrase. They all joined in for bringing them back to "doe." The next verse, to the same music and in the same order, introduced each one. "Hi. I'm Tom, the oldest son…" and so forth, down to "Kiri, the family's youngest babe," and that brought them back to "Doe." The next verse told something about each one, their vocation or avocation or characteristics. The choreography involved alternate bobbing and straightening in synch, with Kiri to be constantly out of step.

The last round involved a switch from "Doe…" to "So long… Adios," as they ambled offstage slowly in step, waving to the audience—all except for Kiri who held back smiling, giggling, and licking her lolly until Michael came back to get her. He did, and she found herself over his shoulder just as she had been only hours before at the airport. This time he gave her a spank on the bottom and paraded her around for a few moments before taking her offstage and returning her to their table. She was astonished and showed it. She tried to wriggle away from him, jab him in the ribs and bonk him on the head with her lollipop, much to the delight of the crowd who laughed and applauded her fruitless efforts.

Back at the table, Michael gave her a hug and pulled out her chair. "You were great!" he said, tugging on a pigtail and giving her a noogie, an ear-to-ear smile crossing his face.

"And your knees are showing," Kiri joshed, plunging the lollipop into that broad smile. "Hold this for me, will you?" she asked as she turned to leave.

"Where are you going? You aren't angry with me… again, are you?" he worried.

"No, Michael. Not angry. Just humiliated," she said calmly. "I'm going to change. I refuse to sit here like a baby doll for the rest of the evening." It was apparent the sisters did not intend to relinquish their dainty dresses, for no one got up to leave with her. The men slipped into V-necks right there. "I'll be back to see if anyone else suffers greater mortification than I tonight."

Kiri made her way out of the Great Hall along the wall at the far end of the tables. She tried to make herself invisible but was not successful, as several she passed nodded or stated their approval of her performance.

"You have one good sport for a sister," Michael commented to Kurt. "A whale of a trooper and a lot of fun. You don't think she's upset with me, do you?"

"Kiri? Naw. She just needs to relax for a few minutes. Take a time-out. Put on something she feels presentable in. She pretends more disgust than she really feels—a little guilt thrown your way," Kurt assured his roommate. "Kiri's a ham to the bone. She'll be fine and back in no time."

She did return a few minutes later in slacks and sweater as before, hair brushed to a rich luster and tucked behind her ears, rouge and freckles sucked down the drain. Kiri slipped into her seat beside Michael. With the hard part over, she was determined to enjoy the rest of the evening.

* * *

At Thomas' house, all the wee ones were in bed, their energies spent on noisemakers and sparklers at the bewitching hour of 9p.m. "It must be midnight somewhere in the world," Paula reasoned. The four oldest were glued to a 3D movie in the den. She and Thomas relaxed in the living room by the fire, feet up on an ottoman, recounting their successful celebration, when Paula's phone rang first... and then Thomas' sounded.

Kurt... and Michael exclaimed simultaneously, "Mom/Father! You've got to see this! The cousins videoed our hilarious skit. Sending it now. Talk to you later. Kurt/Michael."

The video came through, and the couple watched with rapt attention. They smiled throughout, and then roared at Michael's and Kiri's antics at the end. After they watched again... and again, Thomas grabbed her into an embrace. "Oh, Paula. How did you manage to raise such terrific children without me? A family is born!"

"I hope you don't expect me to invite those 200 guests over to celebrate a christening with us!" she said, and returned his favor.

*   *   *

Copley Castle's host brought an end to the skits with a round of applause for everyone—the best program they had seen in many years. Thanks to all. The second segment of entertainment would be audience participation— karaoke, something they had never done before but was reputed to be great fun. They would have two microphones going—one for the current singer and one for the next man up. First round, each table was expected to select one family member to represent them—no holding back because of embarrassment. This was all in good fun, remember.

"Anyone who needs a drink first, just raise your glass and you'll be taken care of. We've obtained a huge music log and a professional to pull up the music and cue you. Video screens are being set up at the sides of the platform as we speak. Our family will go first; the rest of you begin deciding who will defend your family's honor with voice. Second round will be voluntary, anyone who wants to, in turn, around the room again, and so on. "Let's begin!" He handed the mike over to his table and sat down.

The music blared. The O'Connell table was alive with discussion as to who would represent them. Anne would not dare. Meghan just laughed it off. Tommy said "No way!" and Emily put her hands over her eyes as if to disappear behind them. Anne looked to the cousins who shook their heads. They would not be O'Connells now when it counted most.

The "next up" mike arrived at their table. The siblings and guests passed it from one to another. Michael and Kurt tossed it between them like a game of "hot potato," until Kiri grabbed it from them.

"For heaven's sake, people. Lighten up. This is not that big a deal; it's only a song!" She got up from the table in a huff and strode to the music man to select her piece. Surprised no one had sung it yet, she picked possibly the number one karaoke favorite of all time, performed repeatedly throughout any evening by vocalist wannabes.

When the Uilleann pipes began, the audience immediately recognized the romantic theme from *Titanic*. Kiri did her best Dion impersonation with breathy tones, serious countenance and doleful eyes to begin. Then she belted out the lyrics with a strong voice and emotion building to a crescendo of dramatic exaggeration, intending her performance to be a caricature. The open-mouthed group took her seriously, however, and broke into effusive applause and whistles as she curtsied and exited quickly from the raised platform.

"Now that was embarrassing," she said to herself. A Colorado crowd would laugh at her good-natured intention; not take her seriously. "What century do these people live in?" she asked herself again.

Before Kiri touched down in her seat, Michael yanked her up by the hand and led her brusquely from the Great Hall. A man on a mission, he pulled her from sitting room after sitting room on their way to the Library. "Stop! What's wrong?" she half-shouted. "I'm sorry if I embarrassed you. I meant it as a joke! Slow down!"

Michael swung the library door open with a flourish, then slammed it shut, its reverberations sounding down the long hall. He flung Kiri against the wall and pinned her there with his muscular forearms, squeezing her head between his powerful hands. Not an inch from her face, he stared into her eyes and bellowed, "No more twins! No more brother and sister!" Without another moment's hesitation, he pressed himself against her forcefully and kissed her full on the lips.

"What the hell are you doing?" Kiri spat out, trying to break his hold, but Michael was the stronger. He released her slightly, then forced another ardent embrace. Finally she used a knee on him. He drew back immediately, stunned. "So this is the *true* Mighty Mike," she accused. "The Michael who uses force to have his way! Who's going to pull his trusty sword and defend me now? Back off!"

Michael was in denial. "Oh, Kiri. I'm sorry! God, what have I done?"

"You've drunk too much and embarrassed yourself, that's what you've done. And you've scared me witless. If this is part of your father's plan to keep me happy and entertained, you take your responsibility too seriously. As if tonight weren't already humiliating enough, you've really put a cap on it. What were you thinking?"

"I... I don't know. We had such a great time. Dinner... wine... conversation... skits. They were so much fun. And then you sang that song. It was powerful. I foolishly assumed you were speaking to me. I... I don't know what I was thinking." He tried to rub the remorse from his face.

"It was a joke, Michael. My song was a joke... an impersonation... make believe. You'd better rethink what just happened here, and when you sober up, I'll expect an apology."

Hurt and chagrin flushed across her assailant's face. He felt a shame he had not known for many years.

Kiri sensed his discomfort. "You're a charming man, Michael. You don't need to use force. Why not use your innate charm and just ask a girl.

She might say 'yes.'" Kiri straightened her sweater and ran her fingers through her hair to fluff it. Then she started for the door. "Let's get back. I don't want my reputation 'spoiled' any more than it already is."

"Now, that hurt. I promise. I will never force myself on you again. You have my word."

"Convince me with your behavior, then. Let's go." She opened the door, and they left. Generations of peering eyes followed them again, back along the corridor to the Great Hall.

"Where have you two been?" Kurt asked, worried. He searched Kiri's eyes for a sign of distress. "You missed some good songs, but nothing as great as yours, Sis. Anything wrong?"

"I needed a quick time-out. Too much pressure. I'm okay now," she assured him.

"Come over here and sit by me," Kurt suggested.

"No, I'm fine. Really. Let's watch."

*   *   *

Paula and Thomas tried not to doze off, but it was a struggle. First, Paula's phone rang… and then Thomas' sounded. Kurt/Michael called again.

"Hey, Mom/Father. Get a load of your daughter! Later. Kurt/Michael."

The older couple watched the video, amazed at the performance. What fun those young people must be having.

*   *   *

The volunteer round of karaoke began, and the "next up" mike got closer and closer to the O'Connell table. All eyes were on Kiri, but she declined. "Not on your life! That last was disaster; I'm not doing it again. Michael? Kurt? Don't you think you owe me?"

Michael looked at Kurt, and Kurt at Michael. Michael won. "You do it, Kurt. You know the gang would love to hear you, now that they've seen your sister."

"OK. I will, if Kiri will. A duet." He turned to her and grinned. "If the crowd expects hokey, let's give them hokey. Something like 'Achy Breaky' and we'll throw in a lotta twang and a little line dance. Come on," he coaxed. "These up-tights will love it."

"Please, Kiri. That would be great. I promise to be on good behavior," Michael offered.

"Oh, what the heck. This night couldn't get any worse," she agreed. "Give me your shirt."

"What?"

"Take off your shirt and give it to me, Michael," she insisted.

"How am I supposed to do that here in public?"

Exasperated, Kiri explained, "You put your hands under your sweater, unbutton the shirt, wriggle out, and pull it out the bottom. Get busy. It's almost our turn." She divided her hair in two bunches, braided it, secured the ends with elastic napkin rings from the table, and pulled the braids forward across her shoulders to bounce on her chest. She put Michael's shirt over her sweater, buttoned it part way, then tied the tails at her waist and rolled up the sleeves. She used a bright table napkin for a neckerchief and rolled her pant legs to her calves. She was set. Kurt grabbed his cowboy hat, and they were ready to go.

The Koyle duo touched base with the music man and took the stage. They did two verses and a chorus with their country voices and demeanor, then a full rotation of a simple line dance with hands in their back pockets. They finished with a last chorus, Kurt down on one knee, Kiri sitting on his other, and his hat flung high in the air with a "wahoo!" The down home number was a hit. They exited to exuberant applause, and returned to the O'Connell table.

Kiri was in the midst of removing Michael's shirt and her braids when he pulled her chair closer and rested his arm along the back of it. "That was fabulous!" he said. "You two are just great!" Then he whispered to her, "Please notice that I am cold sober and in control. I apologize for my abhorrent behavior earlier. I will not compromise you again." He played on her back with his thumb. "Now, I want to know what you would say."

"Say?"

"If I asked."

"Asked what?"

"If I asked to kiss… a certain girl," he said shyly.

"Try her sometime," Kiri taunted.

*   *   *

Paula and Thomas were spent but did not dare leave the four grandchildren downstairs alone while they went to bed. First, Paula's phone rang… and then, Thomas' sounded.

"Mom/Father. You won't believe this. Hokey to the max! Don't wait up. Kurt/Michael."

Paula and Thomas watched until they were giddy with laughter. Who could sleep after that!

*   *   *

The entertainment wound down. There were more passers than takers. A finale was needed, but no one would step up to do it. The microphone kept making its way back to the O'Connell table into Kiri's hands. She passed it along to the next table, and it made its way back again. She passed it to another, and it came back again. Kiri shook her head. "I cannot do this one more time," she whispered to Michael.

"Yes, you can. There must be a grand finale, and who better to do it. Your public demands it," he urged.

"My public? My *friends* are skiing about now, and that's where I should be too. I think I've more than satisfied my family obligation tonight."

"But you have new friends here too, and we all need a fitting end to this marvelous time. Please. For your new friends. For *this* friend, if for no one else. I'll owe you."

"You're being a bit melodramatic, don't you think?"

"Whatever it takes," Michael grinned.

Kiri reached deep into her pocket where her fingers played with the cord of Thomas' Celtic compass. "Your mother's spirit... your own inner strength," he had said. Finding one's direction in life was not about doing what you want all the time; it was about doing what was right most of the time. She had no fear of singing in front of a crowd. Goodness knows, she could ham it up and keep a party going all night if need be. But these poor little rich girls in their dainty dresses could not find the courage to stand up for the family and expected someone else to... a foreigner, at that. How would they be able to sleep at night knowing they handed their duty over to a stranger? The alien invader would sleep just fine.

"One last song, then—good humor, no complaints. 'The End' until Saturday night. And when we get to the sing-along, Michael, you'd better be the first one up on stage beside me... and your brother, sisters and cousins, too. You all owe me." She twirled a pointed finger directly at each sibling and cousin. She was not bullied; she was challenged, and she expected the rest of them to rise or fall with her.

At Michael's nod, Kiri fluffed her hair again, tossed her head, grabbed the microphone and took the stage with a determined smile. She found her sultry, mellow voice and calmed the room as she began the Carole King standard about having a friend who will be there. Her brilliant blue eyes stared straight into Michael's each time she sang the chorus.

He melted. Every phrase entered his head, twizzled its way down the back of his throat into his chest, and twined around his heart. This time Kiri did sing to him, no question.

When the applause subsided, she took an instant for one more deep breath and then called out, "OK, everyone. You're used to a grand finale sing-along, so here it is. Everybody up. O'Connells, on stage to form the beginnings of a circle. The rest of you, complete the circle around the room. That's right—everybody. I've had to sing for my supper tonight. Now it's your turn. I'll do the verses; you all join in the chorus."

Kiri turned to Michael—who joined her onstage as promised—and smiled. Kurt and Meghan were on her other side, and the remainder of the family trailed along behind. Gradually, the rest of the room followed suit. "Grab hands and start to sway—left... right," she demonstrated. "That's it.

We're going to sing a New Year's wish, sixties-style. How many of *you* remember the sixties?"

Several nodded.

"I don't. I wasn't there."

They laughed.

"But our folks were. Sex... drugs... protests... riots... crazy clothes... and music. If your parents tell you they don't remember, they are lying. How could they miss a whole decade? Left... right," she directed.

More laughter.

"I'm going to let you in on a secret—not even my prospective brother and sisters know this." She eyed them mysteriously... "Our two parents *first* met in the sixties." ...and noted their surprise. "Your folks probably did too. So this last song is dedicated to them—a New Year's wish as poignant today as it was then." And she began, "Love..." with several repetitions until the entire circle moved with her.

Smiles broke out all around as that reserved and proper group swayed and sang together.

Kiri continued with verses, some very topical ones she made up. Reluctant participants became willing and joined in the chorus. Heads swayed lazily a beat behind their bodies. Clasped hands became arms around shoulders and waists, the ambiance dreamy, even hopeful. She wondered if this was how it had been, way back then... in the olden days... in those troubled times when their parents were young... and in love.

She interrupted the echoing refrain and broke the spell to end the party. "That's right. Love. It's all we need, so grab your honey. Spread a little love tonight. Happy New Year, everyone!"

Unwilling to disperse, the guests continued to sway to the music. Some hugged and danced. Others stood in contemplation. Their subdued host announced, "I don't know what to say after that. Thanks, O'Connells. Thanks, everyone. Dancing begins in the Grand Ballroom in half an hour."

* * *

Paula and Thomas sat erect, fast asleep, their chins on their chests. The quartet of movie-watchers pointed and giggled at them. Paula's phone rang... and then Thomas' sounded.

"Mom/Father. This one's for you. Happy New Year! Kurt/Michael."

After watching, they closed their eyes and dreamed again... of the olden days... when they were young... and in love.

* * *

"That was remarkable, Kiri. Truly remarkable." Michael pulled her close as they continued to weave to the last strains of music. He whispered, "Thank you so much for making this stupendous, a New Year's dream come true. I think you should stay in Dublin with us forever."

117

"Not a chance. Not... a... chance! I'm headed upstairs to bed. Happy New Year!"

"You can't! You must come to the dance. We have to ring in the New Year together!"

"Do you have any idea how exhausted I am? Emotionally and physically? I need rest. I've done my duty by your father and the rest of the family, and now I need rest."

"Take a break... a time-out." He tilted her chin upward with a finger. "I'll take you up to your room. You'll lie down and rest. I'll come and get you in an hour. What do you say?"

"I say, get me upstairs now and check back in an hour. If you can rouse me, you can have me."

"Upstairs it is, then." He guided her up the grand staircase, his arm around her waist and her head on his shoulder. They stopped at her door.

"Well, what's your answer? May I?" Michael asked.

"Brother and sister?"

"Not on your life."

She sang softly, "A friend...?"

"Not enough." He shook his head. "That's not enough for me now."

Kiri lifted her chin and put her hand out to touch his chest.

Michael raised it to his lips and kissed her hand gently.

"But I thought..."

"I wanted to make sure you were ready to say 'yes' when I move in for the real deal... later."

Chapter 15

Kiri lay spread-eagle face down on her bed. About to doze off after a hot shower, she heard a knock on the door. "Go away, Michael. I'm not dressed."

"It's me, Meghan," she said as she entered. "We've been looking for you, wondering why you aren't at the dance. Everyone is still raving about the party and what a star you were. We've accepted accolades on your behalf, but it would be nice if you could come enjoy some of them yourself. Kurt certainly is."

"I didn't do it for the applause, Meghan. I did it to put an end to the party, so we could move on. I don't handle attention well. I'm more the stand-on-the-sidelines kind of person."

"Whatever the reason, we're all grateful to you. Tommy and Anne don't know how to express their emotion. Emily is full of giggles; she's never had so much notice. But I'm proud you're a part of the family and appreciate that you rallied to support us tonight," Meghan explained.

"Thanks for the sentiment. I suppose I should try to join the festivities, but I'm so tired," Kiri sighed.

"What can I do to help? A cup of tea?"

"Could you rub my shoulders and neck for a minute? That would feel heavenly. I'm still in knots."

"Sure thing. I'm not very good at it, but I'll try." Meghan sat beside Kiri on the bed, pulled down the bath towel and began a gentle massage. "You know Michael has called 'family only' on you tonight."

"What on earth is that?" Kiri asked as she felt herself relaxing into the mattress.

"'Family only?' That means only family members are allowed to dance with you tonight. Hands off to all those unrelated."

"That will cramp Kurt's style, if I do get down to the dance. Does he know about this?"

Meghan laughed. "Family includes the O'Connells too, of course. Michael is busy spreading the word; then he'll be up here to get you."

"Have you ever had 'family only' called on you?"

"My ex did once, before we were engaged."

"Did you ever call 'family only' on him?" Kiri asked innocently.

"Why would I do that?" Meghan asked, surprised, "I'm a woman."

"You mean, a man can restrict a woman's access to the opposite sex, but a woman can't do likewise? I don't believe it!" Amazed, she admitted, "I keep forgetting we're from different worlds."

"Why would a woman need to? Men don't require our protection."

"Don't tell me that when you look across a room at a table of women who are eyeing your guy, you can't tell which of them imagine he would make a great lay? And you don't think he senses that?"

"Kiri! Such words!"

"Well, women are just as lecherous as men, and men are less wary. Your brother has no right to restrict my activity tonight... or any other time."

Meghan sensed her anger and tried to make amends. "He just wants to keep you from being bothered by the unseemly sorts, since he knows most of the guys here. He's not trying to control you, I'm sure. He is responsible for you this weekend." She finished and got up to leave. "I'll get out of here before I expose poor Michael any further. I hope you'll join us soon."

"Thanks. Your magic fingers really helped. And your comments were very enlightening. See you in a bit."

After a short nap, Kiri tried to force herself up and dressed, a struggle that lasted twice as long as usual. Under normal circumstances, she could be ready in twenty minutes. Tonight it seemed an eternity. She added final touches to her makeup and bent over to brush her hair back to life when she heard another knock at her door.

"Kiri? It's Michael. Are you awake?"

"Barely. Come on in," she said and straightened up, tossing her hair back.

"My goodness. What's going on... up there?" He indicated her head with a twirl of his fingers near his own.

"Bad hair night. I'm trying to shock some zing back into it. Of course, I forgot my curling iron... and my pjs. Bad night all around." She looked him over while working tangles out. "You look good in pants."

He flushed slightly. "You don't like my knees?"

"I do. Very much. But I'm not sure I want you sharing those cuties with any other gals tonight." Michael flinched. He sensed the confrontation Meghan warned him about.

"I don't intend to. Nor any other parts of me. Not with anyone but you," he laughed nervously. "I want you all to myself. I don't want to be bothered by other guys trying to cut in." He tried to read Kiri's reaction from her face, but she did not reveal any. "If you get tired of me and want me out of your sight, just say the word, and I'll turn you loose. Deal?"

"We'll see how it goes," she considered. Confrontation averted for the moment. "What do you think—up or down?"

"Up or down?

"My hair—up or down?" She modeled an 'up' and a 'down' style.

Was this a test, or a service rendered by brothers? "My opinion... I think you should save a fancy 'up' for the Ball and go casual and comfortable 'down' tonight. What do you think?"

"I'm glad someone can make a decision. I can't." and Kiri went to work. She brushed her hair until it bounced, gathered a few strands from each side, plaited them and joined them into one long thin maiden's braid down the back of her head atop her curls. She pulled a few wisps forward, wet them, and wound them tightly around her fingers.

Once she slid the tiny curls off, Kiri truly looked like a medieval maiden waiting for her knight to return. The large cowl neck of her pearlescent satin blouse slipped over one shoulder and then the other as she moved around the room searching for her accessories. She found the necklace she sought—big bulky rounds of mother of pearl—and fastened it around her neck. The string of shells fell just inside the curve of her blouse.

Michael approached and pulled her into a tight dance hold. "Put your head on my shoulder," he said as he swayed her back and forth. Then he clenched her tightly. "I'm going to be very bold here and ask you to change your necklace." Kiri stiffened, but he plunged ahead. "I don't want there to be any dead sea creatures poking us when we're dancing. Where's your jewel case?"

Kiri laughed, "You mean, my plastic zip baggie?" She retrieved the pint-sized sack from her carryon.

"You don't haul your jewels around in plastic, do you?" he asked, shocked.

"My jewels, as you call them, are craft fair specials. They are very safe in plastic."

"Let me look through them, then." He carefully fingered each piece until he found the ideal bauble. "Ah, this will be perfect." He untangled the single faux-pearl from the other pieces, removed the showy shell necklace, and gently fastened the delicate bead and chain at her nape. The dainty nacreous sphere, elegant in its simplicity, nestled in the notch at the base of her long slender neck.

Michael moved Kiri to face their reflections in the looking glass. He stood behind her, his head showing over her shoulder and his arms around her at the waist. She placed her arms atop his and laced his fingers with hers. They fit into the oval frame of the mirror as if they belonged there... together... two people who knew each other intimately, enjoyed the ease of familiarity, and best of all, understood one another.

"Enchanting," he said and kissed her cheek.

Kiri turned to repay his favor when he asked, "May I...?" His eyes were alight with anticipation of the real deal.

"We're entering dangerous territory," she tried to protest.

"I thrive on danger," Michael said seductively. He gathered Kiri to him, unhindered by pesky sea creatures, to share the passion he felt from the first note she sang.

*   *   *

Kiri and Michael took the floor well after most other couples. They danced easily to a mixture of rock, swing, slow and Latin numbers. Between dances, she marveled at the surroundings. Pedestals topped with gigantic floral bouquets in holiday colors surrounded the dance floor. White columns wound with evergreen garlands alternated with the pedestals, and crystal and gold chandeliers hung from above.

At one point, as she admired the well-polished, recently parqueted wooden floor, Michael's feet caught her eye. "You mended your shoe!" she exclaimed.

"For my own protection," he responded. "I was afraid you might step all over my feet tonight. I had no idea you were so smooth."

"Only by comparison to you," she said. Michael laughed and twirled her around as the music resumed. She took notice of the stares and whispers their antics on the dance floor evoked.

During a pause in the musical numbers, he found them places at a small table and left to get refreshments. "Just water for me, thanks," Kiri reminded him.

"But this is a celebration."

"OK. I'll have soda water with lemon and a cherry for now, and I'll drink two fingers of champagne with you at midnight."

"Sounds perfect," he said and headed for the bar.

Meghan immediately sat down with Kiri, her eyes darting about trying to spot would-be spoilers. "Glad to see you two made it down. Looks like you're having a lot of fun."

"Oh, I am! Michael is great to dance with and easy to talk to, especially tonight when I'm only half aware of what's going on. This room is so amazing... so lavish. I feel like a princess," she admitted.

"The rest of the room is well aware of what's going on between you two, even if you are not. You've really set tongues to wagging."

"Well, let them. It's no one's business but ours. If we want to have a little fun, who's to stop us?" Kiri tossed her head.

"That may be true where you're from, but not here. All of Michael's friends and family are keeping a close eye on him tonight whether he likes it that way or not." Kiri noted the seriousness of her tone.

A blonde, svelte young woman in a low-cut dress, front and back, approached the table and sat down. "Hi, Meg," she said. "Having a good time tonight... babysitting?" Kiri recognized the inference and the glare in her eyes.

"Kiri, this is Alice Richardson, an old... friend of the family. Alice, this is Kiri as you are no doubt aware. We're waiting for Michael. He'll be back in just a minute, I'm sure."

"I'm sure he will be, knowing *you're* waiting for him." Alice directed her comments and her glower at Kiri. "I gather Mighty Mike has you wrapped up for the rest of the evening as well. Better watch out for that one—the love 'em and leave 'em type, you know."

"I gather you have first-hand experience with that," Kiri shot back confidently.

Alice rose quickly and left without any proper farewells. Meghan and Kiri exchanged glances. This gal was tougher than she looked, Meghan recognized.

The music continued, and Kiri felt the fatigue of her endless day. She barely kept from dancing all over Michael's feet, as he feared. When the countdown was announced, the crowd passed around hats, noisemakers and flutes of champagne. The two declined all but the champagne. They did not have enough hands to manage anything more than holding one another and sharing a drink.

At the stroke of midnight, the room erupted in noise and cheers. The band played "Auld Lang Syne" and couples cuddled, but none longer nor more romantically than Kiri and Michael. They were the only two people in the room, awash in the glitter of chandelier and candlelight, swirling 'round and 'round, locked in ardent embrace.

When they finally separated, Michael grabbed her hand and jogged for the doors to the garden. "Come on. Let's get a head start," he said.

"Where are we going?" she asked, confused.

"To find the perfect viewing platform for the fireworks."

"Fireworks!" she exclaimed. "I love fireworks! I didn't expect this kind of fun."

Michael pulled her toward the statuary lining the steps to the expansive lawn below and chose the massive granite lion to the left. He formed a stirrup with his hands to give her a lift up.

"On top?" she asked. She kicked off her shoes, stepped into his hands and flung a leg across the giant cat's back. She reached for his hand to help him, but he did not need it. He found foot- and hand-hold enough to hoist himself up beside her.

"You've done this before," she observed. He nodded shyly. "And I don't suppose you were alone," she intimated. He nodded again. She scrambled away from him and stood up on the lion's head, steadying her feet between its ears.

"Kiri! What are you doing? You'll fall! Don't be upset with me," he shouted.

"No!" she laughed back. "This is marvelous! I feel like I can touch the stars!" She flung her arms wide as if to gather in the galaxy. "The unicorn in me wants to tempt fate. Do you know, when hunted a unicorn can only be entrapped by a virgin? When it is pursued or in danger of capture, it throws itself from a precipice like this," and Kiri pretended a dive off the lion's head. "Miraculously it escapes unscathed. That's the way I feel... like I could fling myself over this cliff and be swallowed up in the celestial sea to run free another day."

The skies came alive as fireworks exploded in brilliant colors all around them. Kiri appeared to dance among the bursts, her arms conducting the extravaganza and her feet now balancing one and then the other on the giant beast's nose. Michael grabbed her from behind and pulled her back toward its haunches. "Get back here," he cried. "You're frightening me. You look like you're about to fly away, wings or no."

"Maybe I do take my namesake too seriously. That would explain my tendency toward risky behavior. I trust I'll have the strength to save myself with the help of a little magic. Michael, this is exhilarating! You'll have to hold me down if you don't want me to vanish into this beautiful night."

Kiri sat down in front of him and snuggled her back against his chest. He curled his arms around her and gathered her legs in with his knees. Her head rested in the hollow beneath his shoulder, and he could feel her pleasure as flares arched toward them amid their "oohs" and "ahs." Excitement built to the grand finale, a sky alive with fire. Then the noise subsided, the smoke cleared, and the crowd dispersed... all but Kiri and Michael who lingered on the lion's back, refusing to leave the fantasy.

"Tell me more about this unicorn within you," he ventured, nesting his face in her hair.

"Mmmm," she thought. "A unicorn is fierce... yet good at heart. It is solitary, selfless if need be, and mysteriously beautiful. I'm still working on that," she giggled. "And, of course, untamable."

"Untamable?"

"No one's tamed me yet," she asserted. "For disbelievers, I can show you my constellation."

"There's no unicorn constellation," Michael protested, shaking his head against hers.

"Oh yes, there is. See Orion's belt? Follow it downward, a few degrees further south... there... and you'll see two stars. That's my horn." She pointed and traced figures in the sky. "My name is Monoceros." She could tell that he still did not believe her. "Look it up sometime. You could have a constellation, too. There's not one for a soldier or savior, but you could be Perseus the Rescuer. Or we could create one for you... use Orion's belt for your sword and my horn for your arm that bears a shield. Then we'd be side by side, against the world," she finished dramatically.

Enthralled with her descriptions and imaginings, Michael did not want to leave their perch near the heavens, but Kiri shivered. He climbed down from the statue and caught her as she attempted to jump. "No diving into oblivion tonight, Miss Unicorn. Let's dance."

They reentered the ballroom, revitalized by the fresh air and excitement. They clung together swaying to the music, be it fast or slow. The tilting and tossing of their heads, nervous laughter at no jokes, embarrassed smiles, longing gazes and tender caresses made it obvious that Kiri and Michael were a couple. No trespassing!

"I'm wooing you, in case you can't tell," he revealed coyly.

"Does that make me a 'wooee'?" she hinted impishly. At Michael's nod, she shouted out a wild western "Whoowee!"

The couple joined Kurt at a table for a last beverage before the bar closed. Michael excused himself. "Keep an eye on her for me, will you Kurt? I'll only be a minute," he asked and left the room.

Kiri decided that sounded like a good idea and got up to leave as well. "Be right back, Bro. Save my seat," she said over her shoulder as she left the room heading in the opposite direction.

When Michael returned, he looked around and asked, "Where's Kiri?"

"She just stepped out for a minute. You know…" Kurt answered.

"I asked you to keep an eye on her." Michael seemed worried.

"She's barely been gone a minute. What did you expect me to do? Go with her?" Kurt asked gruffly.

"Yes!" exclaimed Michael. "That's what any attentive brother does in a crowd like this one. Which way did she go?" He started for the door again.

Kurt caught the implication and jumped up to follow, concern evident as he pointed the way his sister had taken. The two men hurried along the vast, dimly lit hallway until they heard the noises Michael feared coming from an alcove ahead. He recognized Kiri's distress call ricochet down the corridor. "Back off! Don't touch me!"

"Come on, love. Loosen up. You know you want it. Women love to be touched. You've been begging for it all night, and your Mighty Mike hasn't obliged. My turn, now," the rogue harassed, staring into her with his Arctic cold eyes.

"Kiri!" Michael shouted as his heart quickened with his step. The next sounds he heard were an "Ow," an "oomph," and a "whack" as Kiri drove her knee into the assailant's groin, her elbow into his diaphragm, and her fist under his chin.

An astounded Patrick Murphy staggered backward and nearly encountered Michael's fist as well, but she stepped between them. "No, Michael!" she ordered. "No more blows tonight." Turning on Patrick, she commanded, "The next time we meet, Mr. Murphy, I expect an abject apology."

Michael was visibly more shaken than she. Kurt, audibly furious, punched his fist into the wall, forgetting it was stone. Kiri grabbed both her failed protectors by their arms and marched them forcefully back toward the ballroom.

"The name of Patrick Murphy will not be mentioned again tonight. To allow his impropriety to cloud the rest of this beautiful evening awards him a victory he does not deserve," she stated firmly. "Now, who's going to dance with me?" she asked with a smile.

Both men did—in turn. Michael was first. When he opened his mouth to speak, Kiri put her hand there to quiet him. Reduced to gesture, he blew softly on the light curls surrounding her face and smoothed her hair with his fingers, kissing her forehead. He ran his hands gently across her cheeks and kissed her there as well. He reset the alluring bead back in its notch and fluffed the cowl collar of her blouse such that it slipped over her right shoulder exposing another place calling for another kiss. Michael tried to apologize again, but Kiri would have none of it and stopped his words with her lips.

When Kurt's turn came, he told her how proud he was she could defend herself with such class. "Nice moves, Sis. I can't believe I allowed that to happen! If I had even a hint what your going off alone would lead to, I would have held your hand the whole time, even in the stall. Different rules over here, that's for sure."

"I said 'no more,'" Kiri reminded him. "You taught me well. I can defend myself. Now, let's show these foreigners what a couple of hokeys can do." She and Kurt hammed it up on the floor until the tone of the music shifted to slow, romantic numbers signaling the near end to festivities. Kiri spent the rest of the evening in Michael's arms becoming more drowsy by the minute until he literally held her up and slid her feet with his.

The orchestra leader called the last dance. Kiri and Michael barely moved on the floor. When the musicians packed up to leave, the couple still stood there as the rest of the celebrants disbanded. "Thank you, Michael. I've had a wonderful evening, but it's time for my bed," Kiri whispered. "I'm exhausted. I can't dance another step."

"Please don't insist," he appealed. "I'm not ready for the night to end. Let's find a quiet corner and sit for a while."

"I won't be good company. I'm practically asleep now."

"I don't expect scintillating conversation, only companionship. Let's find a spot... just for a while," he coaxed.

They drifted slowly down the corridor toward the grand staircase, checking the intimate chambers along the way. In some, couples, already ensconced on sofas, engaged in activities preliminary to coupling. In others, the clinking of glasses and raucous laughter drove them away. The smoking room was filled with mellow souls and a haze, not from cigars.

"I didn't know sex, drugs and alcohol were accepted as part of the entertainment here. Not my style," Kiri yawned. "Better take me to my room."

"Nor mine. We'll find a place to ourselves down here." He guided her to a small sitting room not connected to the others near the end of the corridor. An inviting alcove beyond was now a staging for background entertainment—a single musician on an Irish harp whose soulful music evoked an earlier age and wafted softly into their space. A long sofa faced the fireplace, a warm fire crackled, and the room was empty... waiting for them. Michael settled himself and drew Kiri close. She shed her shoes and curled up next to him, her head on his shoulder until it slid into his lap. He left it there, ran his fingers through her soft hair, and gazed into the flames.

"I think I'll call you Kirin, my number one unicorn," Michael said quietly.

"Pretty big mouthful," she remarked.

"Well, Miss Unicorn. You have your head in my lap. Does that mean you're ready to be tempered and tamed by me?" he asked with a sly smile.

"Are you a virgin?"

"Hardly!" he laughed.

"Then I guess I'll have to play both roles for us," Kiri said as her eyelids closed and her breathing became measured.

Chapter 16

Michael was not aware of how much time elapsed before he heard his name called quietly from the corridor. Meghan entered and approached from behind. "There you are. I've been looking all over for you. I can't find Kiri anywhere; she's not in our room. I hope she hasn't been accosted by Patrick again." She stopped when Michael raised his arm to point beside him. She peered over the back of the sofa and beheld Kiri fast asleep.

"Oh," she said. "The lost is found. Your little sibling dozed off, I see."

"Kiri is *not* my sibling, as you well know—and as you and the others refuse to admit!" Michael shot at her.

"As you say, Brother," she responded. "Don't you think we ought to get Kiri up to bed?"

"I'm not ready to let her go yet. She's brought so much innocent pleasure to my life this past week. Come sit with us for a bit, Meg."

Meghan scooted in on the other side of her brother. Michael put his feet up on an ottoman and his free arm around his sister's shoulders. "What a blessed man I am, sitting here with my two favorite women at the end of a truly remarkable day—week, actually—in front of this friendly fire, reflecting on what marvelous surprises lie ahead in the New Year. Look at her, Meg. Isn't Kiri lovely?"

"She's exhausted, Michael. She needs to be put to bed."

"Of course she's exhausted. She danced to my drummer—more specifically, to Father's—all week long. She survived more pressure these last few days than any of us can imagine. But look at her now. She's so peaceful, as if all the strain washed right over her. Father said she has a unique inner strength—a Celtic strength—we can't understand. What if it had been Emily gone through this? She would be a wreck. But Kirin..."

"You know all her emotion has to be locked inside somewhere. Woe be unto you, or anyone else who is around, when she erupts. And she will. Maybe not tonight or tomorrow. God help us if she chooses Saturday. I hope you are prepared for the comedown once you realize she's merely mortal like the rest of us."

"You can mock me if you like, Meghan, but I feel affection for this woman, and I don't want to be apart from her. I'm beginning to understand Father, as crazy as that sounds."

"You said it; I didn't. Father would be appalled if he could hear you talk like this, and what do you think Alice will have to say about this new friendship of yours?"

"Alice should have nothing to say about anything I do. We have no commitment to one another. Never have."

"That's not how she sees it. She's been waiting for you for a long time. She was hurt tonight by your obvious favor to Kiri."

"She has no right to be. We've never had a 'defined relationship,' as you would say."

"Have you ever slept with Alice?"

"That's not for a gentleman to reveal." Michael's eyes dropped to Kiri's face. He caressed her cheek and jaw tenderly with his thumb. "How did you know when you were in love and ready for marriage?"

"You can't be serious. Kiri? You're approaching forbidden territory with that, Michael. Father would…"

"Father is not in this conversation. You and I are. It's a simple question, and I would appreciate your answer. When did you know you were in love?"

"I'm surprised you would ask that of the disgraced divorcée in the family," Meghan admitted.

"Who better to ask? You thought you'd found it once, and then you realized you hadn't."

"Well, I know what it is *not*—physical attraction and sex. They bring you babies but not a fulfilling life with a partner," Meghan stated firmly. "I now think tenderness is the most important aspect of love."

"You mean, a soft touch?"

"No. Tenderness is the awareness of what your partner feels and the ability to convey that understanding. Sometimes a soft touch is just right, but sometimes roughness is what's called for."

Michael shook his head. "Roughness? A hard hand?"

"No. Wrong term. Call it brutal honesty. If you try to ignore the prickly issues, they'll jab you to death in the end."

"I'm sure there's more…"

"Respect, kindness, consideration—an awareness of your partner's needs. You must help him or her to feel good about himself."

Michael was silent for a time, pondering deeply. "That's a pretty tall order for a regular guy."

"It's not an order, Michael. It's an ideal—something to strive for."

"If a fellow could realize most of what you cited, would he be ready for… could he expect a successful marriage?"

Meghan laughed, and he looked at her, confused. "If only it were that simple," she said. "For a 'love' to guide you through successful marriage, first all those feelings have to be mutual, and second, you both must have the ability to act on them. You must support one another's needs and decisions, understand the little important things in their lives as well as the obvious, show that you can love them at their worst and accept well-intentioned criticism. You should also make laughter and a sense of play a part of your passion as well as your everyday lives. When you are in love, you have a sense of completeness, of wholeness, and you cannot tolerate being apart."

"Where are we supposed to learn all this stuff?" Michael seemed upset. "We don't get taught in school. It wasn't in our catechism."

"Oh, yes it was! Everything I stated is implicit in our religious teachings. We just don't recognize it as such."

"What went wrong with your marriage? Didn't you and Derek love each other?"

"All of the above. I thought we did… love each other… but obviously not in the same way. During our courtship, we never got around to discussing the important issues. We assumed any differences would work themselves out because we 'loved' each other. The big issue for us was mutual support. I wanted to continue working after we were married and put off having children for a while. Derek wanted his wife at home and his first son right away to carry on the family name. Voilà, Brendan. I didn't support him when he wanted to take advantage of a promotion and move to Cork nearer his family and away from mine. Our marriage went downhill from there, and our love rolled right along with it."

"Wow…" Michael said pensively to himself. "Father and Paula are on pretty weak ground, aren't they?" Then he turned to his sister. "Will you marry again, do you think?"

"I don't know. At my age, it will be hard to find a perfect guy like you." Meghan patted his chest affectionately and inadvertently hit Kiri's head. She stirred, looked up at Michael's chin, smiled, and noticed the top half of his sister in her view.

"Hi, Meghan. What's up?" she yawned.

"Michael and I were just having a brother/sister chat. Join us."

"I couldn't form one coherent sentence right now, but you two go ahead."

"We discussed what makes a good marriage. What do you think?"

Meghan expected Kiri to stammer her way through some indefinite explanation, but Kiri surprised her when she sat straight up and said without hesitation, "Compromise!"

"Compromise? As simple as that?" asked Michael rather shocked at her lively outburst.

"Compromise isn't simple. It involves a willingness to put your partner's needs and desires before your own and the ability to recognize when that will best serve the alliance." Kiri thought for a moment, then added, "Equality. There has to be equality between partners, neither more dominant than the other. I understand that's not the case over here where a man is king of his castle—no pun intended."

"You make marriage sound like a business. Where does love figure in?" Meghan asked.

"Loving someone is the hardest job there is," Kiri stated.

"Job?" Michael questioned.

Kiri nodded her head confidently. "You have to wake up every morning determined to be the best partner you can be every minute of the day, no matter the sacrifices you'll have to make, and go to bed every night praying you will find the strength to do it again. If that's not a hard job, I don't know what is."

"Where did those crazy ideas come from?" his half-grin asked.

"From watching my mother."

"Brother, you'd better close your ears and become invisible," Meghan suggested. "I think Kiri and I have lots to talk about—woman to woman."

He gave both of his girls a squeeze and relaxed with his eyes closed, intending to be bored silly by two women talking nonsense. At least they included him as a physical part of their conversation, he reasoned. The women adjusted their postures to face one another as if Michael were not even there.

"Kiri, have you ever been in love?"

"Not the kind we're talking about, nothing that could be sustained over time. Why do you ask?"

"Michael and I were wondering how to define love," Meghan explained.

"You should know. You're the one who's been married."

"Just because I've been married doesn't mean I understand love any better than a single person. I obviously did not." The two women both glanced at Michael, his eyes still closed but a slight grin creeping across his lips. "What do you think of Michael?" Meghan finally asked. "You obviously like my brother, despite how perverted that is."

Kiri glared at Meghan, then she snuggled against Michael's chest and put her arms around him, causing him to shift and pull her closer. "He's snugglable."

"Is that even a word?"

"Probably not," admitted Kiri. "It's more a feeling. Michael makes me feel safe, like he'll protect me."

"That didn't work so well for you tonight, did it?" Meghan reminded her. "I heard you had to fend off a couple of lusty young men... my brother included."

"Word travels fast around here, doesn't it?"

"Castle walls see and hear everything," Meghan revealed.

"Let's just say, I think they both got the message," Kiri said. "Any woman has to be prepared to defend herself. That part didn't bother me. How a man reacts to such a rejection is more important." Kiri sensed Michael's head barely nod in agreement.

"Anything else you like about him?"

"Many, many things. We've known one another only five days now, yet he seems familiar. Michael is playful... caring... mysterious. And he tolerates my flights of fancy. That shows he understands where I'm coming from," she said finally.

"Anything you don't like?"

Kiri considered carefully, knowing Michael was indeed listening. "He's quick to anger, and he reacts without thinking sometimes. He seems troubled with an open-ended situation when he can't anticipate what is likely to occur. I think he needs to know the endpoint—when a job is complete. There's quite a difference between 'Help me dig a hole' and 'Help me dig a three foot square hole.'" Kiri felt Michael clench her tighter, affirming her observations.

"What about his looks?" Meghan asked.

"What about them? He's a hunk, for sure!" Kiri was definite. "Michael is very handsome in a rugged sort of way, and I crave the sensuousness of running my fingers through his curly mane." She did just that, tantalizing him. His face pinked beneath the favored curl she coaxed down onto his forehead. "But his looks are not as important as his personality. I'm surprised he has not been snatched up and married long before now. I feel very lucky he's had these few days free with me."

"What makes you think he's free?"

"Michael told me he has no special gal right now. Why? Is that not true? Is he going with someone? Alice maybe? She seemed very put out tonight." At the mention of Alice's name, Michael's abdomen tensed.

"They used to be an item," Meghan admitted. "They've known each other since school, and all of us thought... well... that they would eventually make it official. He informed me tonight, however, that is definitely not the case."

"Do you think Michael has ever had sex with Alice?" Kiri felt him tense again when she asked.

"Would it make any difference if he had?"

"Not really. We all have a past. Who has he got his arms around tonight?" Kiri asked confidently. "I don't see Alice here with us." Michael relaxed.

"It would never be acceptable, of course, but would you like Michael to make love to *you*?" Meghan quizzed boldly.

Before Kiri could answer, he jumped to his feet, leaving the women to prop up one another. "All right. That's enough! No more talking about Michael when I'm right here!"

"You're supposed to have your ears closed. You're not to listen to our girl talk," his sister reminded him.

He turned to face them, beet red from embarrassment. "Pretty hard to avoid when you start probing my sex life. It's time for us all to go to bed. Grab your shoes, Kiri, and let's go." She did, and he flung her over his shoulder again for the third time that day. He put his other arm around

Meghan's shoulders, and they set out to climb the grand staircase. "I hope you two will become good friends. You'll be seeing a lot of each other."

The trio arrived at the girls' room. "Do me a favor, Sis, and take another walk along the halls to see who is bedded up with whom. I need a few minutes alone with Kiri."

"Michael, you wouldn't!" Meghan accused.

"No. I won't. I'd like to, but I'm too much of a gentleman to take advantage of a woman who is asleep. I would like a few minutes alone... to wish her a sweet good night."

"Whatever you say." Meghan shook her head and left to browse the halls... again.

Michael slid Kiri from his shoulder and laid her gently on the bed. He removed her skirt and blouse, admired the curves hidden by her slip, and rolled her under the covers. She turned onto her left side, her right arm atop the duvet. He swept her hair behind her ear, stroked her arm and kissed her forehead, reluctant to leave.

Kiri opened her eyes and found Michael staring at her. "Do you want to make love to me?" she asked faintly.

"Not tonight. I want your eyes wide open when I do."

"You're a good man, Michael O'Connell," her smile whispered.

"You're my kind of woman, Kirin Koyle."

"I think I'm going to sleep now." With her next deep breath, she appealed, "May I take your hand with me?"

"If you like." He perched on the edge of the bed and placed his right hand on her chest. She clutched it firmly, smiled, and drifted into a gentle sleep. Michael gazed at her, his fondness growing with each pulsation of her heart.

On Meghan's return, he reluctantly slipped his hand from beneath Kiri's and kissed her shoulder goodbye. "G'night, Sis," he said to Meghan as he left. "Happy New Year!"

Chapter 17

Kiri roused with no recollection of where she was or how she got there. In her slip instead of pajamas, she noticed—"ow!"—her hair tangled in her necklace. Some creature in the bed next to her slept with mask and earplugs, dead to the world. Then she remembered. Far from a dream, she awoke in a private chamber in a castle. That would explain the downy comforters and gilt furnishings.

She stepped out of bed onto the cold floor and skittered over to the steam pipes, icy to her touch. She shivered and rubbed her arms, searching for a sweater. A large window, the only redeeming feature of the room at this point, allowed sunlight to stream in. Oh, happy day! The sun shone on Ireland after all. Kiri could not dress herself fast enough. She grabbed hat, coat, muffler and boots and set out on an adventure.

The guardian at the massive main door interrupted her escapade. "Where ye be goin,' Miss, at this early hour?"

"Out for a walk. It's such a beautiful morning."

"Which family are ye with, then, and why is no one goin' with ye?"

"I'm with the O'Connells, and no one else is up yet." Kiri felt sure of that.

"Yur the young lady what sung so sweet last night, aren't ye?"

"I'm not sure about the 'sweet,' but I did sing. And now I need fresh air and exercise."

"We don't usually let guests wander off alone, especially young ladies. Best to stay safe here."

"You are doing your best to discourage me, aren't you? I expect that's your job. But I will go for a walk outside," she insisted, determined to escape the dank, stifling castle. "I won't be long."

"It's chill out there."

Kiri modeled her hat, muffler and gloves in response.

"It's damp."

She showed the warden her boots.

"You'll take this with ye, then." He handed her a neck chain with a whistle and a small electronic device. "If ye lose yur way, just whistle if yur close by. If yur far, just open this here, and the locator will signal us to come find ye. I'm hopin' we won't be hearin' from ye," he laughed and watched Kiri disappear around the stable, headed for the hills beyond, free at last from the constraints of the ancient stone stronghold.

*   *   *

Michael awoke, looked at his watch, and wondered why his eyes opened at the early hour. Must be the sunlight. Kurt still slept, he noticed. Maybe he would check on the girls. Maybe they would still be in bed. Delicious thought, he fantasized.

No sweet voice invited him in when he knocked on the door, so Michael opened it and peered inside. He found Meghan sound asleep and Kiri, nowhere. He checked the bathroom. With the sink still damp, she could not have been gone long. He perused her possessions; the only apparent missing items—coat and boots. Please do not let her wander outside alone, he appealed to anyone. Surely the watchman halted her at the main door. He hurried back to his room, grabbed his coat and descended the stairs in a flash.

"Ah, Mr. O'Connell. Goin' out to meet up with yur sister, I see."

"My sister?"

"That nice young lady what sung last night. I didna think she should be goin' out on her own."

"You let her go off alone?" Michael accused harshly. Then he stopped himself. "Could you show me which way she's gone, then? I'd like to catch up with her."

"That'll be hard to do. She's almost an hour ahead a ye. She seemed to be takin' the perimeter trail, that way," he pointed.

"Thanks." Michael headed for the stable at a jog.

* * *

Kiri was in her element—lush, dense woodlands, profuse undergrowth and streams of sunlight making patchwork figures on the forest floor. She sauntered from one tree to another, gawking upward through branches, in search of a perfect specimen. She pretended to measure girth by hugging the yew, inhaling their woody fragrance. She caressed the skin of oak saplings, tracing bark designs with her fingers. She whirled in a locus of sunshine the diameter of her wingspan, absorbing warmth and strength. She lurched to a stop, impeded by two strong arms thrusting into her space from behind.

"Michael!"

"Happy New Year!" he murmured in her ear.

"Happy New Year to you! Have you followed me all this way?" she accused, turning to face her marauder.

"Absolutely not. I tracked you. Not hard to do with your big boots. Do you have any idea how far you've come?"

Kiri looked at her watch. "I've been gone an hour and a half, so maybe three or four miles of an uphill climb." She looked to Michael for confirmation.

"You've walked nearly to the next county! Let's head back. Brunch will be on soon."

"How long did it take you to find me?"

" 'Bout thirty minutes."

"You set a pretty hefty pace."

"Tracking... it's my job." He brushed off her quizzical look. "The staff should never have let you leave the grounds alone," he stated angrily. "When I found that out, I did not lose my temper as I would have yesterday. I thanked them for pointing me in your direction and took off."

"I'm proud of you... and I'm perfectly fine," she assured him. "I feel very much at home in these woods."

"But you shouldn't be way out here communing with nature on your own. You had me worried."

"I think I can take care of myself," she said defensively.

"You've proven you can—with supposed gentlemen—but you don't know what's lurking out here. Could be poachers or wildlife. Look, I don't want to make an issue out of this. I'm trying here. Could you... please... if you feel you must go wandering off again, let someone know where you're going?"

Michael was trying, she agreed. He did not immediately jump to criticize or chastise her. "You're right," she said. "I wouldn't go hiking in the mountains at home without a buddy or telling someone. I shouldn't have done it here, but when I looked out the window and saw real sunshine, I couldn't wait to get outside."

"You could have gone lost out here. How did you think you would find your way back?"

"The sun, of course. This whistle and locator, in an emergency. And I've got this." She pulled the small compass from her pocket and set it in the palm of her hand.

The sight of his father's treasured instrument surprised him. "Where did you get this?" he asked, disbelieving that his father would let it out of his possession.

"Your father gave it to me before we left yesterday. He told me not to be bullied by your sisters into doing something I wasn't prepared to do. He called it a Celtic compass to help me find my own direction, my own inner strength. I think he was trying to make amends for his hard line last weekend. It seems very old and well-worn."

"It is. It belonged to my grandfather. Father's uncle gave it to him when grandfather passed, for the same reason—to give him the courage to find his own way. As the only son in his family, he assumed a heady responsibility at a fairly young age."

"I'll return it then, as soon as we get back to his house," she decided. "I tried before, but he insisted."

"No. If he gave it to you, I'm sure he meant for you to have it." Michael looked at her intently. "I don't know what you've done to impress him so greatly, but you have, Kiri. Despite how harsh he has been with you a time or two, he thinks very highly of you and wants you to feel a part of the family, I know. Keep it, and feel kindly toward him." Then her would-be rescuer lightened the mood. "And use it now to show me you can find our way back to the castle."

Kiri checked the angle of the sun and used the compass to orient them to the north. "Should be right over there, just the other side of that ridge."

"Nice job." They linked arms and headed down the hillside and up toward the ridge beyond. They conversed casually and laughed over the events of the previous evening. Michael's recollections were much sharper than her own; he remembered every detail of her performances with great delight. To Kiri, it was all a blur.

"What is your fondest memory from last night?" she asked, thinking it might be their skit, the finale circle or even the fireworks.

"That's easy. Sitting in front of the fire with my feet up and your head in my lap, like an old married couple. I felt the same as lying under the Christmas tree with you watching the flicker of flames through its boughs. I suddenly glimpsed what the future might be, what the New Year might bring. Your taking my hand to bed with you runs a close second."

Surprised at his candor, Kiri was a little discomfited with his assumptions.

"How about you? What is your fondest memory? Do you *have* any memory of last night?" Michael laughed as he asked. He imagined the castle tour or the fireworks.

"I was in a haze most of the time, that's true," she admitted. "Actually, I'm embarrassed to say."

"But you must. I did," he challenged.

"Seeing us framed in that beautiful antique looking glass... that's my memory, the only time I've seen the two of us together. We looked comfortable as a couple, I thought."

"I think we are comfortable as a couple. And I think we ought to celebrate that with our first kiss of this brilliant New Year's Day," he suggested. They reached the base of the wooded hill and were looking up at an incline to the ridge above the castle. The couple took a moment to seal their good wishes to one another with a kiss even more endearing than those of the previous evening.

"Do you want to rest before we begin the uphill?" he asked.

"No. I'm fine. Let's keep going," she said. "We'll rest on the top where we'll have a good view of the grounds below." They did not follow a trail; they cut their own direct route—a short cut—north. Sometimes they climbed abreast; sometimes he led the way. He adjusted his pace to hers, but he found her hearty, not requiring his assistance. Their conversation turned from casual to personal.

"Is it true... what you said last night?" Michael began, a little embarrassed.

"What's that?"

"That you're a virgin?" he asked hesitantly.

"I didn't say that. You can't hold me accountable for anything I said; I was practically comatose," she replied. "Would it make a difference if I were?"

"Yes!"

"Why?"

"It would put such a heavy responsibility on *me*!" Michael exclaimed.

"In what way?"

"To meet your expectations," he attempted to explain.

"You mean, if I'm used goods, you're under no pressure to do your best. But if I'm a virgin, you're not sure your best is good enough?" Kiri demanded. "A little short on self-confidence are you, Mighty Mike?"

"Oh, no! I'm good," he assured her.

"What makes you think I'd be interested in giving myself away to *you*?

"Last night when you were talking to Meghan, she asked if you would like to…"

"And *you* interrupted before I could answer. You have no idea what I would have said," she declared.

"What would you have said?" he wanted to know.

"I asked you if you wanted to make love to me, remember… and *you* said 'no.' "

"I said, 'not last night.' The timing wasn't right. You were almost asleep for heaven's sake! I couldn't take advantage." Michael defended his decision.

"So, if the time *is* right… for *both* of us… you'll have your answer then." Kiri brought a definite end to that topic of conversation.

They reached the top of the ridge with the valley spread out below them. Copley Castle's domain, separated into fields by hedges and rock walls, extended to the fortress beyond where only that one small remnant of the original wall remained with ramparts intact. The wanderers could barely discern activity in the garden and parking area. They settled on a large, flat rock to catch their breath and to admire the pastoral scene.

"Why are you grinning like that?" she quizzed.

Michael put both arms around her, rocking her from side to side. "I know my endpoint now, as you would say."

"You look like you've suddenly discovered the mother lode," she observed, noticing the twinkle in his eyes.

"Even better," he said impishly. "I've just found the mother of my children!"

"What?" Kiri was baffled by his announcement.

"I know it sounds ridiculous, but I thought a lot about what you said to Meghan last night, about my needing to have an endpoint. I awoke this morning knowing the next turn my life would take. I awoke wanting to have someone there beside me… and I'm not talking about your brother," he clarified.

"This last week with you, under the tree and everywhere else we've been—kitchen to castle—has been magical. You said it yourself—who was in my arms last night? I wanted to see you first thing this morning... and tomorrow... and the day after. I'm tired of waking up alone, going to bed alone, dreaming alone and having conversations with myself. I'm ready to share my life, my hopes, my fears and my dreams with someone who is ready to do the same with me."

"*You* are talking nonsense," Kiri accused.

"*You* are going to be the mother of my children," Michael asserted.

"That's preposterous!" The trill of her laughter joined the birds' morning songs. "What a line. Does it usually get you what you want?"

"That's an insult! It is not a line. I know we will make beautiful children together!"

"Aren't you skipping a few steps here? Don't you think I might have something to say about your project?" she inquired. What craziness inhabited this man's mind, she wondered.

"Oh, you will. You'll say 'I do' when the time is right," Michael said with confidence.

"You are crazy. Did you drink your breakfast before you came out here?" she charged.

"Not on your life. I'm as sober as a stone," he defended. "I learned my lesson from you last night. If you want something from a woman—and you're the woman I want—ask her. She just might say yes. I'm cold sober enough right now to know this isn't the time to ask, but I'm giving you fair warning that I intend to. And you will say 'yes.'"

"Be careful what you say," Kiri cautioned. "I think you'd better keep this grand plan of yours under wraps for a while until you consider it more carefully. Your family will lock you up."

"No need. I don't care who knows. I'll shout it out." He shouted to the valley below, "Kiri Koyle will bear my children!"

"Michael, that's absurd!"

"You're right," he admitted. He cupped his hands around his mouth like a megaphone and yelled, "Kirin O'Connell will bear my children!" He waited for his cries to dissipate. "Oh, I like the sound of that—'Kirin O'Connell.' Couldn't be more perfect if I had fashioned it myself." He turned to her with obvious elation. "This is exciting. I'm energized. I can't wait to see what happens next."

She refused to take him seriously. "You do realize you are annoying." Almost laughing she said, "I can't wait to see you manage this across the 5,000 mile expanse between us, and I can imagine your father's face when you announce your plan to him."

"Good points," Michael mused, faced with reality. "We'll have to work on that."

"What makes you think your wacky scheme will work at all?" Kiri challenged. "I'm asking simply as an objective observer here, you understand."

"We're perfect complements to one another," Michael stated as if it were obvious. "You're reasoned; I'm assertive. You see possibility; I'm locked in reality. I'm strong enough to prevent you from jumping off the precipice when you feel trapped, and you are strong enough to survive on your own if I fail." He gazed at Kiri intently and stroked her back. "We're both sensitive and loving… and I know we'll fit together flawlessly to create a perfect being."

He grabbed her, threw her gently to the ground, clutched her tightly to him and rolled with her through the wild grasses a short way downhill. Their rollicking progress ended abruptly against the scanty remains of a rock wall. They unlinked and lay side by side breathing heavily. Michael clapped Kiri's thigh. "Come on, now. Let's get up and go find breakfast. I'm famished, and we've got lots of work ahead of us. We have a life to plan." He stood and brushed dried leaves and dirt from his clothes, then extended his hand to Kiri to help clean her up as well.

"I'm not going anywhere right now; I can't get up," she revealed with embarrassment.

"What's the matter? Did I hurt you?" Michael worried. "Not sick, are you?"

"No," she said shyly. "My legs feel like rubber bands, and I'm… queasy."

He noticed her flushed face, felt her forehead and her trembly tummy. "Why, you sexy vixen. I've barely touched you and you're…."

"I'm humiliated," she lamented, covering her face. "Go away!"

"No need to be humiliated. This is beautiful," he revealed. "We're going to be great together!" He shouted again toward the castle and its occupants, "Kirin Koyle O'Connell is going to have my babies! He tried to pick her up to carry her the rest of the way downhill, but she wrestled away from him, glaring.

"I can stand on my own two feet now, thank you, Michael O'Connell." She continued on her own.

They hiked silently and separately through a field until he caught up to her and whispered in her ear. "You'll be a wonderful mother to my children."

Kiri's moist eyes betrayed her hurt. "Stop it! This is *not* something you joke about with a woman."

Michael locked her eyes in an earnest gaze. "I'm not joking, Kiri. I mean every word I say. I'm willing to wait until you come 'round to my way of thinking, as I know you shall. Whatever it takes." He put his arm around her shoulder and folded her close to his chest. He whispered into her hair, "Michael and Kirin O'Connell will make a formidable pair. You'll see."

* * *

Brunch was well underway by the time the couple reentered the castle. A sleepless staff transformed the Great Hall from the previous evening. Small tables seating four or six replaced the long ones, and a gigantic buffet worthy of the Queen Mary filled the stage.

Michael and Kiri were the only O'Connells she recognized in the food line. A horde of men stood waiting, their women still lost in beauty sleep, no doubt. Their stomachs, apparently, brought the guys down as soon as smells of coffee, bacon and cinnamon wafted through the drafty building. Michael spoke jovially with most and introduced Kiri proudly, allowing her to speak without monitor and move about freely. Conversation with someone other than an O'Connell actually excited her. The previously staid group turned casual and interesting. Michael associated with many very nice people, she decided. She certainly did not feel threatened by anyone.

Kiri filled her plate with far more than she should and turned to Michael with a guilty look on her face. No need. His plate would easily satisfy five growing boys, and he did not hesitate to pile on more. He found a semi-secluded table for them, anticipating private, intimate conversation, but one after another of his friends sat down with coffee while waiting for the line to diminish. Many kindly mentioned her participation in the entertainment with a "nice job," "terrific show," or "can't wait 'til next year." She tolerated such casual appreciation comfortably. Some dared to smile and pat her on the back. Michael did not seem bothered in the least; these folks must be "acceptable," she concluded.

Henry Callaghan took his turn to join the couple. Michael introduced him as a coworker at his network. That made five she had met who knew Michael's job, but none said more than, "Yeah, we work together occasionally." No one expanded on exactly the nature of that work. Henry seemed nice enough. Average hair and expressive gray eyes, a thin mouth and pointy features accented his tall, slim but solid build.

In the midst of touting Dublin's finer aspects, Michael asked if Kiri wanted seconds. "Hardly," she said. "This is more than I usually eat in a week! You can't possibly have room for more either."

"Me? I've only just begun. Can I get you anything, Henry, while I'm there? A sweet bun or something?"

"No. I'm fine. Thanks. I'll be taking off soon for the Plunge. I was just on my way out, in fact, when I thought to stop and say hello."

"Would you mind looking after Kiri, then, until I get back? Keep her company? Thanks." At Henry's friendly nod, Michael broke into the food line again.

"Well, Henry Callaghan. It's nice to finally meet someone considered trustworthy enough to chaperone me," Kiri smiled.

"I'm happy to be of service," he said, evidence of his kind nature.

"Michael has kept me quite constricted, you know. I feel like a child who doesn't have enough sense to stay out of the traffic. But he lightened up this morning."

"Probably has something to do with learning, when you first came in for brunch, that Patrick has already returned to the city. No one else would dare take liberties after last night."

"You mean, you know about last night too?"

"Kiri, everyone knows. Can't keep a secret in a closed society like this. And there's not one who would risk crossing Michael—or you now—without fear of retribution or bodily harm." Henry's shy smile crept across his lean face.

"I'm glad I have this chance to speak to a normal person. I've been confined, restricted and commanded by O'Connells for the past week. It's nice to have a nonjudgmental conversation. If I can survive through tomorrow night, I'll leave Ireland far behind and return to my home and my sanity."

"Is our dear little island really so distasteful?"

"No. I'm sure that if I chose a trip to Ireland for vacation, I would love it. But I'm here under 'commanding' circumstances, shall we say, and wishing I were somewhere else. Nothing personal."

"You're not going to make New Year's at Copley Castle an annual event?"

"Absolutely not!"

"Won't Michael be disappointed and expect you to come?"

"I'm sure he'll survive without me."

"If you're not a couple, then, you might want to do something about all the grass and weeds in your hair," Henry suggested with another shy smile.

Kiri stared at him, obviously embarrassed, as she combed her fingers through her hair until they caught on bits of twig and grass in the back. She flushed and picked out what she could easily, then flung her hands open wide. "I give up. This is truly a very awkward moment. No wonder everyone has been so friendly this morning. Now I have two conflicting reputations to live down. What say we change the subject? Tell me, Henry, what exactly do you and Michael do when you work together?"

"I can't *exactly* tell you, except to say that Patrick and I tell him where to go and when, and he does. He's a very good... reporter and always fulfills his missions in a quality manner."

"None of you, Michael included, will tell me just what it is he does, so I will assume you have some sort of Bond thing going on and you'll have to kill me if you tell me." Henry laughed at that. She insisted on pursuing further. "Can you at least tell me if it is something immoral?"

142

"Definitely not immoral."

"Good. Illegal?"

Henry took his time and hedged an answer. "Mmm... not in the strictest sense."

"An honest answer. Thank you." Kiri considered for a moment. "This is just great. Up until last week I lived a simple, down home kind of existence. I worked at a bank during the week and skied on weekends. I showed up daily, obeyed speed limits, flossed and hit the sack early most nights. Now, I'm involved with a ring of secret agents who don't get along and who operate outside the law... sometimes—a cad, an honest trustworthy soul and a valiant knight who draws his sword first and asks questions later." She shook her head. "I need to go home; this has to be a dream."

"What's this about a dream?" Michael asked as he sat down again with another full plate. "Not a nightmare, I hope," he added, grinning. Henry and Kiri exchanged guarded glances, and he got up to leave.

She caught his arm and stopped him. "Thank you for watching over me, Henry. I felt very safe. I hope, if we meet again and Michael will allow it, that we can share another conversation or even a dance." She glowered at Michael, but he did not seem to notice.

"Absolutely," Michael said. "On your way to the Plunge, you say?"

Henry nodded. "You?"

Michael glanced at Kiri. "Not sure I can make it this year."

"Give it a try. We don't want to lose to that rival network, and with most of our guys gone, I hate for us to rely on Patrick."

"Will you be at the Club Ball on Saturday?"

Henry nodded.

"Good. We'll see you there for sure," Michael continued. "And thanks again." When his friend left, he added, "Nice man, Henry. One of the finest gentlemen in our group in every sense of the word." He looked seriously at Kiri. "You do not have to ask my permission to associate with nice men like Henry."

"Michael!" Meghan startled them as she approached their table. "We've been looking for you two to join us. My goodness! What have you been up to, coming in here looking like you've been rolling in the hay with grass in your hair and mud all over your pants and shoes?" He looked down and saw dried mud up to his calves and telltale signs in Kiri's hair of their roll down the hill.

"Guess we should have made ourselves more presentable after our hike in the woods. We came back with such an appetite, it didn't occur to us. We'll do better next time. Kiri, do you want to join the others?"

"I think I'll pass on that," she said. "I have some packing... and cleaning up to do, it looks like. You go ahead with the family. Don't cut things short on my account." She smiled and rose to leave. "I hope you slept well, Meghan. Later."

*   *   *

An hour slipped by before Michael knew it. He returned to his room and packed, then rushed to the opposite wing to get Kiri. He hoped she would not be stewing because he left her for so long. He should not have worried, because she was not there at all. He found an empty room. Meghan had cleared out, and Kiri's bag lay at the foot of her bed—her precisely arranged bed. "Who made her own bed in a castle?" Michael asked himself. She wiped down the wash basin and tub and neatly folded and stacked the soiled towels at its foot. What was she thinking? Does she not know a castle has maids for cleaning up?

Michael spotted a note on her bag; she remembered his request. "Wandering/snooping. This floor only. Whistle. K." He made a quick run down the hall. Many open rooms, empty of their departed occupants, tempted spies to peek in. He did not want to resort to a whistle, calling her like a dog, so he searched the couples' hall and then the men's. At the far east end, he found Kiri sitting on the floor, bathed in a circle of light, in a sunroom immediately above the ballroom. He whistled softly.

"Oh, Michael!" she exclaimed as she turned to him. "Isn't this the most beautiful room ever? All these tall windows stretching from east to west capture every ray of sunlight, and it all centers right here in this spot. Come here, and feel how warm it is, a perfect spiritual nexus." She stood up, twirled, and reached out to him. "This is absolutely a Cinderella moment. Come. Be my Prince Charming, and waltz with me," she invited, twirling again.

"I don't think so," Michael replied hurriedly, turning to leave. "We've got to hit the road." As an afterthought he added, "And fancy dance isn't really my thing."

Stunned by such an abrupt rejection, Kiri exploded. "Not *your thing*?" Then she gathered her calm and responded with firm deliberation. "I've come 5,000 miles so *you* could go to a party with your family and friends, but giving me two minutes of your time is not *your thing*? I've tried to behave as you wanted, dress as you liked, perform and show up when you asked, not associate or dance with those you thought unsuitable. I've fended off dragons, climbed statuary to sit in the cold, and denied myself sleep because *you* wanted the evening to continue. I interrupted my walk because *you* were hungry for breakfast—not to mention, I listened to your annoying chatter about bearing *your* children.

"Here we are in this marvelous castle, this beautiful room with windows on the world and sunlight streaming down on us, and when I ask you to join me in playing out my fantasy for a couple of minutes, you refuse my modest wish because it's *not your thing*."

Kiri grabbed him by the arm and marched him toward a gigantic mirror on the wall. "Come over here and look long and hard in this glass and tell me just what *your thing* is. While you're at it, consider what that says about the kind of partner you're going to make someone some day. Then go sit in your fancy car and sulk because I've thrown off *your* schedule by two minutes. I intend to stay right here and enjoy my fantasy, because that's what *my thing* is. And I'm sure I can find a ride back with someone else if the wait is too long for you." She turned her back on him and returned to her spot in the center of the sunshine.

Michael stalked out of the room and let the door slam behind him. Kiri's words cut through him like a machete through the heart of a gourd, leaving it in pieces. He stomped down the hallway, fists clenched, jaw tight and face reddening to a deep merlot. He collided with Meghan.

"The others are ready to leave, and Kiri is lost again. Any idea?" She did a double-take. "What has happened to you? You look terrible, Michael!"

He thought to himself, Kiri is not the one who is lost. "You all go on ahead. There's no reason for us to caravan anyway. You take Kurt. I'll find Kiri, and we'll follow shortly. See you back at Father's."

Meghan nodded and started down the staircase. Michael tried to compose himself, waiting for his breathing and pulse to return to normal and his face to reclaim an ordinary shade of red. Then he returned to the sunroom.

Kiri remained exactly as he had left her, standing at the confluence of sunbeams, motes of dust dancing like specks of gold in the light surrounding her silhouette. He approached quietly and grasped her from behind. "May I have the honor of the next dance?"

Turning her head toward him, she smiled demurely, lifted her imaginary skirt by its hem and accepted Michael's hand. She sang softly a waltz from *Sleeping Beauty,* a waltz from once upon a dream, while they attempted a dignified dance in the elegant surroundings. The hazel flecks in her blue eyes reflected the golden sun, and her face beamed.

Chapter 18

"I'm sorry I made you angry," Michael apologized when they drove away from the castle. "I did that 'acting before thinking' thing that has haunted me this weekend."

"I'm not angry with you, just disappointed." Kiri dropped her head into her hands and shook it. "My God, I sound like my mother," she said. "I actually told Meghan (and you heard me) that I thought you understood me—my need for 'flights of fancy.' I can handle a lot, Michael. I can climb mountains, swim rivers, fight dragons. I work hard. I live a healthy life. I don't use drugs or alcohol. I self-medicate by drenching myself in a hot shower, if nothing else works. But for all that, if I can't have a little bit of magic—a smidgen of make-believe in my life—the rest is not enough."

"Do you ever get angry?" he asked.

"All the time. I just don't show it," she answered. "I told your father, you can't control how someone treats you—only how you react."

Michael stared straight down the gravel road in front of them. "What would you have done if I hadn't come back for you?"

"You'd be driving home alone."

They rode in silence for a time and caught up to the rest of the family. "Hang on. Let's have some fun," he said, as he shifted his racer into fifth gear and swerved to the right-hand lane to pass up three cars carrying all the brothers and sisters who raised their fists and pretended to shout at him. He exaggerated a taunting laugh at them, pulled in front and disappeared, enjoying the thrill and the surprise on Kiri's face.

Once they reached the motorway, he slowed to a respectable speed. "Mind if I ask a personal question?" he ventured, still keeping his eyes on the road.

"As long as it has nothing to do with having your children, and as long as you don't mind if I decline to answer," she replied.

"Why don't you drink?"

"Why *do* you drink?"

"Because I always have, I guess," he answered. "The parents regularly had wine with dinner, and as you've seen, stout is always available too. Once confirmed, we were allowed to join the rest of the family in a few sips of wine with our evening meal. Of course, school boys find drink wherever they can, and from that point it becomes habit."

"Not so for me," Kiri began. "I've never liked alcohol or what it does to my body. I can handle two fingers to be sociable at a celebration, but much more and my senses are dulled. If I consumed even half as much alcohol as you did before dinner last night, I might have skipped the dance. Why bother? If I did make an effort—maybe throw on a necklace—I wouldn't have brushed my hair or put on lipstick. I certainly couldn't balance on the lion's back or be thrilled by fireworks. And I'm sure I would not have noticed or appreciated your efforts.

"When you came to escort me to the dance, I noticed that you smelled fresh and clean from a shower. Your skin was smooth from a shave. You tried to comb back your wild hair and put my favorite curl in its proper place. You brushed your teeth instead of chewing gum. You wore a crisp, clean shirt, and you changed your sweater for a beautiful blue one that made your eyes jump out at me. Your clean trousers had a pressed crease, and you buffed your shoes. When you put your hands around my neck to fasten that silly bauble, they were so broad and strong, yet gentle, the nails trim and white. And Michael, an aura of manliness permeated my chamber. Why would I want to miss a single detail for a drink?"

When she stopped to catch her breath, Michael, embarrassed but flattered by her description, joshed, "Has anyone ever told you that you use too many words?"

"Fine!" she shot back. "Short answer... my choice."

She noticed him glance at his watch several times throughout their conversation. "Are you late for something? Have plans?" she asked.

"Not really. If I can get you back to the house in time, I might stop by the Plunge."

"Henry, apparently, hopes you will. What is the Plunge?"

"It's one of those gatherings where a crazy bunch runs into the sea to celebrate the New Year. The local media organization sponsors a charity event for networks and newspapers to compete. Most Polar Bear Plunges are a quick run into and out of the cold waters of winter. We swim an actual 400-meter course out into the bay, around a floating dock and back again. Anyone who wants to can swim, but the times of the first four from each team to cross the finish line are combined for a winning total. The companies donate a hefty fee to enter a team. The only thing we get for a win, though, is a round of drinks from the second place finisher. Our network is the defending champion. We usually field a team of a dozen or so. The five of us who work closely together have a pretty good record, but this year the other four are already on assignment, so we'll have to use the best we can get from the rest of the boys. Our strongest competition, Tommy's Irish national network, will give us a run for it this time."

"Will Tommy be there?"

"No. He doesn't do that sort of thing."

"Anyone else I've met?"

"Some from this morning, and Henry, of course. He does much of the organizing and signing in, and he remembers the towels we swimmers usually forget. Patrick may show up since the others are gone. We never know quite what he will do."

"Then I say we go straight there so you don't miss your chance. You don't have to take me home first."

"Are you sure? Aren't you anxious to get back and crawl into bed?"

"That would be nice, but I can wait until after you've done *your* thing," she joshed.

Michael pinked, turned sharply to the east and flew toward the coast.

"You are a great sport to agree to this," he admitted as he motored into the parking lot. He stripped off most of his clothes and fished a shorty wetsuit out of his bag to squeeze over his boxers and T-shirt. He shut the door, pulled on booties and banged on the window as he left. "Get a move on, or you'll miss the starting gun," he shouted as he ran toward the crowd on the beach.

Kiri peered out the window at the mass of guys and a few gals spreading along the shoreline. She pinched herself. What *had* she agreed to? Did Michael really expect her to get a move on and participate—yet another test of her loyalty to family and her willingness to go the extra distance for them? She shuffled through her bag to find clothes that would not be ruined by salt water and settled on her costume, bound for the trash anyway. In moments she ran barefoot toward the beach to join the others, just as the gun went off.

The horde high-stepped it into the frigid water, splashing and screaming. Last in, Kiri barely spotted the dock in the frenzy of froth in front of her. She passed the trailers and figured she would not get lost with most in front and a few behind her. "Stroke and survive," she repeated with each breath. "Stroke and survive."

By the time the leaders rounded the dock, Michael easily led the pack. He finished the swim strong, sloshed his way to the line and shouted his team name to the timekeeper. Two from the Irish network and a second from his team followed in quick succession. A steady stream of others straggled in, shivering. Michael sought out Henry and looked up and down the beach for Kiri.

"Fine job, Mike, as usual," Henry greeted his friend.

"Thanks. Have you seen Kiri? I expected her to walk down and watch."

"She did come down, but I doubt she's having much fun. Take a look out there," and Henry pointed toward the second wave of swimmers rounding the dock. Kiri's brightly polka-dotted blouse was hard to miss.

"What the hell is she doing out there?" Michael shouted. "She'll freeze to death. She has no idea how to swim in open water."

"Could be, but right now she is shoulder to shoulder with Patrick."

Henry and Michael watched the race between the two play out—side by side until the 300-meter mark—and then Kiri inched ahead for the last 100. Patrick's weight pulled him down as he rolled with his labored strokes, while her lighter body glided on top, pushed forward by the surf. When she hit the beach, Michael and Henry shouted at her to run, their arms urging her toward the finish line. "Run!" Exhausted, Kiri did her best to cross the pebbled sand, and collapsed into the timekeeper's lap five seconds ahead of her pursuer.

Michael threw his damp towel around her. "Fantastic! But what the hell were you doing in the water? You were supposed to stand here and watch."

"You told me to hurry up for the starting gun. I thought this was another trial I had to endure before I could show my face at dinner tonight."

"You *are* crazy. Father will kill me if I bring home an icicle." He rubbed her quivering body roughly with the towel to warm her up.

Henry joined them after congratulating Patrick for finishing fifth for their team. "Wish we could use your time, Kiri, but you aren't a paid employee. We'll have to wait for the final tallies before we know who is buying today. I have to say, you are a real guy's gal—lots of heart, a good sport and a great looker in your sopping, skin tight polka dots."

Michael quickly wrapped her in the towel and tried to cover his own blush as well as hers. "Let's get you back to the car and into warm clothes. Then we'll hit the pub for the announcement of the lucky winners."

"You know I don't drink. I think I'll wait this one out in the car. You go have fun doing *your* thing and be embarrassed for both of us," her blue lips smiled as Michael tossed her over his shoulder once again.

*　　*　　*

The vehicles arrived, one after the other, in birth order: Tommy's first with Margaret, Meghan and Kurt, then Anne and Charles, and finally Emily and Stephen. When the little band let themselves into the house, they were surprised that Michael and Kiri had not yet arrived. "They passed us long ago," Emily said. "What do you suppose happened?"

"Knowing Michael, he probably has them holed up in his flat for a little after-party party," Anne replied.

"Are you implying..." Kurt jumped at the reference to his sister.

"No. I'm sure Kiri is completely innocent in this," Anne replied with contempt in her voice. "But Michael seems to have left his sense of propriety at home the last couple of days. Father will hear about this."

Tommy suggested that while they wait for the two lag-behinds to show, they ask Kurt to play some video of that American football he kept talking about. He obliged with pleasure. He started a bowl game, went to the kitchen for refreshments, and returned to find Tommy, Charles and Stephen on separate sofas and the sisters huddled across the room.

Thomas expected his children to return about this time. He followed their noises downstairs and into the living room where an exciting football game dominated the guys' attention. With the grandchildren resting upstairs and this jovial brood gathered here, he was elated to imagine all of his progeny under one roof for fun and games. Oh Happy New Year! Then he counted and came up two short.

At the sight of their father in the doorway, Anne jumped to her feet. "Father, we need to talk," she said and motioned for all of the women to follow her to the hallway.

"What's up, Annie girl? Not worried about your children, I hope," he asked while escorting his daughters away from the sports party.

"No, Father. We're worried about *yours*. Can we sit somewhere? Maybe the nook?"

The gravity of Anne's tone alerted Thomas to an impending confrontation. When Paula saw all the girls, including Margaret, enter with their father, she interrupted assembling wake-up snacks and offered to leave. "No, my dear," he said. "I have a feeling this concerns both of us. Slide in with the rest."

The five women arranged themselves around the table. Thomas stood at the head like a conductor, ready to orchestrate a great battle. He looked at each one in turn, studying the seriousness of their faces. He could tell Paula's presence made his girls uncomfortable. "We're missing someone. Shouldn't Kiri be here too?" he asked.

"No, Father, she should not," Anne replied. "That's exactly the point."

"I see," he said. "What is on your mind, then, Anne?"

"I'm concerned… We're all concerned about Michael's and Kiri's behavior in public. They give the impression they're in a relationship. You must agree, that is inappropriate," Anne stated firmly. "We think you need to tell Michael that his familiarity with Kiri must stop. It is improper."

Thomas was the uncomfortable one now. He twisted and pulled at his right ear and clenched his jaw. "I charged Michael with watching after Kiri at the castle, insuring she have a good time and be included in all the festivities. Surely you mistake his attentions for fulfilling his responsibility. How do you see the situation, Meghan?"

"I agree that Michael is approaching the limits of propriety. As for Kiri, I don't know her well enough to judge whether she is simply toying with him or developing affection for him. Either way, it's uncomfortable to be in their company."

"Emily?"

"I like Kiri, Father, but I don't think she and Michael should be flirting and carrying on like they do. Dancing close together is one thing—we all do that with one another's husbands—but kissing and hugging without a care for who is watching? Going off alone together? That's creepy; they're practically brother and sister!"

"Impossible," Thomas objected. "Michael is a gentleman. He would never take liberties with a guest of this house."

"Well, he has, Father. The two of them are not back yet, and they were well ahead of us on the road." Anne pursed her lips. "Michael left Kiri's room in the middle of the night—and he wasn't wearing a frown."

Meghan blinked. Anne did not.

Unsettled, the patriarch turned to Tommy's wife.

Margaret had participated in very few family discussions and was reluctant to say anything. Thomas frightened her; he was so commanding. "I think I could handle their being familiar in public—there is so much of that these days, and Kiri and Michael are younger than we—but coupled with being related? That's hard to overlook."

"Paula?"

Paula was startled to hear her name called. She thought herself simply an observer, not a participant. "I've not seen what you all have witnessed. I've watched Kiri and Michael develop a close friendship, but I'm not surprised, given how much time he has been here in the house with us. I know they spent a couple of nights together under the tree last weekend...."

"Father!"

Thomas put a finger to his lips to signal silence.

Paula continued, "...but both my children have done that for years. I read nothing into it. I wonder if this anxiety isn't about more than Michael and Kiri. Perhaps the girls' concern is a substitute for their feelings about the two of us, Thomas. After all, if there is any impropriety in this family, we are the guilty parties. I wonder, girls, do you talk about your father and me the way you're talking about Kiri and Michael now?"

"Well, it seems we're faced with quite a conundrum," Thomas began. "Let's deal with Paula and me first, get that out of the way. We two are mature adults. We are entitled to the same pleasures as the rest of you. That we have chosen to live together before we marry and enjoy one another's company in public is not your concern; it is ours. Deal with it. None of you made it to your marriage beds lily white, so don't you be casting stones.

"Second, I will speak with Michael when he returns. I feel certain that you misunderstand his actions, but if you do, others may also, so I will assure that he modifies his behavior accordingly.

"Third, before you condemn others, take a good look at yourselves. Observe how you do—or do not—show affection for your siblings and your spouses. I want nothing more than for all of you to develop lasting love and friendship—and with Kurt and Kiri, too. We'll be unfortunate losers if we cannot accept one another as friends as well as family. Do not be too critical of those you don't fully understand. Now, you girls get back in that den and tend to your husbands. End of discussion!"

The obedient daughters filed back into the den and took their places beside their spouses. Anne surprised her Charles. Meghan squeezed in with Margaret and Tommy. Emily slithered between Kurt and Stephen. The sofa in back awaited Michael and Kiri—wherever they were.

*   *   *

Michael and Kiri returned within the hour. He ceded first shower to her while he went to the den to deliver news from the Plunge. "Good race today, but freezing—about seven degrees. You should have come by."

"We wondered where you two had gone. I never thought to mention the Plunge," Tommy said. "How did we do?"

"We each took one. I, the individual and you, the team. If they had let us use Kiri's time, we would have won by a smidgen. But we had to take Patrick's, so your network got the nod."

At the mention of his sister's name, Kurt turned his attention from the game to Michael. "What's this about Kiri? What has my sister done?"

"Your crazy sister jumped into the Irish Sea and swam 400 meters with the rest of us at today's Polar Bear Plunge. She did a great job—came in the middle of the pack and beat Patrick—but she sure did look funny when she turned blue," he joked.

"What?" Meghan asked, shocked. "You let Kiri in that frigid water? What were you thinking, Michael?"

"I didn't *let* her. She jumped in on her own. She's fine… upstairs in a hot shower. What are we watching?"

Michael did not find out. Thomas entered from checking on the wee ones and called his son out. "Michael. A word… please." In the hallway, he asked, "Have you done anything at all to compromise Kiri?"

"I'm sorry, Father. I meant to tell you, but it wasn't my fault."

Thomas turned red. "Son, you are a gentleman. I cannot believe you would let yourself get out of hand with a guest of this house. Have you no regard for our family's reputation?"

"But Kiri jumped in on her own, I swear. If I had any idea she would do such a fool thing, I would have locked her in the car."

"What are you talking about?" Thomas asked, confused.

"The Plunge today. What are you talking about?" Michael responded, equally confused.

"Your sisters tell me that your behavior with Kiri at Copley Castle crossed the line of propriety. Witnesses report that you danced too close, kissed and dallied in her room at an unseemly hour. Is that true?"

"My sisters have no right to stick their noses in my business. What do you think young adults do at a New Year's party? We behaved no differently than dozens of other couples there. Kiri deserved to have some fun after all the sisters put her through. I did nothing to compromise our guest. But may I remind you, Father, that you are the one who wanted her to feel welcome, a part of the family. What did you expect me to do? Hang her on a peg on the wall with a sign that said 'Don't Touch?' That wouldn't be very brotherly now, would it?"

"Are you disrespecting your father?"

"No. I'm asking you to stop putting so much stock in the words of my sisters who have shown our guests very little hospitality… and trust your son." With that, Michael took the stairs by twos for his turn in a hot shower.

* * *

Kiri roused to the scent of fresh soap and a bristly tickle on her cheek. "What are you doing in my bed?" Michael asked.

"Little girl things littered mine, and little girls did too. So I took refuge in here. That OK?" she answered from her cocoon in his comforter.

"Fine by me. Your brother has a football party going in the den, and everyone is here, so it would be nice if you could join us for a while. Might be a good opportunity to socialize with the brothers in a less formal setting," he suggested. "Tomorrow night will be awful. Suit yourself."

"Yet another O'Connell test of endurance," she groaned. "Give me five."

"Good girl." Michael kissed her on the cheek and was out the door.

Kiri dragged herself downstairs and flopped onto the sofa in the back row near Michael. Kurt motioned to him to go find his own sister and immediately sat at Kiri's side to wrap her in a throw and a squeeze. "I heard you swam a quarter-mile today in iceberg water."

She nodded.

"What were you thinking?"

"I wasn't, apparently. I assumed yet another family initiation rite required my participation and dove in. Besides, we swim in colder than forty-five degrees in mountain lakes."

"A shout out to Kiri," Tommy announced from the front of the room. "Nice job! Anyone who can best Patrick Murphy is tops in my book. Welcome to the family."

"Hear! Hear!" the others cheered.

"You look exhausted. Why don't you go up to bed," Kurt suggested.

"Family duty calls, remember? We are to participate fully. No complaints," she sighed as she rested her head on her brother's shoulder and closed her eyes.

Thomas and Paula joined the 3D bespectacled group sometime later. No empty seats on the sofas disappointed him, but at least the children behaved as they ought and enjoyed the entertainment, all except Kiri whose head fell into her brother's lap.

Sometime near the beginning of the third quarter, an interception and thrilling runback brought all to their feet… except Kiri, whose head landed on the sofa when Kurt jumped up. When he sat back down right on top of her, she screamed. He leapt back up and turned to her, bumping Meghan's head with his elbow. Her popcorn landed in Tommy's lap and her drink splashed onto Michael and across to Emily who screeched, bringing Anne to her feet scolding… someone.

Paula reached for a towel—anything to wipe up the mess—but Thomas stopped her, snickering until she did too, both enjoying the Rube Goldberg chain reaction unfold before them. Kiri rubbed her smashed ear. Kurt apologized profusely. Meghan shook her head while trying not to laugh. Tommy started eating the popcorn in his lap. Michael tried to wipe the spill off Emily with the tail of his shirt while Stephen sought to dry her from the other side. Anne, still on her feet, scolded... someone. Charles grabbed his wife and told her to sit down; Kurt was embarrassed enough. He did not need her harsh words too. Then he cuddled her until she started smiling.

Emily was a bag full of giggles as Stephen's attempts to clean her up turned into a tickling match. Michael vaulted out of their way in a hurry and bumped into Meghan brushing popcorn off the sofa, toppling her into Tommy's lap. He slid quickly to his right, smashing Margaret against the arm of the sofa. Her squawk brought Anne to her feet again... scolding.

"Enough! Everybody, quiet!" Kurt shouted. "I'm sorry. I know I'm a klutz. I don't need to be reminded; I'm embarrassed enough as it is. If you'll all sit back down and stop hollering at me, I'll clean up the mess as soon as you leave. OK?"

A barrage of popcorn pelted him from all sides. He took cover down on his knees brushing the hair from Kiri's face, trying to apologize. She attempted to stifle her smile so her brother wouldn't feel any worse.

Thomas observed his chaotic brood, then turned to Paula and clutched her tight. Oh, Happy New Year!

"I've had enough of this craziness. I'm going to bed. See you all tomorrow night." Kiri waved as she left.

"It's about time I get upstairs too and help the nanny with the little ones. You coming?" Paula asked the man holding her hand.

"In a few minutes. I want to watch just a little longer," he smiled.

"Is the game that interesting... or is it the family?" Paula grinned as she gave his cheek a pat and followed Kiri to the third floor.

The afternoon wore on. The red team defeated the white team by a field goal in overtime. The exhausted spectators pronounced 3D American football superior entertainment. Everyone applauded Kurt's efforts to introduce them to the game, brutal as it was. Then they went in search of children and found them lined up on the steps, overnight bags in hand, ready to go home.

Meghan, the last to depart, whispered to Michael as her two boys darted out the door, "I don't want to leave. I've had such fun this afternoon that I hate to end New Year's Day at home alone waiting for the clock to tell me it's late enough to go to bed."

"Then stay," Michael said. "We'll find something to do after dinner—play cards or games, just like old times."

"I couldn't do that. Paula..."

"Mom won't mind," Kurt assured her. "Hey, Mom. Meghan is staying for dinner," he hollered through the dining room toward the kitchen.

"Great!" she called back. "Food for eight in about half an hour."

"Make that seven," Michael added. "Kiri is still sleeping."

"But what about the others?" Meghan asked. "What will they say if they know I stayed beyond six?"

"Really, Meg. Why do you worry so much about what the others think? Do what you want for a change. If it bothers you to deviate from following directions, get in your car and drive your boys around the Green. Then come back. Technically you will not have stayed."

"Brilliant!" Meghan squeezed her brother and hurried to her car.

Kurt and Michael made quick work of the mess in the den, gathering empty bottles and bowls of popcorn kernels to dump in the waste bin in the kitchen, and returning with a broom. They swept the errant popcorn into a pile, scooped it up and deposited it in the Christmas tree's tub with last week's cookie crumbs. They were shifting furniture back into proper places when Meghan returned with Brendan and Connor. They enlisted the help of the two small boys to chase down the last of the flying popcorn while Meghan headed to the kitchen "to help Paula," she said without thinking.

Thomas strutted from living room to kitchen and back, observing the homey activity and clapping his hands and rubbing them together with satisfaction as if he had choreographed the entire afternoon and evening.

Michael excused himself for a few minutes and went to search for Kiri. He found her still in his room wrapped up in the comforter. He stretched out next to her and nibbled at her ear until she bat at him like a fly.

"Go away. I'm tired, I ache all over, and I'm dreading tomorrow. I need sleep if I'm to be in good humor for your father." She pulled the cover back over her head.

"Meghan and her boys are staying for dinner. Then we'll play games or something after. We'll have a great time, but we need you as a fourth."

Kiri shook her head.

"We'll get you back to bed early, and you have all day tomorrow to take it easy. What do you say?"

"I'm skipping dinner."

"Then you'll come for the fun?" he urged.

She looked defeated and mumbled, "I refuse to put on a necklace."

Michael rolled onto his back and covered his eyes with his hands. "This is going to cost me, isn't it?" he asked. "How many waltzes?"

"I was thinking of something more open-ended," Kiri replied with a sassy smirk, "...like no complaints, no refusals tomorrow night."

He shook his head and moaned at the thought of committing to all that fancy dance.

Chapter 19

After hungry tummies were full, Kurt and Michael volunteered to clean the kitchen while Meghan settled her boys at the far end of the den for a movie. Thomas turned on the tree lights and the fire, then sank down on a sofa next to Paula who said she was exhausted, no games for her. Every time she opened her eyes she saw hordes of grandchildren jumping all over beds.

He pulled her close. "You've been a real trooper these last two days. Thank you. Tomorrow is yours, remember."

"I remember very well that you promised to give me the whole day with Kiri, and I expect you to keep your promise."

"Not even breakfast together... in bed?"

"Not even."

Kurt and Michael filled the dishwasher, swiped the sink and counter with a cloth... and done. They were quite pleased with themselves at how quickly they disposed of the mess. Guys know how to get down to business! They brought drinks for everyone to the living room where Meghan cleared a coffee table. The guys pulled up four chairs and made a token gesture of asking Thomas if he wanted to play with them. He deferred. Paula's head drowsed on his shoulder.

The participants decided that three quick rounds of play would be about right for time. They chose three different games, each to be played in pairs to move the activity along faster. They would partner in three dyads— brother/sister, couples, guys against girls—combine their totals, and carry them as individual points to the end when some one talented player would be declared the grand champion. Kurt and Meghan both glared at Michael who smiled back innocently. It was he who had devised the unique scoring system. Then he disappeared.

"Awake, my sleeping beauty," Michael whispered as he gently kissed Kiri back to consciousness. He scooped her up and flung her over his shoulder—again—and bounced her down two flights of stairs. He plopped her into a chair and announced, "Let the games begin!"

Michael and Meghan won drawing pictures from words in short order with Kurt and Kiri mere points behind. Next came the dreaded scattered categories again, which did not require special rules since both teams were Irish/English. Michael and Kiri won that, but not by much. For scrambled crosswords, Gaelic words were barred in deference to Kiri's objection: the vowels would be used up before they really got into the game. She called Meghan into a corner to strategize. A plan of attack for crosswords seemed improbable, the guys agreed. Michael reviewed the custom-made rules: the first to lay down all his/her tiles would win the game for the team.

After a few turns around the board, it became apparent that everyone tried to rid himself of tiles as fast as possible with short, simple words...

except for Kiri who hoarded hers, laying down and picking up one tile at a time. A few more turns, and nothing changed. Something was up....

With the board half full, Kurt hesitated to put down a vertical word with a really good vowel, an *O*, open on both sides. Meghan's and Kiri's eyebrows went up and they exchanged a secret glance. Meghan laid down a *C, M,* and *E* for a horizontal "come." Their trap was set. Michael cautiously added *I* and *N* to the word for "income." He had taken the bait. He scribbled his score and waited for Kiri.

She smiled demurely and laid down her tiles—all of them—but not in order, building vertically on Michael's fateful *I*. When she revealed the last two, a *Q* and an *X*, for two triple counts and one triple word score, Michael just stared, incredulous. Their point tally put the girls way over the top of the boys, making Kiri the ultimate winner with Meghan a close second. The women jumped up and launched into an exaggerated girl-power dance, bumping fists and hips and taunting the guys until Michael finally lost it.

"Enough!" he cried. "Too much estrogen, here! I'm not even sure you've won... legally. I challenge your last." He spelled, "*Q... U...I...X...O...T...I...C* is not even a word."

"Of course it is. Quixotic is exactly what you are. Deal with it. This is only a game, you know," Kiri teased, turning his own words from their dart contest on him.

Meghan hurried with a dictionary to verify their winner. "Quixotic: extravagantly chivalrous or romantic; visionary but impractical." She looked at her brother. "That's definitely you, Michael. Admit it."

"All right, all right!" he agreed, trying to summon his good nature. "You girls win." He turned to Kiri with fire in his eyes. "This makes twice you've bested me, Kiri Koyle. Mark my words, there won't be a third time, Miss!" The girls shivered and "oohed" with pretend fright. "Let's get this place cleaned up, gang, and get our champion back to bed before she conjures up another means to outwit us."

"That was great, Kiri," Meghan confided as they put game pieces back in the box. "I'd hate to be up against you with a full night's sleep under your belt."

Kiri just smiled and yawned. At last, it seemed an end to this interminable day was within sight. She staggered to the stairs and found she was third in line behind Paula and Thomas who was still shaking his head and chuckling at the game's outcome.

"Oh, Michael, this has been so jolly!" Meghan exclaimed. "I haven't laughed this much since... well, forever, it seems. Both Kurt and Kiri are lively and such fun to be around. I wish they could come more often. In fact, I wish I knew more guys like Kurt who knew how to show a girl a really good time."

"Be careful what you wish for, Sis. You know Father wouldn't approve," he mocked.

"True. No relations with relations!" she laughed. "I understand, now, your comments from dinner last week and about Kiri last night. Was it just last night? Seems ages ago. You and Kiri are great together. I like her a lot, and I'm sorry I was critical of you to Father. From this point on, I am definitely on your side. Here's a hint for a sweet good night," and she whispered in her brother's ear.

"Thanks for the support; it's nice to know I have my favorite sister on my side. I'm aware the others don't approve, but they better get used to the idea." He gave his sister a final hug and kissed her on the forehead to say goodbye. Then he hefted one sleepy nephew over each shoulder to carry them to her car.

*　　*　　*

Paula perched herself up on her elbows in bed. "Tom! You're thrashing around like a wounded bear. What's the matter?"

"Can't sleep."

"Surely you're as worn out as I am after that marathon session with the grandchildren. What's on your mind?"

"I'm too excited about tomorrow. It is going to be a great day. I know it. I will not say 'I told you so,' but I feel we have a success on our hands. Kiri was right—give them all time to become acquainted. The children got along so well this afternoon—not a cross word between them. And then tonight—your two and my two played mix and match as if they had known one another forever."

"They did have fun, didn't they," she agreed.

"I told you Michael did not take liberties with your daughter. He simply took good care of her, as a gentleman should. My girls overreacted—too much champagne or emotion or both. There is absolutely nothing beyond friendship between our two."

At that response, Paula eased herself down beside Tom, resting her head on his shoulder and her arm on his chest. She scratched her nails through his thick white beard, slowly back and forth, around his chin and beneath his jaws.

Tom loved it when she did that; it was so sensuous and calming at the same time. He stroked her arm. "To be honest, I am worried about Michael and Kiri."

"I thought you settled that this afternoon with your girls and with Michael. You just admitted there was nothing between them. What could be troubling you now?"

"I want all of our children to become close friends, but what if they do and then have a real falling out—more than a slight misunderstanding? I don't want us to be divided by our loyalties to our children. I don't want us to choose sides like Kathryn and I did when Meghan divorced. It's not healthy... for any of those involved."

"You're starting down a dark road before you need to. I don't think it will ever come to that. The holidays have been so fraught with emotion, I believe that once we return to our regular routines—especially Kiri and Michael, miles apart—everything that's taken place over the past week will be a passing memory, and we will all live happily ever after."

"I hope you're right, dear. I do hope you're right. I just wish.... Michael is becoming a good... a fine man. He'll be a wonderful father. It is time for him to settle down and start a family of his own. I hope he doesn't get sidetracked and think he can live vicariously through his nieces and nephews. I just wish...."

"Be careful what you wish for, Tom. Bury your thoughts and go to sleep. We must be in good humor tomorrow. Your orders." Paula would have admonished him further, but there was no need. He was out.

*   *   *

Kiri heard a soft rapping on her door. Assuming Michael came to lure her away from bed for more fun and games, she answered harshly through the keyhole. "Go away! Not interested!"

"But, I thought we'd...."

"Thought we'd what, Michael?" she asked with a hint of disgust.

"I thought we'd sleep under the Christmas tree tonight."

"Again? Christmas was last week. It's not Christmas anymore. The magic is gone."

"Not true. Christmas is whenever we're together. What's the point of being in the same house if we're not together?"

"I feel as if I've been led around on a leash like a puppy dog for most of the day, and I ache from that swim. I'm tired, and I've had enough togetherness. Besides, what would Thomas say?"

"Father? Our congenial afternoon and evening delighted him so, he probably forgot about his stern warning to 'be a gentleman.'"

"Are you... a gentleman?"

"When the situation calls for it. Now, come on out of there and let's put me to the test."

"What could possibly entice me away from this wonderful bed in here?"

Michael was fed up with leaning over talking through a keyhole, when he knew all he had to do was turn the doorknob and push his way in, but he persevered and whispered through the tiny opening a temptation Meghan suggested—one he hoped Kiri could not resist. "I'll give you a backrub."

He almost fell on his face, the door opened so suddenly. "You're on," she smiled.

The couple dragged bedding down the stairs behind them for the third time in a week. He turned on the tree lights, music and fire as before. She laid out their beds side by side and began to roll a blanket into a bolster

159

when Michael grabbed it from her and flung it across the room. "Don't offend me by suggesting I'm not trustworthy," he ordered brusquely. "Now, lie face down. I'm going to sit on your rear."

Kiri followed orders and was soon savoring absolute bliss. He carried most of his weight on his knees and heels, resting just enough on her lower body to center and relax her. He began at her sacrum, massaging each vertebra along her spine with his thumbs, then using the heels of his palms to push the muscle tissue outward from her backbone. He worked methodically but gently for such a brawny man.

Nearly lulled to sleep, she heard him ask, "When will we see each other again?"

"Tomorrow. We're going to a Ball."

"I mean, after that. When will we get together again?"

"At our folks' wedding, probably."

"Sorry you had to give up a second ski weekend. When can you return to the slopes?"

"MLK weekend—Martin Luther King Day, in a couple of weeks. The whole gang will meet up at our condo. I need that time in the mountains to unwind after these hectic holidays."

"After that, when will you make another long ski trip?"

"Not until mid-February—Presidents Day."

Michael reached her shoulders now. She released tension and confided to her blanket, "Ooh, this feels heavenly. How delicious to have a massage like this after a day of skiing. Imagine the possibilities!"

"Maybe I could fly over and join you sometime," he suggested.

"Really? But you don't ski."

"Does it matter? I'm a fast learner, as you know, and always up for a new challenge. Besides, I won't be coming for the skiing."

"It will be very cold—high elevation cold."

"So is Afghanistan, and I survived that. Something tells me Colorado has more to keep me warm at night."

"You would really fly all the way to the States for a ski lesson?"

"And to see you—whatever it takes." He finished at her neck, rolled her over, and against his better judgement sealed the deal with a penetrating, passionate kiss.

Kiri noted the surprise in his eyes when she finally pushed him away. "It's your turn. Roll over. I'll help you relax," she explained. He obeyed immediately, and she began with his shoulders. My word, they are broad and strong, she thought to herself. She had not realized how broad or how strong until she started to work on him. She could sense his contentment when his jaw finally released.

"What can I expect tomorrow?" Kiri asked. "I'm a little scared, you know."

"Nothing to be apprehensive about. As long as we follow the established rules, we'll be fine. This party is not a real Ball in the 19th century sense; it's more of a social. The men show off their women; the women attempt to outdo other women. The music and dance simply add to the drama: who is dancing with whom and what does it mean? My sisters love all the fuss, of course. Tommy and I? We accept the to-do as part of our responsibility to Father."

Kiri worked down below his shoulder blades now.

"Father, by the way, has tomorrow scheduled down to the last minute. I'm surprised he hasn't posted timetables yet. As long as we follow his directions to a tee, the day and evening will proceed without incident. I understand you and Paula have the day to yourselves to get ready."

"We do, and I'm excited for us to have that time together. We have fancy dresses, which we're not used to wearing, by the way. We have shoes and gloves, and Meghan said they rented wraps for us. I don't know what else is expected. We know how to bathe and apply our own sparkle, so we're pretty low maintenance."

"We men should have it so easy. Father will take Kurt and me out mid-morning to pick up his tux at the cleaners and ours at the rental place. There must be time for alterations, if needed; he'll be the one to decide if they're needed. We're free until mid-afternoon when we're scheduled at the barbershop, late enough for those wonderful close shaves to last through the evening. Then we will snack so we won't be ravenous at the dinner. We'll meet up with the rest of the family at the Club."

Michael turned his head to the opposite side and coaxed Kiri to return to his neck. "There will be a reception line, of course. We'll proceed in birth order, so Meghan will introduce Kurt and I will introduce you. The bow and curtsy things aren't done anymore. A smile, slight nod and your hand ready for a shake should get you through just fine. Father will probably take Paula, Kurt and you around to some of the tables for more introductions. Then we'll have dinner and dancing after." He winced at the idea of the waltzes he promised.

"If you're worried about which forks or spoons to use... don't. Follow Anne; she's the etiquette expert."

Kiri's eyes rolled at the memory of Christmas dinner.

"When you see her do or use something, take a deep breath and wait a moment, then do the same thing. I still don't know which fork is which, and I don't much care; I watch Father. I'm willing to fall into line for him once or twice a year if that makes him happy."

Michael explained, "The thing is, Father hasn't attended one of these formal affairs for almost ten years, so he's quite nervous. He knows a lot of attention will focus on all of us. As long as we don't say too much, don't show emotion, keep our hands in our laps and our minds out of the bedroom, we'll be just fine. No big deal."

Kiri threw up her hands and bounced hard on Michael's rear. "No big deal! Lipstick and hairdos are the least of my worries, I see. Lines and nods and forks and manners! I can't remember names. I don't know how to make polite conversation about nothing. I'm rarely on time. I guess I'll spend tomorrow practicing to be socially acceptable—find a character in a movie I can impersonate—or I'll make believe this is only a nightmare. At least, I won't know anyone. There will be no preconceived notion of who or what I am. *You* may not even recognize me when I put on an act."

"That's not altogether true," Michael hesitated to add. "Everyone there will know you. Everyone there has seen you. You are all over the internet, at least here in Dublin. The whole city has watched you dance and sing your way to the New Year from last night at the castle. You're quite the talk. I wasn't going to tell you, but it may come up in conversation tomorrow night."

Kiri slid off Michael and sat down hard on her own bedding. "That does it! I will definitely have the flu tomorrow. So sorry. I will not set foot out of this house, no matter what your father says. He wouldn't dare drag a sickly girl out of bed!"

"Oh, yes he would. And if he won't, he'll send me to do his dirty work for him. You have to go. Besides, I'll need the moral support. I'm the one who'll be walking in there practically bald!"

"That's right! Tomorrow is the day! That extreme? Can't you back out of that haircut some way?"

"Not on your life... a promise made, you know. It doesn't really matter. I need to get one within a couple of weeks anyway, so I'll be back to this length before I go overseas again in April. I should match my passport photos as closely as possible when I travel in the Middle East. Less bother through customs. Plus, the station likes this wild look and a bit of the brogue when I report on location. Drama, you know. I'll survive, as long as you'll still speak to me."

"Roll over and let me see how you'll look." Michael did. She sat up on her knees beside him and laced her fingers into his hair. She pulled it back tight and close to his head, exposing just the structure of his face. "You have freckles up here I haven't seen before." Kiri lightly kissed each new one she found.

"Your brow ridge is wide and more prominent than your father's, your eyes more deep-set and more expressive," she said tracing his brows with her thumbs. "Look at those long, thick eyelashes. Where have you been hiding them?" Kiri attempted to exchange butterfly kisses with him, but his longer lashes kept hers at bay."

She pulled her hands from his hair and smoothed them around the edges of his face. "I've never really studied your face before... and Michael, I like what I see. You'll do just fine! I won't be the least bit embarrassed to be escorted by this baldy," she said, making a fist and rubbing it hard across the top of his head. "Of course, I may have to wear my sunglasses."

"Very funny, Miss Koyle of the ridiculous pigtails," Michael retorted. "Lie down and roll over on your side. Let me pull you close, really close. Relax. Breathe deeply, long slow breaths. In... and out. Let yourself go." He pulled her hair back from her face and kissed her behind the ear. "Now, is there anything else on your mind—besides my hair—that we need to take care of before we go to sleep?"

Kiri shook her head. "Just nervous."

"I assure you that other than all the pomp and manner, it will be a perfectly calm, uneventful evening. We'll come home, have a nice cup of tea and wonder why you worried so much over this—just like an old married couple."

Kiri jabbed him in the ribs with an elbow.

"I'm going to pull you closer, and we'll go to sleep. Can you feel my heart pulsing?" He felt her nod, then he said, "I'm going to put my hand over your heart. You put your hand on mine. We'll breathe in time, letting our energy flow like blood from my heart to yours, to our hands, through our arms and back to our hearts again, until we are perfectly synchronized. Inhale... exhale. I'll slow my breathing way down and then catch up to you. Now we're breathing together. Can you feel it? Our two hearts are beating as one."

"That's nice."

"Kiri?"

"Hmmm?"

"I promise to be a gentleman until after the Ball is over."

"That's nice."

Chapter 20

Thomas awakened with first light. He watched Paula sleep peacefully, but only for a moment. Then he rose, put on his dressing gown and slippers, and walked in to his desk. He had lists to write—several. No time to lose on this most important of days. He gathered several pieces of paper and a marker and began to write:

10:00—Men depart for tux rental shop
Noon—return, free time
3:00—Men depart for barber shop
5:00—return, snack
5:30—shower, dress, etc.
6:45—Men at the foot of the stairs
6:50—Women at the foot of the stairs
7:00—departure
7:30—Enter club with entire family, receiving line, introductions
Midnight—depart for home

There, he thought. The schedule looked good. Only six copies to go, one each for front door, back door, fridge, Paula's bathroom and two for the third floor bathrooms. The young people would probably use both of those. Now, to hang them around before anyone else got up. He wanted no excuses for deviating from the schedule.

Pleased with himself, Thomas straightened his stack, found tape, and returned to the bedroom. Paula still slept. He slipped quietly into clothes, kissed her on the cheek and left to post his commandments.

Paula felt a whiskery kiss on her cheek and heard the door close. Thomas must be up. Just five more minutes, maybe ten. Yesterday's test of endurance with the grandchildren left her drained. Then she remembered. The Ball. Today was The Ball—freedom to spend the day with her daughter, two women being silly. Excited, she rushed to get up and get going. Should she wake Kiri, she wondered. No, let her sleep a little longer. Her daughter went to bed exhausted last night.

She decided on dressing gown and slippers for the morning. Actually they would probably do all day long. Oh, happy day! Paula headed for the kitchen to post her own note to the rest of the household.

Thomas affixed the last of his agendas in the front and noticed the French doors to the living room were closed. Kiri must be sleeping there... again. He started to enter and then thought better of it. She did not have to be up quite yet; he would allow her to sleep a little longer. He let go of the door handle and walked to the kitchen to start the tea.

Kiri heard footsteps outside the living room door and then the handle turn. She stuffed her head under her pillow, expecting Thomas to barge in booming at them again. But the handle released and the footsteps faded. Saved! She turned toward Michael and studied the face of the overgrown man-child sleeping next to her—a nice face, a good-looking face, a sensitive face. She rearranged his curly locks to frame it. What a pity the two of them would move from being carefree children to grownups before the night ended. She kissed him gently on the nose, wriggled out of her bedding and left quietly.

Michael felt a tickle on his nose. He rubbed it, and then reached out for Kiri. Oh, so nice to wake up with her next to him again. But his hand found only empty covers. He rolled onto his back. Too late. She had gone. He probably would not see her until evening when they left for the Ball. She must be a bundle of nerves already, to be awake so early. He stared up through the tree's boughs—its extremely dry boughs. Pine needles shrouded his feet. Maybe he should water the tree. If he added water to the tub, would all the popcorn he'd thrown in there start to grow, he wondered. Better not. Paula would take the tree down in a day or two, for sure.

Kiri tip-toed back into the living room, her hands full. She had a leaning tower of peanut butter toast and two mugs of tea that she set on the floor at the head of their nest. She tried not to wake Michael, but something grabbed her ankle and pulled her down into her bed. He gave her a good morning kiss and then asked, "What's for breakfast?"

"There was a pot of tea waiting and a note on the fridge from Mom saying, *Fend for yourselves today,* so this is what you get if I'm playing cook. As you predicted, your father has schedules posted all over the house. Looks like you're free until ten."

Michael eyed the sorry excuse for a man's meal. "Thanks. This… will do just fine."

Noting his disappointment at the skimpy offering, she laughed and tore off a bite to feed to him.

Michael mouthed the morsel, followed it with a sip of tea and another kiss. He did not need more, after all; Kiri satisfied his cravings. The two continued alternating bites and kisses playfully until they heard noise at the door.

Kurt's stomach awakened him. He showered, dressed and shook his head at Thomas' schedule. He had a different one in mind. Get up, shower, dress, eat, watch football, get fancied up and go. Surely someone could pick up the clown suit for him, and he had not planned on a trip to a barbershop. Probably could not trust an Irish barber if Michael were any example of their expertise. Disappointed to find his mother's note since he hoped for one of her big breakfasts, he rustled around the kitchen, then aimed for the den with a giant OJ in one hand and peanut butter toast in the other. When he walked in on Michael and Kiri, he called out "Break it up, kids. Innocent eyes passing through..." He found the remote and some 3D specs, and keyed up a game.

"Is this an American thing—peanut butter toast for breakfast?" Michael asked.

"Fallback position when Mom's not cooking. Have some more," she replied, tearing off another bite for him.

For a second, but only a second, joining Kurt in front of the TV tempted him. He opted for Kiri's offering instead; he could call up games again tomorrow. Tomorrow. Kurt and Kiri would leave tomorrow. Too soon. Must use every minute of today to advantage, and pray the minutes tick by slowly.

They did not. The instants flew as if on steroids. When it was apparent that time had run out for them, Kiri turned serious. "Thank you for tonight's preview. I'm sorry I'm not looking forward to what should be very special, but I will make an effort not to let you down. I appreciate your allowing me to get used to the idea of you as a different person. Secret surprises are great, but ones that bring drastic change are not my favorites."

"I'll let you play with my hair anytime... that I have some," he chuckled. "Relax and enjoy your day. We'll have a great time tonight, you'll see. Right now, I need to put on clothes and get in line to leave. Can I take a peek at your dress before I go?"

"No, you may not. I think it should remain a mystery. If I'm to be surprised by you, then you can be surprised by me."

"I don't need to see the whole thing; I don't mean to ruin the effect. I'd like to see the color so I can try to match my waistcoat and tie with it. I don't want us to clash if we're going as a couple."

"A couple, are we? Your family might have something to say about that."

"Father's orders, remember. I'm to be your escort for the evening, guard and protect you and keep you happy, so we might as well look like a couple," he smiled with a scampish eye.

*   *   *

Paula knocked on Kiri's door as soon as she heard the car with three men aboard leave the drive. She had her own list of tasks to accomplish while they were absent. First: try on dresses with undergarments to make sure the women fit into them and the dresses over them, with nothing untoward revealed or spilling out. They helped one another with snaps, hooks and buttons, oohed and aahed over colors and styles, and made a few adjustments.

"Let's turn on some music and dance," Paula suggested with a foxy smile. "If these outfits can stand up to some heavy bumping and grinding, then they ought to last through an evening of waltzes with no malfunctions."

Kiri obliged, and the two women played teenager again. Their gyrations included some twist, jitterbug, a little disco, and a couple of tango backbends for good measure, accompanied by giggling. The garments remained stable, all important elements retaining their places. Luckily the women would not have to make a desperate run to the store.

"Mom, I didn't know you could dance like this!"

"There are a lot of things you don't know about me, my dear. Your mother did have a life before children," she smiled suggestively.

They added the expected high heels and quickly found their footwear better suited to a slow waltz than a spicy cha cha. They tried on the long gloves that accented their garments.

"Why do we need these long gloves?" Kiri asked. "I know how to use a napkin."

"I have no idea," Paula replied. "Perhaps to provide an unobtrusive way of removing nervous sweat from our brows and upper lips. Maybe we're to inadvertently drop one so a dashing young gentleman will swoop in and return it, locking us in his gaze thereby igniting love at first sight," she reasoned dramatically. "I thought long gloves went out when I was in college, but Anne mentioned that the girls would wear them, so I thought I'd better be prepared. I guess we watch Anne for the on and off signals. The gloves can easily be stuffed in a man's jacket pocket if they become a nuisance. How did you know to bring some? Did the girls tell you to?"

"Nope. The internet. Apparently gloves are back in."

The women collapsed on Kiri's bed to rest for a moment before removing their gowns. "Mom, I can't undo all these little buttons; my hands aren't in the right place. How did you get yours done so quickly—and they're in the back?" Hers were down her right side.

"Practice, dear. Practice. If you can't do them this evening, let me know and I'll help."

"What's wrong with a good old zipper, anyway?"

"That would be mundane. Remember, this is 'fancy dress.'"

"The only thing fancy about this dress is how hard it is to get on and off," Kiri complained.

The sound of the doorbell caught Paula's attention. "Oh, good! They're right on time. I ordered us a surprise," she hollered over her shoulder as she ran down the stairs to repeated chiming.

"Pizza?" Kiri asked expectantly.

Paula returned with a box that smelled sweet and was not flat—obviously not pizza. She opened it to reveal flowers, lots and lots of small white blossoms with greenery, cold packed for freshness. "Anne said they don't do flowers anymore—corsages, boutonnieres and such. Must be the cold weather this time of year. But I wanted to wear a flower in my hair tonight. That was quite the thing when Tom and I... when Thomas and I were young." She hummed a few bars about going to San Francisco, as she let her memories carry her decades back.

"I thought you might like some, too. I ordered lots of jasmine and gardenias. These flowers are the one extravagance I allowed myself for this affair. Everything else was very reasonably priced. I'll wear one gardenia, the symbol for secret love and joy. See how wonderful it smells. Just one tucked behind the ear means you're either single or taken, I can never remember which. Do you know?"

"No. I've never worn flowers in my hair... or any other sign that said 'available and looking.' Let's search the internet." A single flower worn behind the right ear meant that a girl was single, and behind the left ear, that she was taken, a posting from the South Pacific apprised them.

"OK," said Paula. "Left... left... left. How am I going to remember that?"

"We could put a sticky on your left ear, or you can repeat, 'right is ready and willing; left is loved and looking for more.'" They both laughed as Paula whispered to herself all the way back to Kiri's room.

"I needed to have the flowers here and the ear info before working on hair today. You're welcome to use gardenias too, if you want, but the jasmine is so much more delicate and fragrant, I thought you might like it instead. All the cut ends have been treated and wrapped, so the blossoms should stay fresh through the evening. We'll put any leftovers in bowls in our bedrooms; their perfume will be so... sensuous."

"Jasmine! Jasmine! Jasmine for me! They look like little stars." Kiri fingered the tiny flowers and knew exactly how she would wear her hair.

"Decided then. Let's get started and see what you can do to separate the white from the dark of my hair. Not too drastic; I plan no big surprises for my man tonight. He's nervous enough as it is. He doesn't need a shock from me."

*   *   *

The men's errand run included Kurt, despite his protestations. They picked up Thomas' tuxedo from the cleaners and went to the rental shop for the young men's outfits and the women's wraps. His daughters tried to talk their father into matching waistcoat and bow tie; that combination was currently thought more up-to-date and colorful. Thomas said he would feel uncomfortable; he was used to his black cummerbund and tie. The only point he would give on was color; if he could find a combo that suitably matched the hue of Paula's dress, he would at least opt for color this time.

Kurt was so tall and slender that his pants and jacket sleeves had to be let down slightly. It would not take but a few minutes, the tailor assured them. Michael's tux was fine since he had it fit only a few days previous.

They both tried on black patent leather shoes and scrinched up their faces imagining a whole evening in stiff footwear. Thomas' girls also reserved waistcoats and bow ties in colors they thought would look nice on the young men. Michael exchanged his light blue for a shade closer to that of Kiri's dress. He looked manlier in a darker tone, he thought.

He helped Kurt select something more acceptable than the light lime green the girls favored. By rights, he should probably wear white since he was not coupled and coordinating with anyone, but that seemed too dull. The boys decided that green did complement his eyes. They finally settled on a deep sage—not too flashy but appropriate for someone from "out west," they agreed—an earthy tone for an earthy guy. Kurt could not imagine them in the pleated shirts they would wear. It would take him all afternoon to get the studs in. He accepted the offer to borrow his sidekick's black and silver cuff links so he would not have to rent and worry about losing one. Michael planned to wear gold.

"We can stop by my flat on the way home. I'll nip in for the links, handkerchiefs and silk underwear. I forgot to pack those."

"Silk? Are you kidding me?"

"These stiff suits ride best on silk. Want to try some?"

"Not on your life! No girly stuff on this guy!"

"Suit yourself. You might change your mind by the end of the evening."

While awaiting Kurt's alterations, Thomas took Michael aside. "I don't have to remind you how important tonight is for the family. I'm counting on you to look after Kiri. Keep her entertained and happy, and guard her against inappropriate advances from other young men. Remember the gentleman you are and the tradition you represent. Act with honor and integrity."

Michael nodded out of respect for his father but left the interpretation of *gentleman* open.

* * *

Tromping in the hallway signaled the men's return. They found the women still cloistered in Kiri's room, chattering away. "We're back. Everything is on schedule," Thomas offered through the door.

"Good," Paula replied. "See you at five." That was the end of their exchange. A dejected Thomas walked slowly back down the stairs wondering what two women had to talk about all day long.

Paula and Kiri talked about the afternoon's plan. After deciding on hair, they tackled accessories and nails. Paula thought they should settle on accessories first so they would not mar a fresh nail job pawing through jewelry. Both mother and daughter were "less is more" kind of women, so Paula chose her pearls—not a strand, but single pearls separated by one inch sections of fine antique silver chain. She thought this would coordinate nicely with the white flower and curls in her hair.

Kiri untangled from her assortment a designer-linked thin, gold chain to highlight the golden threads running through the ruffles of her dress. Nails were easy—pearlescent for both. Kiri's included tiny gold flecks.

Just before three o'clock, there was a knock at her door. "Go away. It's not tonight yet," she responded.

"It's Michael, and I'm not under your mother's rules. I've come to let you know we're leaving again. Is there any last-minute item you want us to pick up?"

She opened her door and stepped out. "No. We're good. I just need one more tug on that mane of yours before it disappears." She grabbed a hank of his hair and gave it a hearty pull. Then she threw her arms around him and attempted one of his bear hugs, but he beat her to it. "I can't wait to meet the brand new you and be dazzled," she smiled at him.

"You're sure you're all right with this."

"I'm sure I will be when I know you are. Don't worry yourself over a crazy thing like hair, Michael. I'm just having fun with you. I'm running on nervous energy right now; I'll be so happy to see—really see—your friendly face when you get back."

"I've come with a message for Paula from Father, and for you from me. We'll need to have a few minutes with each of you in your rooms when we get back at five. Then we'll leave you alone again 'til it's time to depart."

"We'll be ready for you…"

The closing of the front door meant the women could draw their bubbly, aromatic baths and settle in to soak and relax, putting their cares aside for an hour. Then they planned to put on makeup so they could be out of the bathrooms by five when the men returned. The men would take their turns in the bath and dressing rooms while the women did their hair in Kiri's bedroom. Once the men cleared out, the women could dress and put a final touch to their makeup and be at the foot of the stairs to meet Thomas' timetable. So much fuss when they could be out walking on the Green!

* * *

Kurt had never had a real barbershop shave before with hot towels, stropping the razor, and someone else doing all the work. He was an instant convert, but he still did not want any scissors coming close to his hair. Thomas insisted in a friendly sort of way, so Kurt agreed to the slightest of trims around his ears and neck, and was gratified to find a barber who followed directions.

Thomas instructed his barber to give him a clean shave, lose the beard, when Michael stopped him. "Hold on, Father. I don't think that's such a wise idea. Too drastic."

"What do you mean, Son?"

"If Paula does not expect a beardless escort, it's not fair to shock her with a completely different appearance. She's nervous enough about tonight without having to reestablish a comfort level with you. How would you feel if you got home this afternoon and she'd dyed her hair red without warning you? You might come to like it eventually, but the initial surprise would take all the ease out of your relationship for the evening. Give her a break. Return to her the same man she fell in love with last summer."

"You're speaking rather passionately, Michael. Is keeping your Christmas pledge a problem? Do you want to renege on your promise?"

"Absolutely not! I intend to keep my word—a gentleman's word."

"You don't have to get a short cut, you know. Styled a little shorter would do."

"I've never found anyone who could do a decent job. I always end up looking spiky and weird. Nope. I'm going for the usual because I know what the result will be. You should do the same."

*   *   *

Kiri expected the knock on her door at five o'clock, but she was not prepared for it. She knew that her first reaction to Michael's new do would be the most important look she gave him all night. She did not want his self-esteem to be hurt by her reaction. She knew her eyes would betray her if she felt disappointment or shock, so she practiced being calm. This will be fine, she said to herself. Michael might look nice. After all, it's only hair. Take a deep breath and relax.

She answered his second series of knocks. "Come on in," she invited as she tightened her robe around her waist. He entered hesitantly. She went to him, put her hands on his face and examined it closely. She cupped her hands around his head and ran them back and forth atop his bristles, staring him straight in the eyes—his beautiful blue, agitated eyes.

"Oh, Michael," she said softly. "Someone has sheared my guy within a half-inch of his life... and returned to me a veritable Prince Charming."

His bearing reflected a new confidence when he heard her words and saw the smile in her eyes. Two inches taller, he strode into the room. "You really think I look okay?"

"Absolutely. More than okay. You look terrific. You've lost your playful look, but this new one is so... sexy. I don't know if I'll be able to keep my hands off you. Dress you in your tux, now, and you'll be positively irresistible. Maybe I'll lock you up here and go by myself; I don't want any other woman's hands on you tonight."

"What a relief. I can breathe now. I was so tense since seeing all my kinks and curls on the floor of the shop. You're really okay with this?" Michael asked, needing further assurance.

"No doubt. Relax and go away so I can finish getting ready. It's going to take me much longer than I planned to even approach your standard."

"No can do. I'm not finished here yet. I have something for you. Sit down in front of the mirror," he instructed as he reached into his pocket. "Now close your eyes."

Kiri did as she was told. Michael opened her robe slightly until it fell around her shoulders. She felt a cold tickle on her chest just below the notch in her collarbone. Then she felt his fingers at the nape of her neck.

"Open," he said. "And take a look at that beautiful woman in the mirror."

Kiri opened her eyes and bent nearer to examine more closely the ornament he placed around her neck. Celtic interlacings formed the outer of two concentric circles, its size about that of a one Euro coin. Four slender Kite-shaped diamonds pointing outward in the four cardinal directions were imbedded there and fixed to a golden inner face, as were four smaller, similarly shaped sapphires indicating the four intercardinal ones. The solid central circle was no larger than the tip of Kiri's little finger, just enough to balance a needle. The elegant piece hung from a delicate antique gold chain.

"Michael, this is beautiful. Tell me it's not real."

"Absolutely genuine. This trinket is also a true Celtic compass like Father's, except this one has gold thinly painted on the top of the magnetic needle instead of an eye."

"I hope you rented it."

"Not a chance. One of a kind. A beautiful woman deserves precious jewels."

"But I can't possibly accept such an expensive gift."

"Of course you can. I'm quixotic, remember? Think of it as an investment, if nothing else. I can't have my princess going around in craft fair baubles. It wouldn't be fitting for a man of my station. Prince Charming, you know."

Their two pairs of brilliant blue eyes joined in smiling at their reflections in the mirror. They did make a handsome couple.

"I almost forgot. A fancy jewel requires a fancy jewel box." He took a fresh new, plastic zip baggie from his pocket and handed it to her with great fanfare. "For you, dear Kirin," he grinned as he turned and left her room.

*   *   *

Paula anticipated Thomas' knock and opened the door to him while his hand rapped the air. "Oh... Thomas," she said taking that hand and leading him into their room. "What a handsome man you are." She ran her fingers along the clean smoothness under his chin, then along his jawbone where his beard now began. She traced the precise line below his cheekbones that paralleled his jaw, defining the perimeter of his neatly trimmed, shortened white beard. "How is it you remain so attractive after all these years?"

Thomas lifted her chin and met her lips in a tender kiss. "It is you who make me what I am," he replied. "Sit down, please. I have something for you. It is time we do this properly."

* * *

"Thirty minutes to departure," Thomas' voice rang out through the hallways. "Thirty minutes," he warned everyone on the second and third floors. He paced nervously now. Calm all afternoon with his schedule maintained, he allowed his nerves to overtake his ease as the hour approached when his whole family would be critically scrutinized.

"Fifteen minutes to departure," Thomas boomed. "Fifteen minutes." A thunder of patent leather shoes answered his command, the young men racing to their inspection at the foot of the stairs. Thomas looked them over. Dressed similarly, the differences between the two good-looking young men stood out.

Long and lean Kurt had the deep green eyes and the prominent cheekbones of his mother, his skin tanned from days on the ski slopes. He wore his sandy blond hair neatly combed, Thomas noticed, and his bow tie only slightly askew. Thomas righted it with a gentle tug to each side, then he patted Kurt on the shoulder. "You appear quite sophisticated for a casual guy. You do your mother proud." Kurt returned his smile, relieved that he passed muster.

The shorter and stockier Michael carried the broad chest of his father at the same age. He had Thomas' deep-set dancing blue eyes, but lighter and not so gray. His ruddy, wholesome complexion bespoke the Irish in him. Extremely attractive tonight when all spruced up, he spread a smile across his face in nervous anticipation of Kiri's arrival.

The three men straightened to attention when a wail emanating from Kiri's room followed her streak of blue down one flight of stairs and across the second floor landing. "Mo....ther!" she cried, pounding on Paula's door. It opened quickly and closed just as fast. The yowls became agitated babbles. Thomas checked his pocket watch. Whatever the crisis, he prayed it could be resolved in under ten minutes, for he had only built that much extra time into his schedule. All three men grew fidgety.

"Mother, help! I'm stuck! I attempted to fasten these dratted buttons myself, but I must have gone off track because I ended with two more loops than buttons. I tried to undo them, but I can't. I'm afraid I'll either rip my dress or pop off these demons in the process. Help!"

"Rest your arm on my shoulder, dear, and I'll see what I can do." She worked skillfully to free Kiri; then Paula deftly positioned each fabric sphere into its proper loop. "We may have to cut you out of this later; your gown is so tight." She stood back from her daughter and gazed on her admiringly. "Kirin, you look absolutely radiant."

"Thanks, Mom. You're quite a babe yourself. Have a good time with Thomas tonight." As swiftly as she had come, she was gone. Crisis averted.

Thomas checked his watch. 6:49. He debated whether to call the next minute or let the drama above play out, when the boys gasped in wonder.

A vision in ethereal midnight blue silk chiffon descended the staircase. Layers of two-inch diaphanous ruffles floated down with Kiri in waves extending from her left shoulder to beneath her right arm, front and back, leaving her right shoulder bare. The same angle and layers repeated at the hemline, flowing from below the knee on her left to mid-calf on her right. The fabric of the draped fitted bodice let go at her hips, moving freely with her graceful gait. Her gilded necklace highlighted the hazel flecks in her blue eyes and the tiny golden threads edging the ruffles.

Michael's face glowed with adoration as he met her halfway down to act as escort. The symbolism in her hair struck him when she turned her long neck and head toward his open-mouthed stare. She had pulled it severely from her face upward into a mass of curls covering the crown of her head like the decorated mane of a parade pony. Where others might place a tiara, delicate white star-like flowers formed a small pyramid centered on an arc just above short wisps angled across her forehead. More fragrant blossoms nestled in her curls here and there. She swept her locks up off her neck in back, pinned them, and then allowed them to cascade down in a train of rich brown tresses that swayed with her every step.

"Kirin, my number one unicorn," Michael cooed as he kissed her gloved hand. "You are beautiful beyond words. Truly my princess."

She smiled and lowered her eyelashes in response, then looked to Thomas for approval. Her loveliness obviously pleased him, but the compass necklace immediately caught his attention. He smiled admiringly at her. "Very nice," he said, and turned to his son. "Well done, Michael. Well done, indeed."

Thomas had no time to expound further, for now Paula posed at the head of the staircase to begin her own descent. She was dressed in the same midnight green—the shadowy hue that settles over a forest just before the moon rises—she wore that night in Rome forty years ago when he realized she was not simply a wandering carefree girl; she was a woman. The simple yet elegant design featured a low curved neck in front with lower curved back where covered buttons led all the way to the hemline that also followed a curve from front to rear. The slightly fitted bodice of her gown relaxed at her waist into long folds of silvery shimmer when stirred by movement. Loose three-quarter length sleeves camouflaged her least attractive feature, she felt, her upper arms beginning to show their years.

The scooped revealing neckline, however, enhanced one of her best features, her long slender neck like Kiri's, the skin still tight and unblemished by age creating a perfect foundation for the tasteful diamonds

Thomas placed there earlier. The third finger of her left hand sparkled, too, with evidence of his proper proposal. The streaks of sugar-white in her hair, separated from the dark chocolate, gathered in curls on the left side of her head surrounding... a luscious white gardenia. She wore a flower in her hair! Tom was the first man ever to dare weave flowers in her hair, Paula confessed to him on Puffin Island.

Thomas' heart stopped. Four decades washed away. Paula stood before him as young and beautiful—and in love with him—as she was so long ago. Speechless, he wanted to kiss her cheeks, smell the fragrance of her blossom, run his fingers through her curls and his hands down her bare back. Instead, he composed himself. "Paula, you are twenty-three again and just as stunning—even more so—an apparition of our youth."

Chapter 21

The O'Connell party dazzled the receiving line. With Paula at the front and Kiri at the rear, august heads snapped back and forth, to and fro, as if following a championship tennis match, admiring the two new glamorous additions to Thomas' flock. The men who received them held hands longer than they should; the women eyed gowns and jewels as long as they could. Introductions passed without incident except for the line backing up behind Thomas' group.

The gold and glitter of Copley Castle did not greatly overshadow the Club, elegantly dressed in silver, white, red and green. Paula appeared to be a part of the décor, so well did her gown and hair blend with it. Kiri was the eye-catching accent in her blue and gold, a standout in the crowd. The O'Connells filled a round table for twelve, Michael seated opposite Thomas and Kiri opposite Paula, with the rest of the party alternately placed husband and wife around the remaining curves.

Thomas' daughters were relieved, even pleased, that Paula and Kiri comported themselves so well. Gowns, makeup, hair, accessories, and demeanor—nothing warranted criticism. Envious of the flowers the two wore in their hair, the sisters wondered why they had not thought to do such a clever thing. The girls were proud to be in their company for all the positive attention they attracted. Kurt turned heads as well with his rugged good looks and golden tan, outstanding in the otherwise pasty crowd. The tuxedo gave him quite a regal bearing. Even the sisters looked forward to a remarkable family occasion.

The stiff but determined approach of Patrick Murphy interjected the first interruption to their pleasant evening. Michael jumped to his feet to stand between Kiri and her accoster, but she moved him aside and indicated she would handle this encounter.

"Kiri, good evening. You look stunning," Patrick smiled faintly. "Congratulations on your fine swim yesterday." At her nod, he continued, "I wish to apologize for my ungentlemanly and brutish behavior at the castle. I can assure you, that will never happen again."

"Apology accepted," she stated without emotion. "I can assure you, the opportunity will never present itself again."

Patrick bowed slightly, turned, and left without another word to Kiri or anyone else at the table. Michael resumed his seat. The offensive man's departure brought relief to the O'Connells who returned to their chatter critiquing attire and attendance throughout the vast room.

Thomas signaled to the young Koyles to join Paula and him for introductions at other tables. Michael regarded Kiri move effortlessly among the staid celebrants, smiling, nodding, offering her hand and saying very little while still drawing laughter and obvious acceptance. He admired her ability to adapt to this atypical situation, standing alone in the crowd with her head held high. He marveled at her...

...sudden stiffness as she turned quickly from the others and returned to her place ahead of them, her smile glued beneath an icy glare. He wanted to touch her but could not; that would be improper in formal company. "Kiri, what's the matter," he asked, worried. "Is this you melting down? Meghan warned you might."

"No. This is me trying to hide my anger at *that man* my mother is engaged to."

"Father? What has he done? The evening's gone so well up to now."

"*That man* committed me to providing tonight's entertainment. That's what he did. Without so much as a 'would you,' 'could you,' or even a 'please,' those two... men informed me I will sing in front of this austere audience at their behest," she charged angrily.

"How did this happen? What did Father say to you?"

"Nothing. He said absolutely nothing," Kiri accused. "He did not speak out to defend me when that other man—the one in the red sash angled across his chest—ordered me to perform. 'We're all anxious to hear you sing 'Titanic' as you did for the young people the other night... and any other two or three songs of your choosing will be fine. Delighted to meet you,' he said. That was it. Not a word from your father."

Michael did not hesitate to act by calling Thomas out. "Father, a word in the foyer, please."

Discomfited by his son's reaction to Kiri's report, Thomas hurried to catch up with him. Determined to avoid a scene at all costs, he could only hope for a quiet, rational discussion before dinner commenced. Paula and Kurt eyed one another across the table, understanding—but not accepting—the wrong Thomas foisted on Kiri.

"Father, what have you done?" Michael demanded. "How could you not refuse on Kiri's behalf? It is unconscionable of you to expect her to defend our family's honor when you wouldn't stand up and do it yourself."

"I did, Son. I tried," Thomas assured him. "The 'request' came shortly after noon, and I've been on the phone the rest of the day, as you may have noticed, trying to avoid this very confrontation. I offered to take Kiri's place tonight, as uncomfortable as that would be for me, but none would hear of it. The Colonel wanted Kiri. 'Impossible,' I replied and thought my word brought an end to it. But as you saw, the Colonel forced my hand only moments ago."

"You wouldn't expect your own daughters to comply with such an outlandish request. Why Kiri? Is it because she is *not* a daughter that you feel free to coerce her compliance? Good God, Father! What if Emily were in this untenable position?"

"Precisely because Kirin *is* my daughter—or soon will be—I have faith that she will fulfill this obligation for the family with dignity. She has proven she is capable."

"Surely Kiri herself can refuse. She can leave, if need be."

"Yes, she could. And you know how that would reflect on the rest of us."

"Well, who's most important here, Father? Hmm? Your guest or your Colonel?"

"The family's honor is most important, and you should understand that. If Kiri is to be a part of this family, you should help her accept that too."

Michael accepted that no further argument would resolve the situation. The two men returned red-faced to their table where soup was already served and none of the rest in the family dared look up from it. Kiri had not touched a spoonful.

"Here's Father's story," Michael began, as calmly as he could. "You were 'requested' earlier this afternoon. ('Requested' means 'commanded' around here.) Father declined repeatedly and even volunteered to take your place. He played the wedding and funeral go-to guy in his day, so he should have been accepted, but the old geezer wanted you. He must have seen your videos. Father made a final refusal and thought he heard the end of it, so he didn't bother to mention it to you. He found out at the moment you did that his refusal had been... well... refused."

Michael bent closer to Kiri's ear, ignoring his soup as well. "Here are our options, as I see it... two possibilities. We can leave—quietly or in a huff—at a time of your choosing between now and dessert. No one will prevent us. Or... I will take your place. I will wield my trusty sword to defend you by standing up there and singing 'Happy Birthday' and 'Jingle Bells' and 'Christmas Cookies' until I'm shouted down, and we're asked to leave. What do you say?"

Kiri could not say a word. She bent over in laughter at the image of Michael belting out choruses in his atonal voice, sword raised to the chandeliers and shield covering his bow tie—exceedingly out of place for a gallant knight. "Thank you anyway, but I'm not liking either of those options," she grinned at him. "You wouldn't be able to show your face again here at the Club or anywhere else in Dublin after a scene like that. There's got to be another option to save face."

The rest of the table relaxed as they detected a change in their guest's mood, and salads were served. Second near-disaster averted. Kiri stared at her mother with a "what am I supposed to do now?" kind of look. Paula shook her head and mouthed back, "Whatever you decide is okay by me. I love you, and I'll be proud of you either way."

"What I really resent is the disrespect with which I'm being treated," Kiri whispered to Michael. "For a group whose social standards are so high and for whom manner is all-important, their conduct toward me is despicable. They've shown no consideration for me as an individual. I don't respond to orders; I prefer to be asked with a 'please.'"

Her apprehension stuttered through. "I don't mind the singing, Michael. You know I'm a ham when there's a karaoke machine to follow and a few cowboy hats and boots in the crowd. But being up there alone in front of a subdued gathering with no lyrics to read and unfamiliar musical arrangements.... How can I convince anyone that I know what I'm doing when I don't even know what to do with these darn gloves?" She tugged to remove the silky strictures from her arms and stuff them in her lap, noting Anne had placed hers there. She appealed to Michael with fearful doubt in her eyes, "I don't think I'd come off very well. You'd be disappointed and I'd be embarrassed."

"We're not going to let *that* happen," he assured her. "Let's work with what we've got, then. If you don't want to stand alone, I'll stand up with you. I'll be by your side to wield my trusty sword and cut down anyone who dares to smirk or yawn while you're singing." Kiri burst out laughing again. "Alternately," he stammered, "we could con your brother into pairing with you. You've sung together before, I remember." Kurt's ears pricked up, and he joined the conversation.

Michael continued his assessment of the situation. "No lyric means you must choose something very familiar with few verses, short and simple. No unfamiliar arrangement suggests you either sing with no accompaniment or provide your own. Kurt, how are you two going to manage this?"

Kurt leaned forward to weigh in on the discussion. The trio whispered, heads nodded and shook, waiters cleared salads and served the main course. One of them asked Kiri, "red or white," indicating her choice of wine with the meal.

"Both!" she exclaimed in reply.

Michael hurriedly placed his hand over her glass and ordered, "Lemon water—a pitcher, for the two of us. Please."

She protested, "Tonight I *want* to be numbed. I don't want to remember anything more—let the evening be a blur."

"And I want you to remember every minute... how gutsy you are to stand before this wretched audience to support our family. Don't allow yourself to be a victim here. Be the savior. If your self-confidence should falter, take hold of your brother's shoulder or look into my adoring eyes as if there were no one else in the room and you gain your strength from me." Michael paused for dramatic effect.

"Rather over-played, don't you think?" she accused.

"Did it work?" wily Michael asked.

"Yes, Michael. I will straighten my horn and prance forward to save this day," she laughed. "Good humor, no complaints. And in return, you owe me big time. There are not enough hours left in this night for all the waltzes you must dance with me."

The matter settled, Kiri's two voracious partners attacked their plates while she rehearsed lyrics in her head and traced patterns in her peas.

*   *   *

Michael squeezed Kiri's hand under the table and helped her into her gloves. She might as well use them for something, she decided. She took a final sip of water, lubricated her lips with a dab of whipped cream, smoothed her hair and tossed her curls, inhaled a deep cleansing breath, held and released it. She fingered her compass necklace for strength and reassurance and smiled at Michael. "Whatever it takes," she said.

Kurt had spent the last few minutes conferring with musicians from the small dance orchestra retained for the evening's festivities. He laid out Kiri's plan and dismayed the string section by testing several of their instruments, both classic and folk, until he found one with four gut strings tuned most like his ukulele. He won them over with his engaging smile and heartfelt thanks, and returned to the dinner table. "All set to go, Sis."

When the grisly old man in the red sash came forward to introduce her, Kiri trembled at the thought of what she must do. Michael steadied her with his hand and whispered, "Imagine him as a failed knight with no armor, a broken sword and only his rusty shield to cover his aged, naked body. Of course, he'll still have his red sash, now tied 'round his waist, hanging down his hairy rump and lodged in his crack like a scolded dog's tail."

A guffaw escaped her lips as her brother escorted her front and center.

They began with a popular, nontraditional Hawaiian version of "Over the Rainbow." Kiri kept it short with no extra verses, choruses and no repeats. Kurt perched on a stool to accompany his sister, with Kiri standing beside him, her free hand initially squeezing his shoulder. Her other held the mike. His light-hearted strumming introduced the upbeat piece, unfamiliar to the old-timers but idolized by the young people. Her jazzy, fanciful interpretation was a crowd-pleaser; she was that happy little blue bird flying high.

Kurt cued the master of the woodwinds who used his Uilleann pipes to usher in the next song, eagerly awaited by those aware that Kiri would sing for them. She reprised a toned-down Dion impersonation, and when she began *Titanic's* theme a lone fiddler accompanied her. He had assured Kurt he could match Kiri's key and tempo without disrupting her performance; besides, he had seen her on the "net." She finished to rapturous applause. "Even better than New Year's Eve," several whispered, and Michael sensed that this night she did, indeed, sing to him.

For their next selection, the duo chose an inspirational piece derived from a traditional Irish tune. Again Uilleann pipes played the last two phrases of the chorus to introduce this number. Kurt ceased strumming and only plucked chords forcefully to create a strong, throbbing rhythm like a beating heart. Michael recognized the symbolism immediately and traded places with Charles to put himself practically at Kiri's feet. He wanted to watch her eyes carefully through this one.

She summoned her folk song voice for "You Raise Me Up" through one verse and two choruses, the first soft and the second emphatic. Then she paused, the throbbing halted, and she whisper-sang a drawn-out repeat of the last phrase to the accompaniment of wailing pipes. Thomas clutched Paula tightly, moved by Kiri's rendition of the song, and Michael wanted to snatch her by the ankles, throw her over his shoulder and make off with her again.

"For our finale tonight," she announced, "we'd like help from all of you and from our family's head in particular, Thomas O'Connell." Kurt and Michael immediately shot to his sides, grasped Thomas by the arms, and led him to the front.

"I can't do this," he protested. "It's been too long." Although practiced in his younger and middle years, Thomas had not sung in public since before his wife passed almost six years earlier. Most in the gathering anticipated his anxiety as the two young men ushered him forward.

"Yes, you can, Father. It's time. It's *your* turn to support the family," his son stated.

When Thomas reached Kiri, she whispered, "Payback!" He emitted a nervous laugh and then listened to her instructions carefully. She shared her plan with the spectators who, she reminded them, were expected to participate when signaled. Two musicians were enlisted to help direct. Kurt returned to his stool. He would pluck individual strings in the chords in a steady 6/8 rhythm and let the voices carry the melody in ¾ time. She announced the piece—"Dona Nobis Pacem," one of Thomas' standards— and the crowd hushed.

Only eight measures long, the song allowed for numerous repeats. Kurt began, the melody barely discernible among the notes he plucked. Kiri sang alone in a soft, soothing voice, then Thomas alone. His voice wavered over the first three notes, but when she squeezed his hand and smiled at him, he found his stride and his strength came through. They sang together as a duet, then in harmony, then as a round.

The musicians indicated audience participation time, first for everyone... and practically everyone joined in as they had so many times before. Next the women sang with their light soprano voices and then the men with their rich low ones. They all chanted a round, the women beginning and the men ending it. Finally, Kiri and Thomas combined in a partial duet again, the first phrase with both of them. Thomas soloed the last. He resurrected his tenor voice, and with a deep breath for that final note, reached its highest *F* pitch, strong and true.

The grand finale came to its climactic conclusion. Thomas bowed to Kiri and kissed her hand leaving teardrop stains on her glove. Kiri smiled demurely and accepted her brother's hug. The audience stood and applauded its approval, including a few shouts of "Hear! Hear!" Propriety be damned, the daughters encircled their father with weeping embraces, overjoyed that he was restored to them in full. The sons clapped Thomas' back when they could find it. Paula, overwhelmed by the composure of her children, remained seated and waited patiently for her own turn with the man who revealed so engaging a hidden facet of himself. Michael tried to reach Kiri to embrace her, but she was with the orchestra and then with her mother, so he crowded into the thicket of family to congratulate his father.

Thomas finally broke away to find Paula. He still trembled with excitement when he pulled her up from her chair into his arms. She had nothing but praise for him; he had nothing but praise for her children.

"Remarkable, Thomas. Truly remarkable!" she said.

"Yes, they were. Weren't they? We have so much to be proud of—and thankful for—tonight. We are truly blessed."

When the Koyle kids clustered with the rest, they received sincere compliments at their overwhelming acceptance by the Club crowd. The O'Connell girls understood that, by association, they themselves just skipped several rungs to the top of the ladder that night. They admired Kiri's pluck and humility, but Kurt's good looks, easygoing personality, and now instantaneous popularity marked him as the newfound hero. They could not fawn over him enough.

Michael coaxed Kiri to escape from the jubilant throng so he could lavish his own praises on her—not simply for dramatic effect. "I am overwhelmed! Absolutely thunderstruck by your talents!" he exclaimed once they were in the hall. "Never mind what you've done for the family. You sang to me tonight; I know it—directly to me. Every day I discover something new and captivating about you. I can't wait to see what surprise you have in store for me next. I've half a mind to fling you against this wall and have my way with you, right here and now."

"Please do" Kiri invited, "but you might want to ask that waiter with scarlet apology all over his face to close his eyes while we're busy."

Chapter 22

When the music commenced, Michael, who earlier in the week proclaimed his aversion to fancy dance, could not take the floor with his princess fast enough. He did know how to dance, he proved, and quite well with the aid of an orchestra and a festive ambiance. He even exposed the loop near the hem of Kiri's gown meant for her finger to lift her ruffled skirt in a graceful arc, so their swirling and dipping would not soil its hem nor trip them up. Their first dance blended into their second and their waltzing into slow dancing, more of a slow-motion embrace, inappropriate for the setting.

Kurt begged a dance from his sister, so Michael complied. He was her big brother, after all. Michael sought out Meghan for himself, but returned to Kiri at the last beat. The next, a waltz again, had them swirling, twirling and dipping a time or two, punctuated by suggestive glances and giggles. At its end, Michael motioned to Henry Callaghan who joined them.

"I believe Kiri promised you a dance yesterday morning, and I need to take a quick break. Would now be a good time?"

"Perfect for me," Henry smiled, "if the lady so desires."

"Absolutely," she replied with a slight curtsy.

He took her by the hand, and they moved into the crowd. He matched, if not surpassed, Michael on the dance floor, but he seemed more interested in conversation. "Nice choice of..."

"Don't you dare say 'sing, song or music," Kiri warned.

"Sing? Did you sing tonight? Hadn't noticed. I was about to say 'Nice choice of accessories.' Flowers look much more attractive in your hair than grass and weeds, and this frock beats your polka dots."

She laughed, "Thank you, Henry. I appreciate your humor right now."

"I thought you might prefer a laugh to a compliment. I should also say, awfully nice of you to help Thomas out tonight. He's had a rough go of it for the last few years, but he seems to have conquered that final hurdle. That man still has a magnificent voice. Yours is passable too, by the way."

Kiri laughed again. She so enjoyed the comic relief Henry provided to her otherwise emotion-filled evening. "You've known him for some time?"

"For about as long as I have Michael. I'm sorry you two—you and Thomas, that is—don't see eye to eye."

"Don't see eye to eye? How perceptive of you. How could you tell?"

"That's my job. Hard to miss your reaction earlier. It's a pity the Colonel coerced Thomas to put you on the spot like that."

"You know what happened?"

"Kiri, everyone knows. Can't keep a secret in a closed society like this. I told you that yesterday. You received reprehensible treatment this evening, but you handled yourself with dignity and grace and managed to reclaim the same for Thomas in the process. Very well done."

"Thank you, again. But I don't know how dignified or graceful I could be after the battle I've been through." Henry flicked her bare right shoulder rather harshly and repeatedly. "What are you doing?" she asked.

"I'm trying to knock that chip off your shoulder—the one with Thomas' name on it. You shouldn't be so hard on him. You'll find his heart is in the right place. He just can't manage to get his feet into this century yet. He's taken a major first step by shacking up with your mother."

"What!"

"Oh, do you Americans use a different term for two unmarried people living together?" Henry pretended ignorance. "Why not call it what it is? Other than that bold move, Thomas faults on the side of old rules and traditional ways. Give him time and understanding, and you'll find you have a loyal ally in that man." They glided around the dance floor easily until they neared Thomas and Paula who displayed moves revealing time spent dancing together before. "And he does have excellent taste in women. Look at that gorgeous green goddess he's with tonight!"

"That goddess is my mother, I'm sure you know, given how perceptive you claim to be," she charged.

"I do. And I intend to have a dance with her tonight to compare how you two lovely ladies move."

"What makes you think Thomas would approve or that my mother would accept your offer?"

"They will when I tell them you promised me. They both owe you for tonight, you know. They won't refuse me if I use your name."

"You're very confident, as well as trustworthy. How did you get mixed up with this crazy, pretentious bunch?"

"Don't forget humorous," Henry reminded her. "Work, I guess. Patrick takes me along to various functions when he doesn't want to go alone and may need someone to drive him home. I'm surprised you accepted his apology before dinner."

"You know about that, too?"

"Everybody knows. Can't keep...."

"...a secret in a closed society. I know. But you seem to be more aware of what's happening around you than most other people—certainly more than Patrick or Michael."

"That's my business. Assess a situation and formulate a plan of action."

"Michael seems to do it the other way around—act first and think after. How do you two manage to work with Patrick?"

"Easy. I assess. Michael acts. And if all goes well, Patrick takes the credit. If not, he puts the blame on us."

"Sounds like the cad that he is."

"Kiri," he said sharply. "That attitude is not becoming. Do not denigrate the little people who surround you here tonight. They are not worth the breath it takes. You have more character and—at the risk of repeating myself—dignity and grace than anyone else in this room, save possibly your mother. Do not let anything that happens to you this weekend taint your fine qualities."

"Are you scolding me, Henry?"

"Not really. Just trying to pass along a bit of unsolicited Callaghan wisdom. Much has been asked of you this weekend, Kiri, and you have gone above and beyond what could be expected of a normal person. But you're not normal... you're extraordinary. I'm sorry. I apologize if I'm overstepping my bounds here, but these are not the worst transgressions to beset a beautiful young woman, nor the worst you'll endure in your life."

Henry paused mid-twirl to face Kiri directly. "You've been bandied about at two parties. That's all they are—two little parties that don't mean a whit in the grand scheme of things. This one happens to be called a Ball. I daresay you didn't want to come at all. But you are here, and now you think there's some kind of magic to it, that if you don't have a marvelous and fanciful time that meets your expectations, the evening is a loss. Well, that's not true. A Ball is just a blip on the radar screen of your life. 'Happily ever after' never happens at a Ball. That's only in fairy tales. 'Happily ever after' takes place *after* the Ball," he finished, resuming dance posture.

"You're pretty solemn for a guy who wanted to be thought as humorous only moments ago."

"I am trying to prepare you, Kiri. You are about to be tested again."

"I don't understand. Tested? By whom?"

"By everyone here. You are the 'Belle of the Ball' tonight. Every man here wants a piece of you—and every woman here, a piece of your brother. I'm lucky we've had this dance together. I thank you for it while I can."

"You are making no sense."

"See that older man speaking with Thomas, the one in the red sash? He just passed his wife off to your brother, and now he is coming for you."

Kiri turned quickly in the direction of Henry's nod. The horrid, grisly old man in the red sash strode toward them with a sickly grin on his face. "Quickly, Henry. Dance me away from him. We'll escape."

"Sorry, I can't oblige. He's an elder, so I must defer to him."

"What in the world does that mean?"

"He is older than I, my senior, and of higher station, so I must turn you over to him if he so desires."

"What about *my* desires? I don't want to dance with him. I'm having a great time with you."

"I'm having a great time with you too; however, I have no choice but to stand down. Remember, dignity and grace. 'Happily ever after' comes... after. I'll go find Michael and see if I can't stop him from acting foolish before thinking. It's been a pleasure," Henry said as he handed Kiri off to the Colonel.

Luckily for Kiri, her time in his clammy hands was short-lived, for that dance ended within a minute or so. But when it did, the Colonel would not let go of her. Michael came to her quickly, but when he saw her bridled by their elder, he turned back, leaving her to endure a second dance.

Propriety demanded that she submit. The Colonel's revolting smile and fetid breath disgusted her. He forced her in close so his rough cheek brushed hers, and his palsied hands inched toward where they should not. She tried to engage him in conversation, but he only uttered, "delightful, delightful," while hiking his bushy eyebrows repeatedly in invitation. To maintain her sanity, she continued to picture him with his red sash hanging down his rear. By the dance's end, Kiri, drenched in cold sweat, contemplated a mad dash for her sanctuary... in Colorado!

Michael intercepted the mismatched couple and told the Colonel he would escort his guest back to her seat, thank you very much. "Are you all right?" he asked her, looking worried. "You seem limp."

"Nothing that a dance with you wouldn't cure."

They took some light refreshment and hit the dance floor again when the music resumed. Within moments a second older man interrupted the couple, and for the next dance a third, and so on. Michael and Kiri had only a minute between numbers to exchange a few words. Frustrated, he said, "Something's up. I'm going to Father."

"Don't be surprised if he won't help. Where are my gloves? I can't stand those old men touching me," she complained. Soon one such elderly gent whisked her from Michael again.

"Excuse me, Paula," he interrupted the older couple. "A word, Father... in the foyer, please." Determined to control his temper this time, Michael summoned his calm. "Father, Kiri and I are well aware of what's going on, and it needs to be stopped."

Thomas anticipated his son's concern. "Kiri is sought after by every man here. You should be honored that she is so popular and in demand. It speaks well for her and for all of us."

"I don't see you sharing Paula around. Surely she is as much admired and certainly of a more appropriate age for the partners you've sent Kiri's way. And what about my sisters? Shouldn't they be enjoying the attentions of your many distinguished friends tonight?" Despite his attempt to placate it, Michael's spirit asserted itself.

"Son, you are insulting our women," Thomas shot back.

"And you are not? Is not Kiri one of our women? What you expect of her is insulting. Not two hours ago you called her almost your daughter, and now you separate her from the rest by failing to act on her behalf... again. She's not your chattel, Father, nor a prize filly in your stable to be trotted out and stroked by anyone who asks. She deserves your respect and consideration, especially after standing up for the family earlier."

Unmoved by Michael's allegations, Thomas spoke sternly. "There are times when the obligation to family supercedes that to the individual. You speak from your heart instead of your head, and that is unacceptable. Kiri will soon be your sister—and nothing more. Your duty to her and to your family is to look after her in that capacity. Do you understand me?"

"No, I do not!"

"Are you disrespecting your father?"

"No, I am not. My father is not here tonight. An alien inhabits his fancy suit. The father I know is compassionate and honors his family. You charged me with keeping Kiri happy and guarding her against inappropriate advances. She is not happy... and your so-called friends are out of line!"

"My friends are not young and foolish. They understand the rules of this game well, and they have all paid their dues. You cannot tamper with tradition of 200 years standing. I did not anticipate Kiri's popularity any more than you, but we are honor-bound to let this adulation for her play out. If you cannot handle it, then leave. There is nothing I can do." Thomas returned to the festivities leaving Michael fuming but unable to explode in public. That would not be proper.

"Kiri, I spoke to Father," Michael said when he caught a few minutes with her during the next interlude. His flushed face marked his anger. "He seems unwilling to call the old dogs off."

"Then it's time he and I had a chat." She turned from him immediately and approached Thomas and Paula. "Excuse me, Mom. I'm going to steal away your beau for a dance. OK?" Before her mother could reply, Kiri led Thomas to the floor. No one cut in on them. Thomas, a distinguished older man and their friend, was practically her father.

She appeared very calm, much as she had on Christmas night. "We're going to have a conversation, Thomas. I'll do the conversing and you'll do the listening. As I gauge it, we have about five minutes to come to agreement. I have very obligingly played by your rules so far tonight. Now, it's time to play by mine. I do not dance with any man more than five years older than I."

Very matter-of-fact, she continued their one-sided conversation while Thomas moved her around the dance floor. "You gave me your word that you would not put me on the spot again." Kiri pulled her necklace forward and flashed it at him. "I've danced with every man here over fifty, and some more than once. I think that should suffice. You have until intermission to figure out how to break my decision to your friends. Practice saying 'No,' Thomas, or I will," she warned. "I take you as a man of your word."

"Kirin, that's not how it's done here," he professed.

"Well maybe it should be. Try it, Thomas. It's easy. Try: 'No. I'm sorry. It's not possible. Kiri is promised to Michael for the rest of the evening.' Or, 'No. I'm sorry. You know how young people are these days.

No respect for the old ways.' Or, 'Sorry. I'm going out on a limb here to let the young people enjoy one another for the rest of the evening. Catch you next time.' Understand this," Kiri stated, without a hint of anger or emotion in her voice. "I'll smile, dance with whomever you choose and be as charming as I can force myself to be until intermission. After that, I'm with Michael only or I'm leaving. Oh, and Thomas, if one more of your friends tries to grab my butt, I'll tell him to go play with his own wife—and he won't be the only one to hear me."

With that declaration, Kiri returned her surprised partner to Paula. "Thanks for the dance, Thomas," she smiled. "You're very smooth on the floor. I'll bet you also sing to Mom while you're swaying. Enjoy the rest of your evening. I intend to." Another aged partner swooped in to intercept her before she found Michael, so she smiled bravely, accepted his fulsome flatteries, and danced.

* * *

The orchestra signaled an intermission, and dancers returned to their tables where refreshments awaited them. When Kiri arrived at the O'Connell contingent, she struggled to wrest herself from her gloves, damp from her sweat. She held both of them firmly in her right hand, caught Thomas' eye, and threw them down forcefully onto the table. Astonished faces watched her leave the room, alone.

When she failed to return within a few minutes, Thomas ordered, "Find Kirin, Son, and bring her back."

Michael checked the hallway and then the restrooms. No Kiri. He thought bringing her back would be the hard part, but discovering her hiding place really tested him. He checked with the doorman to see if a taxi had picked up a young lady within the last few minutes but learned no pretty girls had departed. Red-faced, and pacing with his hands in his pockets, he had no idea where to try next when a waiter pointed to the service stairs. He followed them down and heard mild epithets and stomping emanating from the staff restroom.

"Kiri? Are you in here?" he asked meekly as he knocked.

Silence. Then, "Thank God, Michael! Get in here and lock the door behind you. I need help!" her voice pleaded.

He opened the door cautiously, expecting to find Kiri in tears and not knowing quite how he should handle such a situation. Instead, he found her covered in soapsuds, lathered all up her arms, over her face and neck and dripping onto the floor. Her arms, spread out in a T, gave her the appearance of a frothy white victim of a bad pie-in-the-face joke—absolutely ridiculous. Michael tried not to laugh at her; that would not be polite. "What in the world has happened here?" he dared to ask. "Is this you melting down?"

"No! This is me trying to wash all those old men away! Take off your jacket and help me out of this dress before I drip all over and stain it beyond repair. I can't get these dratted buttons undone," she wailed.

Michael did as she ordered. He hung his jacket on a hook and bent over to work on her buttons. "These are impossible. How did you ever get into this gown? I'm never going to get you out with my fat fingers."

"Mom got me in. You can get me out," she insisted. "Tear them all off if you need to; I don't care. I just need this dress off and a good scrubbing before I scream."

"I don't understand why you're soaped all over. What happened?"

"All my distinguished dance partners happened. Their hands groped all over—arms, shoulder, back, neck—you name it and they tried it. I felt disgustingly dirty. I couldn't find a shower, so I came in here to wash. One body part led to another, and the next thing I knew suds covered me everywhere. I attempted to scrub under my shoulder strap and inside the bodice, but when I tried to unfasten the dress to make it easier, I couldn't undo the buttons. I didn't know what to do, and then you knocked. Please hurry. I cannot stand this," she babbled.

"Success!"

"Thank goodness. Slide the dress off my shoulder—without getting it wet, if you can—and let the top fall down. Roll up the hem and hold it tight so I can step out without its touching the soppy floor."

He followed her directions and managed a satisfactory disrobing.

"Hang it up, please. Grab a hand towel and start scrubbing."

Michael hung the gown out of the way and pulled up his sleeves as far as the cuff links would allow. Then he turned and smiled at Kiri, standing there like a ghostly scarecrow.

"What are you looking at? Don't pretend you've never seen a woman in a fancy slip before."

"You have no idea how sexy you look standing there in this mess."

"You have no idea how humiliated I feel. Lather up a cloth, please, and start scrubbing—every bit of skin you can find. And scrub hard. I want it to hurt. I want every drop of old codger sucked down the drain. The only man-scent I want on me tonight is yours!"

Michael had never washed a woman like this before, but he figured it could not be too much different from giving his nephews a bath—only, more surface area. He took Kiri at her word, and rubbed the soapy cloth roughly over her skin, turning it red. "Too hard?"

She shook her head. "Keep going. Make sure you get all the way down my back… and the back of my neck under my hair… and behind my ears… and inside my right ear."

"Inside your ear!"

"Just do it! I've been fodder for every man over fifty whose wife hasn't given him any for too long. Believe me, I'm as disgusted as you are. See if there are any clean towels left so I don't have to drip dry."

He found a couple and rubbed her backside while Kiri took care of the front. Then she stood over the sink and scrubbed her face again. When Michael started to help her back into her dress, she stopped him. "Smell me."

"What?"

"Sniff me. I want my fragrance to be fresh soap and not old geezer."

Michael obliged by running his cheek over her, front and back, lingering here and there to nibble at her ear lobe, neck and shoulder. "The fresh scent of Irish soap is all I detect. You are almost good to go." He unhooked her compass necklace, soaped it up, rinsed and dried it, ignoring her exasperated protests against the harsh treatment he was giving her new and treasured ornament. He replaced the chain around her neck whispering, "A fine jewel is like a good woman. If it can't stand up to a hard scrubbing now and then, and still keep its shine, it's not worth the investment. You are priceless."

Kiri stepped into her gown while he held it off the floor and attacked the buttons again. "Thank you, Michael. I hope you aren't so disgusted that you don't want to dance with me. Your father and I have an understanding: either he calls off the dogs or I leave. Are you with me or not?"

"You are asking me to play by rules that are unfamiliar to me. I'm willing. I'm just unsure how to proceed against decades of tradition."

"Set your own rules. Establish your own traditions. Defy those that seem unjust. You are bright, strong and loyal, but you don't have to be blind too. At some point you must make a stand for what is right for you."

"You can't take Father too seriously tonight. He is not himself. Being in an old familiar place in a new situation has him unsettled."

"I don't intend to come between you and your father. I will not ask you to defy your family but to define your own place in it. I've done virtually everything that has been asked of me over the holidays to comply with your family's notion of grand tradition. I can't do that anymore. It's time I do what is right for me. I'm going back out there, and I'm going to dance with whomever *I* choose."

"My dear Kirin, even if you were still in your underwear covered in soapsuds, I would gladly escort you to the dance floor. I will wield my trusty sword and cut anyone off at the knees who dares to stop us from being together. If that means we must flee, so be it."

"Despite your valiant overtures, that trusty sword of yours has remained locked in its sheath tonight, too heavy for you to lift."

Brutal honesty, Michael remembered.

"I won't subject myself to your father's unreasonable standards any longer. You are either with me or you are not."

Chapter 23

Kiri rested in a billowy cloud of midnight blue on a cushion in front of the fire, her back against a sofa. Finally, she reflected, a chance to sit and relax free from notice and the pinch of tight shoes. Michael thumped down the stairs with his arms full of bedding and nearly stumbled on the two pairs of footwear they doffed there. He tromped into the living room, dumped his load of covers near the base of the tree and exited again dictating, "Don't move. I'll be back in a flash."

She laughed at the picture, how quickly she and Michael shed the formality of the evening and sought the comfort of the desiccated Christmas tree and a friendly fire. Their return to the Ball, arm in arm, occasioned a few raised eyebrows but no unseemly comments. At Thomas' slight nod, Michael and Kiri took the floor together and danced... and danced... without interruption from other admirers. When their tempo remained the same despite that of the music, they recognized the signs, said their good-byes and departed, her head on his shoulder and his arm around her back, proper or not.

"Here you go—nice hot tea to help you relax," he said, handing her a cup of steaming brew. "You're not still worrying over tonight, are you?" he asked, settling himself on the sofa behind her.

"Mmm," she said as she sipped while resting her head against his knee. "Not worried—just exhausted. I'm trying to relax and let the evening go." Michael sensed from her tone that she was not finished with that thought. After a few moments of silence, she said, "I am such an idiot!"—not quite what he expected. He braced himself for the impending monologue.

"Every ounce of anger, every degree of disgust and discomfort I felt tonight, was my own fault. At one point I was so irate I could have taken your sword and cut your father to bits." Kiri thrashed the air with an invisible rapier. "I was so unbelievably impudent to him; I doubt he'll ever speak to me again."

"You know that's not true," Michael assured her. "You had every right."

"In Colorado, maybe. But here in Dublin... no way. It's play by your rules or go home." she continued, "Once I let go of the fairy tale and got past the drama, I realized my part as a player in a piece of nonfiction, and not a very good one at that—a victim of my own folly in the midst of a cultural aberration. As violated as I felt, not one old man did anything he'd not done before in this closed little society of yours. Likewise, not one man would allow another to go beyond the bounds of that sanctioned by all. When I accepted that, I looked on the whole affair as a field study with me as the object of some primitive ritual practiced by the elders of your anomalous culture."

"We're all specimens, then, in your scientific endeavor? I'm nothing more than a biological sample to you?" Michael joked as he draped his legs over Kiri's shoulders, clutching her head tightly between his knees. She tried to grasp his legs but could not.

"Your calves are huge!"

"I could crush a man to death between these legs if I had to, but that would make me an abnormal specimen. Better throw me back in the pond."

"No. I'll pull you out rather than throw you back in. I wouldn't want your kind reproducing in that pond. Better to start a whole new massive-calved line." She felt him tugging on her hair. "What are you doing?"

"I'm taking all these hairpins out. I don't want you stabbing me when we roll around on the floor."

Kiri laughed at the suggestion and raised her hands to her head to begin the task herself. "I can do this, Michael. You haven't a clue what I've hidden up there."

"But it will be such fun discovering it all. Besides, I need the practice."

"The practice? For what? I'll never pile it up like this again."

"The practice for being a good father to this new line of little people we'll produce."

"Be careful what you say," she cautioned. "I'm trying to humor you, but you have to know that your constant references to my reproductive future grate at me like a pestering little brother. You're treading on sensitive ground here."

"I'll step carefully." He persisted, "If I'm to be the prototype, our children will be like me, and those poor little girls with hair-trigger tempers will have red kinky curls all over the place. Someone must know how to tame the mess with pins and how to do up their buttons. It's not going to be you, judging by the episode in the restroom."

Kiri could not keep herself from laughing. "Ow!" she cried when Michael stuck her with a pin. She resumed her discourse soberly. "I have not been respectful of your society's accepted practices. They are not right for me; although, the way you treat your women is much less offensive than obliging females to wear burqas or to marry men they've never met."

"Some societies actually sacrifice young maidens, I understand," he interjected. "In that context, spending an evening with lusty Irishmen isn't so bad—especially one in particular," he smiled.

"If I had done my research, I would have seen it coming, but I focused on looking the part—dress and hair and manner. I failed to understand the social implications of 'family obligation.' I can't believe how stupid I am."

Michael grasped her under the chin and tilted her head backward, bent over her until they stared eye-to-upside-down-eye, and stated gruffly in a

Sister Mary Francis tone, "You must write sentences, young lady." At her surprise, he instructed, *I promise to prepare diligently for every party.*

Kiri's trillish laughter ended in a relaxed sigh. "I'm ready to sleep now."

Michael raked a handful of the jasmine from her curls and inhaled their exotic scent. "These dainty blossoms are so lovely. I wish I could save them forever."

"Nothing lasts forever, especially nothing so delicate as a flower." Kiri felt him run his fingers through her hair again to blend her curls. "I learned more what I do and don't want for my life," she admitted. "For one thing, I don't want my man looking forward to a once-a-year occasion for arousal because I can't keep him satisfied at home."

"That's good to know. Once a year is not enough for this Irishman," he joshed.

Footsteps in the hallway marked the return of Thomas and Paula who sauntered up the stairs, speaking in soft tones to one another. They must have enjoyed a very good time and would again soon, Kiri imagined as she tensed at the first sound.

Michael reassured her, "There won't be anyone come to bother us here. Father trusts me to 'remember the tradition I represent and to act with honor and integrity.'"

"And will you?" she asked. "Act with honor and integrity?"

"Don't I always?"

She laughed. "Tell me the best moment of your evening."

"When I first saw you descending the stairs before we left, with every hair, every flower, every ruffle and every fold of your gown in place, I thought surely that beautiful vision would endure forever. Then I saw you standing in your simple satin slip, so innocent and vulnerable, so sudsy and sexy at the same time... needing me. No moment could be more sublime. And for you?"

"When you first came to my rescue and saw what a mess I made, you didn't bolt, show embarrassment or disgust, or run for my mother. You stepped right in and, without one flinch of hesitation, did what needed to be done whether you felt comfortable with it or not. Sometimes a man of action is exactly what a woman needs. Thank you for my fondest memory."

The front door opened and closed again as Kurt took the stairs two at a time as usual. The couple awaited the sound of his third floor door closing. The household complete, Kiri felt free to relax again.

Michael folded his arms around her neck and nuzzled her behind the ear. "Sweet dreams for us both. Time to get ready for bed."

She tried to stand, but he held her there until he could maneuver himself to pick her up – in his arms, this time. He carried her to their heap of blankets and created a jig specifically for arranging bedding with the feet. Kiri could not help giggling at his antics. "Michael, put me down. Did you remember to bring our pjs too?"

"No pjs for us tonight. We'll have to make do with silks and satin," he said setting her on her feet but not allowing her to sit down. He gazed intently at her. "I'm going to prepare you for our bed, and I'll reveal everything I intend to do before I do it. I promise I will not force you into anything that makes you uncomfortable, but I give you fair warning... I'm going to try everything I know. First, I'm going to remove your necklace." Without taking his eyes from hers, Michael unhooked its clasp, and let the chain inch toward her bosom. He clamped it again and hung it over the tree bough that held her unicorn.

Kiri recognized her cue. She had played this game before. Tit for tat. She removed Michael's cuff links and bow tie, sliding the gold fasteners into his pocket and hanging the tie on the branch with her unicorn.

They continued to trade piece for piece, caress for caress, fond tip for tender tap, slowly, in gentleness and affection until Kiri traced the boundaries of his silky under-vest over Michael's shoulders and around the neck. Her hands found the bottom hem and started to work their way upward from his abdomen toward his chest when his hands caught and stopped hers.

"I can't let you go any further. I'm uncomfortable," Michael explained. "I haven't been bare-chested with a woman since... since I was a teenager. I always wear something... a T-shirt or... I'm sorry." He kissed her hands, placed them atop his vest and held them there.

Brave, confident Mighty Mike, embarrassed to bare himself in front of a woman, astounded her. She felt sure she would be first to pull out of their daring game. "Whatever you say, Michael. I definitely don't want to force you into places you don't want to go. Can you help me understand your reluctance?"

"You know how my oversized legs condemned me to your reject gene pool for the overly endowed? The same could be said of my fat fingers, my heavy beard and my thick head of hair. Turns out, my pate isn't the only place I have an overabundance. I have a 'wooly mammoth' kind of thing on my chest—a throwback to my Celtic heritage, no doubt. I'm just more comfortable keeping myself covered."

"Fair enough. I'm not going to push you, but I told you last week that you have no cause to doubt your worth. You have every reason to be proud of everything about your 'self.' You should celebrate your uniqueness; that's what makes you the manly man you are. You overlooked my worst tonight, and I lived through the embarrassment." She regarded him with a glint in her eye. "You may be able to hide yourself from me indefinitely, but once you start prototyping a new line of little urchins, they're going to want to know all about their daddy," she teased gently.

Michael could not help but chuckle at her reasoning. "I... I'm afraid you'll..."

"Afraid I'll what, Michael? Laugh? Show revulsion? Walk out on you, leaving everything behind but my slip? You don't give very much credit to the woman you want to bear your children, do you? Makes me wonder what you see in her."

Michael looked deeply into Kiri's blue eyes, fixating on one hazel fleck in particular, the one that looked starlike. After a long pause, he said haltingly, "I see a woman who understands me and makes me feel safe. Maybe we could go at this slowly—little by little." He grasped her hands and placed them beneath his shirt. He let them find their own way through his forest while he probed her lushness. Then he laid Kiri on their nest of covers and allowed her to roll on top and remove his vest.

"I want your marvelous chest for my pillow tonight," she smiled and nestled her head just beneath his shoulder, her soft hair blanketing him. Michael locked his legs around hers and savored their closeness. His anxiety subsided, and they both relaxed into the pleasant enjoyment of exploring one another.

*   *   *

"You are a happy fellow. Only hours ago, you looked as if Michael had punched you in the stomach, and now you are all smiles," Paula remarked as they closed the door to their bedchamber.

"Just a slight misunderstanding. Nothing to it. Michael is a gentleman and understands his place in this family. Both he and Kiri had unrealistic expectations and were overwhelmed by the excitement of the evening. They have come to their senses, I'm sure. We'll talk no more about it. Especially now. Not one thing could mar the happiness I feel at this moment."

Tom plucked the gardenia from behind Paula's ear and drew in its fragrance. "You know exactly how to titillate me, you minx, and I love every minute of it." He set the flower gently on a small table beside the bed they shared and returned to her. He reached around her neck to unclasp her new jewels and circled the blossom with them.

She smiled, stroked his beard and removed his bow tie to loop it around the diamonds and the flower.

He encircled her slim body with his arms to unfasten the row of buttons falling nearly to her ankles.

She removed his shirt studs and cufflinks and put them in his pocket.

They traded piece for piece and caress for caress until they lay in bed together, the gardenia between them on the pillow.

"Our children were wonderful tonight, Paula. Handsome, beautiful, well-mannered, charming—all of them a credit to our family. Not yours, not mine, but ours. All seven of them. How I wish there were time left to us to make seven more just like them... or eight," he added wistfully. "Do you think the good Lord might bless us—like Abraham and Sarah, with both of us so old now—to create just one more from the two of us?"

"You are an incurable romantic, Tom. I doubt even my god can manage the impossible. But," she replied coyly, "we could do our part."

"My thought exactly," his eyes twinkled. "My thought exactly."

*   *   *

"I want to make love to you, Kiri."

Her heart lurched to a stop, and her fingers froze. There it was, that declaration of desire that preceded one of commitment. The mood was perfect. The moment was perfect, and the man, perfect, but she was old-fashioned and conservative enough to believe that the two yearnings intertwined. They should come as a package. And she refused to apologize for her beliefs.

"I want you to... but not yet. I don't mean to disappoint you, Michael, but I can't give you what you want. I'm not really keen on the idea of multiple partners, so I'm not protected..."

"I have some..."

"...and I won't have anything between us when we do. Open flesh or not at all."

"That's very Catholic of you."

"No. That's natural. Please, let's do this my way tonight. Trust me?"

Michael did put his faith in Kiri and succumbed to the gentle touch of her magic hands. Fingers and palms, they created a swirl of scintillating sensations and evocative visions he had never before experienced. *Every night... two bluebirds... in my dreams... happy blue-eyed bluebirds... flying high together... over the rainbow... I feel you... tenderness... riding the waves... kindness... standing on mountains... waltzing on a cloud... the unicorn and her gallant knight... throbbing... raise me up... more than I can be... exhilaration... ecstasy... dreams... really do... come true.*

When Kiri sensed Michael's body limp beneath her, she draped a cover over them, cuddled him and whispered, "Pacem..."

After a few moments they rolled onto their sides facing one another. "Michael, are you asleep?"

"No, just relaxed. So... completely... relaxed. Kiri, where did you? I thought you were..."

"... 'as pure as the driven snow,' as you so decorously put it to your father? I may be, but that doesn't mean I'm not experienced. I've learned to compensate for my unwillingness to give myself freely... yet. I hope you were gratified."

"Absolutely! I can't believe you brought me such pleasure... such bliss... so simply. I only wish I could do the same for you."

"You will. Soon, you will."

Neither Kiri nor Michael knew how much time passed or if they dozed or slept, but it was still dark outside when he nudged her. "Kiri?"

"Hmmm?"

"Are you awake?"

"Umm hmm."

"I wonder... If I'm the aberrant gene pool specimen here, what will we tell them when our fierce-tempered, red-headed little cherubs begin to grow unicorn horns?"

That brought her up wide awake and laughing. "Oh, you are an incorrigible tease!" she accused, struggling to find her own side of their bed and yanking covers away.

"Don't go," he appealed. "You know I speak in jest. Come back here and lie against me so I can make our hearts beat together again."

Remembering how soothing that felt, Kiri scooted until her back rubbed his chest. She began breathing deeply and regularly. Michael slowed his breaths and then caught up to hers like the previous night. Soon their bodies pulsed in synch again.

"Kiri?"

"Hmmm?"

"Your hair still smells of jasmine."

"That's nice. You have no hair left on your head to sniff!"

Playfulness in passion, Michael thought with delight. Perfection. "Kiri?"

"Hmmm?"

"We're not going to lose each other through time and distance like Father and Paula did so long ago, are we?" He waited for her to shake her head. "I want for us always to return to a nest beneath a tree to find one another again and live happily ever after. Forever. Agreed?"

Michael waited for her nod. Satisfied, the couple turned to their backs and thoughtfully looked up through the branches of the tree—all those pathways to dreams.

Chapter 24

Somewhere over the North Atlantic, Kurt nudged Kiri. "Sis, are you awake?"

"You know I am. What's on your mind?"

"You. You and Michael. You two put on quite a show this weekend, what with all the flirting—a little too cozy, in my opinion. I hope you're not going further than that," Kurt admonished with a hard stare at his sister. "I'm not quite sure what the glove thing was all about. Overly dramatic, don't you think? At least we won't be seeing most of those folks for a long time—time enough to let memory of your foolishness fade away."

"Speak for yourself." Kiri returned his stare. "You're the one who came in late last night. Anything I should know?"

"We all went out for a drink after. Meghan brought me home."

"And? Is that all there is to tell?" she taunted.

"For the time being, yes. Besides, this isn't about me. This is about you. As your big brother, I'm telling you that you'd be wise to cool it with Michael. Don't expect more than a good time from him. I like him a lot, but I know guys just like him—quick into and out of a relationship—and all I see ahead for you is heartbreak with that character. His goodbye was typical of the type."

Kiri absorbed the sting of those last words without reaction. "When you find me a guy like Michael in Denver, I'll listen. Until then, keep your opinions to yourself."

"I'm just saying…."

"You've had your say. Now go to sleep."

Disappointed with their parting at the airport, Kiri wondered if her brother could be right about Michael. She wrestled with her seatbelt in frustration and finally settled back for another sleepless flight home.

*   *   *

Paula's urgency to pack away Christmas befuddled Thomas. When he returned from the attic with the decorations box, she already had a pile of cones and candles from the mantle waiting for him on the hearth. A dusky gloom settled over the long room the minute he disconnected the tree lights. She removed the grandchildren's ornaments and stacked them near the tree to be discarded. He shuffled through the scatter of dry needles to reach the one near the top and tossed it on the stack with the others. Paula startled him when she snatched it up and put it into her pocket. "Not that one. *If* Kiri ever returns, she will expect to see it in the exact same spot."

Thomas attempted to make light of the tension he felt building between them. "Our children are off—all of them—not yours, not mine, but ours. This old house is empty once again. Just the two of us are left to keep the fires burning. The holidays are history, and by all accounts they were a success," he maintained with a smile.

Paula closed the box on his hand. "Is that truly your assessment?"

Thomas noted her glare. "The family is united for the most part, but I'm not sure I can claim absolute victory," he admitted. "There is one twist—one flaw in the picture—I did not see coming. Perhaps success is not the proper term."

"That depends on how you measure success. If you are talking harmony among family members, that is one thing. If you insist on the outcome conforming to your—and only your—prescribed plan… well, most grand plans don't fall into that category."

"I don't know what went wrong." Thomas shook his head. "The rift is more than a slight misunderstanding this time. Michael intended to pursue a close friendship with Kiri despite my objections. I cannot permit it!"

Paula sympathized with him as he struggled against himself. "I told you to be careful what you wished for. It seems you got that one big happy family you wanted, and now you are the only holdout. You are the traditional one standing against the forces of human nature."

"I forbid it!"

"You cannot forbid affection between two young people any more than you can will it. Could *your* family?"

He blanched at the reference. "I want so much for Michael to settle down and begin a family of his own, but with Kiri?"

"Isn't my American daughter good enough for your Irish son?"

"That's not what I mean, and you know it," he snapped, frustrated by her word play.

"How do you think I feel? Do you imagine I like the idea of my daughter taking up with some man who has a secret for a job and lives thousands of miles away? A couple of nights ago, Kiri could do no wrong—the star of the show—and now you speak of her as some *femme fatale*, foiling your plans for your son's future. *Your* plans, Thomas, not his. It seems to me that Michael and Kiri are merely exploring new dimensions of the perfect blended family you set out to create."

"How can you be so calm about this new revelation?"

"My every organ is constricted, every fiber of my being, twisted until I can't think or breathe, but one of us has to appear calm to prevent the other from doing or saying something really foolish."

He rubbed his cheekbone with the back of his hand. "I've already done that, for sure."

"Yes, Thomas. You have."

He lifted the Christmas box and made the long trek upstairs to the fourth floor. He slid it into its place on a shelf and faced the label bearing his wife's handwriting outward. Thomas lingered awhile among the packed remains of his previous life and wiped his hand across his eyes. Such a different celebration this year, he mused. Almost perfect in a unique way. Maybe he did expect too much too fast, push too hard, ask the impossible of those he held most dear. After a shaky start, the holiday proceeded smoothly for the most part. Then it ended abruptly. No, the truth was, he ended it. He forbade his beloved son Michael a repeat of Thomas' own past. Duty to family demanded it. How would he repair that cataclysmic breach, he wondered as he returned to the dark and empty main floor.

Paula removed the crude ornament from her pocket and held it in the palm of her hand. She recognized the symbolism immediately when she spotted Kiri's necklace and Michael's forgotten bow tie hanging with the unicorn on her daughter's branch. She hurriedly tucked the jewel and tie into her sweater before Thomas noticed when they began the undecorating process earlier. Now, she unpocketed them as well, wrapped the three items together in tissue, and climbed the stairs to the room she and her daughter played in so joyfully just the day before. She asked herself if children were condemned to relive the trials of their parents. Did each generation have the same obstacles to happiness: war, protest, economic downturn, social battles and family conflict? Could not parents fight to survive those challenges, then pass their experience to future generations to protect their children from repeating the same? She found herself at the door to the suite she shared with her chosen partner, unsure of the answers.

Thomas returned to their chamber to find Paula lying on the floor in *viparita karani,* legs up the wall, with her head in a hood. "You look like you are ready to turn in. Why so early?"

"For you it may seem early, Thomas, but for me it may be too late."

"You called me Thomas."

"Today you are a man I don't know. I knew a young man once named Tom who dared to dream, who dared to question his family, his traditions and his religious teachings, who dared to search for his own direction."

"That man stands beside you trying to hold our lives together in the only way he knows."

"Maybe so, but he was unrecognizable the moment the first door slammed and warring family members collided. He slipped into his former role just like all the children did."

"I'm still that man."

"Then reach deep, find him and bring him back quickly. You cannot forge new bonds with old ways. Face this new reality with freshness, willing to compromise. Michael is so much like I imagine you at his age. It is no wonder Kiri finds him attractive. You must allow him to dream too. She may not be his ideal at all, but he needs to discover that for himself."

Paula crossed her legs and lowered them, turned to her side and pushed herself up. She traded the hood for her nightgown and crawled into bed pulling the covers clear up to her chin. Thomas sat on the edge of the bed beside her.

"I'm not happy about this turn our lives have taken, Thomas, not one bit, but there are no grounds on which to oppose it. Michael and Kiri are two young healthy adults thrown together by circumstance. They have not grown up under the same roof. Suppose our two children met and fell in love before we found each other last June. If we subsequently reacquainted at a celebration of theirs, would you deny us the happiness we now share simply because their bond preceded ours? To our knowledge, they have not committed a mortal sin by your book, and it wouldn't matter if they had. That's their business, just as what we do in this bedroom is ours. If they were any other two, you would say they are accountable only to their God and to themselves. They do not share one iota of DNA; they are not blood related, which should be the only consideration—not what other people may think or what tradition deems appropriate."

Thomas' chin dropped to his chest as he mulled over what Paula said. Her hand reached out to take his and pulled it under the covers to her. "You know what frightens me most, Thomas? Not what a relationship between our two children would mean for them or for the family, but what it would mean for us. I am scared to death that arguments over our children will eventually tear us apart, and we have so little time left to be together. I don't want that time filled with rancor."

"Nor I, Paula, nor I. But as deeply as I search my heart, I cannot sanctify a relationship between the two."

"Sanctify! Is that really your right? It seems to me you hang on tenaciously to things that have little relevance in this 21st century and let go of the most precious. I could not believe my ears this afternoon when you spoke so harshly to Michael. I'm thankful my children did not hear."

"I have no idea what came over me. I could not stop myself. The thought of Michael and Kiri together offends my sense of propriety, but I had no call to treat him as I did." Thomas grimaced and leaned back to take a deep breath. "Do we need to read some Yeats to get us through this?"

"No, we need you to come to your senses." Paula moved his hand to snuggle it between her cheek and shoulder. "There is so much to love in you, Tom. So much. But sometimes you make it a real challenge. You are one stubborn man, still fighting the battle between tradition and religious teachings on the one side and what is right for you on the other. Maybe you should listen to your own words and reach back to your roots—your Celtic roots—to find your own inner strength and direction. Summon your ancestral heritage to find the true meaning of family. You might be surprised at what you find."

"You called me Tom again."

"Tom is the man I agreed to marry. I think he deserves a second chance. He's going to need lots of practice to get this 'family' thing right," she smiled.

"You are my soul mate, Paula, my *anam ċara*, my best friend. I can share my innermost self with you. You understand me as I am, and when I am understood, I feel safe at home. I need your help to open my eyes to new views and my heart to new ways."

"Come home beside me, then, and we'll see what we can do." When they were close, Paula ran her fingers through his hair, pulled him nose-to-nose and gently shook his head. "Approve of it or not, you've got a situation on your hands, Tom O'Connell—one that is completely out of your control. Now see if you can sleep!"

*   *   *

Michael sat alone in the middle of his cold, empty flat—no fire, no fireplace, no festive atmosphere, and no tree. Only one day ago the New Year promised so much. Then he argued with his father—his recalcitrant father. A loyal Irish son did not challenge his own father, but Michael had—three times in the last day, four if one counted their conversation on his return from the castle, provoked by his meddling sisters.

Their last confrontation was the worst. Just before Michael drove the Koyles to the airport, his father ordered him outside and demanded that his son drop all intention of pursuing any kind of relationship with Kiri beyond that of the sister she would become. Their blatant disregard for tradition at the Ball was unconscionable, only tolerated to spare Paula and the rest of the family embarrassment.

"Your spectacle was outrageous! Any close friendship with Kiri goes beyond the bounds of propriety. It is unnatural and against God's laws!"

Michael challenged him to name which ones, but that only angered Thomas further. When the son labeled his father a hypocrite for living with a woman "without benefit of clergy," Thomas became enraged. He forbade his son to entertain any notion of friendship with Kiri.

"Take her to the airport and break it off!" he commanded.

How far-reaching is one's obligation to respect and obey his elder, Michael wondered. When would he be considered mature enough to make decisions for himself? He rubbed his chin, ran his fingers through the hair that was not there, and contemplated his next move.

*   *   *

Kirin Koyle gazed up through the branches of her Christmas tree. From her vantage point on the floor beneath it, she beheld disaster—unmitigated disaster—and not just in the tree. The holidays turned out that way too—a litter of dried needles and broken dreams. When things go bad, take refuge under the tree, she reminded herself. That's what she did in Dublin, and that is what she would do here... for one more night.

She stewed all the way home on the flight back to Denver. Her sleeplessness provided lots of time to think—to think about the festivities and about Michael. Then she walked in the door and was home. Home! In her own environment, she could be herself. She dropped her bag and went straight for the tree, turned on the lights and crawled beneath it. Safe at last.

A snicker somersaulted up from her belly as she recalled one of the last things Michael whispered to her: "We're not going to lose each other through time and distance." Lose each other? You had to have a thing before you could lose it, and apparently they had nothing, judging from the peck on the forehead and the shove down the jetway she got from him when the time arrived to say goodbye at the airport.

Kurt was right. Kiri performed admirably as Michael's fling. The Casanova came home for the holidays looking for a good time, and she was fool enough to be his fool... until she said "no." One word. Two letters. Why could it not be different just one time? Why could a guy not proclaim his love first and his desire after? Not in the male DNA, she decided. Could Kurt be the same and she just not know it? Not her brother, she shook her head. Nor this newfound brother, she wished.

Kiri laughed at herself. She chided Thomas numerous times for living in another century, yet here she was struggling to hold onto a time when the morality of waiting for one's partner was a norm, not an anomaly. Maybe it was time for her to rethink standing alone on a hard rock of principle, to revisit the give in option even though it was too late for her with Michael.

"Merry Christmas, Mom," Kiri muttered. "You got what you wanted. Heaven knows you deserve it." But moms were not supposed to have a romantic life at her age. They had lived their chance. It was Kiri's turn now, and what she wanted was a life forbidden to her—too close for comfort—with a guy who was not interested. She reached into her pocket to twine the cord of the compass around her finger—the compass with the eye pointed in the direction right for her. She found her own direction all right, straight out of a fairy tale and back to the fringe of the forest... alone.

Kiri expelled a final cleansing breath, closed her eyes and relaxed into a deep sleep—her body and senses too exhausted, too depraved, too oblivious of time and place to hear the ringing of the phone in her ear.

~

What's next for Paula and Tom?
Kiri and Michael?
Find out in *Celtic Compass, Part II,*
a novel by Sherry Schubert, currently available

AWARD WINNING AUTHOR SHERRY SCHUBERT, named 2012 Writer of the Year by Idaho Writer's League and a recipient of an Editors' Choice award from Idaho Author Awards, is a graduate of the University of California at Berkeley, Class of 1967. Subsequently, she spent two years hitchhiking abroad, gathering grist for stories and a packful of dreams. "Life" called her back to her home state of Idaho where she raised a family and taught teenagers to solve quadratic equations.

Ms. Schubert's yen to write fiction during retirement is precipitated by her daughter's observation, "I have no idea who you were before you were Mom." The author specializes in fiction appealing to Baby Boomers and their Children.

Puffin Island relates how the historical events and social issues of the Sixties shaped the author and still reverberate in her children's lives today. *Celtic Compass, Part 1,* applies her experience in a Sixties "blended family"—before that term was coined—to present-day holiday conflicts. *Celtic Compass, Part II,* explores the challenge of divided loyalties faced by members of a blended family in a time of crisis.
Celtic Circle~for Better, for Worse examines how antagonistic members of a blended family channel their bitterness and grief.
In *Celtic Circle~Forever,* hostile members of a blended family seek pathways to reconciliation following tragedy.

In addition to her five novels, Ms. Schubert is a contributing author to the short story anthologies, *Hauntings from the Snake River Plain* and *Family Recipes from the Snake River Plain*. All of her works are available as ebooks or paperbacks from Amazon or http://sunwaypress.com.

Sherry continues to live and write on the family farm. For the record, she did shake the hand of President Kennedy, and she did play the guitar... badly.

www.ingramcontent.com/pod-product-compliance
Lightning Source LLC
Chambersburg PA
CBHW060807120626
46557CB00001B/123